DRAGONWATCH

CHAMPION OF THE TITAN GAMES

ALSO BY BRANDON MULL

DRAGONWATCH
CHAMPION OF THE TITAN GAMES

BRANDON MULL

ILLUSTRATED BY
BRANDON DORMAN

SHADOW
MOUNTAIN

Library of Congress Cataloging-in-Publication Data

(CIP data on file)
ISBN 978-1-62972-788-2

Printed in the United States of America   7/2020
LSC Communications, Crawfordsville, IN

10   9   8   7   6   5   4   3   2   1

For my extraordinary Rose—I adore you now and always

Contents

CONTENTS

CHAPTER ONE

Paradise

Twisting supports of gleaming adamant buttressed the crystal towers of the Fairy Queen's palace. The fanciful structure seemed less like it had been built, more like it had grown and then been hollowed out by the elements. Rooms tapered and curved unpredictably, delicate bridges connected unexpected terraces, and rounded corridors wound like elaborate root systems.

Kendra walked along a pale hallway that might have been carved by wind or water. At her side, Bracken strolled with the relaxed ease of being at home. Less than a day ago, they had traveled through the fairy shrine at Crescent Lagoon and entered the protected realm of the Fairy Queen—one of the five known monarchs of the magical world.

Kendra felt like a foreigner. The women here were tall,

slender specimens of ethereal beauty, garbed in artful collages of fallen leaves or masterpieces woven by silkworms. Men were sparse, though she saw an occasional astrid, golden wings tucked behind polished armor.

Bracken had exuded an extra glow since they entered the Fairy Realm, as if his body could barely contain the brightness within. He was always dashing, but at the moment he appeared particularly breathtaking—his fair skin and tousled white hair looked best suffused with light. If Kendra hadn't already known him, she might have suspected he was an angel.

"It looks more complete than last time," Kendra remarked as they passed a wide window, trying not to focus helplessly on Bracken's irresistible appearance.

The fairies were rebuilding their realm within the space that had formerly served as the demon prison, after having lured the demons into their former homeland. When Kendra had last visited this domain, the trees and bushes had looked younger and had not yet spread to cover so much of the landscape. Kendra knew fairies could encourage vegetation to flourish, but the abundant fields of flowers and the mature forests still took her by surprise.

"We have more work to do," Bracken said. "But the palace is done for now, and much of the filth left by the demons has been expunged. I expect Mother will provide a full update."

Kendra held up the jeweled circlet in her hands. "She'll be happy to see this."

"I still can't believe she loaned you her crown," Bracken said.

"It was so I could rescue you," Kendra said.

"She has left me to languish in prison before," Bracken said. "The dangers of the dragon war to the Fairy Realm must be significant. Otherwise she would not have taken such a risk."

Kendra noticed that the palace almost totally lacked doors. Rather, the windings of passageways or freestanding partitions helped differentiate rooms. At the end of one meandering hall, Kendra and Bracken walked around an intricately painted screen and into a tremendous open area. Translucent walls sloped away to outrageous heights and distances.

Though it was daytime outside, this room felt like twilight. Before Kendra was a still, reedy pond bordered by a grassy field and a wood where stately trees with silver trunks were clad in gilded leaves. She smelled blossoms, sap, and wet earth.

"Are we still inside the castle?" Kendra asked.

Bracken laughed gently. "This palace contains several rooms that are much larger than they should be."

"Huge spaces inside small containers," Kendra mused. "The Fairy Queen will meet us here?"

"Far from the throne room," Bracken said. "Mother prefers to hold significant meetings away from formality."

"I'm surprised she allowed me to come to the palace," Kendra said.

"You have her crown," Bracken said.

"Some of the fairies gave me looks," Kendra said.

"They're burning with envy," Bracken said.

"Because I'm with you," Kendra said.

"They can't help feeling respect," Bracken replied. "To be entrusted with the crown makes you utterly unique. Some might even wonder if they have a new queen."

Kendra heard a rustle in the dimness at the edge of the wood, and an elegant unicorn emerged, glowing like moonlight as it paced toward the reedy pond. At the edge of the pond, the unicorn bent forward to drink, the tip of the horn sending concentric ripples across the previously glassy surface.

When the unicorn turned from the water, she was the Fairy Queen, an exquisite fairy more than a head taller than Kendra. Her silver and white wings spread behind her for a moment, like a peacock making a grand display, and then folded to vanish behind her graceful shoulders.

"You have wings?" Kendra asked.

"When I so choose," the Fairy Queen said.

The aromas in the room intensified. Kendra became more acutely aware of the fresh water in the pond, the sap inside the trees, the minerals in the soil, and the perfume of the blossoms.

"My faith in you was justified," the Fairy Queen said as she came around the pond toward Kendra, bare feet treading on rich mud without becoming dirty. Little green sprouts and shoots started worming up from the ground wherever her soles had touched.

"Hello, your majesty," Kendra said, dropping to one knee.

"Rise, my child," the Fairy Queen said. She held out her arms to Bracken, and he advanced into her embrace.

"Hello, Mother," Bracken said.

"You must stop frightening us so," the Fairy Queen said, releasing him and stepping back. "It caused enough grief to have your father imprisoned for so long."

"There is a war," Bracken said.

"Indeed," the Fairy Queen said. Her eyes turned to Kendra, who felt deeply understood by that fathomless gaze. Kendra perceived sorrow for her hardships and losses, admiration for her courage, and gratitude for her heroics.

"Here is your crown," Kendra said, holding it out.

The Fairy Queen knelt before Kendra, head tilted upward. For a moment, Kendra felt too astonished to react. Then, using both hands, Kendra placed the tiara on the queen's brow.

The Fairy Queen rose. "Thank you."

"Why did you risk the crown?" Bracken asked.

"The time had come for decisive action," the Fairy Queen said. "Withholding it would have posed greater dangers. I needed you home. I fear Ronodin has not been idle."

"I purified his third horn," Bracken said, holding it out to her.

The Fairy Queen accepted the pearly white offering. "No small feat." Cradling the glossy horn in both hands, she stared down at it mournfully. "How did one so dear turn so foul? Truly the most devastating blows come from those who have been our allies."

"Whom can we trust if not family?" Bracken said. "My cousin should have remained one of our greatest protectors. Instead, Ronodin started down a ruinous path and appears determined to walk it to completion."

"He fled after your confrontation?" the Fairy Queen asked.

"I know not where," Bracken replied.

"Kendra," the Fairy Queen said, straightening, "you have once again performed a vital service for my people. How can I begin to repay you?"

Kendra glanced at Bracken. "I'm trying to save my brother, Seth. He escaped the Underking but still doesn't have his memories. Can you help us get to Titan Valley?"

The Fairy Queen gazed at Kendra sadly. "You hope to go there with my son."

"Yes," Bracken said. "Seth is traveling by leviathan."

"I wish I could fully accommodate you, Kendra," the Fairy Queen said. "Unfortunately, I need Bracken here for a time."

"What?" Bracken asked.

"We have yet to purge a few demons the way we did Jubaya," the Fairy Queen said. "They were here before we arrived and have a claim to the spaces they occupy. The Fairy Realm will not be secure until it is pure. With the dragon war expanding, we must fully engage our defenses."

"If your best efforts have not ejected these demons, what do you imagine I can accomplish?" Bracken asked.

"Succeed where others have failed," the Fairy Queen said.

"You have other weapons at your disposal," Bracken said. "No unicorn can drive them out? No combination of astrids and fairies? Have you drawn on the Source?"

"What we can borrow from the Source remains limited," the Fairy Queen said. "We have exhausted all options. It is part of why I had to risk my crown to get you back."

"I should have known you had a need to rescue me," Bracken said.

"We must all assume our responsibilities in the upcoming conflict," the Fairy Queen said. "There is potential for an Age of Darkness that could consume leaf and stream."

"Let me find Seth first," Bracken said.

"My apologies, but no," the Fairy Queen said. "Purge the demons and then you may go aid Kendra."

"How long will it take?" Kendra asked.

"Given the failures so far?" Bracken asked. "Impossible to predict."

"It sounds important," Kendra said.

"It is," Bracken replied, resting a hand against the side of her neck. "So are you."

"Kendra, I grant you passage to Titan Valley through my realm," the Fairy Queen said. "Along with any comrades from outside my realm you wish to have accompany you."

"Other outsiders?" Bracken said.

"Our realm is not yet pure," the Fairy Queen said. "There would be no desecration. It is the least I can do."

"Thank you," Kendra said. "If we find him, could you help me restore Seth's memories?"

"The absence of his memories is connected to the Wizenstone," the Fairy Queen said. "That is a power I cannot overturn. But I will aid you as I am able, and after Bracken expels the demons from our realm, you will have his assistance as well."

"Thank you, your majesty," Kendra said with a small curtsy.

"It's not enough," Bracken objected. "After all Kendra has lost? All she risked?"

"This is merely the beginning of my gratitude," the Fairy Queen said. "All things in order, my son. If I do not bring our realm to full strength, the aid I can provide will be grossly limited. The survival of our realm is vital to maintaining balance in the world."

Bracken nodded. "I will do as you say."

The Fairy Queen regarded Kendra. "Do you wish to return to your friends on Timbuli at Crescent Lagoon before proceeding to Titan Valley?"

"Yes," Kendra said. "Especially if it means I can bring some of them with me."

"Very well," the Fairy Queen said. "Bracken can show you the way back. The way to my realm will remain open to you until you cross to Titan Valley with your comrades."

"Thank you," Kendra said.

"Return to me, my son, after you escort Kendra out," the Fairy Queen said.

"As you wish, Mother," Bracken replied.

The Fairy Queen turned and waded into the pond, descending ever deeper with no sign of floating. Her head disappeared without leaving a ripple. The sight reminded Kendra of the Dry Depths potion.

"You realize you could have kept the crown," Bracken said softly.

"What do you mean?" Kendra asked.

"The crown isn't just a symbol," Bracken said. "When you were wearing it, technically, you held the office of Fairy Queen."

"I wouldn't know how to use it like your mother does," Kendra said.

"Of course not," Bracken said. "If you tried to rule the Fairy Realm as a mortal, it would go no better than if you tried to rule the demons. But Mother did more than trust you not to lose the crown. She trusted you to give it back."

"When she knelt, that was a real coronation," Kendra said.

"Yes," Bracken replied, eyes on the woods. "We're not alone."

A figure emerged from the trees, using a staff like a cane as he walked toward them. The man was both mature and ageless, with unblemished skin that seemed untouched by the sun. His hooded robe looked silver or gray depending on how it caught the light.

"Hello, Father," Bracken said.

"I'm glad you've returned," his father said, walking toward them with humble dignity. "Thank you for retrieving him, Kendra. This realm has never been so indebted to a single mortal."

"I am happy to help," Kendra said.

"May I have a word with you two before Kendra departs?" the Fairy King asked.

"Of course," Bracken said.

"I need you to reason with your mother," the Fairy King said.

"About what?" Bracken asked.

"About me," his father said, reaching them and stopping to lean on his staff. "I have wrestled with this matter since I came here, and though the reality pains me deeply, I feel certain that I don't belong here anymore."

"What do you mean?" Bracken asked.

He gazed upon his son with sad, loving eyes. "Your mother refuses to see the truth of the matter. She is the monarch here, and few beings are wiser, but I'm afraid I represent a blind spot in which emotion is clouding her judgment."

"She knows you're still healing," Bracken said.

His father nodded. "But she ignores the peril I represent. Bracken, I was chained to the Demon King for eons. I cannot begin to convey the horrors that uninterrupted exposure to the Demon King in his very prison entailed. He dragged me around on a chain for millennia, together with other dead and dying trophies."

Kendra winced at the thought.

"I would rather not imagine," Bracken said.

"The damage to me, body and soul, was real," the Fairy

King said. "I survived, but in a diminished state. A fallen condition. Once, long ago, my virtue was unblemished. That perfection is irretrievably lost. I am wounded, tainted, and scarred to the core. No amount of waiting or patience will return me to my former state. The Fairy Realm will never be pure while I dwell here, and I will never feel peace as a resident, let alone as a ruler."

"Getting trapped there was not your fault," Bracken said. "You were an innocent victim. How could that make you impure?"

"Not so innocent as you may imagine," the Fairy King said. "I made my share of mistakes to end up there, and my personal defenses broke down amid the torment. I sustained real harm, and I am now vulnerable in ways that do not belong here."

"Father, there must be a way to help you heal," Bracken said.

"It would be my wish," his father said. "I did not intend to fall, but the damage is done. For better and worse, I am not the being of yesteryear. Whatever healing is available will not happen here. The Fairy Realm is meant to be endless and unchanging. If I want transformation, I must go among the mortals."

"Surely you do not intend to go now," Bracken said. "War is raging and will only worsen, and you lack most of your former powers."

"Which is further evidence that I am damaged," the Fairy King said. "Your mother does not see it. Bracken, you will never drive those demons out while I dwell here. I am a barrier to purity, an obstacle to the Source. While I dwell here, this cannot truly be the Fairy Realm. My presence desecrates it."

"Can't Mother heal you?" Bracken asked.

"She has tried, and I have tried," the Fairy King said. "My form is whole. My inner self is beyond her reach, or mine."

"What can I do?" Bracken asked.

"Help your mother see," the Fairy King said. "Help her understand. I have tried to leave against her wishes, but she is too powerful here. Even without her crown. You must convince her to let me go."

Bracken had tears in his eyes. "Who is going to convince me?"

"Have compassion, Son," his father said. "I love you and your mother. I adore this realm. I protected it for ages. Don't let me be the means of its undoing. I can conceive of no worse punishment. Give me a chance to heal."

"It's not my decision to make," Bracken said.

"But you could help me persuade her," the Fairy King said.

Bracken gave a pensive nod. "Perhaps, if I fail against the demons, and if the situation becomes sufficiently grim. Are you sure you're right?"

"Have I ever been a fool?" the Fairy King asked.

"No, but you might imagine that sacrificing yourself would be preferable to feeling like a burden," Bracken said.

"I'm trying to heal," his father said. "I have tried. I will try. I hope restoration will happen. I trust it can happen. But

I am certain it will not happen here, and that my presence compromises our defenses."

"I need to escort Kendra back to Timbuli," Bracken said.

"Of course," his father said. "I wanted to speak with you before you became immersed in your new duties. Kendra, I am forever indebted to you and your brother for freeing me from Gorgrog. I thought the darkness would have no end. It didn't . . . and then it did. Thanks to you mortals."

"It was my pleasure," Kendra said.

The Fairy King laughed. "A response more fitting for if I had thanked you for passing the cream. I'm sorry about your brother, Kendra. I want him restored. I will not rest until we succeed."

Kendra felt tears spring to her eyes. It was encouraging to hear that somebody so important cared about her brother. "I won't rest either."

"Was it your idea?" Bracken asked. "The crown?"

The Fairy King offered a cryptic smile. "You don't imagine your mother would have come up with that?"

"It was," Bracken said. "You want to talk about destroying the Fairy Realm? Losing the crown would have done the job."

"Yes, it might have," his father said. "Did we lose it?"

Bracken shook his head.

The Fairy King gave a little bow and walked away.

CHAPTER TWO

Landfall

The cask bobbed in the shallow water several yards from the small boat where Seth crouched, turning a potato in his hands. A lantern in the other rowboat illuminated the hermit troll watching curiously, his wide, lipless mouth drooped in a concerned frown. As usual, the leviathan was moving so smoothly that Seth could almost forget he was inside of an enormous sea creature.

Hermo had missed his last throw. If Seth landed the potato inside the cask, he would win.

"You take too long," Hermo blurted. "You forfeit."

"There is a lot riding on this," Seth said, knowing the tension made the hermit troll crazy. "If this potato goes in, I will be the Champion of the Entire Ocean."

"You will be lucky," Hermo said. "Nothing more. But potato will miss, because you no lucky!"

Seth theatrically licked a finger and then held it up to test the air.

"No wind inside fish," Hermo complained.

Seth plucked a sprout out of one of the potato's eyes.

Hermo slapped his green hands over his eyes. "Why you waste tasty part?"

"The sprouts are gross," Seth said.

"You have brains of starfish," Hermo said.

"Can a starfish do this?" Seth asked, raising the potato like a basketball and shooting it at the slightly swaying mouth of the little barrel. He had missed three of his last five throws, but this one dropped inside with a wet, hollow thump.

"No!" Hermo cried, raising his fists above his head. He spread his arms wide. "Why?"

"Because I'm what happens when luck meets skill," Seth said, "and they get into a serious relationship."

"You what happens when tuna barfs," Hermo said.

"Guess you just lost to tuna puke," Seth said. "From now on you can call me Champion of the Entire Ocean."

"I Champion of the Seven Seas at mancala," Hermo said.

"You got lucky at mancala," Seth said. "The rematch is coming."

"Is it time to eat some more potatoes?" Calvin asked. About the size of one of Seth's fingers, the nipsie stood on the gunwale of Seth's boat, balancing casually.

"Another raw potato?" Seth asked.

"Eat fish," Hermo said. "Giant fish swallow plenty fish."

"I'm not going to eat raw fish," Seth said. "I'll get parasites."

"Hookworms," Calvin said. "Or worse."

Hermo waved a disgusted hand at them. "Fish delicious and full of flavor. Parasites have vitamins."

"The parasites will suck me dry from the inside," Seth said. "I'm a person. Not a troll."

"You got that right," Hermo said.

We approach the desired landmass, a low, slow voice spoke in Seth's mind. It came from the leviathan.

"Already?" Seth asked.

I went swiftly.

"Is it talking?" Calvin asked. "What's it saying?"

"Nobody talking," Hermo said.

"The leviathan says we're almost to Titan Valley," Seth said. "How long has it been?"

"Not two days yet," Calvin said. "It's a big fish. Must be fast."

"Can you get us into the sanctuary?" Seth asked the leviathan.

The sanctuary includes a portion of the ocean around the landmass, the leviathan replied. *I am allowed into those waters; therefore, you can enter, since you are within me.*

"He can get us in," Seth reported. "Hopefully someplace where we won't be seen. But not too far from civilization."

As you wish, the leviathan replied.

"Wait," Hermo said. "You go Titan Valley? You leave fish?"

"You'll have your privacy back," Seth said. "I never meant to live here."

"What about rematch?" Hermo asked. "With potato?"

"Maybe someday," Seth said. "For now, I have to retire as the greatest champion the ocean has ever known."

"Why you say Titan Valley?"

"That's where the leviathan is dropping us off."

Hermo stared at him in shock, then laughed. "Titan Valley not for humans. You get eaten."

"We know it's a dragon sanctuary," Seth said.

Hermo shook his head, still laughing. "Titan Valley for trolls. Our queen there."

"There's a troll queen?" Seth asked.

"Titan Valley is managed by the Giant Queen," Calvin said. "She rules over the giants and some of the larger creatures, including trolls."

"Larger creatures?" Seth exclaimed. "Hermo would need a stool to reach my shoulder."

Hermo stopped laughing and folded his arms. "Hermo reach plenty."

"There are different types of trolls," Calvin said. "Hermit trolls are the smallest."

"The leviathan called Titan Valley a landmass," Seth said. "Isn't Titan Valley an island?"

"Every continent is surrounded by water," Calvin said. "New Zealand has hundreds of little islands, but two major ones: North Island and South Island. Titan Valley is on the third major island of New Zealand, larger than the others combined. It's the largest dragon sanctuary. Some have called it the Lost Continent."

"It's that big and no regular humans notice it?" Seth asked.

"Distracter spells can be powerful," Calvin said. "Especially the type that hide a dragon sanctuary and harness the power of all those creatures that mortals do not naturally notice."

"Titan Valley is bestest most famous place," Hermo said.

"Well, I'm excited to visit somewhere new," Seth said. "I don't have many memories."

"If you been there before, you no be here," Hermo said. "You be eaten."

"I guess we'll find out if I can survive," Seth replied.

Hermo gave a start and then cocked his head. "We stop. Why we stop?"

Seth had gotten so used to the subtle motions of the leviathan that the standstill felt unsettling. "This must be where we get off."

Daylight flooded into the fleshy chamber, showing Seth how accustomed his eyes had become to dim lamplight as he squinted against the new brightness.

"The leviathan opened his mouth," Calvin said.

We have arrived, the leviathan declared.

"No leave!" Hermo cried.

"You've complained about us the whole time," Seth said.

"Complain when you win," Hermo said. "Need rematches."

"Sorry," Seth said. "Thanks for the games, but we have to go."

Hermo began to wring his hands. "Where you go in Titan Valley?"

Seth glanced at Calvin, still balancing on the edge of the boat. The nipsie shrugged.

"We'll figure it out," Seth said.

"What look for? Hermo know plenty."

"We'll need to learn about Humbuggle," Seth said, not wanting to reveal too much, but curious to see if the hermit troll might have pointers.

Hermo placed a hand over his eyes. "Me should have known. You here for Games. You even dumber than you look."

"It's no game," Seth assured him.

"Humbuggle makes Games," Hermo said, peeking out from between his fingers. "You not know nothing."

Seth held out a hand to Calvin, who sprang onto his palm. Seth pocketed the nipsie. "We'll play it by ear."

Hermo pointed at Seth emphatically. "You need Troll Tavern. Information there."

"Troll Tavern?"

"Best secrets in Titan Valley," Hermo said, spreading his arms grandly. "Best knowledge in world!"

"Maybe we'll take a look," Seth said.

Hermo doubled over laughing. "They eat you so fast. Only for trolls."

"Then we'll find another way," Seth said. "Goodbye, Hermo."

"It was nice meeting you," Calvin said. "Thanks for sharing the ride with us."

Hermo stood tall and dropped his hands in exasperation. "Fine! Me go with you! Me take you to Troll Tavern."

"Wait," Seth said. "Really?"

"Time to see Titan Valley," Hermo said. "Time for new hideout."

"Many trolls make a pilgrimage to Titan Valley at least once in their lifetimes," Calvin said.

"You want to come with us?" Seth asked.

"Not come with," Hermo said, making a disgusted face. "Lead. And play more games."

They sloshed forward through the inside of the leviathan until the open mouth came into view, with teeth the size of traffic cones. Hermo ran ahead and sniffed the air, then shook his head. "Tell fishy closer to Troll Tavern."

"Can you take us closer to Troll Tavern?" Seth asked.

As you desire, the leviathan replied. The great mouth closed, and Seth felt the sea creature scoot away from the shore and then begin to glide forward again. The lamplight on the boats was too far away to provide more than the faintest glow.

"I thought hermit trolls stayed in their hideouts," Seth said.

"Yes," Hermo said. "Unless don't want to. Unless need new hideout. Unless see Troll Tavern."

"How did you get in this leviathan to begin with?" Seth asked.

"No, no, no," Hermo replied. "Trade secret. You no learn."

Before long, the leviathan stopped again, and the mouth opened. *This is the closest I can deliver you without being seen.*

"Thanks," Seth said.

I will remain in these waters, the leviathan said. *Should you need to leave the sanctuary, call to me.*

"You still work for me?" Seth asked.

You brought me forth, the leviathan replied. *You are my master.*

Seth wished the leviathan could travel on land. He could use some power behind him in a sanctuary full of dragons, giants, and trolls. But at least he had a way to escape. "I'll let you know if we need to bolt."

"You crazy," Hermo said. "Talk to fishy. Fishy crazier. Listen to you."

Seth stepped out of the leviathan's mouth onto pink sand, firm with dampness. A giant loomed before him, tall enough to rival a skyscraper, each sandal-clad foot larger than a bus. Seth resisted the reflex to retreat back into the leviathan. For a terrifying moment, Seth wondered why the leviathan had dropped them at such a dangerous location, until he noticed the unnatural stillness of the giant—and the fact that it was made of stone. The oversized figure was an enormous statue.

"I hope that statue was built beyond the size of actual giants," Seth said.

"Western Sentinel," Hermo said.

Calvin whistled. "I've heard of it. Hard to imagine something that enormous without seeing it."

Hermo waved a dismissive hand. "Waste of rocks."

"It's impressive," Seth said. He turned to Hermo. "Do you know the way to the tavern?"

Hermo picked up some sand and rubbed it between his fingers, letting it sprinkle down. He sniffed the air. "Easy. You follow."

Looking up and down the beach, Seth detected no people or creatures, and no sign of civilization. "Lead the way."

Hermo advanced in a crouch, moving in a zigzag, as if dodging invisible obstacles. In spite of his aversion to going straight, his progress was deceptively quick, forcing Seth to trot in order to keep up.

Seth looked back as the leviathan jackknifed away from the beach, the ocean sloshing around its vast bulk. He watched as the titanic creature turned and vanished beneath the water.

"Do you feel a little stranded?" Seth asked Calvin.

"Nah, we're exactly where we want to be," Calvin said.

"I'll face dragons and giants if it gets my memory back," Seth said.

"Don't forget the trolls," Calvin reminded him.

"You have one job!" Hermo called, frustrated. "Follow. No watch waves."

"Sorry," Seth said, surprised at how far ahead Hermo had gotten. The hermit troll waited, arms folded, while Seth hurriedly closed the distance.

"If you get lost, you get eaten," Hermo said. "Me still go to tavern, have drink."

"I'll stay with you," Seth said.

"You easy to spot on sand," Hermo said. "Look like snack."

"Then let's get over to those trees," Seth suggested.

"Me first," Hermo said. "You after." He started forward again, moving like a running back weaving through traffic.

Shielding his eyes from the sun, Seth craned to look up at the stone giant one more time. He was so close to the statue that Seth saw the bottom of the jaw more than the face.

"I hope that thing is an exaggeration," Seth muttered, picking up his pace to stay with the nimble troll.

CHAPTER THREE

Danger

A steady breeze ruffled the surface of Crescent Lagoon as clouds mounted on the horizon. A large stone head, one of the moai, supervised as Knox stabbed imaginary enemies with a stick while reeling and jumping on the sand.

"Did you get them?" Tess asked her older brother. She knelt in the sand near the water, building a sandcastle with the help of half a dozen fairies.

"I need to have moves figured out," Knox explained, blocking an imagined attack and then delivering the counterblow. "I can't expect to beat the next demon the same way I took out Remulon."

"Do you think you'll have to fight more demons?" Tess asked.

"As long as we're stuck on these magical preserves, who knows?"

"Did you really face Remulon all alone?"

"I had to," Knox said. "The others were captured."

"I still don't understand how you avoided getting captured."

"I told you—I dodged more attacks than the others and found shelter in the razor coral."

Tess huffed. "How did you sneak in there when everybody else got caught?"

"That's why I practice my moves," Knox said, faking right, then spinning to the left. "That's why I'm a hero."

"It would have been so scary," Tess said. "Didn't you want to run away?"

"How could I?" Knox said. "I might not have been the hero they expected, but I was the hero they needed. I stayed quiet for a time. I had to catch such a big demon off guard."

"And you used Kendra's wind bag."

"The sack of gales," Knox said. "Kendra had it but didn't even try."

"She succeeded at other stuff," Tess said. "Like going to the Phantom Isle and rescuing Bracken and Seth from the Underking."

"Hard to succeed at anything if she'd been stuck a prisoner of that underwater demon for a million years," Knox said.

"How would she live a million years?"

"Or until she died. Luckily for her, I was there. I knew if I blew the demon into the razor coral, everyone would be saved. So I did. Wasn't that hard, really. Just took a little Texas ingenuity."

"Do they have sacks of gales in Texas?" Tess asked.

"They have courage," Knox said. "And know-how. And when they were handing them out, I stuck around for seconds."

"How many seconds?"

"No, a second helping. A double portion."

Tess rolled her eyes. "How will you kill the next demon? With that stick?"

"A new problem will need a new solution," Knox said. "I might use some of the moves I'm practicing. Or maybe some other technique. At least I'm not wasting my time with sandcastles."

"Kendra saved us from the spider eels with a sandcastle," Tess said.

"Not one like you're making," Knox scoffed.

"I like it," Tess said. "And the fairies like it. Having fairy friends can be useful too."

As Knox gave the sandcastle a closer look, he had to quietly admit it was impressive. The highest tower was as tall as his waist, sculpted with details like bricks, shingles, crenellations, and windows. Flashes of light signaled fairy magic as the tiny winged women smoothed surfaces and bound sand particles into fanciful shapes.

"I'd rather have friends who know how to fight," Knox said.

"I like friends who play with me," Tess said.

"Hey, Knox," Warren called, exiting the jungle from the direction of the sprawling tree house called the Monkey Maze. "Hi, Tess. Good to see you."

His tone was an odd mix of purposeful and friendly, almost like a bad actor in a community play putting too much expression into his line.

"Is something wrong?" Knox asked.

"Everything is super great," Warren said, again with too much expression. His eyes darted up and down the beach as he strolled toward them.

Now Knox knew something was off. Tess watched Warren curiously as well.

As Warren drew near, he lowered his voice and spoke with urgency. "A pair of sand dullions just attacked Savani. We suspect there are more. You two need to get off the sand, but look casual. Hopefully this is just a precaution."

The fairies started pointing down the beach and chattering over one another. Tess gazed in the direction they indicated.

"Don't look toward—" Warren began as, twenty yards away, a thick figure erupted out of the beach in a gritty geyser. The monster was at least eight feet tall and made of tightly packed sand, with lumpy shoulders and big, three-fingered hands.

"Run!" Warren shouted, motioning the kids toward the trees.

Fairies scattered as Tess dashed for the jungle, bare feet kicking up sand. Knox followed, stout stick held ready. Warren charged the dullion, sword raised. He ducked when the dullion swung a long arm at him, then rose to slash the creature across the torso, sending a spray of sand into the air but otherwise having little effect. The creature punched at

Warren, who narrowly dodged the blow, then failed to avoid a backhand that sent him cartwheeling.

A second dullion surged from the sand up the beach in the opposite direction and raced to cut off Knox's escape into the trees. The sand creature moved with long, loping strides, and Knox saw that it would beat them to the jungle, so he yanked Tess to a stop.

"Head for the water!" he cried, hoping the dullions might hesitate to get immersed. The ocean around the Crescent Lagoon sanctuary teemed with dangerous sea creatures, but the lagoon itself was generally safe—certainly safer than getting bashed by living sand.

The water was much closer than the trees, and the dullions were out of position to block access to the lagoon, but it would still be a challenge to beat them there. Knox knew he could go faster if he released his sister's hand, but instead he squeezed more tightly. No way was he going to leave her behind.

Both dullions closed on them, one from off to the side, the other from behind. Knox heard Vanessa calling, and out of his peripheral vision he noticed Warren getting up, too far behind the dullion to interfere.

Knox and Tess reached the wet sand at the edge of the water and splashed forward, first to their ankles, then to their knees. A quick glance back showed that the dullions had almost reached them and did not appear to be slowing as they approached the water. As Knox sprang forward, a mighty roar hit his eardrums like a cannon blast, only to be muffled as his surface dive took him underwater.

When his head emerged, Knox saw both dullions facing away from him as one of the Himalayan cyclopses stormed toward them, maybe Hobar or Baroi. The cyclops carried a club that was broad and flat on one end, like a cricket bat fringed with sharp stones. Working together, the dullions tried to counterattack, but the cyclops made them look slow, chopping with savage precision as he dodged their swings, hacking off arms, then heads, then legs. Each severed limb dissipated into a cloud of sand, and the torsos disintegrated as well once the limbs and head were gone.

"Come on," Knox said to Tess, pushing her ahead of him before stroking back to the beach.

Very soon it was too shallow to swim, and Knox waded to Warren, who awaited them alongside the cyclops at the edge of the water. Warren had blood leaking from his left nostril, and his eye was swelling shut. Vanessa caught up with them there.

"Are you all right?" Warren asked, taking hold of Knox by the shoulders and looking him up and down.

"I'm fine," Knox said. "I didn't get punched in the face."

"What about you?" Vanessa asked Tess, gripping her hands.

"I'm a little scared," Tess said. "But we're safe, right?"

Vanessa looked at the cyclops. "Baroi?"

"I believe there are no more dullions," Baroi said. "I will patrol the area to be sure."

"Do you know if Kendra is safe?" Vanessa asked.

"She is well," Baroi said. "She is with my brothers, near the Sunset Pearl."

"Four dullions," Warren said.

"Four?" Knox asked.

"Two attacked Savani as she oversaw the expansion of her garden," Vanessa said. "The menehunes helping on the project came to her aid. They fought one dullion, and Baroi battled the other."

"He called for us to go to the beach," Warren said. "He could sense the dullions there."

"Were the dullions targeting the children?" Vanessa asked.

"Difficult to know," Baroi said. "They may simply have been after whoever they found on the sand. I'm sorry it took me so long to overcome the dullion in the garden. It was more evasive than these."

"These directly attacked you," Warren said.

"Their mistake," Baroi remarked.

"How did dullions get in here?" Warren asked. "This area should be protected!"

"They might have been planted when all protections were down," Baroi said. "Before the first moai was revived. Or else it was an inside job. Someone with access could have admitted them."

"Who would do that?" Vanessa asked.

Baroi tilted his face skyward. "I cannot see."

"Do we have a traitor?" Knox asked.

"Possibly," Vanessa said. "Many people went missing when the preserve fell. It could be somebody who had access but is presumed dead. It could also be a high-level member of Dragonwatch."

"Or they might have been brought in when the defenses were down," Warren reminded her.

"If so, why wait so long to deploy them?" Vanessa asked.

"I don't know," Warren said. "Why attack now in the first place?"

"I came running the moment I sensed them," the cyclops said. "Tal and Hobar stayed back to protect Kendra and the pearl."

"How could they have avoided your notice for so long?" Warren asked.

"These dullions seemed to spring into existence," Baroi said. "They were either dormant or created on the spot—or else they snuck into the preserve through a portal. I wish I could have reached you sooner."

"Could other dormant ones still be hiding?" Knox asked.

"I will conduct a thorough search," Baroi said. "We must all consider the likelihood that our defenses have been compromised."

"We barely got our defenses back," Warren complained.

"The defenses of the sanctuary are functional," Baroi said. "But somebody may be granting unwarranted access, or else your enemies have found another way to work around the protections."

"What now?" Knox asked.

"Short term?" Warren replied. "You two need to stay in the tree house."

Knox glanced at where he had dropped his stick before running into the water with Tess. Maybe he wasn't as ready to become a warrior as he had imagined, but did he have to hide in a tree? "Isn't the danger past?"

"We didn't anticipate an attack like this," Vanessa said. "It shouldn't have been possible. Until we figure out what is going on, you ought to stay in our most defensible stronghold."

"Why punish us for getting attacked?" Knox complained.

"Staying alive is not a punishment," Warren said. "If attacks can happen, we have to take more precautions."

"That could have been the last attack," Knox said.

"Or it could just be the beginning," Vanessa countered. "There is a war going on."

"We might be safer on the ground," Knox said. "If I were the bad guys, I'd chop down the trees."

"Good thing you're not them," Warren said. "March."

"Why do safety precautions usually happen after the accidents?" Knox asked.

"It's how we learn," Vanessa said. "Better late than never."

Knox crouched to pick up his stick without stopping.

"Thanks for staying by me," Tess said.

"I wish I could have knocked their heads off," Knox said.

"I wish the same thing," Warren said, raising a hand to gingerly probe his swollen eye. "We'll keep this fair. We'll all stay mostly up in the trees."

CHAPTER FOUR

Disaster

Hobar patted Kendra reassuringly with a hand big enough to crush a watermelon. "Your cousins and friends are safe. Baroi destroyed the last of the dullions."

"Are you sure?" Kendra asked.

The cyclops nodded, then sniffed the air. "Something else is coming, though."

"More dullions?" Kendra asked.

"Something of greater magnitude," Tal said. "Something from the depths."

"We have sensed a growing disturbance," Hobar said. "An imbalance."

"The war?" Kendra guessed.

"Not exactly," Tal said.

Kendra looked to where she had just planted a seed from the Sentient Wood. The hamadryad Eldanore had entrusted her with three seeds—an oak, a redwood, and a banyan. They would grow into thinking trees like those in the ruminating forest at Wyrmroost.

After returning from the Fairy Realm, Kendra had gone directly to the cyclopses. Baroi had suggested she plant the banyan here on Timbuli, within sight of the Sunset Pearl. Scooping the dirt over the seed had felt like her final duty at Crescent Lagoon. As she was searching for a feeling of farewell, the cyclopses had sensed the intrusion, and Baroi had raced away.

Now Kendra stared at the pearl, resting in a shallow basin atop an altar of black, porous rock. The size of a softball, the Sunset Pearl had a rainbow sheen on its milky white surface. Around the clearing where the altar had been raised stood the ten Grand Moai, enormous statues with elongated heads like those on Easter Island. When the pearl was present, the moai around the sanctuary exerted their protective magic. After the pearl had been stolen, the sanctuary had fallen.

"I know now," Hobar and Tal spoke in unison, interrupting her musings.

"You know what?" Kendra asked.

"The cause of the imbalance," Hobar said.

"The coming upheaval we perceived," Tal said.

Kendra heard heavy footfalls approaching. Baroi bounded into view, breathing heavily.

"Yes, they are fine," Baroi said to her unasked question. He laid a gentle palm against her back. "Come to the center of the clearing and witness an event that has not transpired for centuries."

The ground began to tremble as the three cyclopses gathered near the altar. They pointed up at Baga Loa, the volcanic mountain that towered over the island. As the quaking increased, so did Kendra's alarm.

"Is Baga Loa going to blow?" she asked.

"For the first time in many years," Tal said.

"Should we run?" Kendra asked.

"You could not outrun Baga Loa if she erupted in earnest," Hobar said.

"We will be safe here for a time," Baroi said.

Kendra gasped as a column of ash and smoke exploded from the mountaintop. The sound hit a moment later, prompting Kendra to cover her ears. Lava fountained up at the base of the smoke.

The cyclopses placed their hands over their chests and bowed their heads. The ground stopped trembling, but the smoke and lava kept gushing.

"Baga Loa is displeased," Tal said.

"Someone tried to take the Everbloom," Hobar said.

"The eruption will worsen unless the firewalkers soothe it," Baroi said.

Kendra watched in awestruck fascination. What would she do if a river of lava came her way? Would there be anywhere to hide? High ground? Or out in the ocean? Were the cyclopses right that there was no point in running?

"Come," Baroi said. "You grow restless. Let me escort

you back to the Monkey Maze. No harm will come to you today from this eruption."

Kendra accepted the invitation after one last long look. She also gave final glances to the Sunset Pearl and to the spot where she had planted the banyan seed before she walked away.

As Kendra balanced on a platform rising to the elaborate tree house, she listened to the roar of the volcano rumbling like a mighty wind. She could not see the eruption through the layered screen of leaves, but she had caught several glimpses of the towering discharge on her way back to the Monkey Maze with Baroi.

Kendra wondered how long the ancient trees would last against a river of lava. How much shelter could the powerful limbs provide against a pyroclastic flow of sweltering ash? How long before the forest and the hidden dwellings it protected toppled in fiery ruin?

As she neared the top of her ascent, Kendra saw the satyrs Newel and Doren on a platform off to one side, using badminton rackets to swat a shuttlecock back and forth without a net. Newel paused to wave at her before returning to his horseplay.

Kendra's lift drew level with a much bigger platform and stopped. The larger structure was one of many covered platforms, at various elevations, connected by walkways, rope bridges, and ladders, extending out of view in the lush canopy.

"Kendra!" Tess called, running to greet her.

Kendra was glad to see her cousin so exuberant. Behind Tess, Knox seemed calm and unharmed. Tanu acknowledged Kendra from beside Knox, his eyes showing both concern and welcome. The Samoan potion master looked rumpled but unhurt.

Standing apart from the others was a man clad in dark robes, with white hair and a neatly trimmed beard. Kendra had not expected to see Andromadus, and she was relieved by his presence.

"Are you all right?" Kendra asked Tess as they hugged.

"Yes," Tess said. "Except for the sand monsters who tried to kill us. And the erupting volcano."

"We'll keep you safe," Kendra said.

"That's what everyone keeps telling me," Tess said. "It kind of makes me worry."

"We have some reasons to worry," Kendra admitted. She lifted her gaze to Andromadus. "You came."

"We must talk."

"How are my grandparents?"

"The Sorensons remain in the secure room at Blackwell Keep with the others who sought refuge there," Andromadus said.

"Can't you just use magic to teleport them out?" Knox asked.

"The room is impervious to magic, which is part of what makes it secure," Andromadus explained.

"Did you know we were under attack?" Kendra asked.

Andromadus gave a weary sigh. "Everywhere is under attack. I came here to inform you and to recruit your assistance. Can we converse in private with Savani?"

"Sure," Kendra said.

"I want to hear," Knox complained.

"You will learn all you should know," Andromadus assured him.

"Don't forget, if the problem involves unstoppable demons, you might want me around," Knox warned.

"I'll watch Knox and Tess," Tanu offered. "Go."

Andromadus led Kendra over a sturdy bridge to a thatched platform, and then over a long rope bridge that rippled with every step. Pushing aside vines, they climbed a ladder to a higher, smaller landing, birds hooting around them, then crossed to a completely enclosed platform with a door. A menehune stood guard out front, not much taller than Kendra's waist, but with a gruff face and a body crammed with veiny muscles. Unseen through the leafy barriers, Baga Loa continued to grumble.

"Savani expects us," Andromadus announced.

The menehune rapped the door twice with his elbow.

"Send them in," Savani called.

The menehune reached up to open the door and stepped aside. Kendra and Andromadus entered a shuttered room with a tree trunk ascending through its center. Dim hanging lanterns and unshielded candles provided mellow luminance. Savani sat cross-legged before a brazier of red-hot coals, her back to the door, sleek shoulders exposed by a strapless wrap.

Kendra winced as Savani reached into the glowing coals and retrieved two in each hand. "Baga Loa is upset," intoned the caretaker of Crescent Lagoon.

"So we noticed," Andromadus replied.

"A thief tried to steal the Everbloom from her depths," Savani chanted with little inflection, rolling the coals against her palms, fingers caressing them.

Kendra had a sick feeling. "Was it Seth?"

"Your brother did enter Baga Loa," Savani said. "He approached the Everbloom but caused it no harm. The thief came afterward and was consumed by lava in the act of treachery."

"How safe is the Everbloom now?" Andromadus asked.

"The bloom was damaged but will be renewed," Savani said. "Baga Loa is one of the Earth's mightiest chimneys, and she remains in a state of distress."

"How bad will the eruption get?" Kendra asked.

"My people, the firewalkers, are performing the rituals to pacify her," Savani said, replacing the hot coals into the brazier. Without the coals in her hands, she assumed a more conversational tone as she turned to face them. "I believe we will succeed if the volcano receives no further provocation."

"Our enemies would rejoice if Baga Loa exploded," Andromadus said. "Guard her well."

"As always, we will do our duty," Savani said. "Tell me of the war."

Andromadus sighed. "Frosted Peaks has fallen. It

happened quickly. Celebrant grows bolder. He is organizing the dragons from the fallen preserves. The remaining sanctuaries are besieged, whether they know it or not. The wizards of the Small Council have openly joined Celebrant."

"Openly?" Savani asked.

"They have declared war alongside the dragons," Andromadus said.

"What is the Small Council?" Kendra asked.

"Wizards have never been great in number," Andromadus said. "We tend to operate individually, but the Major Council of Wizards forms when we need to work together or take disciplinary action, and every wizard has an equal voice. The Small Council, on the other hand, has long been an unsanctioned group of dissidents among us. Most of the wizards who joined the Society of the Evening Star were members of the Small Council."

"You've learned a lot about wizards in a short while," Kendra said.

"I have consulted with some of the others," Andromadus said. "Most of them were young dragons or not yet hatched back when I was the Dragon King. In fact, they have asked me to oversee the Major Council and to lead Dragonwatch."

"You accepted?" Kendra asked.

"I pledged to do my best," Andromadus said. "You know I didn't want any of this. My longtime attempts to withdraw from world events have utterly failed."

"We're grateful for your aid," Savani said.

"The Small Council formed to champion the rights of dragons," Andromadus said. "I applaud their original mission, but their intent has evolved from protecting the rights of dragons to promoting their darkest ambitions to the detriment of all. The Small Council has now shamelessly joined the fight to help dragons destroy humanity."

"What can the Small Council do?" Kendra asked.

"All kinds of mischief, unfortunately," Andromadus said. "Several members have official access to certain sanctuaries and preserves. One of them was responsible for the dullions that attacked this sanctuary today."

"Aren't the wizards mostly against the dragons?" Kendra asked.

"Do not misunderstand," Andromadus clarified. "None of us are against dragons. We all were once dragons. Our ancestors, our families, our descendants are dragons. But many of us are against the unnatural desire for dragons to combine into a society and raze their hunting ground. Dragons are solitary by nature. Do we hunt? Almost anything. Do we hoard? Everything of value. Do we wreak havoc? On occasion, especially if provoked.

"Before now, we had never sought to rule. We had never tried to organize a nation. And only once had we sought the level of destruction that would leave the world in ruins."

"The dragon war," Kendra said. "After they lost, the dragons were put into sanctuaries."

"I fear this new war is more deliberate and better organized," Andromadus said.

"Do all the dragons want this war?" Kendra asked. "Or mostly Celebrant?"

"I believe this way of thinking originated with him,

largely as a reaction to his incarceration," Andromadus said. "How deeply the other dragons have been indoctrinated, how truly they desire this new pattern of behavior, I cannot guess. But I believe that Celebrant is exploiting our innate desire for dominance to extremes that harm our best interests."

"What chance do we have against them?" Kendra asked.

"Celebrant has organized a hunt for the five legendary Dragon Slayers," Andromadus said. "It is a vulnerable time for those retired heroes—they have essentially been in hibernation since the dragon war. Nobody knows where to find them. Some or all of them might be asleep to their true identities. But the dragons remember them well and wish to eliminate those ancient foes before they can regain their former stature."

"We have to find the Dragon Slayers before they do," Kendra said.

"Just as we must recover the talismans hidden in the dragon temples—the Sage's Gauntlets, the Emperor's Shield, and the Harp of Ages. All dragons fear these items for good reason. And of course, at all cost, we must protect the Sovereign Skull, which augments the unbelief of mortals to potently repel dragons. If those deterrents are lost, Celebrant will ravage the globe."

"Are you ready to fight for us?" Kendra asked, knowing that Andromadus had always been committed to pacifism in the past.

"I will stand with you," Andromadus said, "for as long as

dragons are determined to pursue a course harmful to their kind and to all the world."

"Will you fight?" Kendra repeated.

"You know I am a pacifist," Andromadus said. "I recognize that there are times when even the peaceful must defend themselves from the violence and aggression of others. I cannot commit to physically harm my kind, but I commit to aid in your fight."

Kendra considered the wizard. His direct willingness to help represented progress. "I don't want to fight dragons," she said. "I don't want to fight anyone. But I can't let evil harm those I love."

"I understand that you intend to visit Titan Valley," Andromadus said.

"How did you hear that?" Kendra asked.

"I was talking to Tanu," Andromadus said. "He informed me about Seth."

"I have to find him," Kendra said.

"There is strategic value in you going there," Andromadus said. "For one, Titan Valley is the most secure of the dragon sanctuaries."

"By deplorable means," Savani said.

"What do you mean?" Kendra asked.

"The Giant Queen does not respect the creatures in her care," Savani said. "She doesn't serve them. At best, she views them as resources she controls."

"Few caretakers approve of her methods," Andromadus said. "And no wizards do. But we may need her aid in the war. And it works to our advantage to keep her sanctuary standing."

"How did she become the caretaker?" Kendra asked.

"By treaty, long ago," Andromadus said. "Appointing her to the position made the giants less of a threat and granted them a homeland. It did not go well for the dragons in her care. Before this war, if there were any sanctuary where I might have aided a dragon rebellion, it would have been Titan Valley."

"But you want me to go there?" Kendra asked.

"You are close to the Fairy Queen," Andromadus said. "That is an extraordinarily rare relationship. We will need her help in the upcoming conflict. Kendra, you killed the Demon King, and you wore the crown of the Fairy Queen."

"You heard about that?" Kendra asked.

"Yes, and it is plain to see to those who can perceive such things," Andromadus said. "You are also the former caretaker of a fallen dragon sanctuary. There is a chance you could curry favor with the Giant Queen. Win her to our cause. She has not shown much initiative in protecting anything besides her sanctuary."

"And I need to find my brother," Kendra said.

"Her help could simplify that task," Andromadus said.

"Then of course I'll try to make friends with her," Kendra said.

"I cringe to think of Kendra in company with that tyrant," Savani said.

"I do not wish it for her either," Andromadus said. "But these are desperate times, and Kendra has business at Titan

Valley because of her brother, and it is one of the last secure strongholds where members of Dragonwatch are still welcome."

"It makes sense," Savani said.

"Do you have a way to get there?" Andromadus asked.

"The Fairy Queen will allow me and some companions to travel through her realm," Kendra said.

"Almost unbelievable," Andromadus said. "And most fortunate. Kendra, you must preserve that relationship. Assistance from the Fairy Queen could prove vital in the coming conflict."

"It has saved me in the past," Kendra said. "Can't you teleport us there? Would that be simpler?"

"Sadly, the increase of power that comes with being a newborn wizard has abated," Andromadus said. "I wish I could have done more while at the zenith of my strength, but I was still learning what needed to be done. Even at the height of my power, I could not have sent you all the way to Titan Valley. There are other methods to get you there, but using the Fairy Realm is a simpler, more direct option."

"When should I leave with my friends?" Kendra asked.

"Soon," Andromadus said. "With all the trouble in the world, I have other places to be, but I will see you safely on your way."

"What about Knox and Tess?" Kendra asked.

"They are welcome to remain here for now," Savani said. "I believe the eruption will subside."

"They can stay here or go to Titan Valley," Andromadus

said. "Both locations have their dangers, but few places are safer in these war-torn times."

"We can talk to them about it," Kendra said. "But I need them out of harm's way."

"We will do all we can," Andromadus said. "Come. Titan Valley awaits."

CHAPTER FIVE

Troll Tavern

Are you sure this is the right way?" Seth asked.

"Not far now," Hermo replied.

"I thought you'd never been here before," Seth said.

"Never," Hermo agreed.

"Have you memorized a map?"

Hermo gave a disgusted chuckle. "No map. That slow. This easy."

"Hermit trolls are rumored to have special gifts for finding things," Calvin said from Seth's pocket. "And for hiding."

"Me have gift for everything," Hermo said. "Eat much food. Win prizes. Ride in fish. Jump far. Make speeches."

"That's a lot of gifts," Seth said.

"You second best," Hermo said. "You win when lucky."

"I won that game with the potatoes more than I lost," Seth said.

"Potato bad shape to throw," Hermo said. "Good shape for loser."

"It feels like we're roaming blindly through the bushes," Seth complained, pressing through some thick undergrowth. "Does your sense of direction ever lead to a path?"

"Road dicey," Hermo said. "Big guys see us. Eat you."

"I think we passed that tree before," Seth said. "Are we going in circles?"

"First time that tree," Hermo said. "You see tavern soon. Stop yapping."

Seth held back a reply, but he used his knife to carve a little mark on the tree. Next time he would have proof.

A few paces ahead, Hermo crouched between a pair of dense bushes. He pointed beyond the foliage. "Come see."

Seth came up beside the hermit troll and gazed across a clearing to where a huge structure sprawled beside a road. The haphazard edifice looked like it might have started out as a general store, but then various builders began adding wings, porches, balconies, beams, gables, cupolas, attics, weather vanes, chimneys, and towers without a comprehensive plan. The result was a disjointed monstrosity composed of wood, stone, brick, glass, clay, and thatch, surrounded by seven water towers on stilts of varying heights.

"Troll Tavern?" Seth guessed.

Hermo sniffed, wiping away a tear. "More beautiful than in stories."

"Should we go knock?" Seth asked, stepping forward.

Hermo grabbed his elbow and tugged him back. "Go

knock? A human? If anybody knock, they never let you in. In Troll Tavern, you must belong. You my slave. Only way."

"I have to pose as your slave to get in?" Seth asked.

Hermo nodded. "Be my slave to get in. To stay inside. And to stay alive. Only way."

"The tavern is just for trolls?" Seth asked.

"Only trolls and slaves," Hermo said.

"How do we sell it?" Seth asked. "Do we need a rope?"

"You follow me," Hermo said. "Obey and serve."

"You don't want me to call you master?" Seth checked.

"Good idea," Hermo said. "But no talk much. Bow sometimes."

"I'm not sure I like this plan," Calvin protested from Seth's pocket.

"Little bug say nothing," Hermo insisted.

"I'm not a bug," Calvin griped. "And Seth is no slave."

"Little bugs wait outside if no help," Hermo said. "This only way in."

"Let's play along," Seth said. "If they have good info here, it'll be worth it."

"Another option would be for the little guy to sneak inside," Calvin offered.

"No sneak," Hermo said. "Little bug get squished. We talk trolls. Ask questions. Get gossip."

"Do you know why we're going in there?" Seth checked.

"Legendary rabbit stew," Hermo said, licking his lips.

"No," Seth said.

"Win at cards?"

"We need info about Humbuggle," Seth said. "Where to find him. How to beat him."

"Don't forget Serena," Calvin added.

"Right, we need info about a nipsie called Serena," Seth said.

"What a nipsie?" Hermo asked.

"A little person like me," Calvin clarified.

"And I need to find Humbuggle," Seth said. "I want my memories back."

"I want memory of rabbit stew," Hermo pouted.

"How about we do both, Master?" Seth asked.

"Deal, Slave," Hermo said, spitting on his palm before shaking Seth's hand.

Seth immediately wiped his hand on his pants. "Should we head inside?"

"Yes," Hermo said. "You walk behind. You need slave name. Dirt Face good one."

"Anything to please Master," Seth said.

"I can't stomach this," Calvin said, his tone conveying legitimate suffering.

"Small price to pay if the info is good," Seth said. "Help us succeed."

Seth followed Hermo out into the clearing. He wondered how believable it would be that he was the slave of a stumpy little troll. Hopefully, if he played the role right, he could sell it. As they approached the tavern, Seth wondered if his shadow charming skills could prove useful. He reached out with his senses, trying to perceive any undead, in case he could mine them for information or perhaps gain an ally. None seemed to be in the area.

The road beside the tavern was empty. A squeaky sign swung in the breeze, and several wooden wind chimes clattered. The broad steps out front led to a door so tall Seth would need a ladder to reach the top. He wondered about the size of the trolls inside.

Hermo opened a smaller door to the left of the tall one and entered without a backward glance. Seth crouched to follow his temporary master.

Just inside the door loomed a thick-limbed troll who would have to duck to get through even the tall door. A pair of tusks jutted up from his lower jaw. The troll hunched forward to peer at Seth, making a rumbling sound in his chest like a dog about to attack.

"Him slave," Hermo said, jerking a thumb at Seth. "Him Dirt Face."

The hulking troll backed off, though he kept an unwelcoming eye on Seth. Snugly shuttered windows muted the daylight, and a sparse assortment of candles and torches provided uneven luminance while slowly blackening the rafters and ceiling with soot. Many obstacles limited lines of sight in the expansive room, including wooden beams, potted plants, heavy curtains, and booths built around tables. Niches and alcoves laced the edges of the room, with many doorways and halls leading elsewhere. Stairways climbed to murky galleries and lofts, and others curved down to unseen cellars.

Seth tried not to fixate on any of the occupants of the

shadowy booths huddled in hushed conversation. The variety of trolls astonished him. Most were reptilian in their scales and features, though some were hairy, a few were porcine, and a couple had feathers. The trolls came in varied sizes and builds, though none stood shorter than Hermo. Seth noted sharp claws, crooked fangs, intimidating tusks, gill slits, webbed fingers and toes, mottled markings, horns, spikes, and warty bumps in endless combinations. The trolls dressed simply, with few sporting more than a vest on their upper bodies, and none wearing footwear. Most carried weapons, and a majority displayed sparse items of jewelry— an earring here, a pendant there, an anklet on another.

Seth noticed many trolls stealing glances at him or slyly following him from the sides of their eyes. Trying not to let his gaze rove, he kept his focus on Hermo and waited for chances to show his devotion as a slave. Thanks to his gift with languages, the murmured conversations around him sounded like English, but he could tell the trolls were actually speaking Duggish.

"Why you here, Dog Breath?" challenged an accuser.

Seth saw another hermit troll waddling their way. He was almost as short and stumpy as Hermo, his head too big for his body, wide nostrils flaring.

"Me visiting," Hermo shot back. "Why you out of hole, Snot Lick?"

"Me no Snot Lick," the hermit troll said. "Me Jeff."

"You no Jeff," Hermo said. "What real name?"

"Me Fonnar."

"Me Hermo. You get lost."

"This my lair."

Hermo gave a derisive chuckle. "This for many trolls."

"Me have places here," Fonnar said.

Hermo cocked his head and looked around. "Maybe."

"Why bring human?" Fonnar asked.

"Human my slave," Hermo said. "You get lost or he throw potatoes."

Fonnar sized up Seth. "He no look slave."

"He valet," Hermo said smugly.

Fonnar shooed Hermo away with both hands. "Hermit troll no have valet. No have slave either. No have human."

Hermo puffed out his chest. "You not know what best hermit troll have."

"You no best," Fonnar said.

"I ride in fish," Hermo said. "I have human." Hermo glanced around. "Where your slave?"

"Me busy," Fonnar sputtered, wobbling off. Hermo approached a bar where a stocky gray troll with black stripes filled a mug from a spigot.

"Me want famous rabbit stew," Hermo said. "And brick of rat tallow for human."

"How do you intend to pay?" the bartender asked in a gravelly voice.

"Him pay," Hermo said, jerking a thumb at Seth.

Seth absently patted his pockets and realized the Tiny Hero was no longer in there. Neither was any money.

"How much does the stew cost?" Seth asked.

The bartender leaned forward with a gleam in his eye,

his smile revealing rows of teeth made for shredding. "You speak Duggish?"

"I aim to please," Seth said.

"A slave to this little one, are you?" the bartender asked.

"I strive to serve Master well," Seth said.

"Master, is it? Well, for you and his excellency, the price of a bowl of soup is merely ten pounds of gold and a basket of diamonds. I'll throw in the rat tallow for any ruby larger than a hen's egg."

"Too much," Hermo griped.

"Or else, three healthy human children," the bartender bargained.

"Him no like you," Hermo told Seth. "You go so I eat stew."

"Did either of you notice this is *Troll* Tavern?" the bartender asked through gritted teeth. "We don't take kindly to humans here, nor any who brings one."

"He no human," Hermo said. "He Dirt Face. He slave."

"Where are his chains?" the bartender asked.

"He trained," Hermo said.

The bartender chuckled, then raised his voice. "Anybody spy a human in the room?"

"I smelled something awful," a gruff voice answered, drawing laughs.

"I saw a human," another troll called. "Thought maybe I had too much to drink."

"Anybody claim him?" the bartender asked.

"He my slave," Hermo piped up.

The bartender slapped both hands on the bar and glared

down at Hermo. "Are you standing by that claim in this company?"

"Not now," Hermo muttered, stepping away.

"Anybody else care to speak for the human?" the bartender asked.

The room was quiet.

"Who wants fresh human on the menu?" the bartender asked.

Uproarious cheering greeted the proposition. All eyes were on Seth now, and Hermo was edging away, looking miserable. Seth realized he was on his own.

Searching inside himself, Seth found the cold and darkness Ronodin had taught him to seek, then reached out with his ability to the candles and torches in the room and started dousing them. Startled trolls gasped and murmured, and a moment later the room sank into near-perfect blackness. A sudden chill pierced the air.

"Spellcraft," a voice accused.

"Witchery," another cried.

"I'm no slave," Seth challenged loudly.

"Shadow charmer!" a voice exclaimed.

"Last week I was doing errands for the Underking," Seth said. "Today I'm on business of my own. Take care, you never know what unseen beings are within the call of a shadow charmer. I overthrew Wyrmroost in a day. Maybe I'll let your tavern stand for a while if somebody can answer my questions."

A troll with a face like a bulldog covered in snakeskin

lit a torch. "He's all right," the troll said. "It's the one that killed Graulas. Tornick, today he eats on my tab."

More candles and torches were lit, and trolls started turning back to their own conversations. Seth had failed to inspire much awe, but he seemed to have dodged disaster.

"You still want rabbit stew for the little one?" the bartender asked.

"Are you Tornick?" Seth asked.

The bartender gave a little bow. "What's your business here?"

"I'm looking for Humbuggle," Seth said.

Tornick hawked, spat on the counter, and started wiping it with a grimy rag. "Might be less trouble to let us eat you."

"Shadow charmers taste horrible," Seth said.

Tornick shrugged. "I'll take your word for it. What about the stew? You have an open tab."

"Thanks," Seth said. "Some stew would be great."

"What will you have?" the bartender asked. "Still hungry for rat tallow?"

"Do you have any human food?" Seth asked.

Tornick patted the counter as if imitating a drumroll. "We have bread and cheese."

"I'll take it," Seth said. Then he hesitated. "Is it possum cheese or something?"

"We have several varieties," Tornick said. "The kind I had in mind for you is made with cow's milk."

"Sounds all right," Seth said.

Hermo sidled up to Seth as Tornick moved away.

"Your stew is coming," Seth said.

"Good slave," Hermo said.

"No problem," Seth said. "But I'm not your slave." He felt something brush his ankle and glanced down to find Calvin climbing his pant leg. Seth subtly put a hand down and lifted the nipsie to his shoulder.

"You want Dante," Calvin whispered loud enough for Seth to hear.

"Who is that?" Seth asked.

"A troll in a secret back room," Calvin said. "He has been watching you through peepholes. The other trolls whisper his name with reverence."

"Good job," Seth said.

"They call me Tiny Hero for a reason," Calvin said. "Don't forget to ask about Serena."

"I won't," Seth promised.

"Me almost got to try slave soup," Hermo said.

"Nobody cooks me without a fight," Seth muttered. He regarded the bustling room, dozens of trolls engaged in conspiratorial conversations, more than a few gazes straying his way. "Is this place all you dreamed?"

"It not bad," Hermo said. "Me know more when stew comes."

Tornick returned with half a loaf of bread and a big hunk of white cheese for Seth and a steaming bowl of chunky stew for Hermo. The hermit troll had to kneel on his stool to be tall enough for the counter.

"I need to talk to Dante," Seth mumbled softly.

"What are you going on about?" Tornick asked, matching his quiet tone.

"Dante," Seth repeated. "I need to see Dante."

"Never heard of the guy," Tornick whispered.

"Don't play dumb," Seth said. "Everybody knows Dante."

"Oh, *that* Dante," Tornick acknowledged. "I hear you. The briar troll. He hasn't been seen around these parts in a good while."

"He's in the back room," Seth said. "He'll be glad he saw me."

Tornick couldn't hide his surprise. "You're determined to get yourself into hot water."

"It's where I swim," Seth whispered boldly. "Go tell Dante the shadow charmer wants to have words with him. Or find somebody who can."

Tornick shrugged. "Your funeral."

Seth cut a slice of bread and put cheese on it. The bread was a little stale, but the cheese tasted quite good. A simple meal, but tasty, and different from what he had eaten in the leviathan. Seth chewed slowly, hoping it made him look casual about the surrounding danger.

Hermo finished his stew by tipping the bowl against his lips and licking the interior clean, then wiped his mouth on his sleeve. "Me like this place."

Seth popped a little piece of cheese into his mouth without any bread. "It's growing on me."

Two trolls wearing long coats approached Seth from behind, one on each side, squeezing in close. They matched each other, tall and muscular, with silvery scales and curled horns like a ram's. One leaned in closer than the other, staying in profile as he studied Seth through a narrow eye on the side of his head.

"Alley trolls," Hermo mumbled, leaping one stool farther away.

"Folks who nose around here tend to have accidents," the beefy troll said.

"I want to see Dante," Seth said.

"He doesn't know you," the troll replied. "He wonders how you know him."

"He has a reputation," Seth said.

"Why should he talk to a stinking human?"

Seth forced himself to put some bread in his mouth. He hoped to look relaxed as he gave his answer. "I want his advice before I tear this sanctuary apart."

He chewed as the trolls on either side of him exchanged uncertain glances. "Dante doesn't like strangers."

"Look, if you can't take me to him, go find a troll who can," Seth said.

The trolls shared another glance. "Very well," the spokesman said. "Let's see how long you last."

CHAPTER SIX

Departure

I'm coming with you," Knox insisted. Outside the window of the elevated room, smoke and ash plumed up from Baga Loa. "How can you pretend it is any safer here where sand monsters attack us and a volcano is erupting!"

"Savani is getting things under control," Kendra said.

"But she can't protect us like a Giant Queen could," Knox said.

"I'd love to see a Giant Queen," Tess expressed. "Does she wear fancy gowns?"

"I'm not sure," Kendra said. "Technically the Giant Queen is part of Dragonwatch. But she does things her own way. We're not sure how much we can rely on her."

"But she keeps her dragons under control," Knox said.

"It's supposed to be the most secure sanctuary," Kendra said.

"Then why aren't we there already?" Knox asked. "Tess is just a kid! Don't you want her secure?"

"I'm into double digits," Tess said.

"I'm not new to giants," Knox reminded Kendra. "You were there when we partied with Thronis. Besides, even if Titan Valley is super dangerous, I've proven I can handle emergencies. I want to help you get Seth back."

"It isn't your fault he was taken," Kendra said.

"I'm the reason Ronodin had access to the barrel," Knox said. "I left the keys to the dungeon with the goblin at Fablehaven."

"You made a mistake," Kendra said. "It's good to learn from, but it was Ronodin who took him."

"I can still help save him," Knox argued.

"The dragon war is heating up," Kendra said. "With more preserves falling, the dragons are gaining momentum. I have a feeling Titan Valley could become a battlefield."

"Visiting Remulon turned into a battle," Knox said. "If I hadn't been along, you might still be his prisoner. You need me."

"The more people helping, the better your chances," Tess said. "I want to come too."

Kendra sighed. Knox really had saved the day when they faced Remulon. And he was right that Titan Valley might prove to be a safer sanctuary than Crescent Lagoon. "Fine. If that's what you want, you and Tess can come."

Knox pumped a fist. "Yes."

"You might not thank me in the end," Kendra warned.

"Let me at least enjoy the beginning," Knox said. "We're going through fairyland?"

"We are?" Tess asked breathily, eyes wide.

"Yeah, the Fairy Realm," Kendra said. "We'll just be passing through."

"When?" Tess asked.

"Now," Kendra said. "I'd intended to say goodbye to you, not to bring you along. Grab what you need."

Kendra exited the room and went to the main platform, where Warren, Vanessa, Tanu, Newel, Doren, Savani, and Andromadus awaited her. "Knox and Tess are coming," she announced.

"That confirms it," Newel said. "We're coming too."

"We'd love your help," Kendra said.

"Nobody made life interesting like Seth," Doren said.

"Without him we might never have learned about fast food," Newel said.

"Or video games," Doren said.

"Or gummy candy," Newel added. "He must be rescued."

"So be it," Andromadus said. "Kendra, do you know the story of the Legender?"

"That doesn't sound familiar," she admitted.

"The tale explains the origin of the legendary Dragon Slayers," Andromadus said. "These are the five Dragon Slayers who set the pattern for all others. The ones we hope to find. It might be of value for you to know it." He pulled a large book from within the folds of his robe. "There are many versions of the story. I like this illustrated telling."

Kendra accepted the oversized book and leafed through

it. The book wasn't thick and had fairly large type, with fanciful illustrations and illuminated letters. "I'll read it."

"The dragons are hunting the legendary slayers," Andromadus said. "We need to find the slayers first."

"Don't leave yet," Knox called. "Here we come!"

He and Tess ran into view from across a bridge.

"Should I leave a note for the fairies?" Tess asked.

"I will give them your kind regards," Savani said.

"Shall I transport us to the fairy shrine?" Andromadus asked.

"Sure," Kendra said. "It's nice to have a wizard around."

Andromadus looked at Savani. "You have much to accomplish here."

Savani gave a small bow. "I bid you all a fond farewell and wish you safe travels."

"Thanks for everything," Kendra said.

"Keep that volcano calm," Knox added.

"We will do what we can," Savani said.

"Come," Andromadus said. "The fairy shrine awaits."

Waterfalls spilled from a semicircular embankment into a shallow marsh where large tiki statues waded. They were in different locations from where Kendra had found them on her previous visit. She knew the statues could move, though she had never caught one in the act. Kendra understood that unwanted trespassers into the fairy shrine would be destroyed, but today, she and her friends had permission.

"Freaky statues," Knox said. "Where are the fairies?"

"Did you drink your milk?" Tess asked.

"I drink it every morning," Knox said.

"Then you would see them if they were here," Tess replied.

"I expect we'll see plenty when we cross to the Fairy Realm," Kendra said.

"This is where we part ways," Andromadus said. "I must make assignments to some of the members of Dragonwatch, and the Polar Plains sanctuary has requested my assistance."

"I wish you could come with us," Tess said.

"You will be protected," Andromadus said. "I notified the Giant Queen about your visit. A giant called Rustafet will meet you at the Titan Valley fairy shrine and provide you with safe access to the castle."

"What kind of welcome can we expect from the Giant Queen?" Kendra asked.

"As official visitors from Dragonwatch, you can count on her hospitality," Andromadus said. "If you want a word of advice, she will think you perceptive and intelligent if you recognize her virtues. But don't overdo it. She is no fool." The wizard vanished in a burst of red light.

"So dramatic," Warren said.

"You'd do it if you could," Vanessa teased.

"I'd probably moonwalk first," Warren said. "Maybe throw in a spin."

"I can hardly believe a blix will be allowed to enter the Fairy Realm," Vanessa said. "No matter how briefly."

"The Fairy Queen is letting me bring whoever I want," Kendra said. "This way."

"We have to wade into the water?" Knox asked.

"Going through will dry us off," Kendra told him. "Don't grab any treasure you see along the way. It's a trap." She sloshed deeper into the marsh. The others followed.

"So don't go take that golden shield over there?" Warren asked.

"That's exactly the kind of thing to ignore," Kendra said.

"But I want it," Newel pouted.

"What about a scepter with a big emerald?" Knox asked.

"Resist the urge," Kendra said.

Doren whimpered miserably.

Kendra led them to a curtain of clear water at the rear of the semicircle. The water doused her as she passed through, and the others came after, crowding into the humid alcove, ankle-deep in water. A tiny fairy statue stood near a bronze bowl in a niche opposite the waterfall.

"Ladies and gentlemen," Knox announced, "I give you . . . the back side of water!" He gestured at the waterfall.

Newel and Doren snickered.

"Hush," Kendra said. "This is a sacred place."

"Is that a statue of the Fairy Queen?" Tess asked politely.

"I'm not sure," Kendra said, squinting at it. "But I know it represents her power."

"Where do we go now?" Knox asked.

"We ask her for help," Kendra said, clearing her throat. "Fairy Queen, I am here to cross through your realm to

Titan Valley. I brought my friends and family as we agreed. Can you help us cross over?"

The air stirred and became rich with earthy aromas. A hand reached up out of the water, which seemed impossible because it was so shallow. Tess shrieked.

"It's all right," Kendra said. Crouching and taking the hand, she was pulled down into the water and almost immediately found she was being pulled up out of a pool of water by the Fairy King. The seamless transition from down to up felt strangely natural despite seeming illogical.

"Hello, Kendra," the Fairy King said. "Welcome back." He was dressed like a woodsman, with a dark brown cloak.

As he stooped and placed his hand into the water again, Kendra looked around for Bracken or the Fairy Queen. She saw neither, but there were four astrids standing nearby, golden wings tucked behind gilded armor. Kendra realized she was perfectly dry. The Fairy King helped Knox through, then Tess, Tanu, Vanessa, Newel, Doren, and finally Warren. They arose from the water completely dry.

"Look at the birdmen," Tess whispered loudly. "They're all muscly."

"Welcome," the Fairy King said. "Bracken asked that I apologize on his behalf. He and his mother are combating the remaining demons."

"There are still demons here?" Warren asked. "After all this time?"

"Regrettably, yes," the Fairy King said. "Several were entrenched when we took over the demon prison. A few took time to discover. Three major pockets of darkness remain here, preventing the Fairy Realm from becoming whole."

"Can we help?" Tanu asked.

"I appreciate the sentiment," the Fairy King said. "I do not wish to put you at risk. You have more than enough trouble to contend with outside of this realm. Come, I will lead you to Titan Valley."

He guided them into a cheerful forest of tall, slender trees with silver bark and golden leaves. Abundant wildflowers of endless variety served as undergrowth. Shimmering fairies flitted among the blossoms, coaxing more vibrance out of them. Several drifted over near Tess, tittering.

Vanessa pointed. "The moss on that stone is getting brown. Isn't this supposed to be the undying land?"

The Fairy King gave a nod. "Until darkness is expelled, this realm remains tainted. Sharp eyes will apprehend other examples."

"It's paradise, your majesty," Newel said. "Don't stare at the nymphs," he added to Doren out of the side of his mouth.

"Almost paradise," the Fairy King said sadly.

Kendra began scanning for imperfection amid the beauty. She noticed a few droopy blossoms, but overall the scene came close to a flawless ideal.

On the far side of the forest, the lane emerged onto a brilliant lawn, with flowering shrubs adding variety, along with some colossal sunflowers. In the distance, Kendra observed pillars of dark smoke rising into the pristine sky. Flames licked up at the base of the smoke.

"Those woods are on fire," Kendra said.

"Now you see what consumes Bracken's attention," the Fairy King said.

"The demons are burning down your forest?" Knox asked.

"A great deal of power is colliding to try to expel them," the Fairy King said. "I believe we will succeed, but it will require time and sacrifice."

They turned onto another lane and crossed a brook using a bridge that spanned it in a single, graceful arc. Glancing down as they crossed, Kendra glimpsed a pair of naiads swimming upstream.

"The berries on this bush," Vanessa said, approaching a shrub on the far side of the stream. The small black berries looked grainy. She picked one, and as she rubbed it between her thumb and two fingers, the berry disintegrated into cinders, leaving smudges on her hand.

"Very astute," the Fairy King said. "This way."

"What are those berries supposed to be like?" Kendra asked. "Why would that happen?"

"How are a few holdout demons having so much influence?" Tanu asked.

"Something is awry here," the Fairy King said. "This was the demon prison not long ago. We're working on it."

Kendra kept watch as they continued along the lane. She saw so much beauty, the undying glory of spring she had beheld on previous visits. But she also noticed dead leaves, fallen blossoms, and an occasional dry patch of grass.

Warren pointed out a small tree where a few of the

branches writhed like tentacles, reaching and curling. Knox hustled over for a closer look.

"Stay back," the Fairy King warned. "That tree has fallen under unnatural influences."

The squirming branches stretched toward Knox, but he stopped short of their grasp and moved away. "This place is messed up," he muttered.

At length they reached a small, clear pond. "Your destination awaits," the Fairy King said. "Simply walk into the water."

Kendra looked back at the smoke from the fire. It seemed like the blaze was growing. "Tell Bracken I miss him."

"I hope he will join you soon," the Fairy King said. "Please keep all information about this realm, especially our recent troubles, to yourselves."

"You can count on us," Tanu said.

"Good luck," the Fairy King said, backing away.

Kendra got the feeling he had other duties that needed attention. "Thanks. You too."

She walked into the water. It felt like a normal pond at first, with a muddy bottom, but as the water got deeper, the ground fell away beneath her and she dropped completely under the surface. After a moment of darkness and disorientation, kicking with her legs and sweeping with her arms, Kendra rose up out of the water and stroked to the edge of a different pond.

A colonnade ran in a circle around the pond, the white marble columns supporting a narrow roof that curved into a complete ring. Her companions swam out of the pond as well, Vanessa staying by Tess until they were out of the water. There was no magical drying this time. Newel and Doren sent water flying as they shook their furry haunches.

"Welcome to Titan Valley," Warren said. The pond was located on a flat-topped knoll, affording them a view of the moderately hilly countryside.

"Have any of you been here before?" Knox asked.

They looked at one another.

"I don't think so," Tanu said.

"We're supposed to find a giant," Kendra said.

From off to one side, somebody cleared his throat, and a huge head poked up over the edge of the hilltop. "Don't mean to startle you," the giant said. "I wanted to give you a moment to get your bearings."

The giant was a husky man with a bulbous nose. He could almost have been human, except for the massive scale of his size. Kendra felt sure he was bigger than Thronis.

"Hello!" Warren hailed him, waving a hand. "Are you here to bring us to the Giant Queen?"

"I'm Rustafet," the giant said. "Assistant to her majesty's majordomo."

"I'm Kendra, and these are my companions."

"Welcome to Titan Valley," Rustafet said. He turned around to show that he was wearing a three-story wicker house on his back like a backpack. "If you step inside, I will transport you to Terastios."

"Thank you," Kendra said.

He squatted and maneuvered to bring the base of the

house level with the hilltop. Warren opened the door, and the others filed past him. The wicker home had basic wicker furnishings affixed to the ground and walls. Wicker stairs led to the upper levels.

"Latch the door," Rustafet said. "You probably want to sit down until you're used to the motion. Some passengers have told me it is like being on a rough sea."

Kendra found a sofa, and Tess sat beside her. Knox went to a window. Warren latched the door and sat near Vanessa and Tanu. Newel and Doren raced each other up the stairs, each elbowing to be first.

"We're all set!" Kendra called.

"Hold on," Rustafet said, standing upright and causing the whole house to lurch. Kendra gripped the arm of the sofa to keep from falling off, and Knox clutched the windowsill. In a few steps the giant reached the bottom of the hill, and the jostling of the house smoothed out to a gentle sway.

"I can't believe we're riding in a giant's backpack," Knox called from the window.

"It's a portable domicile," Rustafet corrected. "Sorry if it was a rocky start—that hill was kind of steep. Should be smoother from now on. Won't take very long. Sit back and enjoy the ride!"

CHAPTER SEVEN

Dante

The alley trolls conducted Seth through the dim common room to a recessed door blocked by a barrel. One troll moved the barrel aside while the other stepped forward and used a crooked key to open the door. Seth glanced behind at Hermo, who followed at a distance, holding his empty bowl. Seth pointed at the door, and Hermo took a couple of paces back, shaking his head.

The trolls ushered Seth into a short hall with several doors, lit by a few drippy candles. The fuzzy, striped wallpaper made the walls seem gift wrapped, and dusty paintings of distinguished trolls hung in gaudy frames. The alley trolls escorted Seth to the last door on the left. It opened into a musty broom closet. One troll went to the back of the closet, flipped a hidden switch, then slid the rear wall of the closet aside.

Seth and the trolls stepped into a windowless sitting room illuminated only by the flames within the wide fireplace. A stocky troll relaxed in a leather armchair, long feet propped on an ottoman. Short upturned horns protruded from his face and head, and smaller ones thorned the backs of his hands. He had three bony chins, side by side, and heavy-lidded eyes that regarded Seth indifferently.

"Dante?" Seth asked.

"Why bring a hermit troll?" the seated troll asked, his voice almost a croak.

Seth thought about the question. "He's funny."

"Unwittingly, perhaps," the troll replied. "Is he not a liability?"

"He's the only troll I know."

"And you wanted access here?"

"Sure."

The seated troll glanced at his henchmen. "Leave us. I'll signal when you're needed."

The trolls bowed and exited the room.

"Are you the head alley troll?" Seth asked.

The seated troll gave a snort. "I am Dante, but I am no alley troll. Do you really know so little of our kind?"

"I'm Seth. I've heard of trolls. I don't recall meeting any before the hermit troll."

"You are bold to intrude here unprepared," Dante said. "And foolish. I am a briar troll."

"I need some information," Seth said.

At this Dante gave a chuckle. "Just information? Is

intelligence a casual matter?" He held up a hand, displaying a dark ring, set with a black jewel. "Do you know this ring?"

"It looks valuable," Seth said.

"Indeed," Dante said. "But the material worth pales compared to the symbolic importance. Do you know who owned this ring before me?"

"No."

"This is the signature ring of Ulrik the Intolerable."

"Okay."

"What does my possession of this ring tell you?"

"It's yours now?"

"What else?" the troll asked, his expression inscrutable.

"You're a collector? Black is your color? You killed Ulrik?"

Dante averted his gaze and shook his head sadly. "Ulrik died long ago. He entrusted this ring to me, and it means I know the location of his treasure hoard."

"Did his treasure make you rich?" Seth asked.

"Not exactly," Dante said. "No need. It is more valuable to me where it lies. Ulrik was cunning and wealthy, a troll of great renown. Because I alone know the location of his hoard, no sane troll would wish me harm."

"Or the treasure would be lost," Seth said.

"My knowledge makes it absurd for anyone to cross me," Dante said.

"Anyone who cares about the treasure," Seth corrected.

"Which includes any self-respecting troll," Dante said. "And anyone else with common sense." He held up the hand with the ring, fingers splayed. "I carry several such tokens, making me invaluable. Many a troll hopes I pass on some of my secrets before I go. Perhaps I will. Perhaps I won't."

"Asking for knowledge can be a big deal," Seth said, trying to skip to the conclusion.

"That depends on the information you seek," Dante said. The briar troll lifted a small, ivory container from a stand beside his chair, flipped open the oval lid, and sniffed the contents. His eyes rolled back in his head, and he sagged in his chair, then closed the lid and replaced the container on the stand. "If you ask me what to order from the tavern, I lose little by suggesting a menu item. Then again, I don't like to waste my time with trivialities."

"You want to know my question," Seth said.

"I'd rather learn how I benefit from answering," Dante said.

"I have information too," Seth said.

The briar troll nodded. "I suppose you do. The question is whether you know anything that might prove valuable to me."

"I wonder the same thing," Seth said.

"As is your right," Dante said, "though you sought me out." He gestured to a nearby chair. "Have a seat."

Seth sensed an element of ritual to the invitation, as if the door to negotiation had been opened. He sat down on the edge of the chair and studied Dante by the flickering light of the fire, waiting for him to speak.

"Why chance a visit to Troll Tavern?" Dante asked.

"The hermit troll recommended it as a good place for information," Seth said.

"You understand that hermit trolls are rabble?" Dante asked. "Almost vermin?"

"I like him," Seth said, offended on Hermo's behalf. He was better company than the unfriendly, self-important trolls he had met at the tavern.

"I suppose anyone deserves their pets," Dante said off-handedly. "It was dangerous to come. Trolls are not gentle creatures."

"I really need information," Seth said.

Dante stretched lazily. "And what stops me from throttling you for trespassing here unannounced?"

"Do trolls waste resources?" Seth asked. "Do you know many shadow charmers?"

"A valid argument," Dante said. "And the chief reason you remain alive. It was a good spectacle, dousing the torches. You made the others wonder what else you could do, how you might harm them or help them."

"You saw that?" Seth asked.

"I am aware of what transpires in my tavern," Dante said. "Tell me why you came to Titan Valley."

"Will you keep my secret?" Seth asked.

"Why should I?"

"If you want to hear it," Seth said.

Dante produced a coin and rolled it across his knuckles, first one way, then the other. "I accept that condition."

"Can a troll be trusted to keep his word?" Seth asked.

Dante's feet slapped to the floor and he leaned forward. "Are you baiting me?"

"I'm new to trolls," Seth said.

"To dishonor one's word is instant bankruptcy."

"You promise to keep my business here a secret?" Seth asked.

"Done," Dante said, settling back in his chair. "Proceed."

Seth knew through Ronodin that most magical creatures were much truer to their word than mortals, so he decided to risk confiding in Dante. "I lost my memory. I'm here to regain it."

"Why here?"

"Humbuggle took my identity."

Dante nodded as if the information added up. "Where? How?"

"At Wyrmroost. Inside Stormguard Castle."

"You disturbed his game there," Dante said.

"Yes."

"And you discovered he returned to his former home."

"I'm here to find him and get my memories back," Seth said.

Dante shrugged. "Your motivations may differ from the pack somewhat, but in essence you came here for the same reason most outsiders come—Humbuggle and his Games."

"He has games here?" Seth asked.

Dante gave him a disbelieving look. "You have never heard of the Titan Games?"

"Who knows?" Seth said. "I lost my memories."

This seemed to satisfy the briar troll. "Humbuggle

established the Games centuries ago. Competitors vie for the chance to compete in the Titan Games, with the Wizenstone as the grand prize."

"This is common knowledge?" Seth asked.

"It is no secret," Dante said.

"I don't care about the Games," Seth said. "I just want my memory back."

Dante grinned. "How do you expect to convince Humbuggle to grant your request?"

"I haven't gotten to that part yet," Seth said. "First I have to find him."

"You understand that you are talking about perhaps the most elusive and powerful demon in the world?" Dante asked. "The greatest warriors and adventurers have been trying to thwart Humbuggle for millennia. He has the Wizenstone under his control. He is notoriously clever."

"Do you know how I can find him?" Seth asked.

"There is only one sure way to get close to Humbuggle," Dante said. "Participate in his Games, and, ideally, win."

"Where do I enter?" Seth asked. "How do I win?"

"I am often asked for advice about the Games," Dante said. "Competitors always seek an advantage. The Games are complex. There is more to them than greets the eye. And there is a reason they have been going on for centuries without a victor."

"I'll win the Games if that's what it takes," Seth said.

Dante gave a nod. "You're clearly willing to risk your life, or you would not be inside this tavern."

"I need my memories," Seth said.

"If I lost my memories, I would want them returned," Dante said. "But if I had lost them to Humbuggle? I would be tempted to leave them behind and start making new ones. My free advice ends there."

"What about help I earn?" Seth asked.

"If it benefits me, sure, I could offer extra assistance," Dante said. "There are those who advise prospective competitors in the Games. Some could reveal valuable secrets. Help with the Games is a common request. Why should I take yours seriously?"

"What can I do for you?" Seth asked.

"Do you have riches to offer?" Dante asked.

"None," Seth said. "At least not that I remember."

"You're young," Dante said. "You have had little time to achieve much. It's a surprise that a being of your tender years is a shadow charmer."

"I had some help," Seth said, hoping to be mysterious.

"I'm not interested in your history," Dante said.

"I know things about the dragon war," Seth said. "And the Under Realm."

"Celebrant is abroad," Dante said. "Soaring Cliffs fell. You helped Wyrmroost fall. Crescent Lagoon fell and was reclaimed. Frosted Peaks went down recently. Do you know what Celebrant intends for Titan Valley? Do you still serve his cause?"

"I'm not sure how much to say without an arrangement," Seth said.

"Mortals lie more readily than most," Dante said. "A

disgusting trait. The story about your memories might be fabrication."

"I gave you my word," Seth said.

"Tell me why you helped topple Wyrmroost," Dante said.

"I was in training, working for the Underking," Seth said.

Dante shivered. "I believe you. I can spot a liar. But I doubt you have knowledge I need. I want no dealings with the undead."

"Are there winnings in the Games?" Seth asked. "Could I offer you a share?"

"This troll wants no share of hypothetical prizes," Dante said. "I don't speculate that way. Let others gamble."

"Could I owe you a favor?" Seth asked. "My abilities are useful."

"What favor can a dead boy provide?" Dante countered. "The Games are lethal. Even armed with sound advice, you are heading to your demise. Unless you can offer value now, I see no profit in helping you."

"I'm a shadow charmer," Seth said. "Do you have any problems with the undead?"

Dante rubbed two of his three chins. "As a matter of fact, there is a cottage on the road just east of here with an unruly presence inside."

"A wraith?" Seth asked.

"You pick a name," Dante said. "I don't study these matters. If you expel the presence, I will provide you with an introduction to one who can advise you about the Games."

"Sounds fair," Seth said.

"Brunt will escort you," Dante said, heaving himself to his feet. "Succeed and we both benefit."

"I'll see you soon," Seth assured him.

"I like the confidence," Dante said, slapping Seth on the shoulder. "If you perish, Brunt and I will share a good laugh."

CHAPTER EIGHT

Giant Queen

I s that dragon pulling a wagon?" Knox called from where he stood by the window in the wall of the wicker house.

Kendra crossed the swaying floor and braced herself against the windowsill. The view was out the side of the house. Not far off, moving parallel to them, a giant considerably smaller than Rustafet drove a huge wagon harnessed to an emerald green dragon, the heap of cargo in the back covered by a tarp. Wings pinned down by the harness, the dragon strained to pull the heavy load as the driver swung a lash.

"No way," Kendra said.

"Get used to that sight," Rustafet said. "No free rides for dragons at this sanctuary. They contribute."

Vanessa, Warren, and Tess gathered at another window.

"I never imagined I would see a sight like this," Vanessa said.

"Is it safe to ride in a dragon wagon?" Tess asked.

"I want to ride in one," Warren said. "Pulled by Celebrant. Maybe I'll feed him a carrot."

As Rustafet progressed onward, they passed other dragons hauling other loads, all wearing confining harnesses. Then Kendra spotted a huge brick building with a red dragon chained out back. When the bald giant beside the dragon prodded it with an iron spear, the dragon blew fire through a window into the facility.

"What is happening there?" Knox asked.

"Dragon forge?" Warren guessed.

"Exactly," Rustafet said cheerfully. "We have the last five dragon forges in the world."

"What are those?" Tess asked, pointing upward. "Dragon kites?"

Up ahead Kendra saw a pair of dragons circling in the sky, harnessed to long poles. As they drew nearer, Kendra beheld that the poles attached to a wheel atop a squat tower.

"It's a mill," Tanu said, "powered by dragons in flight."

"Very good," Rustafet said. "The mills are a newer innovation, but we're getting good results. It took time to develop poles that were long enough, light enough, and strong enough. Plenty of magic involved!"

"Don't the dragons fight back?" Kendra asked.

"It's been a long while since we had serious resistance," Rustafet said. "It took the Giant Queen some time to establish order here. But now the reptiles generally know their place. A few rogues are on the loose, but they stay free by hiding, not fighting."

Kendra could hardly believe her ears. Dragons were so proud and fierce! Yet there in front of her was a smallish silver dragon rigged to a plow, managed by a burly giant with a heavy tunic and a tangled black beard.

"What would Celebrant say to this?" Knox asked.

"He would go berserk," Warren said.

"He would burn this sanctuary to the ground," Kendra said.

Rustafet chuckled. "A lot of us actually hope the warring dragons come here. Once we subjugate them, we could expand our industries! Build more forges, mills, and wagons!"

Kendra wondered what a fight between giants and dragons might look like. Having seen dragons in action, she suspected the battle might not be as easy as Rustafet seemed to think. "Can't the dragons burn you?"

"Depends on the giant," Rustafet said. "Some of us have thick hides. Fireproof, even against dragon fire. Don't fret about dragons here. Under our protection, you'll be fine. Terastios is just ahead. I'll turn so you can see it."

Rustafet pivoted, and a vast fortress slid into view, a colossal gray rectangle with no towers and few adornments, flanked by sheer mountains. A massive door was opening as they approached. When Rustafet straightened to face the fort directly, Kendra watched the monumental building swing out of sight.

She hurried to a rear-facing window to see the conscripted dragons recede from view as Rustafet passed through the gaping doorway into the tremendous fortress. A female giant nearly the size of Rustafet closed the doors after they entered, her brown hair in a single thick braid that almost reached her waist.

With the rear view cut off, Kendra returned to the side-facing window beside Knox. They had entered a large chamber.

"Hang on," Rustafet said. "It's time to set you down."

Kendra and Knox clung to the windowsill as the wicker house rocked and lowered, finally settling on the floor. They gathered at the door, where Tanu undid the latch and gripped the handle. He paused.

"It's a big world out there," Tanu said.

"And I want to see it," Tess enthused.

Newel and Doren charged down the stairs from an upper story. "We do too!" Doren called.

Tanu opened the door and stepped out into the gigantic chamber. Kendra felt like she was exploring a room from the perspective of a mouse. The wicker house matched their scale, but nothing else in the giant room came close. Not the table in the corner with the huge guest book propped on a stand. Not the monumental suits of armor flanking the towering gilded doors on the far side of the room. And not the giant who had toted them here.

Rustafet came and stooped over them, an intimidating presence considering that Kendra would have had to jump to reach the middle of his shin. "You look drier than when you arrived," he said.

"Still damp," Kendra said. "Luckily, it's a warm day."

"Such a big man," Tess said softly.

"Big to you," Rustafet said. "You're about to meet some real giants. Be polite to her majesty. Protocol is for visitors like you to bow or curtsy. Her subjects kneel. If she dislikes you, she will expel you from the sanctuary. She prefers to speak more than to listen, unless she asks a direct question. Ready?"

"Will you carry us in there?" Knox asked.

"New visitors enter the throne room at their own height, under their own power," Rustafet said. "By decree. Follow me!"

The knocker on the doors was in the shape of a peasant lugging a heavy cauldron. Rustafet approached and used the cauldron to rap three times. The massive doors swung inward and he stepped aside, admitting Kendra and her companions into a grand hall, the dimensions vast even relative to a giant.

About thirty giants awaited in the room, wearing togas and sandals, a few leaning against pillars or roosting on stools, most standing in groups. All conversation quieted as Kendra and her friends entered, lofty eyes gazing in their direction. The shortest of these giants was a head taller than Rustafet, and some were so colossal that Rustafet's head did not clear the middle of their chests.

At the far end of the room, the Giant Queen sat on her immense throne. Even seated, she was clearly the largest person in the room. Younger and prettier than Kendra expected, if the Giant Queen had been human, she would have been in her late thirties. The elaborate green dress she wore showed off a build like an Olympic swimmer's, with square shoulders, a narrow waist, and athletic limbs. Her auburn hair was caught in looping braids that spilled out beneath her stately crown.

Kendra and her friends approached the Giant Queen along a red carpet roughly the size of an airport runway. As they walked, most of the other giants returned to their conversations. Kendra and her comrades strode briskly, but it took them nearly ten minutes to reach the far end of the carpet near the base of the dais.

As they arrived at the end of the carpet, a giant near the dais jabbed the butt of his halberd against the floor, the loud crack echoing across the voluminous room. Conversation died out.

"Her royal majesty, Queen Imani, recognizes the arrival of Kendra Sorenson, disgraced former caretaker of the fallen sanctuary Wyrmroost, and her assorted cohorts."

Kendra wasn't sure the word *disgraced* had been necessary. If Seth had been here, an argument would almost certainly have followed the comment. But at the moment, Kendra felt keeping the relationship functional was more important than verbally scoring points. She curtsied, as did Vanessa and Tess. The males bowed.

The queen raised a compact golden tube to one eye, using it like a spyglass. "You're all damp," the Giant Queen observed in rich alto tones. "You came through the Fairy Queen's shrine?"

"Yes, your majesty," Kendra said.

"She permitted you to traverse her realm?" the Giant Queen asked.

"She knew it was an emergency," Kendra said.

"She is a very *small* queen," the Giant Queen said.

"So is the Underking, compared to you," Kendra said. "But they're very powerful."

The Giant Queen gave an indulgent laugh. "Everyone is small compared to me. I suppose you would like to see my full height? Most visitors take an interest."

"Yes, please," Kendra said.

The Giant Queen arose, towering almost to the ceiling. When she came down off the dais, she was at least a head taller than the loftiest giant in the room. Her scale was so overwhelming, Kendra could hardly comprehend her as a living being. And yet her proportions were those of a powerfully built human woman. Kendra doubted whether she could reach higher than the top of the queen's ankle.

"I'll give you a moment to absorb the experience," the Giant Queen said from high above. "Astonishment is a forgivable reaction." She twirled. "Too much woman for any man on this planet. Am I right?"

"Dragons must seem like little pets to you," Tess said.

"An astute realization," the Giant Queen said. "Who is this cherub?"

"My cousin Tess," Kendra said.

"We brought family, did we?" the Giant Queen asked, returning to her throne. She turned and sat.

"Yes," Kendra affirmed. "And this is my cousin Knox."

"It's odd to imagine one so tiny living an actual life," the

Giant Queen said. "Having a family, for example. Or hobbies. Or pets."

"Some creatures make us look like giants," Knox said. "Fairies, for one."

"Fairies are invisible specks," the Giant Queen said. "You're not much better. It strains reason to grant significance to anything so minute."

"We're here because of the dragon war," Kendra said.

"I'm well aware," the Giant Queen said. "Celebrant took Wyrmroost from you. And I understand you seek refuge with me."

"Yes, we all do," Kendra said.

The Giant Queen lifted the tube to her eyes. "I see two satyrs. Strange folk."

"Not much normal about us," Newel said.

"At your service," Doren added with a bow.

"At least you appear housebroken," the Giant Queen remarked. "And three others besides the cousins. Are they relatives too?"

"Well, Tanu is an expert potion master—"

"I believe I asked a simple question," the Giant Queen interrupted.

"Not two of them," Kendra said, annoyed by the rudeness of the queen but trying not to let it show. "The other is a second cousin."

"I will grant the refuge you seek," the Giant Queen said. "We can offer accommodations on your scale here at Terastios, and most public spaces here include access for wee folk." She gestured toward an area to one side of the dais with bleachers and couches where human-sized people sat watching. Compared to the Giant Queen, they looked miniscule.

"I'm also searching for my brother," Kendra said.

"The former co-caretaker of Wyrmroost," the Giant Queen said.

"I believe he came here," Kendra said.

"Not to my knowledge," the Giant Queen said. "Many tourists of your size visit for the Games. I cannot keep track of all who come and go. My servant Raza will host you during your stay and acquaint you with your accommodations and our policies here. Direct inquiries about your brother to him."

A man in a white, embroidered sherwani and red harem pants detached from where the human-sized spectators were gathered and came toward Kendra. He had dark hair, suntanned skin, meticulous stubble on his jaw, and looked to be in his forties.

"Do you need help with defensive measures against the dragons?" Kendra asked.

In her peripheral vision, Kendra noticed that several of the giants looked taken aback by the question. Queen Imani leaned forward with an ironic smile.

"There is a reason you are seeking refuge here," the Giant Queen said. "This is the largest and most secure magical preserve on the planet. I have strangled dragons with a single hand. Your entire world will fall long before Titan Valley encounters any trouble from those worms. Dragonwatch asked for me to take you in, and so I have.

Remember, dangers that seem large to you might lack significance to me."

Kendra felt embarrassed by the scolding. She curtsied and said, "Thank you, your majesty."

"Very well," the Giant Queen said. "Raza can address any concerns, and he will arrange for the comfort of your little band. Off you go."

CHAPTER NINE

Presence

I t doesn't look too bad," Seth said, standing between
Hermo and Brunt, staring at the log cottage. Empty flower
boxes hung below the windows. Quaint carvings decorated
the eaves. A path of pebbles led from the road across the
weedy lawn to the red front door.

Brunt harrumphed. "Maybe it won't take long."

Seth looked at the imposing alley troll. "Do you want
to help?"

Brunt shook his head and took a step back. "Nobody
crosses that threshold anymore. Nothing good happens."

"What does happen?" Seth asked.

"They get hurt," Brunt said. "Or disappear."

"Does Dante own this place?" Seth asked.

"He does now," Brunt said. "Bought it cheap before we

departed from the tavern. Your job is to ensure that was a profitable purchase."

Seth nodded. "You want to help, Hermo?"

"Me stay with alley troll," Hermo said. "Guard road."

"I'm not sure the road is in any danger," Seth said.

"Better safe than sorry," Hermo maintained.

The alley troll gave a single chuckle.

Seth shrugged. "If you say so." He walked up the path, pebbles crunching underfoot. The closer he got to the cottage, the less welcoming it appeared. The red paint on the front door was cracked and flaking off in places. Spiderwebs laced many of the carved eaves. The windows were dirty, the inside of the glass smeared with grime, as if grubby hands had wiped them hastily.

Seth paused at the door. "How do you feel?" he muttered.

"Like a bully who all sensible people avoid is waiting in ambush," Calvin replied quietly. "And we're walking into the trap. Let's hope this is something we can handle."

"Ronodin never taught me about 'presences,'" Seth said.

"It might be a phantom," Calvin said. "I don't think Dante knows what's haunting the place."

Seth reached out with his power, searching for any undead. He didn't sense a wraith inside the cottage, but there was . . . something. Could it be a phantom? To what extent could they disguise themselves?

"I feel something in there," Seth said.

"A presence?" Calvin ventured.

"I'm not sure what."

"Probably something new to you," Calvin said.

"Do I knock?" Seth asked.

"I guess, if it's locked," Calvin said.

Seth tried the handle and pushed the door inward. Sunshine filtered through the grimy windows to dimly light the interior of the cottage. Some of the furniture was overturned in the large front room. One armchair had been slashed open and bled fluffy wads of stuffing. Seth noticed cobwebs, and in many places wide streaks interrupted the dust on the floor, as if large objects had been dragged across it. A doorway led to a kitchen, and an open door granted access to a bedroom. Some unnameable quality in the musty air felt unsafe.

Seth stepped fully into the cottage and felt a sudden breeze as the front door slammed shut behind him. The room appeared empty. Engaging his senses, he could not pinpoint an entity.

Just walk in? a voice spoke in his mind. *Is that polite?*

A painting flew off the wall and frisbeed straight at him. Seth sidestepped and ducked, barely avoiding it. The picture crashed against the floor, cracking the frame.

"Stop it," Seth said. "I came to talk."

How do we talk when you can't hear me? the voice complained.

An incorporeal force shoved Seth into the center of the room. He staggered to stay on his feet.

"I hear you fine," Seth said. "Sorry I barged in. I'm here to help."

The room immediately grew still. The hostile feeling in the space had changed.

You hear me?

"I hear you."

Stand on one foot.

Seth lifted a foot.

Turn around.

"Can I put my foot down?"

Yes.

Seth turned around.

You hear me.

"And you hear me too."

The voice became small. *I can hardly believe it. Please, who am I?*

"I'm not sure," Seth said. "You tell me."

I can't. Please help me. Who am I?

Seth wondered if the being could read his mind and was mocking him because of his lost memories. *Can you hear me?* Seth projected.

There came no response.

"Can you hear what I'm thinking?" Seth asked.

No, the presence answered. *Who am I?*

"That is for you to know."

But I don't know. I need help. Please. Have mercy. Who am I?

"I wish I could tell you."

The atmosphere in the room became intense again. The door flew open, and Seth was lifted into the air and catapulted out to land half on the pebbly path, half on the weedy lawn. He skidded and rolled to a stop as the door banged shut.

"How it go?" Hermo asked.

Seth stood up and dusted himself off. He could tell his legs had been bruised and scraped. "You okay, Calvin?" he whispered.

"I'm fine," Calvin said. "You?"

"I'm doing well," Seth said. "I think we're hitting it off."

"You need more charm," Brunt said.

"You need lucky potato," Hermo said.

"This is all part of my technique," Seth insisted.

"Flying out door?" Hermo asked.

"Showing flexibility," Seth corrected. "Rolling with the punches."

"That big punch," Hermo said.

"More of a push, really," Seth said. "Or a fling."

"Did you fail?" Brunt asked. His expression became menacing. "Dante won't like it if you fail."

"Who mentioned failing?" Seth replied. "Phase one went great. We established contact. Measured up each other. Phase two is more important. I'm going on a short walk. You two guard the road."

Seth went around behind the cottage. A path led into the trees where an outhouse stood.

"Do you have a plan?" Calvin asked.

"Could *you* hear him?" Seth asked quietly.

"Was it a him?"

"The voice in my head sounded male."

"I heard no voice."

"He wants to know who he is," Seth said. "He sounds desperate. How could we figure it out?"

"Dante didn't know *what* this thing is," Calvin said, "let alone who."

"Right," Seth said. "Since they just call it a presence, I bet nobody knows much about it."

"Strange that you lost your identity and this presence did too," Calvin said.

"Coincidence?" Seth asked. "Could he have been mirroring me?"

"Who knows?" Calvin said.

"I need to find out who I am," Seth said. "My mission can't turn into uncovering the history of this presence."

"Unless it won't take much to find out."

Seth walked around the house and to the road where the trolls stood. Brunt and Hermo watched him approach.

"Do you know anything about the history of this cottage?" Seth asked.

"Many years ago, an old alley troll named Merglebrax lived there," Brunt said. "He fled when the presence arrived."

"Has the presence spoken to anyone?" Seth asked.

"Not that I know of," Brunt said. "Are you stumped? Bested?"

"Just asking questions," Seth said. "Preparing for round two."

Seth walked back to the red door, gravel crunching underfoot.

"Are you sure about this?" Calvin asked quietly.

"Nope," Seth said. "But I'll try to bluff my way through it." He knocked, then raised his voice. "Can I come in?"

Come in, Seth heard in his mind.

Seth entered and shut the door behind him. "I've come to help you. I can hear you."

Who am I?

"I was hoping my presence would jog your memory," Seth said.

Tell me who I am!

"You're my assistant," Seth said. "I've been looking all over for you."

Your assistant?

"I wasn't sure at first," Seth said. "I had to be certain. How long have you been here?"

Not sure. Too long. What's my name?

"Reggie," Seth invented.

What's your name?

"I'm Seth. I've been looking for you."

You found me.

"You don't want to be here, Reggie. This place is no good for you."

This is where I am now. This is what I have.

Seth looked around at the cottage, unimpressed. "This place is a dump. This place is no good. The Reggie I know wouldn't want to live here."

You know me. I am Reggie.

"You sure are," Seth said. "You're sounding more like yourself every minute."

What is Reggie?

"My trusty assistant," Seth said.

What is Reggie made of?

"What do you think?" Seth tried.

I don't know. Please tell me what I'm made of.

"You're made of dirt," Seth improvised. "You belong outside."

Dirt?

"Yeah, dirt," Seth said. "You lost your dirt, though. That confused you. Reggie, you wandered off and got lost. You need a shape."

I belong outside.

"You sure do, Reggie," Seth said. "Should we go out?"

I belong. Outside.

Seth opened the door.

Yes. I am made of dirt. I belong outside.

Seth felt something whoosh past him, and then he exited, closing the door.

The ground to the right of the pebble path began to tremble and churn, as if being aggressively tilled by invisible tools. Grassy chunks of earth and clods of dusty soil merged together and rose up into a vaguely humanoid form, about the height of Seth. The trolls retreated to the far side of the road, poised to run away.

I am Reggie, the earthen figure spoke to Seth's mind. *I am made of dirt. I am your assistant.*

"Good to see you again, Reggie," Seth said, baffled that the entity had successfully taken shape.

You see me, Reggie said. *You hear me. I exist! I knew it!*

"You exist."

What now, Master?

Seth had to silently admit he liked the sound of that. "You stand there for a minute. I have to talk to some trolls. Then we go on a journey."

I will stand here until our journey, Reggie said resolutely.

"If one of the trolls gives me trouble, I'll call you," Seth said.

Nobody troubles Master, Reggie said.

Seth started walking to the trolls.

"He's coming with us?" Calvin whispered.

"I guess so," Seth said. "He's eager to help. We don't want him returning to the cottage and making Dante mad. You still can't hear him?"

"No, but I guess a friend made of dirt could come in handy."

"I got the presence out of the cottage," Seth told Brunt. "We're buddies now."

"So I see," Brunt said. "Not bad."

"He wants to serve me for a while," Seth said. "You know how these things go. What now? Do we go back to Dante?"

"No need," Brunt said, producing an envelope. "This letter of introduction will secure assistance from an expert on the Games. Virgil, son of Galdo, can be found at the address on the envelope, in the town of Humburgh, not far from the arena. Head down this lane to the crossroads, then go left. If in doubt, follow the signs or ask the way to Humburgh. Should the presence return to the cottage, you should forever sleep lightly."

"Thanks for the letter," Seth said, accepting it. "Give Dante my regards."

Brunt replied with a snort, then turned and trudged off.

"We go Humburgh?" Hermo asked.

"Are you sticking with me?" Seth asked.

"You survive Dante," Hermo said. "You survive presence. You survivor."

"Time will tell," Seth said.

"And you have little helper," Hermo said.

"I do my best," Calvin said. "But don't blow my cover. Sometimes it's smarter for me to hide and listen."

"Are you sure you're done with Troll Tavern?" Seth asked. "You were pretty excited to go there."

Hermo waved a disgusted hand toward the tavern. "Stew good. Trolls rude. Humburgh famous. Humburgh better."

"Come on, Reggie," Seth called. "We're going to Humburgh."

The figure of dirt came walking toward him.

Where is that?

"We'll find it together," Seth assured him.

CHAPTER TEN

Giselle

L ast, but certainly not least, Miss Kendra, we will find the door to your suite up here on the left," Raza said, leading her down a hall constructed to human scale. A few inches taller than Kendra, Raza moved with grace and formality, keeping his body unusually erect. A female servant stayed with him, about his same height, with fair skin, fiery red hair, and turquoise eyes. She wore a flattering cheongsam dress and, just like Raza, had a snug silver choker around her neck.

Although the others had already been escorted to their rooms, Vanessa had skipped settling in to remain with Kendra. Raza used a key to open the door.

"Forgive us, Miss Vanessa, if your habitation is not equal to Miss Kendra's," Raza said, ushering them into a spacious salon. "As a former caretaker, she merits elite accommodations."

"No offense taken," Vanessa said.

"Giselle will be your personal attendant," Raza told Kendra. "Inquire about anything you need, including food, laundry, security, navigating Terastios, sightseeing, and privacy."

Giselle gave a small curtsy, red tresses swaying. "I am at your service, day and night, throughout your stay."

"Thank you," Kendra said.

"I will leave you in Giselle's care," Raza said with a small bow. "You can find me or a fellow servant inside the first door of the hall that I showed you, or else through Giselle."

"Thanks," Kendra said.

Raza handed Kendra the key to her room, glanced at Vanessa, and departed.

"Allow me to show you the suite," Giselle said. Kendra and Vanessa followed Giselle into a bedchamber where a veil screened a lavish circular bed piled with cushions. The attendant led them to a bathroom, a kitchen, a sunroom, and finally to a large, tiled space dominated by a waist-deep pool accented by tiled pillars.

"My own pool?" Kendra asked.

"You may swim or bathe here, as you choose," Giselle said.

Kendra noticed the piles of thick towels and the cabinet full of fluffy robes. Cakes of soap waited alongside fragrant lotions and ointments.

"You're living the good life," Vanessa said, fingering a robe.

"You have to come here and swim with me," Kendra said. With her glamorous appearance, Kendra thought Vanessa would look more at home in this glossy paradise than anyone.

"It's not just for pool parties," Vanessa said. "You can wash up."

"I wouldn't want to get the water soapy," Kendra said. "It's too nice."

"We will clean the water after each use, of course," Giselle said.

"Or I guess I could save you the trouble," Kendra said softly, patting her unicorn horn.

"Tell us about the collar you are wearing," Vanessa invited.

"All palace servants wear one, milady," Giselle said.

"Is its purpose more than adornment?" Vanessa asked.

"If I knowingly lie, the choker will constrict and strangle me," Giselle said.

"I thought I recognized the nature of it," Vanessa said. "The giant Thronis at Wyrmroost gave out similar collars."

"They are an application of magic devised by giants," Giselle said. "Thronis wore one when he was exiled to Wyrmroost and placed in the care of Agad."

"How did you become a servant here?" Vanessa asked.

"It is a long story," Giselle said.

"Are you mortal?" Vanessa asked.

"I need not answer personal questions," Giselle said, lowering her eyes.

"You're a dragon," Vanessa guessed.

Giselle raised her eyes and gazed at Vanessa steadily. "I have not taken dragon shape for centuries. The choker would kill me if I tried. I took an oath to serve Imani, and if I break that vow, the choker will ensure I perish."

"Raza too?" Kendra asked.

"All servants in silver collars are dragons," Giselle said.

"It doesn't seem like dragons are treated fairly here," Kendra said.

"I appreciate your opinion," Giselle said.

"At Wyrmroost the dragons were free to live as they chose," Kendra said. "To hunt, or sleep, or hoard treasure. They had their own society."

"I have heard rumors," Giselle said. "Forgive me if it is difficult to believe."

"The dragons rebelled and overthrew the sanctuary," Kendra said.

A small smile flickered on Giselle's lips. "I have heard rumors," she repeated.

Kendra could see that the idea of a dragon rebellion appealed to her. Considering how dragons were treated at Titan Valley, Kendra couldn't blame her.

"Do you think the dragons here are treated fairly?" Kendra asked quietly.

"I cannot give an accurate answer to that question," Giselle said.

"A *yes* would be a lie, and a *no* would break her loyalty oath," Vanessa said.

"You have the right idea," Giselle said.

"Would you harm me if you could?" Kendra asked.

"I cannot harm you," Giselle said. "I am assigned to serve you."

"Will you be spying on me for the Giant Queen?" Kendra asked.

"I serve you under her instructions," Giselle said. "Her royal majesty Imani is my true master."

"Would you prefer not to serve me?" Kendra asked. "Would it be better if I send you away?"

Giselle looked distressed. "There could be punishments if I am dismissed. Another will be chosen to serve you. I would much rather serve you than be dismissed from this task."

"Can you promise not to spy for Imani?" Kendra asked. "Can you promise to do me no harm?"

"I cannot make that promise," Giselle said. "My first loyalty is to Queen Imani. I can only assure you that I am currently assigned to serve and protect you."

"Well, you should know that I wouldn't treat dragons the way Imani does," Kendra said.

"Perhaps that is why your sanctuary fell," Giselle said.

Kendra paused. "Maybe."

"Dragons do not want a cage, however considerate the keeper," Giselle said.

"Leave us," Vanessa said. "I wish to talk to Kendra in private."

Giselle looked to Kendra.

"Yes, please," Kendra said. "And would you promise not to listen to this conversation?"

"I promise," Giselle said. "It is wise to give specific instructions. Consider the possibility that, at some level, I do not wish to work against you or to help the Giant Queen in any way. Remember that though I must be loyal to the queen, I am assigned to obey your direct orders like a good servant. Sensible commands can limit my opportunities to gather information. I cannot avoid helping the Giant Queen when you leave the opportunity available."

"Thanks, Giselle," Kendra said.

Giselle gave a small curtsy and left the room.

Vanessa stepped near Kendra and spoke quietly. "We're in the middle of some delicate politics here."

"I can't believe I'm being served by a dragon," Kendra said.

"Believe it, but stay on guard," Vanessa said. "The Giant Queen might be our ally, but she is not our friend. Giselle will serve her as required. And if Giselle were freed, she would immediately turn on any of us."

"I got that feeling," Kendra said.

"I'm going to visit my room and then do some reconnaissance," Vanessa said. "Rest while you can."

"Andromadus gave me a book," Kendra said. "I'll do some reading."

"It would be worthwhile for you to learn that story," Vanessa said. "Either Warren, Tanu, or I will always be available right down the hall. Enjoy your book."

Giselle opened the front door for Vanessa's departure.

After closing it, she turned to Kendra. "May I prepare any food for you?"

"Sure," Kendra said. "What are the options?"

"I will do my best to prepare whatever you want," Giselle said.

"How about a sandwich?" Kendra asked.

"What kind?"

"Turkey with avocado," Kendra said.

"Mayo? Mustard?" Giselle asked.

"A little of each," Kendra said.

"Cheese? Lettuce? Tomatoes? Oil? Salt? Pepper? Vinegar?"

"Some cheese and lettuce," Kendra said.

"Anything on the side?" Giselle asked.

"A salad with ranch," Kendra said.

"No problem," Giselle said. "Any potato chips?"

"Sure," Kendra said. "What did you look like as a dragon?"

Giselle gave a shy smile. "It has been too long. I hardly remember."

"You didn't forget," Kendra said.

"Mostly red scales," Giselle said. "I was long and slender. Streamlined. Very fast."

"Did you breathe fire?"

"You would call it fire," Giselle said. "Mine was hotter and more liquid than some dragon fire."

"Like lava," Kendra said.

"Yes and no," Giselle said. "Would you care for privacy?"

"Yes, please," Kendra said. "I'm going to read. Promise not to spy on me?"

"I will see and hear only what I must to perform my duties as your attendant," Giselle said. "Take care what you show and say at those times. At present, I will avoid gathering information per your request. May I intrude to bring in your sandwich?"

"I'll come get it when I finish," Kendra said.

"Very well," Giselle acknowledged with a curtsy.

Kendra went into her bedroom and closed the door. She opened the sports bag that held some spare clothes, the sack of gales, and the book Andromadus had given her.

Flopping onto her bed, Kendra found the mattress a little firmer than she would have chosen, but all the soft covers and cushions allowed her to get really comfortable. She studied the elaborate book cover for a moment, then opened it and began to read.

LEGEND OF THE DRAGON SLAYER

Long ago, before the world had been properly mapped, King Titus feared for the kingdom he ruled. His beloved realm of Selona enjoyed modest prosperity but was hemmed in on all sides by terrible dangers. To the north, fierce yeti guarded their icy peaks. A merciless vampire haunted the eastern waterways. Access to the southern swamp was impeded by the arcane powers of the gorgon. And in the west, a deadly phoenix scorched his rocky domain.

Gorgon

One day in the late spring, the king issued a proclamation: "Selona is growing, but we lack room to expand. My engineers believe we could drain the swamp to the south if only we had safe access. If any man will overthrow the gorgon, I shall grant him the title Earl of Farcastle, along with the associated estate and all pertaining lands, including the mill and the village of Drygap. This offer will stand for the next three days."

Many in the nation of Selona were astonished at the news, for the earldom of Farcastle was among the most prosperous in the kingdom, and though the recently deceased earl had left no direct heirs, the majority assumed the property would pass to one of many surviving nephews. But in Selona, the word of the king was law, and the people waited to see what brave soldier would come forward to claim the prize.

On the first day, many a seasoned soldier was heard grumbling that if he were ten years younger, he would slay the gorgon simply on principle. And plenty of tenderfoot soldiers were heard boasting that after gaining a bit more experience, they would make short work of the threat to the south and then donate the earldom to orphans. But not a single person accepted the challenge.

On day two, the proclamation was repeated by commanders to their companies, who encouraged the best of their men to rise up and accept the challenge of the king. Wives spoke of the opportunity to husbands, fathers repeated the challenge to sons, and sons fantasized with friends about becoming heroes. When it came to actual volunteers, a drunkard made some vague boasts before staggering away, and a child of seven years tried to sign up until his mother carried him off, but not a single viable applicant came forward.

By day three, the king and his closest advisers began to worry that perhaps the bravest and best of the men of Selona had already attempted to dispose of the threats and failed, leaving behind none bold enough to fill their boots. Near the end of the third day, as the shadows grew long across the town square, an unlikely candidate approached to volunteer.

Konrad, the cobbler's son, was a tall and gangly youth of seventeen. Given to reading more than to action, he had taken up three different apprenticeships only to get dismissed—twice for trying to invent new processes before mastering the basics, and once for talking too much. He was liked well enough by the children who listened to his stories, but many in the older generation felt sorry for the cobbler, whose only offspring seemed a lazy dreamer.

"I may be untested, and I admittedly lack training as a soldier, but I have a willing hand and strength to bear a sword," Konrad said. "I have wrestled with my impulse to step forward since the proclamation was issued, but I can resist no longer. I will slay the gorgon, though I have neither weaponry nor supplies."

After a stunned silence, and some muffled laughs from bystanders, the recruiters realized this might be the only offer they would receive. So, after the sun went down, Konrad was ushered to stand before the king. The candidate was met with graciousness on the surface and despair behind closed doors, for nobody expected the untried youth to succeed where seasoned mercenaries had failed. Nevertheless, Konrad received a horse, leather armor, new boots, a dagger, and a short sword. More imposing armaments were offered, but they seemed cumbersome to Konrad, who also rejected the weight of a helm and a shield.

The following day at first light, Konrad rode away, leaving behind the cheers of the village and the tears of his mother. Not one person expected to see him again, and, besides the cobbler's household, nobody bothered to mourn him. Weeks went by and the days grew hotter, leaving his departure mostly forgotten until, late one blistering afternoon, Konrad returned, gaunt, bedraggled, clothes soiled and torn. Once his identity had been established, the beggarly figure was escorted into the castle to recount his tale before a small, impromptu audience, including the king.

"I left my horse at the brink of the swamp and proceeded on foot, squelching through mud that gripped to the knee, eventually swimming more than walking. Whoever endeavors to drain that swamp has a mighty labor ahead. I will not tell all the tales I could of leeches and snakes, of quicksand and spiders, of pagan totems and scattered bones. Let it suffice to say that after languishing in fetid water for days, my body an exhibition of rashes, bites, and sores, I discovered an expanse of deep water in the midst of the bog.

"Out toward the middle of this pond, I spied a primitive hut adrift on a wooden raft. Human skeletons dangled from crude rafters. I approached with caution, though an unseen splash hinted that my presence was no mystery. My friends will tell you that I am a standout swimmer, but as I stroked toward the hut, strong hands seized me and pulled me deep, to my supposed doom.

"I awoke caged at the rear of a warm room that reeked of unsavory spices. My hair still wet, I'd been stripped to the waist, boots and weapons gone. From the slow rotation of the room, I understood that I was now inside the hut I had identified.

"A foul cauldron frothed in the center of the room, and beside it coiled a grotesque woman. From the waist down she was a huge snake, with a row of sharp quills bristling along the top ridge of her serpent tail. Tightly knit scales sheathed her humanoid torso, and her hideous face was wretched beyond description, with needle teeth and black, soulless eyes. Slime entangled her long, weedy hair.

"Some say the gaze of a gorgon can turn a man to stone. I can only report that, although my body remained fleshy, I lost the ability to move at the sight of her, so great was my loss of courage.

"As I watched the gorgon add bizarre ingredients to her roiling cauldron—crushed herbs and carved stones and pickled organs—her glances at me soon suggested that I would be the final inclusion to her devilish stew. While stirring the hellbroth, she howled out the window, provoking savage replies from the denizens of the swamp. When at last she approached my cage, fiendishly grinning, I withdrew to the rear of the rusty enclosure.

"Why not try to overpower her when she opened the cage door? Allow me to clarify that from her waist to her crown she was taller than I, and I'd sampled her brutal strength in the water. Terror overtook me as her long tail entered the cage, curled about my waist, and withdrew me as if I weighed no more than a bag of straw.

"I have no doubt I would have exited to my death had I not reacted quickly. Driven by instinct more than design, I plucked a quill from the snake tail and plunged it into the back of her human torso, whereupon she let out a shriek to send nightmares scurrying. Immediately the gorgon dropped me and scrambled from the hut, her lashing tail overturning furnishings and sending crockery crashing. From the doorway, I watched her traverse the pond to a muddy patch of shore, where she turned entirely to stone.

"I will not elaborate on my careful verification that she had indeed become a statue, my treacherous journey out of the swamp, or the successful recovery of my horse. Let me assure you that if you send an expedition deep into the swamp, you will find the pond, the hut, and the corpse of the gorgon exactly as described. In my hand is the very quill I used to stab the villain. I invite the king to handle it if he wishes. The swamp is now safe to be drained, though I warn all who venture therein to beware of natural dangers such as snakes and disease."

In the following days the story was confirmed, and work began to drain the swamp and farm the lands near the brink. Konrad received his earldom amid considerable pageantry, no prouder mother than his could be found in all the land, and the kingdom of Selona rejoiced at their chance to enlarge their southern boundaries.

Yeti

A few years passed, and the kingdom of Selona prospered. But there were limits to how much swampland could be made habitable, and in time King Titus turned his gaze northward.

A proclamation again went forth: "To the north lie vales to inhabit, slopes where flocks could graze, and mountains to mine. If any man will lead an expedition north and destroy the yetis who patrol the mountain passes, I will name him the Duke of Hinterhill and bequeath to him all lands and titles associated with that fair castle. This offer will stand for the next three days."

The proclamation generated much talk and little action, until near the end of the third day, when Konrad, the Earl of Faircastle, came forward. Dressed respectably, and having filled out admirably since he was seventeen, the young nobleman was taken more seriously than when he had volunteered to go south.

This time, Konrad needed no assistance to outfit himself, for he had managed his estate well and was able to gather warm clothes and climbing gear, though none in his employ had enough courage to undertake the dangerous mission alongside him. Again, he was alone, and many supposed that he rode to his demise.

Some hunters worried Konrad should have waited for full summer instead of making the trek in the spring. Among townsfolk, reminders were issued that a person could get lucky once, but expecting similar luck again was an affront to fate. But six weeks later, to the astonishment of most, Konrad returned looking leaner, limping slightly, lips chapped, but otherwise unhurt. He was promptly ushered into the throne room, where a large group gathered to hear him.

"I wish I had better heeded some of the elder members of the community, for winter lingers long in the mountain passes. I left my noble mount in a frosty meadow to proceed up an icy slope on foot. There is no need to bore you with complaints of freezing temperatures, blinding blizzards, and rumbling avalanches. I will not dwell upon details of hollowing out snowbanks with frozen fingers to create shelter, nor recount the mournful howls of wolves in the night, nor belabor the perils of scaling crystalline faces of ice.

"After I spent a fierce night huddled in a shallow ice cave, the air became still and the sun peeked out, turning the mountain snowfields into blazing diamonds. That morning, I found a footprint large enough for me to sit inside. As I encountered more oversized tracks, I began to question whether I wanted to locate a creature who made such large, deep impressions in the snow. Before I could fully refine my intent, the creature found me.

"And it was not alone.

"The yetis had shaggy, apelike bodies and heads like arctic wolves with shortened muzzles. They moved over the snow with ease and showed signs of cunning if not great intelligence. I would have preferred to lead an army of men to attack a single yeti—instead, a pack of them had found me. The grizzliest of bears would seem a modest pet beside the smallest of their number.

"With no hope of prevailing in combat, I attempted to flee. One glance at their fluid strides told me I would not outrun them, so with a prayer that recklessness might triumph where ability was lacking, I flung myself down the steepest nearby slope. The world spun and powdery snow sprayed haphazardly until I came to rest near the mouth of a cave. The mountain vibrated with the roars of the yetis as they bounded down the slope after me.

"Lacking superior options, I dashed into the opening and soon discovered the cavity to be no minor snow tunnel, but rather a long and winding cave that burrowed deep into the rock of the mountainside. Although the darkness deepened as the entrance receded, still I opted to plunge ahead blindly in hopes my pursuers would not follow. Though generally the cave was roomy, my heart swelled with gratitude when I passed through any narrow opening that might hamper their pursuit.

"Once the darkness became complete, my progress slowed dramatically, not only because of unseen obstacles on the cavern floor, but because it soon became impossible to anticipate where I would find the next opening through which to advance. Before long, I could not tell which direction I was facing. The subterranean atmosphere, though not warm, was well above freezing, and when my heavy coat became a burden, I shrugged it off.

"The bellows of the yetis echoed through the cave, reflecting horrifically off unseen stone surfaces. Fumbling through my belongings, I found flint and steel, and then a small oil lamp. Frantic sparks led to modest illumination, and I rushed deeper into the cavern.

"By the mellow light of my lamp, the yetis behind me were not yet visible, though their caterwauling seemed to come from all directions. I knew the light made me an easy target, but I needed the glow to advance and realized that the yetis might track me as easily by smell as by sight.

"I believe that at first, the yetis did hesitate to follow me underground. As I progressed, the roars from behind drew rapidly nearer. I began to run recklessly, fearful of turning an ankle, but more frightened of being torn limb from limb.

"Beyond a narrow passage, I reached a vast chamber decorated with stalactites and stalagmites and littered with stones. Not halfway across the broad floor, I saw several yetis appear behind me, lamplight glinting off ferocious teeth and eyes. Their triumphant bellows assaulted my ears, and I noticed creaking and cracking from above. A hasty glance showed webs of fissures in the uneven ceiling where chandeliers of stone dangled precariously.

"My last hope was to find an aperture in the wall large enough to accommodate me but cramped enough to prevent the yeti pack from following. I remember a surge of regret that I would not cheat death as I had in the swamp but would instead perish alone in a dark cavern within a remote mountain.

"And then the roof collapsed with a thunder that overpowered the yowls of the yetis. I dove for cover in the lee of a large boulder, which almost certainly saved my life, for though most of the collapse occurred behind me, a multitude of stone fragments scattered wildly around the room. Dust saturated the air as a pair of aftershocks followed the main cave-in. I kept my face to the ground, hands over my mouth and nose to filter my breathing, and still I seemed to inhale mostly particles.

"To my dismay, after the pounding ceased and the rocks settled, the roaring of the yetis persisted. I doubted I had much time before they found their way to me through the rubble and the polluted air. I considered extinguishing my lamp, which for the moment revealed only a brown curtain of dust. As seconds passed, and the roaring came no nearer, I noticed it displayed an uncommon uniformity.

"Hesitantly, I began to relax, and then to hope. After the worst of the dust cleared, I emerged from my shelter beside the boulder. Clambering over the detritus on the cave floor, I found my way to a view of a stunning, underground waterfall—the source of the endless roar.

"Returning to where the ceiling of the cave had fallen, I searched for evidence of yetis in the massive jumble of stone. At one edge, I found a head and an arm protruding from beneath a misshapen boulder. None of the other yetis were visible, and no others appeared to threaten me.

"Evidently, the whole pack lay entombed beneath the rockfall. I had unwittingly led them into a perfect trap, where their savage bellows disturbed an equilibrium made fragile over time. My instinct to flee and survive had accomplished what I could never have hoped to achieve with my sword.

"I had brought my quill from the swamp with me for luck, and it reminded me to claim another prize. As you can see, I used my dagger to remove a fang from the partially exposed yeti and brought it back as evidence. I conducted more explorations of the mountain passes after the events inside the cave, and though I nearly met my end from cold and avalanches, I saw no further indications of yetis. You are welcome to conduct your own investigations, but today I pronounce the northern mountains safe to inhabit."

By the time summer was hot and the snows had released their grip on all but the loftiest peaks, the cave was found, along with the rockfall and the partial skeleton of a yeti. Some of the more adventurous from Selona moved to the mountains as herdsmen or to support logging and mining operations. Using funds from his earldom and newly acquired duchy, Konrad invested in many of these ventures, and though some failed, others paid off handsomely, making him second only to the king in wealth.

Vampire

More years passed, and though the northern mountains granted many resources, they offered limited space for new settlements, and the winters were fierce at high altitudes. Before long, the eyes of King Titus strayed eastward.

A proclamation went forth: "The eastern river lands have ample fields and forests to inhabit and waterways to harness for power and irrigation. If any man will go and vanquish the dread vampire, he will have my blessing to pursue the hand of my daughter, Princess Lilianna. The offer becomes void at the end of three days."

The debate in town primarily concerned whether Konrad would come forward or be content having thwarted death twice and gained so much. Some could not imagine a man of his position risking everything for any reason. Others could not envision a man of his character resisting the urge to again prove his valor. All agreed that a chance to win the hand of Princess Lilianna would be enough to tempt any man, especially since she already seemed to favor Konrad.

The Duke of Hinterhill kept his own counsel and let the town wonder until he came forward on the third day, wholly equipped and in the full bloom of manhood. Court gossips spoke of the approving glances Konrad received from the princess before he departed. Several young men boasted that they had been on the verge of accepting the challenge but that Konrad had narrowly beaten them to the opportunity. But, as on previous adventures, no man offered to accompany him.

When Konrad rode away to best the dread vampire, the majority who worked with him or for him voiced their expectations that he would return. Others reminded the public that luck had played a role in his former victories, and they recounted gruesome tales of the vampire and his sinister exploits in the eastern reaches. Wagers were placed about whether Konrad would again survive, with the majority lamenting that the duke had finally taken one risk too many. But those who bet on his success were rewarded in hardly more than a fortnight, when Konrad rode back into town looking not only unharmed but unruffled. This time the king summoned his court to the town square to hear the tale before a huge crowd.

"I see no need to regale you with the hardships met along the way to Blackthorn Manor. I won't remind you how overgrown the former paths through the forests have become, or the variety of wild beasts roaming that friendless territory—not merely boars, wildcats, and bears, but enchanted creatures as well, clever satyrs and devious nymphs, not to mention the river trolls.

"At length I established camp in the abandoned village of Tremonton, where owls and badgers have replaced men and women.

I was struck that the town must have emptied suddenly, for I found tables set for meals, half-completed handicrafts, and plows deserted in the fields. Of people I saw none, save a single jabbering madman who escaped into the woods at my approach.

"Those who know the legends may be interested to learn that I found Blackthorn Manor exactly as described, upon a slender island in the midst of the Silver River. The stone bridge from the riverbank to the manor was in good repair, and the gates into the fortified residence stood open. The entire scene appeared much too inviting for my liking, but for the thickets of pikes topped with human skulls.

"I approached the manor under the noonday sun, carrying a wooden spear and several wooden stakes. For luck, I also had the gorgon's quill and the yeti's fang. Beyond the gate, I found the courtyard tidy, though the walls were overgrown with ivy. The elegant stronghold appeared utterly derelict. I noted no bones, nor blood, nor signs of violence, though I did not forget that outside were skulls enough to fill an ossuary.

"Spear held ready, I entered the manor. Progressing from room to room, I flung open curtains to admit daylight. Except for a film of dust interrupted by occasional mouse prints, all appeared in order. I detected no evidence of looters—the rooms appeared fully furnished and decorated, without so much as a broken window. This was troubling, because the gates stood open and no door within the manor was locked. Some unseen threat must have held potential interlopers at a distance.

"Toward the end of my disquieting tour of the manor, I located a stone stairway descending into an ancient cellar. Before reaching the bottom step, by the light of my torch I beheld the beginnings of not a cellar but a crypt. A dragging scrape of stone against stone from the darkness beyond my light brought me to a halt. I was already retreating up the stairs when I heard the crash of a heavy slab, presumably the lid of a sarcophagus.

"I bolted for the courtyard and did not look back until I stood in the full light of day, wooden spear held ready. The fiend came to the doorway, grotesquely human with hairless, pallid skin and jutting bones. Though he wore no shirt, his tattered pants looked to be made of fine fabric. Fierce eyes glared out of a gaunt, knobby head. Tendons stood out on the back of long hands as contorted fingers twisted and jerked.

"Keeping out of the direct sunlight, the abomination studied me, then beckoned with a gesture. I unwittingly took several steps toward him before resisting with a major effort of will. As I backed away, I saw hate and desperation flash into those baleful eyes, and I realized the creature was starving.

"The vampire beckoned again, but with less effect. Baring sharp teeth, the unholy atrocity charged into the sun after me. Fumes rose from his bubbling flesh as the sun seared it, and his violent shriek set my teeth on edge as the fiend approached with alarming speed.

"I raced out through the gates and onto the bridge with the vampire closing fast. Turning at the last moment, I planted my feet and leveled my spear. My assailant flailed forward, blinded, snarling, sizzling, and I impaled his upper chest beside his shoulder only to have the spear wrenched from my grasp.

"The vampire pawed at the spear, screaming, and while his back was turned to me, I plunged a stake just to one side of his spine. I cannot confirm how much of the damage was caused by my attacks, and how much depletion resulted from exposure to direct sunlight and his malnourished state, but the wretched creature dissolved into a cloud of foul particles.

"I stood for a time in disbelief that I had survived. Catching my breath and gathering courage, I returned to the crypt and investigated the vaults and sarcophagi within. None of the desiccated bodies I uncovered showed signs of life, but I staked them to be sure. As a token of my adventure, I brought back the stake that slew the fiend, which I hold now in my hand. No amount of scrubbing has removed the dark stain from the wood.

"I am relieved to announce that the vampire of Blackthorn Manor is no more. The eastern reaches are reopened to development."

Once again, the story was verified, and the kingdom of Selona gained new industry and territory. Villages were rebuilt, roads refurbished, mills constructed, bridges raised, farms irrigated, and trees felled. Expansion was somewhat limited by impenetrable forests and wildlands, and certain groves were avoided where satyrs frolicked and nymphs dwelt, but overall the kingdom of Selona enjoyed a new era of greater prosperity. Some unknown wit labeled Konrad the Legender, since he had ended three long-standing legends, and the name spread.

The Legender courted Princess Lilianna, and, in time, their affection deepened into a true and abiding love. The kingdom rejoiced when they were married amidst much fanfare. Lilianna birthed two daughters, who received the doting attention of their father until the fateful day when the king approached Konrad in private.

Phoenix

"The final threat to our kingdom is the phoenix of the western waste," the king explained. "The waste holds salt mines, as you know, along with our best trade routes. If we can be rid of the phoenix, the kingdom will be secure, and my reign a success. Age has made me weary, and I am desirous enough to be rid of this final scourge that, if you will destroy the phoenix, I will step down and deliver my crown to you."

"I will accomplish your wish," the Legender replied, "not only in order to secure the throne but out of respect for your desires as my king and my father."

A proclamation went out that the Legender would venture forth on one final mission, and at last the people of Selona believed he would succeed. Konrad had been lionized into a folk hero capable of anything, so destroying the phoenix seemed like a feat he might undertake simply for recreation. Few were shocked at the offer of the king to step down, since Konrad had wed his eldest daughter. Some cautious voices warned that a phoenix was no creature to trifle with, but when Konrad rode away to the west, his departure was met primarily with merriment and high expectations.

As weeks passed, the people of Selona began to doubt. After the first month, Princess Lilianna could often be found weeping in her garden. But after nearly three months away, the Legender returned, hair and beard grown out, skinny and sunburned, but very much alive. He spoke his last tale from the castle balcony to a sea of onlookers that spread beyond the sound of his voice.

"Some of you may recall I ventured west into arid wasteland with my trusty steed and a pack mule in tow. As I beheld the stark scarcity of that stony wilderness, I began to carefully ration my stores of food and water. I shall not rhapsodize about scorching sands and sunbaked rocks, or scraggly plants surviving through some miracle of adaptation, or the meager comforts found on the shady side of a bluff. I will skip recounting the abundance of scorpions and venomous vipers or the false promises offered by shimmering mirages and parched gulches.

"I reached a particularly tortured landscape where pools of hot sludge simmered, lava oozed from cinder cones, and towering geysers of scalding steam surged rebelliously skyward. My first glimpses of the phoenix resembled a distant spark in the sky. At night the bird became more distinct, a fiery comet among the stars.

"I tracked the phoenix for days, paying closest attention to where it landed and from whence it rose. I took care not to get too close, but I soon came to appreciate that the fiery bird was at least the size of my horse. I also noted that when hunting or agitated, the phoenix burned brighter, occasionally shedding showers of sparks or exhaling fire.

"My patient observations were rewarded when I located the nest—composed of blackened stones, and large enough to accommodate many full-grown phoenixes. There were no visible eggs, but the phoenix returned to the nest every night. On one occasion I observed a mountain lion stray into the nest, and the phoenix erupted into a blazing inferno. Though the cougar fought fiercely, claws and teeth flashing, the doomed feline was charred beyond recognition and consumed.

"I realized that if I was to have a chance against such a fiery opponent, more patience would be required. It took merely two weeks to find the nest, but I waited nearly two months for a respectable rainstorm, conserving my stores and foraging to survive. Rain is not frequent in that arid landscape, but eventually the air grew humid, leaden clouds filled the sky, and water began to fall.

"I approached the nest warily but with purpose. I did not know when I might get another opportunity to attack in wet conditions. I reached the nest as the downpour intensified, my clothing already soaked. The phoenix glowed faintly, having sought the limited shelter of an overhang, low flames flickering among iridescent plumage. Water pooled at the bottom of the depression.

"I climbed into the nest and attacked the bird with a spear. The phoenix had its head tucked under a wing and did not sense me coming. I drove the spear in deep, then backed away and began firing arrows.

"With a wailing screech, the phoenix blazed brighter, gouts of flame issuing from where the spear had penetrated and where the arrows struck. The bird came out from its shelter, and the pouring rain hissed as the droplets were vaporized. Falling back, I continued to launch arrows as the downpour quenched the flames. The phoenix collapsed in the pool, wings flapping feebly, and, with sword drawn, I advanced and severed the head.

"The bird took on a peculiar glow, as if an inferno raged internally, and then collapsed into flaky ashes. As the pile of ash began to absorb water and turn to sludge, I remembered tales of phoenixes being reborn from their cinders. I gathered an armful of sodden ashes, then hurried to the edge of the nest and scattered them. I repeated the process many times, hurling goopy handfuls in various directions.

"I wanted to disperse the remains as completely as I could. I packed some of the soggy ashes back to my horse and my donkey, mixed the remnants with their oats, and fed the combination to them. My horse refused to consume much, but the donkey ate with gusto, perhaps because I had not been generous with the feed until that point. In the spirit of camaraderie, and quietly hoping to perhaps derive some benefit, I also ingested some of the ashes.

"My donkey became sluggish and died the next day. I feared my horse and I might suffer the same fate, but though I endured a debilitating stomachache, we survived. Evidently I scattered the ashes sufficiently, because though the pool at the bottom of the nest turned into boiling sludge, the phoenix was not reborn. I waited several days to be sure. Under the overhang in the nest, I recovered a single magnificent feather, which I display to you now. I declare the threat of the phoenix over and the western waste open to all who care to venture there."

Konrad came down from the balcony, and the crowd pressed forward to view the phoenix feather, easily the most impressive of the Legender's mementos, glinting red and orange with an inner light. True to his word, within a year the king abdicated, replaced by King Konrad, Lord Protector of Selona. In the following years, Lilianna bore him two sons. His daughters grew tall and fair, and the Legender governed well. Selona prospered under his leadership, free from the major threats that had once frightened the populace and frustrated expansion.

Dragon

Some might argue that the kingdom prospered too much, for just after Konrad's eldest daughter, Nadia, celebrated her seventeenth birthday, the Rambling Horde approached Selona. Led by the warlord Kula Bakar, known more commonly as the Dragon, the Rambling Horde had been sacking cities for more than twenty years. Before each conquest, the Dragon gave the targeted kingdom a chance to send a champion to face him in single combat. Thus far, no individual had triumphed against him, and no armies or city walls had withstood his horde.

More powerful countries than Selona had fallen to the Rambling Horde, so news of the oncoming riders terrified many in the kingdom.

But for every person who quailed, another reminded listeners that Selona enjoyed protection no other country possessed. Selona had the Legender.

When an invitation to combat arrived at the royal palace, King Konrad took the message to his quarters and did not emerge. That evening, Queen Lilianna knocked on his door, and he admitted her. She had never seen her husband looking so disheveled and distraught.

His wife approached and laid a comforting hand on his arm. "Konrad, surely the warlord of the Rambling Horde is no more deadly than the phoenix, no more fearsome than the vampire, no more ferocious than the yeti, and no more dangerous than the gorgon."

"I expect you are right," Konrad said.

"Then you will vanquish him in combat?"

King Konrad dragged both hands through his hair, still thick, but graying. "It is my fondest wish, Lili."

"You are still young and strong," Lilianna said. "You slew four legends. Why not a fifth?"

"I ended four legends," Konrad said, face contorting as if with pain. "But none know the whole tale."

"Tell me," she said.

"The stories about me have grown since I first told them. And they were exaggerations from the start, colored by a young man's fantasies."

"What do you mean?"

"I ventured into the swamp to slay the gorgon, it is true. I took the risk; I braved the leeches and the snakes, the quicksand and the spiders. I found the floating hut, empty, abandoned, adrift. Nearby I discovered the stone gorgon and a single quill. The rest of my tale was invention."

"You never fought the gorgon?" Lilianna exclaimed.

"I never saw her alive," Konrad said. "For all I know, it is possible she never lived. I searched the area until I felt sure there was no threat. I worried that without a fight and a victory, I would not receive my prize, so I embellished."

"But you bested the other three foes," Lilianna said.

"I searched those mountains for weeks," Konrad said. "In the end, I found a cave—that much was true. The cave held a tremendous waterfall, large enough to sound like the roars of a yeti. I overcame freezing temperatures and snowy conditions. I approached that roaring, uncertain of what I would find. I came upon a rockfall and a skeleton of what might have been a yeti, from which I claimed a fang. I debunked another legend and I told another story."

Lilianna regarded her husband, perplexed. "The vampire?"

"I saw satyrs and nymphs," King Konrad said. "I beheld a river troll from a distance. I found the town of Tremonton and Blackthorn Manor, much as I described. The crypt as well. But instead of a vampire, I discovered a sarcophagus full of dust, with the blood-stained stake inside. Who killed the vampire and when, I have no idea. Assuming he ever existed at all."

"And the phoenix?" Lilianna whispered.

"I found what might once have been a nest of rocks, with boiling sludge inside. My horse sampled the sludge, and the donkey tried even more, which prompted me to have a taste. The donkey died and I grew ill. The feather was uncovered beneath a rock as part of my careful search. I had courage, my love, and I was a thorough investigator, but I know little of combat. I ended four legends without fighting or killing anything."

"I must confess, I have long wondered at the grandness of your adventures," Lilianna said. "It comes as little surprise that there was some enhancement to the tales. They have grown on their own since you originally told them."

"I don't believe I ever repeated any of them," Konrad said. "Others have aggrandized them for me, with even more flair than I initially employed."

"You were so young," Lilianna said. "Even with the phoenix."

"I became an earl, a duke," Konrad said. "I married you, gained a crown . . ."

"And you did end those legends. You returned having succeeded. The gorgon, the yetis, the vampire, and the phoenix were all no more. Because of you."

"Perhaps your father would still have made me an earl had I conveyed the precise truth," Konrad said. "And maybe not. Perchance others would have been emboldened as they heard one or two of the legendary enemies were less impressive than expected. We can never know. That history is written."

"But now . . ." Lilianna said.

"Currently I face an actual threat of flesh and bones," Konrad said. "A renowned warrior who has never lost a fight. I myself have never drawn blood and know little about the ways of warfare. If I accept this challenge, my incompetence will be exposed and the kingdom pillaged. If I refuse this duel, none will go where the Legender feared to tread. Truly, I wish I had never been born."

"Do not speak such nonsense."

Konrad hung his head. "I feel as if I have already failed."

Lilianna shook her head. "The kingdom prospered because of your courage. You are a good king, beloved by your family and your people. You have governed well. Tall tales about your exploits were inevitable. You just gave them a head start."

"And now I face the consequences of exaggeration. Any choice I make will lead to ruin."

Lilianna folded her arms. "What chance did you have against the gorgon? If she had been real?"

"Little to none," King Konrad confessed.

"What chance against the yetis? The vampire? The phoenix?"

"Very little."

"And yet you ventured out to confront them," Lilianna said. "Alone. Did you know any of them had been destroyed?"

"I expected to encounter them."

"It was not your fault they had already fallen. You have a new foe. Why not ride out to meet him with the same bravery?"

"When I rode south, north, east, and west, I risked only my own life. I was naive enough to have confidence that I would find a way to triumph. But now I am being asked to risk the fate of all Selona on my untested abilities. My people have unrealistic faith in me."

Lilianna hugged her husband. "This is no different from your previous escapades. The only differences are the audience and your fears regarding the consequences. You still have a willing hand and strength to bear a sword."

"I do believe I would have found a way," Konrad said.

"Don't let your courage fail when it is most needed. Go forward now, in the same spirit as you went forth to rescue the kingdom and win renown, remembering that when a hero is needed, any chance is better than none."

King Konrad gave a nod, resolution in his gaze. "I will prepare."

A response traveled to the Dragon, and the next day the Legender emerged from his castle and rode to the chosen battlefield with a small entourage. Those who watched the procession noted the king's lack of heavy arms and armor. Instead he wore traveling clothes and carried a short sword. The phoenix feather gleamed in his hat, the yeti fang hung from his neck on a cord, the vampire stake and the gorgon's quill were holstered on his belt.

Some whispered he had gone mad, approaching such an important duel so underequipped. Others accused him of overconfidence. A few who were close to him suspected he was playing to his strengths—since Konrad had little formal training in armed combat, and little experience with heavy arms and armor, they reasoned he was staying with what he knew.

Some citizens expressed outrage. After all, the Legender was the last line of defense against a merciless horde. What right had he to enter the fight with no armor? If he wanted mobility, he could at least have worn leather armor, carried a light shield. And why not bring a sword substantial enough to cause real harm?

At the appointed hour, the Legender found the Dragon awaiting him on the field of battle, standing alone, his horde watching from a distance. Kula Bakar was an enormous man, both tall and broad. He wore a great helmet with a cage hiding his face, and he was armored to withstand a landslide. After beholding the size of his sword, it became easy to believe the stories of him chopping a horse in half with a single stroke.

Leaving his attendants behind, King Konrad rode out to meet his opponent. Those near him maintain that Konrad managed to approach with a smile.

"What stratagem is this?" the Dragon called to the Legender. "Do you expect me to strip off my armor and fight you with lesser weapons? This is single combat for the right to sack your kingdom, and I will fight as I have always fought—fully prepared."

"I have everything I need to defeat you," the Legender replied, dismounting from his horse.

"If you lack proper armaments, I will outfit you myself," the Dragon offered.

"I had plenty of weapons and armor at my disposal," the Legender said. "I have brought all I require."

"Is this an insult?" the Dragon asked. "Perhaps you hope to protect your legacy by claiming the contest was unfair? Excuses will not spare your kingdom."

"The insult is your invasion," the Legender said. "I am here to stop you, unless you wish to withdraw."

"Very well," the Dragon said. "Meet your fate as you see fit."

Short sword in hand, King Konrad approached Kula Bakar. The Legender was considered taller than average, but his face was level with the Dragon's mighty chest. Kula Bakar was massive across all dimensions—tall, broad, and thick. The Legender looked like a child confronting an ogre.

"Announce the start of combat at your leisure," the Dragon announced.

"Begin," the Legender said without pause.

Raising his shield and hefting his sword, the Dragon began to circle his quarry. Some who knew his fighting style commented later that it was an uncharacteristically wary approach, perhaps an adjustment to the mystifying preparations of his opponent in anticipation of some trick or trap.

The mobility of the Legender proved valuable as he dodged several attacks. The first time their swords clashed, the Legender lost hold of his blade. The Dragon paused to let him retrieve it, then knocked it from his grasp two more times. After the third drop, the Dragon rushed his opponent. The Legender ducked and whirled, feinted and leapt, avoiding many swipes and thrusts, some by a close margin, until he stumbled and the Dragon planted his sword in his chest.

Pinned to the ground, the Legender twitched a few times, legs spasming, then grew still. Panting, the Dragon withdrew his sword and raised it high. He ended all his fights by decapitation, and this one would be no exception.

But the Dragon staggered back when the Legender was spontaneously engulfed in flame. Confused bystanders raised their hands to shield their eyes from the startling blaze. Out of the intense conflagration emerged King Konrad, his shirt bloody but unburned, his body whole.

"What sorcery is this?" the Dragon asked.

The fire behind the Legender vanished as quickly as it had appeared. With an inhuman roar, the Legender took the gorgon's quill from his belt and stuck it through a gap in the armor near the Dragon's waist.

After the prick, Kula Bakar went rigid, making no motion to dodge or protect himself as the Legender pulled out the yeti's fang and used it to punch a hole in the Dragon's breastplate. Then Konrad plunged the vampire's stake through the hole, deep into the Dragon's chest. The Legender stepped back, and the Dragon remained on his feet for a prolonged moment.

The armor of the Dragon made his fall clangorous on the silent battlefield. Ignoring the enemy horde, the Legender withdrew the quill and the stake, returned them to his belt, and then claimed the Dragon's sword before walking away.

In the years that followed, the Legender offered no explanation of how he had survived, though many inquired. Some guessed he had visited a witch or a wizard who had enchanted the items from his previous adventures. Others proposed that the act of sacrificing his life to save his kingdom activated the powers of his talismans.

All that can be confirmed is that the Dragon fell that day, and the Legender walked away. Witnesses swear that the Legender received a fatal blow and inexplicably burst into flames before achieving victory. Tales spread that he had risen from death like a phoenix and bellowed like a yeti. Stories spoke of Kula Bakar paralyzed by a gorgon's quill and then slain like a vampire, wood improbably penetrating metal.

As always with the Legender, the tales grew over time. Storytellers claimed the leader of the Rambling Horde really was the avatar of a powerful dragon, and they attributed his previous successes to supernatural abilities. Bards sang of a king in Selona who could not die, and of a bloodline armed with mighty talismans.

The Legender gained a new title in the aftermath of his successful defense of Selona—Dragon Slayer. After the Rambling Horde withdrew from Selona, no mortal country attacked the kingdom again. Konrad kept the sword of the Dragon and passed his other talismans to his two daughters and two sons, who also gained renown as Dragon Slayers. The Legender and his four children were summoned to help as dragons became more aggressive in subsequent years.

Over time, the kingdom of Selona gained prominence in the magical community, and the generations who came after Konrad became known as the Fair Folk. Though the Legender did not remain their king, neither was his death recorded. Ever since, as you well know, when dragons have united to plague the world, five legendary Dragon Slayers have stood against them.

CHAPTER ELEVEN

Green Ogres

Hermo proved invaluable on the road. He knew ahead of time when a troop of bulky giants with tusks like boars approached from the other direction. Seth, Hermo, and Reggie got off the road into a stand of trees before the giants were in sight, and they watched from safe cover as the giants marched past.

Shortly after they got going again, Hermo sensed the presence of three ogres hiding off the road to ambush travelers and led Seth in a circuitous route before rejoining the road beyond their sight. Later in the day, the hermit troll hurried them to take cover before a giant driving a vast wagon pulled by a dragon rolled into view. Seth could hardly believe the sight of a dragon harnessed like a draft horse.

The road crossed prairies and low hills, sometimes meandering into forests. Mountains remained distantly visible

in one direction or another. Many of the trees were without leaves, and dry, dead grasses covered most fields, with very few blossoms.

As the sun plunged toward the horizon, the day became cold and the breeze grew into gusts of wind that hurled gritty dust at them. "Why is it so cold?" Seth asked. "Isn't it July?"

"Southern hemisphere," Calvin said from his pocket. "It's winter down here."

The wind strips away some of my mass, Reggie said. *But dirt is easily replaced.*

"Me no like cold," Hermo said, stomping his feet and rubbing his hands together. "Me no like wind."

"Me no like it either," Seth said. "Especially with night coming and no place to sleep."

"Always places," Hermo said. "Have to find them."

"We don't have blankets or tents," Seth said. "Or very warm clothes. Can you find us shelter for the night?"

"Easy," Hermo said. "I lead. You follow."

I don't like how he talks to you, Reggie communicated to Seth.

Seth looked at the humanoid figure of dirt. Considering how dingy Reggie appeared as he shambled along the road, with no face and little grace in his movements, it remained a surprise to perceive coherent words from him. "It's just his way," Seth said.

Before long, Hermo guided them off the road. While crossing a sloping field, Hermo paused, picked up a rock, subtly licked it, then tossed it aside. With daylight fading, they crested a low rise, and a large farmhouse came into view. Beside the house, Seth saw a barn, a big wagon, a well, an outhouse, and a simple windmill.

Hermo pointed at the barn. "Shelter."

"Looks like somebody lives here," Seth said. "By the scale of things, somebody big."

Hermo shook his head. "Nobody home. Shutters closed. No horsey for cart. No fires. No lights."

"It's abandoned?" Seth asked. Hermo was right that the little compound seemed still. The farmhouse had two chimneys and a stovepipe. With the temperature dropping and the wind rising, wouldn't someone light a fire against the chill if there were people inside? Wouldn't they be cooking dinner? Wouldn't a lamp be lit to brighten a room as twilight faded?

"Empty," Hermo assured him. He started down the gentle slope to the farmhouse.

A gust of wind stripped away enough warmth to make Seth's teeth chatter, and he followed. He could run from a giant. Freezing to death might be harder to dodge.

Seth stepped quietly as he entered the barnyard. The owner could be asleep inside. Maybe he didn't get cold. Maybe he preferred his meat raw. Maybe he could see in the dark. Seth looked around tensely, half expecting a door to fly open or a dog to start barking. But the little farm remained quiet.

Hermo led them to a large door on the side of the barn. Judging from the dimensions of the door, Seth estimated the farmer was at least twice his height. Hermo laid a palm against the door and bowed his head. "Door locked. I find way in."

Seth focused on the dark power inside of himself, then reached out mentally to locate the lock inside the door. With a small exertion of power, he disengaged the lock.

At the sound, Hermo leaped away as if he had been shocked, falling flat to the ground and blending in with the dry leaves. Seth stared in amazement—Hermo hadn't changed color, but the way he melded with the ground was uncanny.

"Nobody is coming," Seth said quietly. "I undid the lock."

Hermo raised his head as if considering a new possibility, then gave a little nod. He had to jump to reach the handle and open the door. Seth and Reggie entered behind Hermo; then Seth surveyed the still barnyard one last time before shutting the door.

The barn smelled of hay and old wood and seemed no warmer than the air outside, except that the walls held the wind back. Hermo motioned for Seth to follow, then stalked over to a far corner of the barn. The whole building creaked when the wind gusted, but it seemed tight and solid, because Seth felt no drafts.

Hermo yanked aside a mat on the floor to reveal a hidden trapdoor. Seth helped him pull it open, and they went down some stairs to a snug room with four beds made out of patchwork quilts stuffed with straw. A precarious stack of folded quilts occupied one corner.

"Shelter," Hermo said, holding up a lantern he had discovered.

"Good work," Seth said. "It's warmer down here. This will work for tonight. Should we cover up the trapdoor?"

"Me do it," Hermo said, puffing out his chest. "Expert hider."

With the lantern lit, Seth could see there was not a single fancy thing about the little room Hermo had discovered. But it was plenty cozy, with an abundance of quilts. Hermo left and returned with some salty strips of jerky along with a bunch of root vegetables and a bucket of water.

After eating, Hermo secured the trapdoor, then bundled up in one of the rudimentary beds and began to snore softly.

"Are you tired?" Seth whispered to Reggie.

I am made of dirt, Reggie replied. *I am your assistant. We are traveling to Humburgh.*

"Do you need sleep?" Seth asked.

Should I need sleep?

"If not, you can stand guard," Seth said quietly. "Let us know if anybody comes."

I don't know how to sleep, Reggie communicated. *I will stand guard.* He went over and stood at the base of the stairs.

Seth settled onto a bed of straw beneath two quilts and on top of one. Getting comfortable took some squirming, but, compared to sleeping in a rowboat in the belly of a leviathan, it felt heavenly. Seth wondered how easily he would be able to fall asleep while trespassing. There was real danger of the owner returning. Maybe the farm was abandoned for the winter. Maybe nobody would ever return. Or maybe he would hear a wagon pull up at any moment. At least Reggie was standing guard.

"How about you, Seth?" Calvin asked quietly. "Are you tired?"

"Sure," Seth whispered. "It was a long day."

"Your companions don't look like much," Calvin said, "but they're more useful than a glance could reveal."

"Hermo helps us hide and can find shelter," Seth said.

"Reggie can watch for danger," Calvin said.

"And you're someone I can actually talk to," Seth said.

"Hey," Calvin complained. "I found Dante!"

"You're valuable for lots of reasons," Seth said. "It's nice to know I have a real friend."

"Especially when he is your loyal vassal," Calvin said. "You're actually a lot like yourself, even without your memories."

"That's good to hear," Seth said. "Hopefully getting them back won't be too big of a shock."

"You'll be glad to have them," Calvin said. "I would hate to lose my memories."

"I hope it will help me better understand what to do next," Seth said, shifting his position, brittle straw crinkling beneath the quilt.

"A lot of people miss you," Calvin said. "Kendra would do anything for you, as would many other friends and family members. You may have forgotten, but I remember. You're not as alone as you feel. And there is a war to fight against the dragons."

"One step at a time," Seth said. "We also have to help you find Serena."

"Yes," Calvin said. "And break the nipsie curse. To think she might be here at this sanctuary someplace makes me restless! But like you said—one step at a time."

"Good night, Calvin."

"Good night, Seth."

Wake up! came the anxious demand. *Master Seth, wake up!*

Seth opened his eyes to the unsettling sight of a pile of dirt leaning over him. A lumpy portion of the pile rocked against his shoulder, jostling him. A heap of dirt could show no expression to convey urgency, but the emotion came across clearly through the words in Seth's mind.

Somebody is here!

Seth reached for the tube of walrus butter Ronodin had given him. He had to eat a little each morning in order to open his eyes to beings of a magical nature. As soon as he tasted the fatty substance, the pile of dirt resolved into the crude, humanoid form of Reggie.

Up above, in the barn, Seth heard a door open and the clomp of heavy footfalls, followed by the clang and clatter of somebody rummaging through a pile of tools.

"Are you sure it's a human?" a male voice asked, speaking Jiganti, the language of the giants.

"Undoubtedly," a husky female voice answered. "It came into our yard and into this barn and I feel sure it's still here."

"Why would a human enter our barn?" the male voice asked. "Don't they usually want to live?"

"Follow my sniffer," the female said. "We'll find him."

"I smell the intruder too," the male said. "It just makes no sense."

Seth winced as heavy footfalls tromped over to the trapdoor.

Hermo crawled over to the lamp and put it out, plunging the room into darkness.

"I'd bet my boots it's down there," the female said.

"Through the hidden door?" the male asked. "In the old slave quarters?"

"I'd bet my boots," the female repeated.

"Maybe all we're smelling is the humans who were down there once upon a time," the male said.

"It's fresh," the female said.

Seth heard the mat being tossed aside, and the trapdoor opened at the top of the stairs, letting light into the enclosure. Seth could not see Hermo, and he tried to lie flat with the quilts over him.

"You're right," the male said. "That's fresh human. Plenty scared."

"Told you so," the female said.

"We could grind it up and make bread," the male said. "You get to keep your boots."

"Was there ever any doubt?"

"Do I have to go down there?"

"How else do you expect to get him out?" the female asked.

Seth knew the quilts were a flimsy hiding place. He decided it would be better to take the initiative rather than be discovered cowering.

"You could ask nicely," Seth called in Jiganti.

There was no response for a moment.

"Who is down there?" the male voice called.

"A traveling shadow charmer," Seth replied. "Just roaming around, looking for work."

"Show yourself," the male demanded.

Seth got out from under the quilts and walked to the foot of the stairs. He stared up at two huge creatures, humanoids with stout bodies and thick limbs, at least twice his height. Their countenances looked like somebody had sculpted ugly faces out of dough, and then someone else had come along and pulled them out of shape. They wore homespun clothes with work boots and had dirt-rimmed fingernails.

"You speak Jiganti?" the male asked.

"One of the best languages," Seth said.

"You don't have to lay it on so thick," the male said. "But I'll admit it is nice to hear Jiganti from a human. Proper accent and everything. Amazing that humans come to the home of the giants from all parts and don't even bother learning how to say 'hello' or 'thank you.'"

"It's barbaric," the female said. "Not to mention insulting."

"It would be hard to ask for work if I couldn't speak the language," Seth said.

"Funny place to ask for work," the male said. "In a hidden cellar under the barn."

"Nobody was home," Seth said. "It was getting dark."

"Barn was locked," the male said.

"Nothing is locked for a shadow charmer," Seth replied.

"That might be reason enough to be rid of you," the male said.

"I didn't bother your home," Seth said. "Didn't damage or take anything."

"If that's true, it's better than nothing," the male said.

"See for yourself," Seth said.

"I reckon you ate from the supplies in the cellar," the male said.

"A little. Sorry for the imposition. Happy to pay you back. I'm Seth."

"Bogdun," the male said. "What work can a shadow charmer do?"

"Have you been haunted by the undead?" Seth asked. "Any phantoms in the vegetable garden?"

"We wouldn't want ghosts troubling the zucchini," the female said.

"Quackery," Bogdun said. "What sort of payment are you after?"

"Just trying to make my way in the world," Seth said. "A little food. Some shelter. Not being made into bread."

"We don't have any trouble with the undead," Bogdun

said, hefting a large pickax. "I don't need a shadow charmer. But I always have an appetite for bread."

"That would be a waste," Seth said. "There aren't many shadow charmers."

"Special bread," Bogdun said. "Rare ingredients."

"You have quite a farm here," Seth said. "Looks like you need help. You had slaves?"

"Tried human slaves," Bogdun said. "Slow workers. It got too tempting."

"We ate them," the female said. "Pies, bread, muffins."

"Fun while it lasted," Bogdun said.

Seth thought of Hermo's warning, astonished that he really might get eaten!

"Do I have to come down there and get you?" Bogdun asked. "I won't be gentle. Save me the trouble. Come up. Quick and painless."

"He is very polite," the female said. "No need to be cruel."

"Not if he comes up like a gentleman," Bogdun said.

"You have zucchini," Seth said. "You have this farm. Why eat me?"

"Do you know what goes great with zucchini?" the female asked.

"Pot roast?" Seth tried.

"Roast human," she said, licking her lips. "Piping hot, on a stick."

"We're what folk call green ogres," Bogdun said. "Some of our kind call us dull ogres. Because we work the land. But that doesn't mean we don't like a bit of meat in the porridge, so to speak."

"Or you could let me go," Seth said. "Do me that favor, and someday I can do one back."

"I already did you a favor," Bogdun said. "Gave you a warm night, a final meal. This is the last time I ask. You won't like it if I come down there."

Seth knew maybe he could back out of sight and try to shade walk. Blend into the shadows and attempt to slip around the ogre. Or he could try the invisibility glove. But the confines of the little room were snug, and the ogres seemed to smell him as easily as they could see him. With Bogdun coming for him and his wife at the top of the stairs, slipping by them wasn't realistic.

"It's time to do some haunting," Seth said. "Get him, Reggie."

As you command, Master, the dirtman said, charging up the stairs.

"Now what is this?" Bogdun asked, swinging his pickax and smashing the top third of Reggie to dust. A return stroke pulverized most of the rest, and what remained of the legs crumbled.

"What a strange little creature," the female remarked. "Smelled exactly like dirt."

"It'll take more than that," Bogdun said, striding toward the stairs, pickax held ready.

GET AWAY FROM MY MASTER! Reggie bellowed.

The ogre was lifted into the air and hurled across the room. A moment later the female left her feet and slammed against a large handcart. Seth hurried up the stairs in time to see Bogdun rocket out the door backwards to tumble in the dust. The female exited under her own power through a different doorway.

Roaring with rage, murder in his eyes, Bogdun came storming back inside, only to sail out the door again, bouncing and sliding farther in the dust this time. He sat up, glaring into the barn, but made no move to enter.

"Looks like your barn is haunted," Seth called. "Too bad there isn't a shadow charmer around!"

Bogdun stood and dusted himself off. He put his hands on his hips, then folded his arms, then put his hands back on his hips. "All right. What'll it take to get that ghost out of my barn?"

Seth smiled. "I think we can reach an arrangement."

CHAPTER TWELVE

Dectus

N o fair!" Knox exclaimed. "Kendra gets her own pool?"

Kendra looked up from her chocolate croissant to the doorway where Knox stood. Vanessa, Warren, Knox, Tess, and the satyrs had gathered to her room for breakfast. According to Warren, Tanu was exploring the fortress.

"Kendra is a former dragon sanctuary caretaker," Newel said.

"Rank has its privileges," Doren added.

"I wish I could be in charge of a dragon sanctuary," Knox said.

"Be careful what you wish for," Warren said. "It gets complicated when people you love start dying."

"Or losing their memories," Kendra said.

"I'm sure it's hard, but that pool looks like it belongs to a sheik!" Knox exclaimed.

"You're welcome to use it," Kendra said.

"How cool to be you," Knox said. "Stumble out of bed and plop into your pool while your servant makes breakfast."

"You can stumble out of bed, walk down the hall to my suite, and do the same thing," Kendra said. "I haven't tried the pool yet."

Knox smacked his hand to his forehead. "What good are luxuries you never use? That pool is wasted on you."

"I never asked for it," Kendra said.

"What is the pool policy for goatmen?" Newel asked.

"We shed much less than strangers assume," Doren said.

"So little that shedding is hardly worth mentioning," Newel said, jabbing the other satyr with his elbow.

"I don't shy away from the hard topics," Doren said. "We're hairy guys, it's no secret."

"Anyone can use the pool," Kendra said. "The servants clean it."

"Dragons clean your pool?" Tess asked in wonder.

"I guess," Kendra said. "Unless some of the servants aren't dragons."

"I still can't believe how dragons are treated here," Vanessa said. "The Giant Queen is more a prison warden than a caretaker."

"It's pretty extreme," Kendra agreed.

"Whatever," Knox said, coming over to the table and spooning scrambled eggs onto his plate. "We're at war. Be glad the local dragons are on a short leash."

"It works as long as the leash holds," Warren muttered.

"We have to make sure the leash holds," Knox said. "Too many sanctuaries are falling. Someplace has to survive."

Kendra had instructed Giselle not to spy on their breakfast. Still, she looked around, hoping her servant could not hear Knox's insensitive comments. "I don't think the Giant Queen is open to much help from us," she said.

"She may not need it," Vanessa said. "A prison is probably more secure than a sanctuary."

"The Giant Queen doesn't understand how bad this war could get," Kendra said. "But I'm not here just to keep this sanctuary safe. I'm here to find Seth."

"I second the motion," Newel said.

"Thirded," Doren chimed in. "Everything is better with Seth around."

"We all want that," Warren said. "We'll stay on high alert for Seth no matter what else we do. It will help to learn how things work here. Then we can start to organize our search."

"I have a chance to get some useful information," Kendra said.

"How?" Vanessa asked.

"Giselle delivered a message to me this morning from a sky giant named Dectus," Kendra said. "According to her, he is one of the wisest and most reasonable of the Giant Queen's councilors."

"That sounds promising," Warren said. "When can you meet?"

"Open invitation," Kendra said. "As soon as I want. I thought I might go after breakfast."

"Do you mind if I join you?" Vanessa asked.

"He wants me to come alone," Kendra said. "Giselle encouraged me to go."

"She's a dragon," Vanessa said. "Is her approval good or bad?"

"You should meet with him," Warren said. "The sky giants have always honored their allegiance to Dragonwatch. From what I can tell so far, I think we're in more danger of being ignored than betrayed."

"I get the same feeling," Kendra said, wiping her lips with a napkin.

"Have you heard about the giant killer?" Newel asked. "Doren and I keep overhearing giants and servants talking about him."

"Not that we have been skulking about the kitchens looking for extra food and listening to the gossip," Doren said. "He keeps visiting the Giant Queen."

"I've heard mention of him," Warren said. "I don't know much."

"Why would giants want visits from a killer?" Tess asked.

"Who knows?" Kendra said. "We need better information." She went to her bedroom and opened the door. "You can join us now," she called.

"I stayed out of earshot, as requested," Giselle said.

"I'm ready to see Dectus," Kendra said.

"Excellent choice," Giselle said. "Learn all you can."

🦅 🦅 🦅

Raza came to escort Kendra to the meeting with Dectus. She walked beside him in silence until he spoke.

"I trust Giselle is attending to your needs?" he asked.

"Giselle is wonderful," Kendra said. "I was surprised to learn you are dragons."

Raza rubbed the silver collar around his neck. "No great shock once you get to know Titan Valley."

"Do you like some giants better than others?" Kendra asked.

"That is fair to say," Raza replied.

"Where does Dectus rank?" Kendra asked.

"I was compelled to swear allegiance to the Giant Queen," Raza said. "Now that I pledged my loyalty, she has it, along with power to punish me if I stray. Were I to voluntarily give my allegiance to any giant, Dectus would be my choice. When he speaks, listen well."

That gave Kendra plenty to wonder about as they returned to the areas of the fortress designed for giants. Dectus led Kendra onto a system of catwalks that stretched high along the walls of tremendous corridors and chambers. At last a catwalk ended at a white, human-sized door. Raza tugged a rope that rang a bell.

"Enter," boomed a friendly voice.

"I'll wait for you out here," Raza said, opening the door for Kendra and motioning her inside. He closed the door behind her without following.

A giant sat at a massive desk writing on a huge piece of

parchment. Dressed in a light blue toga, he hunched over his work, showing Kendra his curly white hair partially wreathed by a laurel. After finishing his sentence, he blew on the parchment, then pinched some sand onto it.

When he looked up at Kendra, the giant smiled, creating deep creases in his aged face. "Kendra Sorenson, I presume?"

"Yes, sir," Kendra said.

He nodded and stood, taking a moment to stretch and shake out his hands. Despite his apparent age, his body looked sturdy and strong. "I am Dectus, a senior member of the Council." His voice sounded so well matched for making speeches that it was almost too resonant for casual conversation. "Would you prefer to talk from there, or shall I bring you to my desk?"

"Either way," Kendra said.

He crossed to her, and Kendra climbed onto a hand large enough to cradle her entire body. Dectus carefully shuttled her to the desk and set her down. He reached down to the floor and picked up a human-sized chair, setting it beside her. "Have a seat, if you please."

Kendra accepted the seat, and Dectus sat as well. "How much do you know about the Council?" he asked.

"Not much," Kendra admitted.

"You came here on short notice, the result of emergency circumstances," Dectus acknowledged. "Nine of us advise the queen: four senior councilors, five junior. Her decisions override even our unanimous opinion, but she delegates many of the practical details of governance to us."

"So you have an important job," Kendra said.

"My role is important only to those who want the kingdom to function," Dectus said. "You might be amazed how small that group seems at times."

"Did you hear when I spoke to the queen?" Kendra asked.

"All nine councilors were present," Dectus said. "I took particular notice of your concerns about the dragon war."

"I felt like the queen ignored them," Kendra said.

Dectus smiled. "I have experienced the same feeling."

"I only meant to help," Kendra said.

"I believe you," Dectus said. "Save a few clever rogues who have learned to stay out of our way, the dragons have long been subjugated at Titan Valley. I fear the queen has concluded that just because the dragons at this sanctuary are under control, any dragons who intrude will fall to her as well."

"Celebrant is powerful, and his army is growing," Kendra said.

"And Celebrant hates the conditions at Titan Valley more than the situation at any other sanctuary," Dectus said.

"You see the danger," Kendra said.

"I do, but the majority of my fellow sky giants side with the queen," Dectus said. "They prefer to assume we are above such lowly concerns. I believe we giants need to take this war more seriously. If we continue to pretend all is well outside this sanctuary simply because we have firmly established authority within our borders, we run the risk of an attack finding us unprepared."

"Titan Valley has to hold," Kendra said. "Too many other preserves have fallen or are teetering."

"And if Titan Valley should fall, we need to be in a position to fight and win a war," Dectus said. "If dragons overrun this world, neither humans nor giants will have a place in it."

Kendra felt comforted to be grouped with such enormous allies. "Can giants really kill dragons with their bare hands?"

"We can kill dragons in many ways," Dectus said. "Especially those of our kind with hides resistant to their breath weapons, or who are armored to withstand them. But some giants forget that dragons can slay us as well."

"I've heard talk of a giant killer," Kendra said.

Dectus shook his head and covered a smile. "There is plenty of gossip about him."

"Who is he?" Kendra pressed.

"To understand the giant killer, one must know the queen," Dectus said. "Imani has never married. Sizeism has always been an issue among the giants."

"Sizeism?"

Dectus scowled and beat his chest. "Bigger is better. Smaller is worse. This thinking extends beyond humans and goblins to our own kind. A major reason Imani is our monarch is because she is easily the largest of us. She regards herself as superior to any suitor brave enough to apply."

"Do other giants want to marry her?" Kendra asked.

"Nearly every giant I know would do anything to wed

her," Dectus said. "But she mocks romantic attention. Pats her suitors on the head and suggests they get on a stool if they want a kiss. There is only so much humiliation a giant can take."

"She won't take any giants seriously," Kendra said.

"Our queen is more than head and shoulders taller than the largest of us," Dectus said. "She may not look it, but she is the strongest of our number as well. She is the only daughter of the titan for which this sanctuary is named. We giants gave up trying to woo her ages ago. Then along comes the giant killer."

"Was he a spurned lover?" Kendra asked. "Did he try to slay her?"

"The title is a jest," Dectus said. "The giant killer is your size. Prince Doranio from Selona. He is romancing her. And having a surprising measure of success."

"A prince my size!" Kendra exclaimed.

"He is shockingly bold," Dectus said. "Her jibes and insults have no effect on him. He is a brilliant conversationalist. He began as a novelty to her, a toy, but I believe she has grown to sincerely enjoy his attentions."

"What about sizeism?" Kendra asked.

"In a way, his tiny stature works to his advantage," Dectus said. "Responding to his interest has given the queen a new method to insult the rest of us. It's yet another way to emphasize that none of us are big enough for her. Her flirtations imply that our value is less than his pathetic size. More than a few giants would squash the miniscule suitor given the chance. But of course, none would risk the wrath of the queen."

"Could she be serious about him?" Kendra asked.

Dectus laughed. "No, Kendra, she isn't serious. But she does enjoy his company. The toy will eventually lose its shine, but he has held her interest much longer than any of us expected."

"Is he around now?" Kendra asked.

"He comes and goes," Dectus said. "He understands the game he is playing. His limited availability prolongs her interest."

"What does he want?"

"I often consider that question," Dectus said. "Could he sincerely be after her hand? I suspect not. The logistics are ludicrous, and he plays it too much like a game. I would be interested to hear your reactions to him."

"I admit I'm curious," Kendra said.

Dectus scratched the side of his head above his ear. "Would you wait here a moment? Let me go see if I can arrange a meeting."

"All right," Kendra said, a little intimidated by the prospect of how dashing and handsome this prince might be to successfully flatter a powerful woman of such inhuman proportions. Then again, nobody could be more absurdly perfect than Bracken.

"I will return shortly," Dectus said. "No offense intended."

CHAPTER THIRTEEN

Humburgh

As the hulking wagon rumbled across the countryside, Seth reclined in the capacious bed atop a payload of turnips. Hermo hunched off to one side, Calvin relaxed in Seth's pocket, and Reggie lay on his back, having borrowed dirt from the barnyard to fashion a new body, this version somewhat dustier than his previous incarnation.

Bogdun had invited Seth to sit up front with him, but Seth felt wary enough to stay out of easy reach. The ogre held reins attached to a monstrous ox, its shaggy hair a golden orange. Iron trinkets decorated the wide white horns, jangling as the beast walked.

That ogre calls me a ghost, Reggie communicated.

"Without any substance, you seem like a ghost," Seth said.

But I am your assistant, Reggie maintained.

"Assistants aren't always visible," Seth said. "You really saved us back there."

My other body was destroyed in the fight, Reggie conveyed.

"That's an advantage to being made of dirt," Seth said. "There is usually more when you need it."

We are going to Humburgh, Reggie expressed.

"Bogdun agreed to take us," Seth said.

Shifting in his seat, Bogdun spoke over his shoulder. "I agreed to get rid of you. Conjure no more hauntings and we can become strangers."

"Him might still smash you," Hermo cautioned.

"If he does, Reggie will haunt his farm forever," Seth said.

At least as long as the buildings stand, Reggie communicated.

"Never attack shadow charmers," Seth advised. "Most of us have an army of undead ready to curse anyone who harms us. We make better friends than enemies."

"This is too much chatter," Bogdun said. "The miles go faster without the yapping."

Seth watched the countryside pass. Sometimes Bogdun followed a road; sometimes he made his own path over field and prairie. They forded a couple of streams.

Hermo bit into a turnip the size of a cantaloupe, crunching loudly. He took another large bite. "Why you no eat?"

"I had a little," Seth said.

"Almost none," Hermo said.

"I negotiated that we could eat all the turnips we want

during the ride," Seth said. "I didn't know how they tasted. I'm just not hungry enough yet. You enjoy."

"You crazy," Hermo said. "Delicious and free."

Seth saw a lonely farm go by. He noticed some ogres toiling in a stony field with hoes.

"Isn't winter a bad time to farm?" Seth asked.

"Mild winters here," Bogdun said. "The Giant Queen manipulates the weather. We can grow worthwhile crops all year. These winter turnips are nice."

The turnip Seth tried had tasted sharply bitter. "They're big."

Bogdun grunted. "Maybe to a pipsqueak like you. I wanted my crop out of the ground before the Perennial Storm hits. Certain seeds will sprout only when the storm of all storms arrives."

"What's the Perennial Storm?" Seth asked.

Bogdun shook his head. "Ignorance is not charming."

Seth waited for more, but the conversation ended there, and he doubted whether asking again would yield additional information. After some time, Seth spotted a trio of giants tramping through deep underbrush among slender trees, each led by his own smallish green dragon tugging against a chain.

"Do giants keep dragons as pets here?" Seth asked.

Bogdun chuckled derisively. "The dragons serve the giants. Those three are hunting pancake mushrooms, a rare delicacy that grows just below the surface. They are very hard to find without the senses of a trained fungus hunter."

"The dragons are sniffing out mushrooms?" Seth asked.

"Hard to beat a fresh pancake mushroom," Bogdun said.

They reached an especially broad road, and Bogdun stayed on it. Coming toward them from the opposite direction, ogres driving empty wagons grunted greetings to Bogdun as they passed. Seth hunkered down to be less conspicuous. Hermo settled deep into the turnips, blending so well that Seth could no longer see him. Bogdun steered his ox to the edge of the road as a huge coach rumbled toward him, massive wheels churning. A beefy female giant with her hair in a sloppy bun handled the reins of a chocolate brown dragon.

The sun had moved well past midday, and Seth became hungry enough to gnaw on a turnip. With some trial and error, he discovered that the smallest ones were less bitter, with a hint of sweetness. Hermo had shared a canteen with him, but it was empty now, and Seth saw no way to refill it.

Up ahead, a black castle with spindly towers rose into view. A lumpy gray dragon with misshapen horns was chained out front, apparently to guard the entrance. Seth heard desperate roars issuing from within the castle.

"Sounds like a party," Seth said, having noticed that direct questions seldom got answers, but wrong guesses or offhand comments could lure Bogdun into conversation.

"It's always lively at the Alchemy Academy," the ogre said.

"Turning dragons into mice?" Seth guessed.

"The alchemists extract rare substances from the dragons there," Bogdun said. "I hear they use a stench giant to elicit dragon tears."

"Seems tough being a dragon at Titan Valley," Seth said.

Bogdun harrumphed. "Welcome to reality. It's tough all around."

Before long, a town came into view, more expansive than Seth had anticipated. From a distance, the municipality looked lopsided, as if some neighborhoods had swollen disproportionately. Seth realized that most of the town was built to human scale, but at least one district had been constructed to accommodate giants. A wall encircled the town, with farms and mills outside and a jumble of rooftops, turrets, chimneys, and towers within. Though the human-sized portion of the town had some impressive buildings, the giant side featured structures at least ten times larger.

Do I like townships? Reggie asked.

"You like them," Seth said. "But you know that people in towns can be superstitious about those who are made of dirt. You avoid too much attention. And if people destroy your dirt body, you form a new one."

Right.

"We're meeting someone in town," Seth said, speaking louder. He pulled out the envelope from Dante and read the address. "We're going to 49 Pinnacle Street, not far from the arena."

"I'm heading to the market," Bogdun said. "You find your street yourself."

"No worry," Hermo said quietly. "Me find."

Seth decided to drop the matter. He considered getting out his invisibility glove but decided it might draw too much attention from Bogdun. Instead he nestled back into the turnips and sought to appear nondescript.

A sign on the wall above the city gate announced HUMBURGH in wrought-iron letters. Beneath the name of the town, in smaller letters, Seth read END NO LIFE. Armored trolls waved the wagon through the city gate with only a grunt or two from Bogdun.

As the ox pulled the wagon along the cobblestone road, Seth stopped trying to hide and sat forward, staring at the assortment of people thronging the streets. He saw humans and dwarfs, trolls and goblins, satyrs and centaurs, nymphs and fairies, and, standing notably taller than the others, an occasional ogre. Some in the crowd carried weapons and looked ready for a fight, but most seemed to be regular folk going about their daily business.

"I don't see any giants," Seth said.

Bogdun guffawed as if the observation were ludicrous. "You want giants, head over to Big Side."

"Is this Small Side?" Seth asked.

"Small Town," Bogdun corrected. "Unless an ogre is around." He sat up straighter and rolled his heavy shoulders. "Then it becomes at least medium."

The structures on either side of the street were packed in close and piled several stories high in a manner that suggested each story had been constructed by different builders at different times. Carved wooden animal heads projected from the facade of a wide building on the right like hunting trophies. The various heads chattered boisterously at passersby, inviting them inside. On the other side of the street, an eatery built on a scale for ogres had swinging bat-wing doors in the front. While ogres swaggered in and out, smaller folk scurried out of the way.

Up ahead, a troll in a bowler hat and plaid vest stood on the balcony of a morose building. The architect must have hated straight lines, because every column was twisted, every railing warped, every window droopy, as if the somber structure were slowly melting.

"Step inside the Mystery House," the troll invited bois-terously. "See the hidden wonders. Learn of treasures un-told. Uncover the deepest secrets of the Games. Enigmas and opportunity await within the Humburgh Mystery House. Today, you have a date with destiny!"

Seth leaned forward with interest. Below the balcony, a young woman approached a painting of a black door on the wall at street level. She knocked on the painted door and it became real, then opened. After she entered, the door closed and became a painted image again.

"Can we get off here?" Seth asked.

"I agreed to ferry you to the marketplace," Bogdun said. "You want to hop off early, so much the better."

"Deal," Seth said.

"I'll slow but I won't stop," Bogdun said. "I could get cited if I halt without good reason. Off you go. May the Games claim you."

The wagon slowed slightly. "Come on," Seth invited, climbing down as low as he could before jumping off. From the ground he marveled anew at the enormity of the shaggy ox pulling the wagon. The bucket-sized hooves picked up their pace.

Hermo and Reggie landed beside Seth, and they moved away from the street. Drawing on his power, Seth scanned the area for the undead, but he could sense no entities.

"Me find Virgil?" Hermo asked.

"Just a second," Seth said, approaching the painted front door of the Humburgh Mystery House. He knocked, but his knuckles thumped against a solid stone wall, and the door remained a painting.

"You want in, Junior?" the troll called down from his balcony. He pointed to an alley with his cane. "Head around the side."

Seth looked in the direction the troll had pointed and saw a figure dressed in layers of dark rags, a black veil obscuring the face, skulking by the far corner of the Mystery House. The troll returned to barking out invitations to the crowd, and Seth went over to the veiled figure.

"Do I go through you to get inside?" Seth asked.

"To use my entrance, you must pay admission," replied a creaky female voice.

"What's the price?" Seth asked.

The veiled hag cackled. "Something I consider valuable."

"Like money?" Seth asked.

"Make an offer," the hag replied.

Seth had kept a single turnip in his pocket in case of an emergency. He had only taken a couple of bites from it. He pulled it from his pocket and held it out to the hag.

The hag made a fist and the turnip caught fire. Seth tossed it aside before he got burned, and the flaming turnip rolled to a stop in the alley beside the Mystery House.

"Insulting," the hag said. "I will consider no more offers from you today."

The hag withdrew into the alley and Seth walked off, not wanting to prolong the interaction. He felt foolish for offering an item he didn't even like.

"It was worth a try," Calvin said from Seth's pocket. "If she'd been starving, a turnip might have seemed valuable."

"Or if she had a taste for partially eaten roots," Seth said.

"At least you didn't lose something you'll miss," Calvin said.

"This way," Hermo said, stabbing a grubby finger down the street.

"How do you know?" Seth asked.

"Follow," Hermo said.

They passed a mercantile where the sale of armaments extended out onto the walkway. A dwarf haggled with a troll over a mail shirt. A centaur hefted a broadsword, sighting along the blade. A goblin rummaged through a bin of used boots.

As Seth paid attention, he noticed several enterprises devoted to outfitting contestants for the Games. He also passed inns and banks, eateries, a gambling house, and several ambiguous establishments, like the one where pungent fumes drifted out through beaded curtains, or the brick wall where people climbed knotted ropes to entrances high above the street.

As the little group made their way through the crowded avenues, many eyes strayed to Reggie, as if a figure made of dirt were a novelty even in this diverse crowd. Seth stayed ready for more than glances, but nobody approached Reggie or openly made comments.

Hermo tugged on Seth's sleeve, leading him down a long, narrow alleyway. Somewhere above him a baby cried. A puddle in a depression had a faint glow and a sweet, rotten odor. They came out onto a less populated street where a small band of centaurs laughed loudly.

Seth kept his eyes down and followed Hermo. Hoping to find a wraith or phantom who could give him information, Seth reached out with his power, but he still sensed no undead nearby, though several of the dilapidated townhouses on the street had a peculiar energy, and he suspected he was being watched by someone who meant him harm.

Hermo led them on a winding route down other streets, including a shabby dirt footpath behind some noisy inns. When they reached a street lined with identical brick residences, Seth noticed a street sign that labeled it Pinnacle, and he pointed it out to Hermo.

"Yes," Hermo said, stopping in front of a doorway. "Number forty-nine."

Seth pulled out the envelope addressed to Virgil and confirmed that Hermo had the correct number. "Let's go," Seth said, starting toward the door.

Do I know Virgil? Reggie wondered.

"I think we're all meeting him for the first time," Seth said.

Can I try introducing us? Reggie asked.

Seth stared at the crude dirt figure. "I think only I can hear you."

I am your assistant, Reggie conveyed. *I should speak. I should be heard. I'll do my best.*

"Go ahead," Seth invited.

Reggie took the lead and knocked. As he was raising his hand a second time, a satyr answered, holding a sandwich. The goatman might have been in his twenties, with thick, messy hair and a green, unbuttoned shirt with the sleeves rolled up.

"Can I help you?" the satyr asked.

We are looking for Virgil, Reggie communicated earnestly.

The satyr glanced past Reggie to Seth. "Small for a golem," he commented.

I am Reggie. My master wishes to speak with Virgil.

"Are you all mute?" the satyr asked.

He doesn't hear me, Reggie concluded.

Seth motioned at the dirtman. "Reggie is my assistant."

"And a hermit troll?" the satyr asked. "How'd you lure him out of hiding?"

"We're looking for Virgil," Seth said.

"You found him," the satyr said, seeming a little more guarded. "You're not here about the Games, are you?"

"We're new to Titan Valley," Seth said.

"You're a kid," Virgil said. "And a hermit troll. And a dirt guy."

"I have a letter for you," Seth said, handing over the envelope.

Virgil held it up. "Dante?" He gave Seth a more interested look, then opened the envelope and started reading. He looked up from the page. "You're a shadow charmer?"

"Yes," Seth said.

"Why come to Humburgh?" Virgil asked. "We have no undead."

Seth glanced at Reggie. "I came to learn about the Games."

"That's what I live and breathe," Virgil said. "Dante has a good track record with me, but I would hate to encourage a kid toward the Games. Those who get involved in the Games tend to die."

"I'm involved with or without you," Seth said. "Dante thought you might be able to give me a better chance."

Virgil swatted the letter from Dante against his palm, glanced up and down the street, then gave a nod. "All right. Come inside. And prepare to have your mind blown!"

CHAPTER FOURTEEN

Giant Killer

Kendra stood near the edge of the enormous desk, tossing bits of wax she had broken off a candle and watching them fall to the floor. The study door opened and Dectus swept back into the room.

"Good news," the giant declared. "When I brought up your name to the Giant Queen, the giant killer showed interest in meeting you. I have been instructed to bring you to the audience chamber at once."

"In the throne room?" Kendra asked.

"Yes, it will afford you a chance to see the paramour in action," Dectus said. "I might be biased, but I don't trust him."

"Let's go," Kendra said.

Dectus picked up a silver chain attached to a silver cage.

When he placed the cylindrical cage in front of Kendra, she saw a cushioned chair inside.

"We giants carry honored guests in such containers," Dectus said, opening the door to the cage. "The chair is firmly attached to the base for your comfort, and the bars are there for your safety. Most prefer it to being transported by hand. The way you wish to travel is your decision, including if you would rather walk. I offer this receptacle for your convenience."

"All right," Kendra said, uncertain about voluntarily entering a cage. She ducked inside and sat on the chair. Dectus carefully fastened the chain around his neck, wearing the container like a pendant.

From her cushy chair, Kendra watched Dectus exit the room and head down a hall. He strolled smoothly, but the cage still wobbled. He entered the audience chamber through a side door, where other gigantic members of the court were gathered.

The Giant Queen presided from her throne, eyes attentive to her armrest. Her demeanor was different from the last time Kendra had seen the monarch. Gone was the stiff formality. Her cheeks were flushed, and she seemed to be resisting a girlish smile. Her eyes twinkled.

Kendra was not close enough to see clearly the little fellow lounging on a chair situated on the armrest of the queen's throne. Clad in black, he appeared to be human-sized.

The Giant Queen glanced at Dectus and straightened slightly. "I see you have brought our visitor," the queen said, her voice softer and more melodious than Kendra recalled. "Bring her forward."

Prince Doranio rose from his chair and pivoted to face Kendra as Dectus drew nearer. Kendra gasped. She knew that self-satisfied grin. The last time she had seen this face was amid horrible peril in the Under Realm. She could not believe it was Ronodin! He wore courtly attire fashioned from black leather, embellished with golden accents.

"Kendra Sorenson!" he greeted grandly. "How charming to see you again!"

"Hello," Kendra said, fighting to keep her voice steady.

"What have we here?" the Giant Queen asked with a delighted clap. "Am I to understand you two are acquainted? My prince is so shrouded in mystery."

"Many women have sought my attention over the years," Ronodin said. He raised his eyes to meet the queen's gaze. "I have sought only one."

Kendra's head swam at his audacity. She hardly knew what to say.

"Tell me, how is your family?" Ronodin inquired politely.

Kendra knew she should have the advantage. She could expose him at her whim! Ronodin was operating under a false identity and undoubtedly up to no good. But the dark unicorn was keeping her off-balance. Shouldn't he be worried about what she might say?

"My family is well, though the war places a strain on everyone," Kendra said.

"Almost everyone," Ronodin corrected with a glance at

the Giant Queen. "There are those with presence enough to rise above such disputes."

The Giant Queen's eyes shone as she relished the praise. She turned her attention to Kendra. "Little one, you have found the greatest oasis in the world. You need only visit my highest battlement to behold safety and prosperity as far as the eye can see."

"You are truly fortunate to be here," Ronodin told Kendra, sipping from a goblet. "But how have you been? I am curious to hear all your news."

"You've always taken such an interest in my family," Kendra said.

"Why not?" the Giant Queen said. "He is enamored by news of all variety."

"You know me well," Ronodin said with a gallant bow. "And yet news comes and goes. Only you hold my prolonged attention."

"You flatter me," the Giant Queen said.

"Is it flattery if I proceed to while away my hours at your side?" Ronodin asked.

"You have done so on many occasions," the Giant Queen said warmly.

"I live to enjoy you," Ronodin said.

"You are awed by my scale, like all who encounter me," the Giant Queen said.

"Your size is but one facet of a perfect jewel," Ronodin professed. "Deeper examination endlessly yields more to admire."

"Enough," the Giant Queen declared with a satisfied

smile. "There are children present." She gave a pointed glance at Kendra. "Go babysit my guest while I attend to royal affairs."

Ronodin bowed deeply. "I am yours to command," he vowed.

"Dectus, you may take the pint-sized prince away," the Giant Queen said. "Be careful with him. He is precious."

"Perhaps he should be careful of me," Ronodin said with bravado. "I can be a lot to handle."

The Giant Queen snickered delightedly. "My feisty prince."

Ronodin strode forward and kissed the queen's ring with a bow. Dectus approached and let Ronodin leap onto the palm of his hand. "My regular parlor would be preferred," Ronodin directed crisply.

"We will go there at once," Dectus said.

The giant exited the audience chamber, passed through a corridor full of mirrors, and set Ronodin down beside a human-sized door. Kendra gripped the arms of her chair as Dectus took the chain from around his neck, rocking her cage. He set the container on the floor and opened the door.

Ronodin extended his hand to help her step out, but Kendra ignored it. He looked dashing in his perfectly tailored outfit, but his good looks did nothing to charm her.

"I will place a servant outside the door should you require anything, Kendra," Dectus said.

"Thank you," Kendra replied.

Ronodin opened the door, and Kendra entered a lavishly appointed parlor that could have comfortably seated ten. After closing the door, Ronodin plopped down on a sofa and put his feet up on a low table with an air of casual ownership.

"Prince Doranio?" Kendra asked flatly.

"Not a perfect anagram of my real name," Ronodin said. "But I like the ring of it."

"Will we be overheard in here?" Kendra asked.

"A prudent question in this fortress," Ronodin said. "I have taken measures to make this parlor secure, so long as we do not raise our voices."

"How much time do you spend here, flirting with her majesty?" Kendra asked.

"Enough," Ronodin said. "You know the servants are all dragons." He pantomimed a choker around his neck.

"Thanks for the obvious," Kendra said. "What's your game here, Ronodin?"

"I've always gravitated to the highest circles," Ronodin said.

"Only to disrupt them," Kendra said. "You look absurd romancing her."

"Ours is primarily a love affair of words," Ronodin said. "I have kissed her hand on occasion."

"She giggles like a schoolgirl around you," Kendra said.

Ronodin winked. "They don't call me the giant killer for nothing. The bigger they are . . ."

Kendra rolled her eyes. "Who are you working with? Celebrant?"

"I have allies everywhere," Ronodin said. "I build bridges, Kendra. And if I burn one, I repair it."

"You were a crow the last time I saw you," Kendra said.

"After butting heads with your boyfriend," Ronodin said.

"My boyfriend?" Kendra asked.

"Bracken has never taken any girl to meet his parents," Ronodin said.

Kendra felt her face grow hot. "I needed to return something."

"I know my cousin," Ronodin said. "He has it bad for you."

Kendra had done her best to bury her feelings for Bracken, but she secretly wanted Ronodin to be right. "How do you know he took me to the Fairy Realm?"

"Little escapes my notice," Ronodin said. "Beings from the magical realm have romanced mortals. Ask Patton. It's unconventional, it requires sacrifice, but it can be done." Ronodin dropped his feet to the floor and leaned forward. "How did it feel to wear the Fairy Queen's crown?"

Kendra hesitated to answer.

Ronodin closed his eyes. "It must have been an exquisite rush."

"I didn't keep it very long," Kendra said.

Ronodin opened his eyes. "Just long enough to accomplish your purposes. How did you squander such an opportunity? You realize that with the crown on, by definition, you were the Fairy Queen?"

"I wasn't after her job," Kendra said.

Ronodin shook his head. "You and I are very different. That crown would have been mine forever."

"Which is why she didn't give it to you," Kendra said.

"Bracken's mother is no fool," Ronodin said. "But she is having trouble purifying her realm."

"What do you mean?" Kendra asked.

Ronodin stayed silent, nonchalantly checking his fingernails.

"Where is Seth?" Kendra asked.

"I wondered when that topic would arise," Ronodin said. "You know, as an apprentice, Seth left much to be desired."

"You know so much," Kendra said. "Where is he?"

"I'm suddenly drawing a blank," Ronodin said. "I remember he was at the volcano."

"Did he cause Baga Loa to erupt?" Kendra asked.

"He had the chance," Ronodin said. "But your little brother chickened out. I sent another agent after the Everbloom, who became an unfortunate casualty."

"What if I tell Dectus all I know about you?"

"I would become much less cooperative," Ronodin said. "Do you think we would be having this conversation had you not played along?"

"I want answers," Kendra said.

"Take a seat," Ronodin said. "Have some fruit from that bowl. I don't know where they source the pears, but you will find them surprisingly refreshing."

"I would rather stand," Kendra said. "If you want me to keep quiet, start with where I can find Seth."

"Somewhere on this preserve?" Ronodin guessed. "He

meant to come here. How should I know? Seth has served his purposes."

"As your slave," Kendra accused.

"As my willing apprentice," Ronodin said. "I did want Seth to free the undead from the Blackwell. He performed perfectly. Everything else was a bonus."

Fighting back tears, Kendra clenched her fists. Ronodin had overthrown Wyrmroost. He had imprisoned Bracken. He had abducted Seth. And here he sat in comfortable luxury. Suddenly the bowl of fruit held new appeal. She crossed to the bowl, picked up an apple, and hurled it at him.

Shrinking and raising his hands, Ronodin deflected the fruit. Kendra pelted him in the side with a pear, narrowly missed his head with an orange, and then he caught the next apple, tossing it aside. Ronodin leaped over the back of the sofa, crouching out of sight. The moment his head popped up, Kendra chucked a kiwi at him.

"Seriously, Kendra?" Ronodin said. "This is very unlike you."

She dumped out the fruit, then charged the sofa, wielding the golden bowl. Ronodin scrambled away as she drew near, then picked up a pillow off a chair and used it to block a swing of the bowl. Kendra lunged at him, but he dodged aside. Her momentum carried her down into the corner of a marble tabletop, opening a long gash on her forearm.

"What have you done?" Ronodin accused.

Kendra staggered to her feet, blood oozing between the fingers clutching her injury. "You're a monster," Kendra accused, panting. "You do evil wherever you go. You're going to destroy Titan Valley."

"I'll do as I see fit," Ronodin said.

"So will I," Kendra said. "Help!" she yelled. "I'm being attacked!"

The door flew open and a brawny man wearing a silver choker entered.

"Out!" Ronodin demanded. "Or I will make your life an endless misery."

The brawny man glanced at the overturned bowl, the scattered fruit, and Kendra's bleeding arm, and his gaze landed on Ronodin.

"Sorry, Giant Killer," the servant said, approaching. "I am under strict orders to protect the caretaker."

"*She* attacked *me*," Ronodin accused.

The brawny servant looked from Ronodin, polished and calm, to Kendra, disheveled, clutching her injured arm with tears in her eyes.

"You damage everything you touch," Kendra spat, still fuming.

"I've seen enough," the servant said. "Her wound requires attention."

"Be wise in what you share," Ronodin said to Kendra.

"Be wise in who you cross," Kendra replied as she exited.

CHAPTER FIFTEEN

Virgil

"Have a seat," Virgil said. "Are you hungry?"

"Actually, yes," Seth said, sitting down on a bench beside a table cluttered with dishes, mugs, utensils, papers, maps, spent candles, and several books. The satyr slid some hefty tomes aside to clear a space in front of Seth.

"You like fish?" Virgil asked.

"I like anything," Seth said. "Except turnips."

"Have you been going hungry?" Virgil asked.

"Yes," Seth said.

"Then you get the works," Virgil said. "Hungry young adventurers deserve some breaks."

The room connected to the little kitchen was overcrowded. Seth counted five ottomans, four clocks, three globes, two hat racks, and an abundance of pillows on the worn furniture. Rows of paintings leaned against the base of a wall. An easel in one corner supported a half-finished landscape.

"Your hermit troll isn't going upstairs, is he?" Virgil asked.

Seth hadn't noticed, but Virgil was right. "Sorry. Hermo, where are you going?"

"Me look around," Hermo replied.

"What are you hoping to find?" Virgil called.

"Me no steal," Hermo said. "Me find stuff."

"Hermo, Virgil is our host," Seth said.

"Let him go," Virgil said.

"Reggie, would you watch Hermo?" Seth asked. "Make sure he doesn't take anything?"

The dirt figure saluted and followed the hermit troll up the stairs.

Virgil brought a platter to the table laden with bread, butter, jam, and cheese. He also produced a plate with three cooked, deboned fish fillets.

"Who names a hermit troll 'Hermo'?" Virgil whispered. "His parents weren't very creative."

Seth chuckled as he buttered a piece of bread. "Thanks for this food. I hope Hermo doesn't get into mischief."

"Between you and me," Virgil said, "I don't have anything of great material value in this house. And I have trouble discarding items, so if he wants something, he will most likely do me a favor by claiming it."

Seth took a bite of bread and felt his appetite roar to life. He made an effort to pace himself and squirreled away a few morsels for Calvin.

"You want to learn about the Games," Virgil said. "Tell me what you already know."

"Humbuggle runs them," Seth replied. "They're really hard to beat. People get killed all the time." Seth's voice trailed off.

Virgil stared at him in amazement. "You're kidding. Don't you at least know the prize?"

Seth added cheese to his bread and took another bite. He shook his head.

"The Wizenstone?" Virgil prompted. "The most powerful talisman in the world? Does that ring a bell?"

"I don't know much about it," Seth said.

Virgil laughed. "Seth, if you haven't heard of the Wizenstone, why enter the Games?"

"I've heard of it," Seth said. He paused, deciding he would need to extend some trust to get the information he desired. "I'm here for Humbuggle. He took my memories."

"Really?" Virgil asked. "When? How?"

"At Stormguard Castle," Seth said.

Virgil pressed his fingers to his temples and then released the pose. "You survived the cursed castle? What happened?"

"I don't remember much," Seth said. "But I saw my sister send the Wizenstone away."

Virgil rushed over to a stack of parchment on an end table, shuffled through many sheets, and returned with a drawing of a mighty castle. "Look familiar?"

"Is that Stormguard?" Seth verified. "I don't remember it from the outside. My memories start in the room where the Wizenstone was kept."

"Your sister sent it away?" Virgil asked. "How?"

"With a magical staff," Seth said. "After some guys tried to grab the Wizenstone and got turned to dust."

"You're kidding me," Virgil said. "Did Dante put you up to this prank?"

"This isn't a joke. Dante doesn't even know this much."

"Scholars of the Games have theorized that the Wizenstone could be difficult to claim," Virgil said. "What action turned these men to dust? Did they try to wield the stone?"

"They reached for it," Seth remembered. "As soon as they touched it, they disintegrated."

"You were an eyewitness?" Virgil confirmed.

"I'm sharing some of my first memories," Seth said. "My identity was wiped right before I entered the room with the Wizenstone."

"How did you know the girl was your sister?" Virgil asked.

"I didn't at first," Seth said. "I learned a lot afterwards. I'm still piecing things together. It's been hard to figure out who anybody is, or who is being honest with me."

"And now you've come here chasing Humbuggle," Virgil said. "Hoping to retrieve your lost memories."

"Yes."

"You're not a rookie of Humbuggle's Games," Virgil said. "Just these particular Games. The Titan Games."

"That might be true," Seth said around a bite of fish. "Then again, thanks to my memory loss, I feel like a rookie at most things."

Virgil jumped up, rubbing his hands with excitement. "Seth, you have come to the right place. There are those who say I'm crazy. But I'm just more awake than most students of the Games, willing to chase down odd possibilities. The Games are much more complicated than the vast majority imagine."

"The Humburgh Mystery House claimed to have secrets about the Games," Seth said.

Virgil huffed and shook his head. "This town has more suckers than an octopus. Starstruck hopefuls arrive eager to garner instant fame and fortune. A whole industry has sprung up to prey on their delusions."

"The Mystery House is a sham?"

"Mostly," Virgil said. "It's better than some of the sideshows in town. Lots of people peddle the same generic information labeled as secrets. Some are total scams. This whole town is part of the Games, and legitimate hints can sometimes be found in surprising places. The Diviner inside the Humburgh Mystery House can provide real help, but good luck finding him."

"Who is the Diviner?" Seth asked.

"We're straying into advanced topics," Virgil said. "Basics first. The Titan Games are portrayed as gladiator combat with the prize being the Wizenstone. If any combatant wins a hundred consecutive fights, the Wizenstone is theirs."

"Did Humbuggle set it up recently?" Seth asked.

Virgil shook his head, a small smile on his lips. "No. The Titan Games have gone on for centuries."

"But the Wizenstone was at Stormguard Castle," Seth said. "People were competing for it there."

"Exactly," Virgil said. "Humbuggle has established multiple Games, all with the Wizenstone as the prize. Some are less possible to win than others."

"How can simultaneous Games be played for the same prize?" Seth asked.

"Fair question," Virgil said. "Ask Humbuggle. He has been doing it for centuries."

"Does that mean the Games are rigged?" Seth asked.

"Not completely rigged," Virgil said. "If there were no way to win, the magic sustaining them would unravel. But the Games are riddled with devious tricks and loopholes."

"How much have you figured out?" Seth asked.

Virgil gave a huge laugh. "Not nearly enough. But at least I'm trying to make sense of the complexities. Plenty of people don't even know to investigate."

"I don't have to win the Games," Seth said. "I just need Humbuggle."

"Good luck finding Humbuggle outside of his Games," Virgil said. "I've never heard of it happening. All his time and attention are focused on the Games. We have only vague descriptions of what he looks like."

"I've seen him," Seth said.

"Don't tease me," Virgil said with a nervous laugh.

"At Stormguard Castle, when my sister sent the Wizenstone away, Humbuggle was there. He looks like a dwarf."

"Everyone knows that much," Virgil complained.

"If I had the ability to draw his face, I could show it to you," Seth said. "He had a forked beard."

"I'm impressed you have seen his true form," Virgil said. "It's a rarity."

"If I need to enter the Games to find Humbuggle, what's my next step?"

"First you need to learn all you can," Virgil said. "The Games began ages ago. Originally the demon dwarf held them in the kingdom of Selona. Several hundred years ago, the Giant Queen invited Humbuggle to stage the Games here. I think she hoped it would give giants a better chance at obtaining the Wizenstone."

"Did it work?" Seth asked.

Virgil shrugged. "The Giants do have more convenient access to the Games than most. Of course, in exchange for hosting the Games, the Giant Queen must admit an annual quota of participants and spectators into her sanctuary, which gives her the weakest borders of any enchanted preserve. She also gifted Humbuggle the land on which Humburgh stands."

"Does he live here in Humburgh?" Seth asked.

"He has a mansion in town," Virgil said. "I don't know of anyone who ever saw him inside of it."

"Is it abandoned?" Seth asked.

"The house is fully staffed," Virgil said.

"That might be a good place to investigate," Seth said.

"They're secretive," Virgil said. "But anything is worth trying."

Seth took another bite of bread and chewed thought-fully. A few minutes before, it had seemed like he might never feel full again, but he was already almost sated. "Will I have to learn to fight like a gladiator?"

"That's one option," Virgil said. "It's the most obvious way into the Games. We should go to the arena and let you watch a round or two before you make any choices in that direction."

"You mentioned there are other Games," Seth said.

"There have been, over the years," Virgil said. "Storm-guard Castle is one example. Before that there was the Travertine Library. There are many rumors of other contests."

"So many Games for the same prize?" Seth asked.

"That is part of what makes winning complicated," Virgil said. "When he uses magic to create a competition, there must be a real possibility to win. So Humbuggle's goal is to make the Games *almost* impossible to win. It's conceivable that winning certain Games leads to the start of others. Since the Games have continued for centuries, with a grand enough prize to draw some of the greatest heroes the world has known, I would say Humbuggle has accomplished his aim."

"Have you discovered any of his deeper secrets?" Seth asked.

"Only hints," Virgil said. "But Humbuggle openly adores tricks and riddles. You should do all the research you can before taking action."

"Have you considered joining the Games?" Seth asked.

Virgil chuckled. "I know my limits. I'm a brilliant re-searcher. And a fan. I advise those who intend to join the

Games. I don't participate directly. That's the only reason I'm still around."

"If I want, I can go sign up and fight in the arena?" Seth checked.

"The arena is always accepting new combatants," Virgil said.

"Can we catch a fight today?" Seth asked.

"It's too late," Virgil said. "We can go in the morning."

"Are tickets expensive?" Seth asked.

"Do you have money?" Virgil asked.

"I'm broke," Seth said.

"There are ways in without money," Virgil said. "Do you have a place to stay?"

Seth shifted uncomfortably. "Not yet. We just got to town."

"You can have one of my couches," Virgil said. "It isn't fancy, but you can't beat the price."

"Maybe I could get rid of wraiths for somebody," Seth said. "Then I could pay you something."

"The undead can't enter Humburgh," Virgil said. "You'll have a hard time finding your kind of work here."

Seth thought about Virgil's assertion. Did a presence like Reggie not count as one of the undead?

"What about me?" Calvin asked from Seth's pocket. "Could I sneak inside the Games as a passenger?"

Virgil gasped, then crouched to observe the pocket where Calvin was peeking out. "And who are you?"

"Calvin, the Tiny Hero, avowed liegeman of Seth Sorenson."

"You must be a nipsie," Virgil said.

"I can sometimes sneak past magical defenses," Calvin said. "They're not usually attuned to invaders my size."

"You haven't come up against Humbuggle," Virgil said.

"Actually, I sort of have," Calvin replied. "I couldn't enter Stormguard Castle."

"I think it would go similarly if you tried to sneak into the arena," Virgil said. "Humbuggle is remarkably thorough, especially where the Games are involved."

"Calvin must like you," Seth said. "He sometimes lies low."

"Virgil is our kind of guy," Calvin said. "It's written all over him. You haven't heard of other nipsies around here, have you? Perhaps a female named Serena?"

Virgil scowled in thought. "Now that you mention it, I heard tell of a nipsie spotted at Humbuggle's manor. The rumor stood out because we don't see your kind in Humburgh. Meeting a nipsie is a first for me."

"I'm encouraged that you heard about a nipsie," Calvin said.

"At least it's a lead," Virgil said.

"Thanks for your help," Seth said.

"My thanks go to you," Virgil said. "Without heroes who brave the Games, I would have nothing to study. We'll help each other. Should we go find the hermit troll and the little golem?"

"I have weird friends," Seth said.

Virgil smiled. "You can add one more to the list."

CHAPTER SIXTEEN

Waystar

K endra waited on a bench near a towering urn in the study where she had first met Dectus, her arm bandaged. After receiving medical attention, she had been escorted here by the servant who had intervened with Ronodin.

The alchemist who dressed Kendra's arm had commented that without his healing solutions, stitches would have been required. Instead he packed the gash with a gelatinous substance, glued the skin together, and wrapped her forearm with gauze.

She had been waiting for Dectus much longer than she expected. Had the giant been notified she was here? Did he not care?

Kendra took out Bracken's first horn, gripping it tightly. Bracken had warned that even with the horn she wouldn't be able to communicate with the Fairy Realm because it was too effectively sealed off from the mortal world. She wondered if Bracken was close to completing his work expelling the demons. She worried about the fire she had seen when crossing the Fairy Realm on her way to Titan Valley. And it bothered her that Ronodin seemed to know about the upheaval there.

Was it possible that Bracken really loved her? Could his full affection simply be on hold? Or was Ronodin messing with her mind? She knew she couldn't trust anything he said.

Kendra gently scratched at the edge of her bandages. If she could leave her mortality behind and join the fairies, would she do it? Was the option even possible? What would such an action do to her ties with her family? Might it not be worth any cost if the transformation meant getting to spend eons with Bracken? Teens grew up to eventually leave home and become adults. In many ways Kendra was already on her own. Maybe her destiny would take her farther from home than anyone could have guessed. Kendra wondered if Bracken cared enough for the issue to ever be relevant.

Finally Dectus burst through the door. He relaxed a bit when he saw her, straightening his robe before closing the door gently. As he crossed to her, Kendra had a clear sense that he was trying to conceal how rattled he was.

"You've had an eventful time," Dectus said, crouching to scoop Kendra into his palm.

"That's one way to put it," Kendra said, raising her injured arm. "The giant killer attacked me."

Dectus carried her to his desk and set her down carefully. "I'm aware of the altercation. What did you learn?"

"He is Ronodin, the dark unicorn," Kendra said. "He was behind the fall of Wyrmroost and other dragon sanctuaries."

Dectus nodded. "That is useful information. Unfortunately, the Giant Queen has placed me on probation as a member of her Council."

"Wait, why?" Kendra asked. "For protecting Titan Valley?"

"That isn't how the queen views it," Dectus said. "She thinks I encouraged you to create a scene that would make Prince Doranio look bad."

"But you had no part in it!" Kendra exclaimed.

"Word of what the servant saw got back to the queen immediately," Dectus said. "Everything her servants observe gets reported. She was angry with the giant killer, but he insisted she put a silver collar on him and then testified that you started the fight. The giant killer claimed he was only resisting your attack."

Kendra opened her mouth to defend herself and then paused to reconsider her words. "I guess I did throw fruit at him. And I tried to whack him with a bowl."

"Were you lying when you claimed he attacked you?" Dectus asked.

Kendra avoided his gaze. "Well, Ronodin has attacked me and my family in so many ways, but technically I fell and hurt myself while trying to hit him."

"The Giant Queen knows the truth because Ronodin wasn't strangled," Dectus said.

"He kidnapped my brother," Kendra said. "He destroyed Wyrmroost and got Agad killed."

"I don't like him either," Dectus said. "But you must not make false accusations. To the queen, you have been established as disreputable. Your testimony against Ronodin will mean little."

Kendra winced. She hadn't anticipated the consequences of starting a fight with Ronodin, nor had she foreseen the implications of her false accusation. She had responded to problems of the moment instinctively and let her anger take over, and it had weakened her ability to help protect Titan Valley. Dectus had paid a price as well.

"I'm sorry," Kendra said.

"Consider it a lesson in politics," Dectus said. "If you claim the moral high ground, the chinks in your armor become targets. You mustn't give your enemies wrong behavior to exploit."

"Someone like Ronodin will always take advantage," Kendra said.

"Precisely," Dectus said. "And a ruler like the queen has her biases, meaning even perfect arguments get ignored at times, leaving little chance for flawed ones."

"Whether she knows it or not, with Ronodin here, Titan Valley is in danger," Kendra said. "How long has he been courting the queen?"

"Off and on for several months now," Dectus said.

"Does she trust him?" Kendra asked. "Does she share secrets with him?"

"The queen would not reveal matters of highest sensitivity to him," Dectus said. "But he is in a position to learn much."

"And Ronodin can figure out a lot from a little," Kendra said. "Underestimating him could be a fatal mistake."

"This sanctuary is mighty," Dectus said. "Our dragons are in no position to make trouble. Scattered renegades in the back country remain free, but their liberty relies on hiding. Nevertheless, when a war is brewing, a responsible leader prepares for every contingency, eliminating weaknesses and shoring up defenses."

"The Giant Queen does not act interested in protecting Titan Valley," Kendra said. "Or in helping with the war. She would rather flirt with a spy."

"The Giant Queen has little interest in any war outside of her boundaries," Dectus said. "She knows her sanctuary is secure, and she intends to give any dragons who venture here the same treatment as the ones already in her care."

"That might not be as simple as she imagines," Kendra said.

"I agree," Dectus said. "I want to help defend Titan Valley and to support the war effort against the dragons."

"What can you do?"

"Much, if you help me first."

"How?"

"You are new to Titan Valley. Do you know what this fortress protects?"

"The sky giants? The Giant Queen?"

"The entrance to Stratos," Dectus said. "Terastios guards the only gap in the mountainous barrier that separates Stratos from the rest of the sanctuary."

"Stratos is a land?"

"The realm of the sky giants," Dectus said. "Long ago it floated high above the world, a vast island in the sky. That power was lost, and now our realm is grounded here in Titan Valley."

"The sky giants still live there?" Kendra asked.

"Only we sky giants and our livestock. Animals on our same scale. Vegetables large enough to really feed us. It is where we properly fit. The one place where we really belong. Stratos is our true home."

"Do you live in Stratos?" Kendra asked.

"As a member of the Council, I live here in Terastios," Dectus said. "But I do have a modest home in Stratos. Immense by your reckoning."

"It must be a big land," Kendra said.

"Large enough to house the biggest citizens around," Dectus said. "Kendra, I need something from Stratos. A treasure called the Waystar. I cannot obtain it myself. If you fetch the jewel for me, I can help with your war."

"How will the jewel help?" Kendra asked.

"I have a great work for you and your friends," Dectus said. "I believe in your integrity. You were the caretaker of a sanctuary. At least two of your comrades are members of the Knights of the Dawn. If you can accomplish this task, I will entrust you with a quest that could alter the war."

"Is this a test?" Kendra asked.

"View it that way if the idea makes sense to you," Dectus said. "Or else consider this the first phase of a greater mission."

"Is the Waystar hidden?" Kendra asked.

"The jewel is in the possession of Madam Ladonna," Dectus said. "The chief spellbinder of the sky giants."

"We have to steal the Waystar from a giant sorceress?" Kendra asked.

"Borrow it," Dectus corrected. "We won't keep it or sell it. We just need it for a time."

"How will I find it?" Kendra asked.

"Make a fist," Dectus said.

Kendra held up a fist. Dectus leaned in for a close look.

"The Waystar is a beautiful gemstone slightly larger than your fist," Dectus said. "It will be your favorite color."

"How do you know my favorite color?" Kendra asked.

"I don't," Dectus said. "The Waystar always looks like your favorite shade of your favorite color. No matter who you are."

"My favorite color changes sometimes," Kendra said.

"If that is true, the Waystar will transform to suit your fancy," Dectus said.

"Can you tell me where Madam Ladonna lives?" Kendra asked.

"Easy," Dectus said. "And I can sneak you into Stratos."

"Do you know where she keeps the Waystar?" Kendra asked.

"I'm not sure," Dectus said. "But expect it to be on display."

"Can I bring some friends?" Kendra asked.

"Whoever you fully trust," Dectus said.

Kendra nodded. With Warren, Vanessa, and Tanu along, she suspected she could succeed. Having help from Dectus with the dragon war would be important, especially since Ronodin had gained the Giant Queen's trust. The dark unicorn had to be setting up Titan Valley for a fall. Maybe Dectus could help her track down Seth as well.

"I'll do it," Kendra said.

Dectus scowled. "If you get caught, I won't be able to help you. I will disavow all knowledge of this conversation."

"What will Madam Ladonna do to us if she catches us?" Kendra asked.

Dectus shuddered. "Don't get caught."

"Would she put a spell on us?" Kendra pursued.

"Don't get caught," Dectus repeated.

"Tomorrow morning?" Kendra asked.

"Bring those who will accompany you to my office before daybreak," Dectus said. "I'll trust your judgment on whom you select."

"And I'll trust that the Waystar is important enough to risk our lives," Kendra said.

Dectus nodded. "It is, if you hope to win the dragon war."

CHAPTER SEVENTEEN

Entry Tokens

I f we arrive early, there are extra ways to earn access tokens for the arena," Virgil said as they moved along the
street in the crisp, predawn twilight.

"You mentioned there's no rule against sneaking in,"
Seth said.

"As long as you don't get caught at the door," Virgil
said. "The guards are really vigilant, though. I don't know
a reliable way to avoid them. It's better to earn admission."

Hermo and Reggie remained back at Virgil's place. Seth
had been worried about having to earn tickets for too many
individuals. And Calvin had wanted to do some exploring
on his own. "Don't you get in free?" Seth asked. "You're a
researcher!"

"To some extent, everyone in Humburgh studies the
Titan Games," Virgil said. "Some hope to participate.

Others make money off the contestants. Many profit from those who come to watch."

"Where do you fit in?" Seth asked.

"I hope to help solve the Games," Virgil said. "Without participating. That puts me in the minority. I'm not trying to personally win or to profit financially, either, though a satyr has to eat."

"Why did Dante recommend you?" Seth asked.

Virgil chuckled. "Dante sees one value to me. I'm good at picking winners and losers. And Dante runs most of the betting in Humburgh."

"People can bet on the Games?" Seth asked.

"It's a big business," Virgil said. "I'm one of the experts Dante checks with before setting odds. He listens to several of the best."

"He pays you?" Seth asked.

"Yes, to consult," Virgil said. "I make enough to get by. I pay my way into the Games about half the time. Otherwise I earn free admission."

"Why not just bet on the Games yourself?" Seth asked.

"Gambling isn't my style," Virgil said. "It can ruin a person." He pointed up ahead. "Here is the Arena Plaza."

The street ended at a sprawling square with more people milling about than Seth had expected so early in the morning. Businesses lined the sides of the square, some with their doors already open, and vendors were setting up booths and carts. One storefront had an outer wall made entirely of barrels, another was covered in thick fur, and a third had a maze of ladders as the facade.

At the center of a park in the middle of the plaza stood a bronze statue of a centaur battling a minotaur, shields raised, weapons swiping, frozen in a moment of desperate combat. Around the statue stood four modest stone buildings with large doors facing outward. The doors were closed, with a pair of armed guards in front of each.

Virgil led Seth over to a blank wall between two businesses. "This is one of the most interesting stores in the plaza."

"The wall? Are you serious?"

"I'm sharing a secret," Virgil said. "Stand right here."

Seth complied.

"Don't face the wall," Virgil said. "Face me. Watch my finger."

Seth turned so the wall was on his left. He stared at Virgil's finger, which moved slowly toward him, then to one side, then down, then away.

"Keep your focus on my finger," Virgil said. "But pay attention to the wall."

Seth fought the urge to glance directly at the wall while trying to stay aware of it. As his gaze tracked the moving finger, out of the corner of his eye, he noticed a door that he had not previously seen. When he glanced at it, the door was no longer there.

"You saw it?" Virgil asked.

"A door," Seth said.

"Very good," Virgil said. "That was quick. Try to spot it again without my finger."

Seth focused in a similar direction to where the satyr's

finger had been, and after a moment he caught sight of the door again. "I see it."

"Don't look at it directly, but approach it," Virgil coached. "Keep it on the edge of your vision. Walk sideways."

Seth kept the door in his peripheral vision and started toward it, legs crossing every other step. He found it unsettling to approach a door he sensed more than saw. He wanted to look right at it but maintained the discipline of looking away.

"You're doing great," Virgil said. "Keep your eyes averted, and then take the handle once you get close enough."

After a couple more steps, Seth reached out, his fingers curling around the rough wooden handle. "Got it."

"I know, because I can't see you anymore," Virgil said. "If you keep hold of the handle, you can look at the door."

The door was made of thick, reddish wood, battered and scarred. The handle was meant only for pulling, not for turning. He tugged, but the door refused to budge.

"It's locked," Virgil said. "It will open when the sun is at its zenith and again when the moon is at its zenith. Two different stores, depending on the time. Otherwise, nothing."

"That is so bizarre," Seth said.

"Welcome to Humburgh," Virgil said.

"What does the shop sell?" Seth asked.

"Different things to different people," Virgil said. "The price is always outrageous."

"Have you shopped here?" Seth asked.

"Once or twice," Virgil said.

"What did you buy?" Seth asked.

"Maybe I'll tell you someday," Virgil said.

"Should I shop here?" Seth asked.

"Up to you," Virgil said. "Not right now, obviously. The sun will rise soon, but there is a long time before midday."

Seth released the handle, and the door immediately vanished. He felt the stony texture of the wall, searching for where the handle used to be. He ran a finger along the mortar between the blocks. "It isn't just invisible. The door is gone."

"And it's still there, if you look correctly," Virgil said. "Want to go to the arena?"

Seth looked around. "I don't see an arena."

"You will," Virgil said.

"When I look out of the corner of my eye?" Seth asked.

"This one is different," Virgil said. "But we need admission. How are you at chess?"

"I don't remember," Seth admitted.

Virgil pointed out an old woman seated in front of a chess table. "Beat her and she gives you an entry token. No fee to play, but I've never seen anyone beat her. Supposedly she has lost a few times."

"What else can we do?" Seth asked.

Virgil pursed his lips toward a fat troll. "Bombus trades in tasks. If you complete one of the tasks, you get your ticket into the arena."

"Are the tasks hard?" Seth asked.

"That depends," Virgil said. "I usually find them harder than an entry token is worth."

"How do you normally get inside without money?" Seth asked.

"I catch a rabbit," Virgil said.

"What?" Seth asked.

"This way," Virgil said.

The sun had crested the snow-topped mountains on the horizon, and Seth stood in a sunken, dusty square toward one end of Arena Plaza Park. Nineteen other participants waited in the square as well, including Virgil. Makeshift bleachers had been raised just beyond the edges of the square, half full of onlookers, some of them eating roasted nuts or popcorn balls.

A troll wearing a dirty military jacket and a red wig raised both hands, partly succeeding at quieting the bystanders. "Five rabbits," the troll called out. "Twenty contestants. Each rabbit caught means an entry token to the Titan Games. The contest will commence at my signal."

Five rabbits, two of them gray, three white with dark splotches, were placed into the square by two trolls. Seth glanced at the other competitors, trying to assess who might be the veterans. Virgil had explained that people could only enter this contest once per week. He emphasized that the regulars would be much more skilled at catching rabbits than the newcomers.

"Let the chaos begin!" the troll in the jacket cried, exiting the square up a short ladder built into one wall.

Contestants rushed at the rabbits, and the frightened animals dodged and darted away. For the first few seconds, Seth only watched. Virgil and a couple of the other contestants studied the situation as well. Most participants were trying to corral the rabbits against the sides, but the nimble targets sprang away too quickly.

Virgil nodded toward a black and white rabbit that had separated from the others and most of the crowd. He had told Seth that they should work to drive the rabbits toward each other, so Virgil approached from one direction, and Seth hurried to the opposite side. The rabbit bolted toward Seth, who shuffled sideways in a crouch, hands wide and low, like an infielder ready for a ground ball. The rabbit reversed direction, and Virgil lunged, snatching a rear leg and quickly gaining control of the squirming creature.

"Great job!" Seth shouted. It was the first rabbit anyone had caught.

"By rule I can't hand it off," Virgil said. "But I could release it and help until you catch one."

"Keep it," Seth said. "One ticket in is much better than none."

"Remember what I taught you," Virgil said, running for the ladder.

Someone in the middle of a mob of contestants cheered, and the crowd clapped as well. There were three rabbits left.

Virgil had told Seth that without a partner, rather than charge directly at the rabbits, he should anticipate where the rabbits would flee as others chased them. Three bunches of contestants had formed, one after each of the rabbits. Two other contestants worked the fringes like Seth, waiting for a chance to strike.

One cluster of contestants drove a gray rabbit along a nearby wall, and Seth maneuvered ahead of it. Before reaching him, the rabbit cut toward the middle of the square, and Seth dove, but his outstretched hand came up short. Rising quickly, Seth found another rabbit scampering his way and dove again. This time his fingers brushed fur. The crowd groaned at the near miss.

Several contestants trapped a rabbit in a corner, and one of them caught it, to the delight of the onlookers. Seth got a chance to dive at a gray rabbit, but it changed direction just as he lunged, and he didn't land anywhere close. As he rose, Seth heard laughs at his expense and noticed some kids pointing at him.

Slapping the worst of the dust from his clothes, Seth decided that he lacked the experience to succeed with his current technique. He needed to try something new.

The low angle of the rising sun left one side of the square deep in the shadow of the five-foot wall and the bleachers. Seth moved into the shadow, crouched, accessed his power, and willed himself to blend into the gloom. He could feel it working and knew he was shade walking. Nobody would notice him now without considerable effort.

Seth waited. Everything now depended on a rabbit coming his way. He could shift around a little, but he knew that when he held still, he was almost invisible. The two remaining groups of contestants could not be farther from him at the moment. If they pinned and caught the rabbits, his strategy would fail.

The remaining gray rabbit evaded the mob, and then the last black and white one did as well. Contestants stormed in pursuit, and the gray rabbit came directly at Seth, seemingly unaware of his presence. Seth wondered if some animal instinct would kick in, causing the rabbit to dodge around him, but instead it paused near him, head up, ears twitching.

Seth sprang and grabbed the rabbit around the midsection with both hands. The crowd gasped, and Seth realized he must have seemed to appear out of nowhere. Muscles and bones churned beneath the soft fur, but Seth held on tight. He kept both hands on the rabbit as he climbed out of the depression, using his elbows to steady himself on the rungs. A troll guided Seth to a basket, where he deposited the gray rabbit, receiving an entry token in return. Made of marble inlaid with silver, the coin had "Admit One" printed on both sides.

Seth stood beside Virgil watching from the side until the last rabbit was caught by a girl who looked no older than twelve. She climbed out contentedly while the other contestants grumbled in varied extremes of disappointment. One husky, bearded man threw his hat to the dust and stomped on it.

"We have our five winners," the troll in the military jacket proclaimed. "Congratulations to all of our contestants for their earnest attempts. Don't walk away yet, because in fifteen minutes, the minotaurs will wrestle. Bet on the victor to make some money, or, if you're feeling brave and you're not an ogre, wrestle one yourself to win an entry token!"

"Have you ever wrestled a minotaur?" Seth asked.

"I hope my answer to that question will forever be 'no,'" Virgil said. "Nifty trick out there. I lost sight of you!"

"I guess we all have our specialties," Seth said.

"Not many have that one," Virgil said. "I feel a little foolish for giving you advice."

"Your advice was good," Seth said, brushing off more dust. "We both came out with a token to the Games."

Virgil craned his neck. "And the arena is open. Shall we?"

Seth followed his gaze. "Is it underground?"

"You'll see."

CHAPTER EIGHTEEN

Stratos

K endra sat on a padded bench alongside Warren, Vanessa, and Tanu, within a wood and leather compartment ventilated by numerous air slits. The compartment was affixed to Dectus's leg, just below his knee, hidden by his toga, swaying with his steps.

"How do we get into these situations?" Warren asked quietly. "This is a new one for me—being smuggled by a giant."

"It's the price if we want to help save the world," Tanu said. "We take what comes."

"You could always retire," Vanessa suggested.

"From saving the world?" Warren asked. "Where do I retire in a world full of rampaging dragons? Sounds like a great way to get eaten while relaxing on a beach, or burned to death in a happy little cottage."

"Let's finish the job," Tanu said. "Then we can peruse retirement packages."

Dectus stopped walking. "What a beautiful morning," he muttered to himself.

Kendra looked to the others. That was the signal!

Warren opened a door in the side of the compartment and unrolled the ladder. Down he climbed, followed by Vanessa. Kendra leaned over the side, staring from above at huge sandaled feet standing on a patch of grass. She started down, hand over hand, rung by rung. The ladder swayed and jerked as Tanu descended above her.

Warren steadied Kendra at the bottom, and Tanu landed beside her. The blades of grass came up to her hips and were wider than her hand. Off to one side, a dandelion slightly taller than her looked ready to disperse its fuzzy globe of seeds.

Vanessa led them out from under the toga. They dashed through waist-deep grass until they huddled behind a discarded brick at the base of a soaring wall. Dectus casually strolled away without a backward glance.

"We have two hours until Dectus returns to this spot to shuttle us out of Stratos," Vanessa said. "If we miss the rendezvous, we're on our own."

"Look at that house," Warren said, pointing down the lane to a dignified home large enough to contain a professional basketball arena. "And the one beyond it. And the tower over there. We're squirrels in this world. We're chipmunks."

"Dragons make us look tiny too," Tanu said.

"Dragons don't have neighborhoods," Warren said. "They don't have streets and windows and yards. This makes me feel like a little pest creeping around a community of my superiors."

"If the shoe fits," Vanessa murmured.

"I don't want to be killed by an exterminator," Warren complained.

"Then we had better get the Waystar and catch our ride back with Dectus," Vanessa said.

"Madam Ladonna's house lies behind this wall?" Kendra asked.

"Her manor, as Dectus called it," Vanessa said.

"She has a big garden," Warren said. "A stable out back. Lots of land. As a spellbinder, she could have any number of protections against intruders."

"Dectus had few details to prep us for her defenses," Tanu said.

"Could you bite her?" Kendra asked Vanessa. "Then control her in her sleep?"

"In theory, yes," Vanessa said. "Giants have tough hides. I've tried to claim giants before but have never succeeded."

"You'd need to target a weak spot," Tanu said. "The eyelids, or maybe the corner of the eye. Inside the ear canal. Vulnerable places."

"It would be a rush," Vanessa said. "Of course, if a subject is too powerful, trying to establish control could break my mind. A giant would be risky, especially a spellbinder."

"You controlled me for a time," Tanu said.

Vanessa frowned. "Sorry, Tanu. I've controlled many. We should get moving. Time is short."

"Dectus mentioned that the wall has a gate we can slip through," Kendra said.

"Follow me," Warren instructed.

Staying low, they hurried along the base of the wall, pausing when they found cover. Kendra noticed a raven on a fence across the lane that looked big enough to carry any of them away. "Do you see the bird?" she whispered.

"I'm not going to die by raven," Warren said. "I refuse."

"Then you'll have to avoid it or fight it off," Vanessa said. "That bird is big enough to kill any of us."

"I came prepared," Tanu said, crouching between the wall and a large stone. After briefly rummaging in his pouches, he produced a vial. "Kendra should take a swallow of this. It will make her smell dangerous or poisonous to most animals."

"Dogs?" Vanessa asked. "Cats?"

"Ravens?" Warren added.

"Yes," Tanu said.

"Giant ravens?" Kendra asked.

Tanu handed Kendra the vial. "I believe it will work on giant versions of animals. The rest of us will have reasonable protection if we stay near her, leaving us free to use other potions."

Kendra found that the potion tasted almost painfully minty.

"Will this make me smell like mouthwash?" Kendra asked.

Tanu took the vial back. "You'll notice hints of pepper-mint, lavender, vinegar, citrus, and other more subtle notes. It shouldn't bother human nostrils."

"What other potions did you bring?" Vanessa asked.

"Some of my standards," Tanu said. "I have some gas-eous potions for worst-case scenarios. I have an augmented version of my giant potion, which still won't make me much higher than the knee of a sky giant. I have some of the speed potions we used on Timbuli. And something new." Tanu passed a flask to Warren. "I call it my gummy potion. Developed it with Uma. The potion puts your whole body into a gummy state. Your skin becomes almost impossible to pierce or tear, your bones will stretch or bend instead of breaking, and your sense of pain will be dulled. The cost is a reduction in motor skills."

"I'll keep it handy," Warren said.

They continued along the base of the wall until they reached a wrought-iron gate. Beyond the metal bars, a wide path wound through a garden up to a manor house with broad front steps and white pillars. From where Kendra stood, she could see pumpkins and watermelons two stories tall, raspberries the size of soccer balls, and tomatoes that she would not be able to reach both arms around.

Kendra sniffed the back of her hand. It smelled like she had been sampling a multitude of essential oils.

"Want me to go in solo?" Warren asked. "I can drink this gummy potion."

"We should stick together," Tanu said. "We have a bet-ter chance working as a team."

"Time is passing," Vanessa reminded everyone.

"I'll take the lead," Warren said, charging between the bars of the gate. The others followed, eventually taking shelter in a patch of strawberries the size of bed pillows. Tanu used his knife to cut away part of a strawberry and stashed it in a pouch.

"Collecting ingredients?" Kendra asked.

"Why not?" Tanu said. "I'm interested in size potions."

They paralleled the path toward the house, staying just off it, forcing their way through the greenery of the garden. As they passed a particularly large, oblong pumpkin, Kendra ran a hand across its smooth surface. "We could live inside of this," she said.

"Good luck hollowing it out," Warren said.

"Look at the butterfly," Tanu said, jerking a thumb.

Yellow with black and orange markings, the butterfly's wings looked big enough for a human to wear as part of a fairy costume. After fluttering about, the butterfly alighted on a blossoming vine.

"What're you doing here?" shouted a gruff voice. "This is a private garden! Begone!"

Kendra whirled to face the speaker and saw a man with a gray, wiry beard and a bulbous nose. He was a few inches shorter than her and wore a bright blue coat, red pants, and wooden shoes. He shook a hoe to emphasize his words.

Vanessa hushed him, then turned to speak to the others. "Anybody understand this guy?"

"Is he a garden gnome?" Warren asked.

"Don't shush me," the man griped. "I don't need no shushing on account of I ain't no trespasser."

"If so, he's a big gnome," Tanu said.

"It's a big garden," Warren reminded him.

"We're not here to harm the garden," Kendra said, speaking his gnomish dialect.

The man glared at her. "You're fairykind?"

"You're a garden gnome?" Kendra asked.

"Course I'm a garden gnome!" the man replied. "You're traipsing around a private garden! You should've knowed better than to enter uninvited. You all need to scram!"

"We're not here to harm the garden," Kendra said.

The gnome narrowed his eyes. "These three got the look of berry pinchers. The big one reeks of strawberry."

"We're just passing through," Kendra said.

"Passing through?" the gnome exclaimed. "Have you any notion what Madam would do to us all if she caught you trampling her private garden? We'd be fertilizing the rutabagas!"

"What's he saying?" Tanu asked.

"He's trying to throw us out," Warren said. "You don't need to speak garden gnome to know that."

"We're here on giant business," Kendra said, trying to sound official.

"You're awful small for giant business," the gnome said. "What do you take me for? You meddlers have the aspect of root filchers."

"We're protectors of Titan Valley," Kendra said. "We

have to make it into the house to get help from Madam Ladonna."

The gnome cupped a hand beside his ear. "*Into* the house."

"Yes, we need to get inside," Kendra said.

The gnome cackled and danced a little jig. "If I conduct you up to the house, you'll be going inside? On purpose?"

"Yes," Kendra said.

The gnome scrunched his forehead. "What'll you pilfer from the garden?"

"Nothing," Kendra said. "Tanu can give back the pieces of strawberry."

"You can't unpick fruit," the gnome said. "What's done is done. You have a fair manner of speech. Do you know our mistress, the Fairy Queen?"

"I do," Kendra said. "And we need your help."

The gnome tugged at his beard. "Well, seeing as the cats won't come near you, and you've been blessed by her ladyship, I'll take you to the house. I'll show you a way in. Once you're inside, it's up to you."

"Thank you," Kendra said. She turned to the others. "He'll show us a way into the house."

"Really?" Vanessa asked.

"I think he figures we'll die in there," Kendra said.

"Death would be a courtesy if you're caught indoors," the gnome said.

"Now you understand English?" Kendra asked.

"I understand more than I let on," the gnome said. "Follow me. Don't stomp nothing."

The gnome led them on a route past long rows of carrots, towering cornstalks, and winding grapevines. They roamed far from the path, pushing past oversized leaves, occasionally catching glimpses of other gnomes. Kendra noticed a huge striped cat watching them with interest from a distance. A leaner brown cat prowled their way, then retreated as if bitten. Kendra assumed it was reacting to her scent.

The gnome guided them onto a brick path that led to the back of the manor house. White wooden stairs accessed the back porch, each step a little taller than Kendra.

"The back door's got a portal for cats," the gnome said. "You should be able to wriggle through."

"Thanks," Kendra said. "What's your name?"

"Oh no you don't," the gnome said. "My name is my business, thank you very much." He gestured at the house. "Off to your doom."

"The trellis will be easier than the stairs," Warren said, indicating the flourishing grapevines along the perimeter of the porch.

Warren started up first. Kendra found the climbing fairly easy—the gaps in the trellis were not too big, and the grapevines added extra handholds. Warren helped her onto the porch, where she found a white wooden swing suspended by chains, dangling out of reach. The foursome gathered at the back door near a rectangular opening covered by a cloth.

"The old cat-door routine," Warren said.

"Have you done this before?" Tanu asked.

"Not on this scale," Warren said. "Usually the trick is getting your shoulders through."

"The gnome got eager when I asked him to bring us here," Kendra said. "I'm pretty sure he thinks we're goners."

Vanessa jogged away from the door and peered off the porch. "He is watching us expectantly." She gave a little wave.

"I'll go in first," Warren said, holding up the gummy potion. "How much time do we have left?"

Tanu checked his wristwatch. "Just under eighty minutes."

Warren shoved through the cloth. Kendra pushed in next. They entered an enormous kitchen with a cold tile floor. Kendra felt horribly exposed on the empty expanse. Vanessa led a dash to take modest cover behind a table leg.

"This place is gigantic," Tanu whispered, panting slightly. "Where do we start?"

"Should we split up?" Warren asked.

"Only if somebody else ingests the repellent scent," Tanu said. "A cat door means cats could be inside. And who knows what else?"

"What's that box by the other table leg?" Kendra asked, pointing. The metal crate looked big enough to accommodate a human or two if they crouched.

"Let's find out," Warren said, leading the charge.

They reached the crate and ducked to peek inside. A raw steak sat on a tin plate.

"It's a trap," Tanu said. "This hatch at the front of the crate is rigged to slam shut."

"If they had cooked the bait, I might be tempted," Warren said, rubbing his belly.

Kendra heard growling, and she turned to find a pack of five wolves approaching from over by the pantry. They were not giant wolves, but regular-sized wolves were enough to make Kendra freeze. The intent canines showed teeth and hunkered low as they approached, but they stopped advancing about twenty yards away.

"The smell works to repel wolves?" Kendra asked.

"Yes," Tanu said. "Can't you tell they want to come closer?"

"The box might be a wolf trap," Warren guessed.

"Right now they seem hungry for us," Vanessa said. "Or maybe they're being territorial."

"Out!" called a rich soprano voice from high above. A giant woman padded into the kitchen, making the tiles tremble. She had gray, curly hair and wore a long housecoat and furry slippers. "Shoo! Out you go!"

The wolves began to whine and yelp as she used a broom to sweep them toward the door. Compared to the woman, the wolf pack seemed like mice or rats. Her efficient strokes forced them to the doorway and redirected any wolf that tried to make a break for it. She opened the door and whisked the whining pack outside.

"And stay out," the woman said, nudging the door closed with her hip.

Kendra and her companions crouched low behind the wolf trap and the table leg. As the woman approached the table, only her bottom half remained in view, including the spidery veins on her legs above her slippers.

"I suppose you four think you're hiding from me," the

giant scolded. "Enough nonsense. Come out from under the table."

Warren held a finger to his lips. Kendra stopped breathing.

"Don't make me move the table," the giant woman warned. "I'll be much more cross if you treat me like a fool. I know you're there. I know you hear me. Come out. All four of you. I will count to five." She reversed her broom and tapped the handle on the floor. "One." She tapped it again. "Two."

Vanessa gave a nod. Tanu shrugged.

Another tap. "Three."

Kendra and her friends raced out from under the cover of the table. The farther they ran, the more of the giant came into view.

Tap. "Four." Tap. "Ah, just in time."

Warren, Vanessa, Tanu, and Kendra slowed as the giant's face came into sight. In one hand she held the broom. In the other she clutched a bucket.

"Enter my private abode uninvited, will you?" the woman asked.

Flipping the bucket upside down, she crouched and used it to cover Kendra and her friends, shutting out almost all light. Vanessa placed a reassuring hand on Kendra's shoulder.

"I'll get to the bottom of this in no time," the giant said, her voice somewhat muffled by the bucket. "Or my name isn't Madam Ladonna."

CHAPTER NINETEEN

Arena

Seth and Virgil approached one of the smallish stone buildings situated in Arena Plaza Park. Each of the four buildings had a line of people that would pack the available space well beyond capacity.

"This must lead underground," Seth said.

"You're about to find out," Virgil said.

They reached the back of the nearest line. "Just tell me! I'm sure I guessed it."

"Then you don't need confirmation," Virgil said.

"Why the mystery?" Seth asked.

"I want to give you the full experience," Virgil said.

Large trolls and minotaurs provided security at the entrances. Seth held his token ready. Up at the front of the line, he saw a minotaur pick up a goblin, haul him away from the building, and fling him onto the lawn.

"Some attendees try to beg their way inside," Virgil said. "Making it more confusing, sometimes they succeed. The guards have a few entrance tokens to give out at their discretion."

A trio of centaurs got in line behind Seth. They crowded too close for his liking, raucously boasting about how the statue of the centaur was clearly about to slaughter the minotaur. The group smelled strongly of sweat and horses.

Most attendees ahead of Seth had tokens and handed them over routinely. The line moved slowly but steadily. Just before Seth and Virgil reached the gate, a dark-haired man fell to his knees before one of the troll guards.

"Please, mighty Dronis, grant me leave to pass," the man pleaded. He bent forward and began peppering the guard's bare feet with kisses.

"Why should I let you enter without a token?" the troll asked. "What message does it send to those who earned the right to enter?"

"My money is spent," the man lamented. "I'm living in alleys, eating scraps. I missed catching a rabbit, failed at a challenge, and found no favor to accomplish." He kissed the feet some more.

"I like that you know your place," the troll said, flexing one of his feet. "But you have entered this way before." The troll turned to those waiting to enter. "What says the line?"

"Off with him," one of the centaurs cried.

"Don't reward him for slowing us down," another centaur bellowed.

The troll nodded at a nearby minotaur. "You heard the consensus," the troll said.

The minotaur grabbed the man by the ankles, dragged him away from the entrance, then swung him into the air, sending him flying onto the lawn. The man scrambled to his feet and darted away. Seth wondered if he might go try a different entrance.

"Token," a minotaur demanded, thrusting a hand out to Virgil as he reached the front. The satyr tossed it to him, and the minotaur waved him through.

Seth held out his token to the troll the man had kissed, but the guard refused to accept it. "Players don't pay."

"What?" Seth asked.

"In you go," the troll said, looking beyond him. "Next."

Seth caught up to Virgil and held up his token. The satyr looked excited. "You got in free! That must mean you're considered an active participant in the Games!"

Seth stopped advancing. "What do you mean? Will they try to make me fight?"

Virgil laughed. "Normally, fighting is the only way to get in as a contestant. But your involvement with Humbuggle at Stormguard Castle must have marked you as an active player. I've never met anyone who played any of his other Games. They usually die."

"How am I marked?" Seth asked.

"I've researched this," Virgil said. "Remember, Humbuggle controls this domain. Those who work for him see an aura around active participants. You automatically carry identification wherever you go. My contacts wouldn't share exactly how it looks because they don't want anyone trying to counterfeit it."

"Out of the way," a centaur demanded. Seth and Virgil moved over against the wall, and several centaurs clopped by.

"But the game I played is over," Seth said.

"Is it?" Virgil asked. "What was the prize?"

"The Wizenstone," Seth said.

"Did somebody win the Wizenstone?" Virgil asked.

"Not exactly," Seth said.

Virgil pointed at him. "Then that game isn't over, whether you knew it or not. This validates one of my main theories: the Games are a collection of contests that reach beyond any individual competition." He clapped Seth on the back. "You're my best evidence yet. Come on."

The stone hallway stretched ahead of them well beyond where the building should have ended. In the distance, sunlight was visible through a coral archway.

"This place is bigger inside than it looks from outside," Seth said.

"Let's not dally," Virgil said.

Seth and Virgil hurried forward, exiting onto a broad patio in front of a tremendous coliseum. Turning in a full circle, Seth absorbed the improbable view. They stood atop a mesa overlooking the ocean on all sides. Extensive walkways, patios, and rose gardens surrounded the limestone coliseum.

"Where are we?" Seth asked.

"Definitely not underground," the satyr replied.

"Where is Humburgh?"

"Welcome to the Arena," Virgil said, spreading his arms proudly. "There are several pocket dimensions within Humburgh. This is the largest I know about."

Shielding his eyes from the sun with one hand, Seth looked out over the beach and the crashing waves, off to where the swells looked like wrinkles before flattening into a horizon line. "How far does the ocean go?"

"I haven't explored it myself," Virgil said. "Some claim you reach a point where you inexplicably start heading back to shore."

"It's part illusion," Seth said.

"Probably," Virgil said. "Or else magical barriers protect what lies beyond. Maybe with the help of distracter spells."

"Ocean in all directions," Seth said. "All inside the Arena Plaza."

"Essentially, yes," Virgil said. "Remember, it's a pocket dimension. Come on. The first event starts soon."

Seth followed Virgil to one of the coliseum entrances, trying not to despair over how powerful Humbuggle must be if he could create such a grand arena on his own private island. A gray minotaur standing in front of a golden gate directed visitors toward the stairs. His nostrils flared as Seth and Virgil approached, and the minotaur opened the golden gate and stepped aside.

"For us?" Seth asked.

"For *you*," the minotaur replied. "The satyr can join you if he is your guest."

"Yes," Seth said.

The minotaur dipped his horns in acknowledgment.

Seth and Virgil passed through the gate and walked out into the brightness of the lower bowl of the coliseum. They paused at the top of a long stairway leading down to the arena floor. Above them, rows of stone benches extended three times higher than where they stood. Below, individual seats offered closer views of the action.

"I should have realized you would have access to this section," Virgil said. "Usually you need a diamond token to get reserved seats. But contestants get privileges. Prospective contestants often receive reserved seats before their first combat."

"Where can we sit?" Seth asked.

"We just have to avoid the boxes," Virgil said, indicating sections of seating surrounded by low railings. The nicest boxes were canopied, rendering a few rows behind them useless. "There are plenty of empty seats in the reserved section. More than anywhere besides the upper reaches."

"Does this place ever fill to capacity?" Seth asked.

"Seldom," Virgil said. "It's really big. But there is always a good crowd. Let's snag prime seats."

They descended the stairs almost to the floor of the arena, then worked their way sideways, selecting cushioned chairs between a couple of canopied boxes. Down on the arena floor, workers raked the dirt level, while others mounted weapons at intervals against the arena wall.

"How many fighters will come out?" Seth asked.

"It varies," Virgil said.

"Can they claim any weapons they want?" Seth asked.

"The gladiators can use any weapon within the arena,"

Virgil said, "including what they bring themselves. If combatants get disarmed, it's rare for them to make it to a new weapon."

Seth absently stroked the arms of his chair. "We're about to see people die?"

"That's the idea," Virgil said. "I'm curious to get your take after you see a few rounds."

Seth wondered how many people would perish in combat today. And for what? A chance to win a magical item? To entertain a crowd? How much did Humbuggle care about the people giving their lives to win his contest? Looking around at the huge coliseum filling with paying spectators, he realized that the demon dwarf seemed more than happy to cash in on the fatalities.

"The Giant Queen is here today," Virgil pointed out.

"Where?" Seth asked.

"See that central box on the far side? Gilded wood with jewels? Only one like it."

"Yes," Seth said. It was the only sheltered box not made of fabric. A stoic woman sat inside, crown on her brow. "I thought she would be larger."

"Nobody over ten feet tall is allowed into the arena," Virgil said. "The only exception is Falstaff the dragon wrangler, who works directly for Humbuggle."

"She shrinks to come here?" Seth asked.

"Giants enjoy their full size over on Big Side," Virgil said. "The Giant Queen has private access from Terastios to Big Side, and from there to the arena. But for giants to enter the arena, or to go anywhere in Small Town, they have to surrender most of their size."

"Can the giants shrink whenever they want?" Seth asked.

"Humbuggle set up a way," Virgil said. "He always does."

"And she comes?" Seth asked.

"Once or twice a week," Virgil said. "Especially when giants compete."

"Is one competing today?" Seth asked.

"Gurnan," Virgil said. "He has thirty-nine wins."

"He needs a hundred?" Seth asked.

"A hundred would get him the Wizenstone," Virgil said.

"Has anyone come close?"

"This place gets wild when anybody racks up more than seventy victories," Virgil said. "Combatants become legendary if they break eighty. The record is ninety-one. The challenges get harder the more a combatant wins. Especially after they pass fifty. The fights get berserk after seventy and almost impossible after eighty. Contestants not only have to climb a mountain to win—the slope gets perpetually steeper."

"Sounds brutal," Seth said.

"Almost seventy percent of competitors are defeated in their first fight," Virgil said. "More than ninety percent don't survive the first ten."

"You know the numbers," Seth said.

Virgil smiled. "It's my area of expertise."

A hefty troll stepped onto a prominent platform, hands upraised. His golden robe flashed with sequins, and pronged antlers projected from his brow. The chatter in the coliseum stilled.

"Welcome to the Titan Games!" the troll shouted, his voice magnified without a visible microphone. It had to be a spell of some sort. The crowd roared in response. He quelled the cheering with downward motions of his hands. The troll bowed low. "We recognize the presence of the caretaker of Titan Valley, her royal majesty, the Giant Queen."

Facing the queen's box, the announcer dropped to a knee. Around the coliseum, everyone slid out of their seats and went down on one or two knees. Seth and Virgil did likewise. Seth even noticed a centaur bowing, the knee of a foreleg touching the ground.

"Have you come for thrills?" the announcer called out, to the delight of the crowd. "Are you ready for battle? Today we will discover if Portia the Improbable can continue her charmed run, and whether Gurnan can secure forty victories, but first, how about six brand-new gladiators going head-to-head, a three-on-three battle royale?"

The crowd responded enthusiastically. Seth cheered along with them, then leaned over to Virgil. "If a gladiator keeps winning, how often do they fight?"

"Normally no more than once per week," Virgil said.

"So it would take around two years for a hundred wins," Seth said.

"That's right," Virgil said.

"As always," the announcer declared, "if you get inspired to participate in the combat, feel free to join the fray."

"Is he serious?" Seth asked.

Virgil nodded. "Anyone can jump down to the arena floor and join the action."

"Does it happen?" Seth asked.

"From time to time," Virgil said. "Not often. It isn't a very strategic move. Combatants get better treatment and advantages if they formally enroll in the Games."

The troll on the platform was announcing gladiators by name. So far there was a bearded human, a hobgoblin, and a reddish minotaur. The crowd cheered them half-heartedly.

"Once the gladiators sign up, can they quit?" Seth asked.

Virgil laughed. "No way! Do you know Humbuggle at all? Whether you join the Titan Games by signing up or by jumping into the combat, once you're in, the only escape is victory. The competitors all live here in the coliseum."

"How can he lay claim to those who jump in?" Seth asked.

"His policies are posted around the coliseum," Virgil said. "I can show you if you want. They serve as a basic contract for anyone who spontaneously joins the fight."

"They just grab a weapon off the wall?" Seth asked.

"Wherever they can get one," Virgil said. "You're not thinking about it, are you?"

"No," Seth said, mostly meaning it.

"It's usually some crazed fan trying to help one of their heroes," Virgil said. "Occasionally somebody thinks they see a favorable situation, like two badly wounded competitors. Attempts to take advantage of injured gladiators usually earn boos, but some people are cutthroat. Those who join the fight spontaneously almost always perish."

The six competitors had been introduced and were squaring up against each other, three on each side. One human had a war hammer, another a battle-ax. The minotaur swung a flail above his head, the hobgoblin brandished a spear, and the two dwarfs wielded swords. All wore various pieces of armor, and all showed some skin (or fur).

"These guys are all newbies?" Seth asked.

"At maximum, three will survive," Virgil said. "At minimum, one."

A horn blew, and the melee commenced. The minotaur barreled toward one of the dwarfs, swiping with his flail. The dwarf tried to repel the attack with his shield, but the minotaur swung so hard, the short defender was blasted to the ground, shield dented. He scuttled away, losing his sword, as the minotaur pounded at him relentlessly. As the embattled dwarf struggled to his feet, turning to run for a wall, the minotaur got a clear shot at the back of his head.

At the moment of impact from the flail, the dwarf vanished in a flash.

"Where did he go?" Seth asked.

"That's what losing looks like," Virgil said.

"Wait, is he dead?" Seth asked.

"Makes you wonder, doesn't it?"

The battle raged on. The minotaur teamed with the axman against the hobgoblin, who retreated until he got cornered against the wall and finally vanished in a flash. The human with the war hammer was evenly matched against a dwarf with a sword, but when the minotaur and the axman closed in, the dwarf got reckless, and the gladiator with the war hammer delivered a blow that made him disappear.

The three surviving teammates raised their fists, accepting the adulation of the crowd. The announcer offered congratulations, and the combatants made their way off the arena floor to ongoing cheers.

"But where are the losers?" Seth asked. "Dead?"

"There is no definitive answer," Virgil said. "We can theorize later. I'd love your guesses."

Masked clowns swarmed onto the arena floor and engaged in physical comedy that Seth felt ran a little too long. After their act, a brawny, armored, full-sized giant strode into the arena, leading a two-headed dragon.

"Giants and dwarfs," the troll announced from his platform, "centaurs and minotaurs, connoisseurs and dilettantes, some of you have seen the dragon Scipio in combat, but never matched against a single foe. In his fortieth contest, Gurnan must pierce one eye of the dragon to secure victory. As always, should Gurnan slay the dragon, it will count as three victories."

"Can the dragon win the Wizenstone?" Seth asked.

"Animals and magical beasts compete only for their freedom," Virgil said. "Thirty-three wins and they go free."

Gurnan sauntered into the ring, fully ten feet tall, and also broad and muscular. Seth wondered how big he would be at his true stature. Gurnan wore a long leather duster, with armor over his chest, and a spiked helm upon his head. He carried a longbow in one hand and a lance in the other, a quiver of arrows slung over one shoulder.

"The dragon is gagged so she can't use her breath weapons," Virgil said. "Gurnan has done really well so far, but this will be a tough contest."

A horn sounded, and the armored giant released the dragon's chains and left the arena floor. Both dragon heads roared, and Seth felt his seat vibrating. Gurnan nocked an arrow, briefly aimed, and fired. One of the dragon heads whipped sideways, and the arrow pinged off its snout.

As Gurnan pulled another arrow, the dragon rushed him. The arrow sailed past the dragon heads and flashed against an invisible barrier that prevented the errant shot from sailing into the crowd. Dropping his bow, Gurnan gripped his lance in both hands and began fending off the heads that lashed at him, teeth glinting. Gurnan dodged and stabbed, coming close to the eyes several times.

"I can't look," Virgil said, partially covering his eyes with one hand.

The dragon swiped down at the lance, pinning it to the ground with lethal claws. Gurnan sprang away from a ferocious bite and produced a sword from beneath his jacket. He jumped over a swipe from the tail of the dragon, but the return swing clipped his legs and knocked him to the dirt.

Both heads of Scipio plunged forward, gripping Gurnan between them. The warrior vanished in a flash as the heads pulled apart.

The crowd roared. Seth noticed the Giant Queen rise from her seat and depart. The armored giant returned to the arena floor, and the dragon submitted to a pair of restraining nooses at the ends of poles.

"Feeling eager to join the Games?" Virgil asked.

"The challenges get harder than this?" Seth asked.

"Some are unbelievable," Virgil said. "It is no coincidence that nobody has won a hundred rounds."

While the dragon was being escorted out, a group of acrobats tumbled onto the arena floor and began to perform. They set up a big seesaw and used it to launch one another high into the air.

Seth thought back to his earliest memories at Stormguard Castle, entering the same chamber as the Wizenstone. How many challenges had he overcome to reach that moment? Was it the equivalent of a hundred gladiator battles?

"I intend to explore all of my options before I commit to these fights," Seth said.

CHAPTER TWENTY

Madam Ladonna

I would speak with the girl," Madam Ladonna said, her voice coming from well above the overturned bucket that entrapped them.

"We have two girls," Warren called.

"Not so," Madam Ladonna replied. "You have a woman and a girl. I would speak with the girl."

"What do you want to know?" Kendra cried out.

"You need not yell," Madam Ladonna said. "Giants have excellent hearing. I am no exception."

"How can I help you?" Kendra asked without shouting.

"Better volume," Madam Ladonna approved. "The rest of you, move away from the girl. I would speak to her in private."

"We stay together," Warren said.

"Then you die together," Madam Ladonna said. "You

were caught trespassing in my home. Ordinarily I would grind you all into seasoning."

"But she's just a child," Tanu said.

"Which is why I might give her a chance to live if the rest of you step away from her," Madam Ladonna explained with exasperation. "Now move."

"Be brave," Vanessa whispered, squeezing Kendra's upper arm.

Vanessa, Warren, and Tanu shuffled to the other side of the bucket.

"We moved!" Warren called.

The bucket lifted, and a huge hand lowered beside Kendra. She looked up into the wrinkled face gazing down at her, then stepped onto the calloused hand. Ladonna lifted Kendra and replaced the bucket over her friends.

Madam Ladonna walked out of the kitchen, down a hall, and into a large study. Loaded bookshelves covered one wall, most of the leather-bound volumes much taller than Kendra. Mermen and dolphins swam in a long aquarium that spanned another wall. In the corner of the room loomed a Quiet Box that must have stood sixty feet tall.

Madam Ladonna set Kendra on a table covered by a purple cloth embroidered with gold thread. Nearby, a crystal ball rested on a three-legged stand, a set of balance scales hung beside a row of weights, and several corked bottles clustered together. The giant picked up a scroll from the table and rolled it up, setting it aside.

Kendra gazed up at Madam Ladonna. "Do you have to keep my friends under a bucket?"

The giant scowled down at Kendra. "If little folk wish to be treated like big folk, why enter our homes like vermin?"

"We're allies of the giants," Kendra said.

"We'll see about that," Madam Ladonna said, grasping Kendra and setting her upon one side of the scale. The tray where Kendra stood dropped and the other one rose. Madam Ladonna eyed Kendra shrewdly, then began selecting cylindrical weights to place on the opposite tray. As she added or subtracted weight, Kendra's side of the scale wobbled up and down, forcing her to hold out her hands and crouch to stay on her feet. After a moment, the two sides of the scale leveled out.

"Why do you care how much I weigh?" Kendra asked.

"I don't," Madam Ladonna said. "I care if you are going to tell me the truth. What is your name?"

"Must I tell you?" Kendra asked.

"Your best chance to live is to answer my questions honestly," Madam Ladonna said. "It also gives your friends their best chance."

"I'm Kendra Sorenson."

"I know," Madam Ladonna said. "Now lie to me. What is your name?"

"Stan," Kendra said.

The scales jerked, lurching enough that Kendra fell to her knees and one of the little weights on the other side toppled over. Madam Ladonna reached out and righted the overturned weight, making the scales sway.

"Very good," Madam Ladonna said. "All appears to be in order. You were the caretaker of Wyrmroost?"

"Yes," Kendra said, rising to her feet.

"Did you come to our sanctuary as a spy?" Madam Ladonna asked.

"No," Kendra said.

"Why did you come?" Madam Ladonna asked.

"I came for refuge and to help defend against the dragon war," Kendra said, leaving Seth out of it.

Madam stared at the scales and nodded. "Some in Dragonwatch do not appreciate the methods of the Giant Queen. Do you approve of how the dragons here are treated?"

Kendra hesitated. "Not entirely. But I like that Titan Valley seems secure."

"Tell me why you came into my house," Madam Ladonna instructed.

"We didn't mean any harm," Kendra said, and the scales lurched enough to make her sit down hard. She hadn't expected the scales to move because she hadn't felt like she was lying. Kendra stared up in fear of how the giant would react. Madam Ladonna frowned as she righted two weights on the other side.

"What harm did you intend?" Madam Ladonna asked, an angry edge to the question.

"We wanted to take the Waystar," Kendra admitted.

Madam Ladonna gasped. "What did you intend to do with my precious jewel?"

"I'm not sure," Kendra said. The scales heaved again, making Kendra glad she had stayed seated. Once again, she had not expected movement.

"Answer me," Madam Ladonna insisted.

"We were getting it for a giant," Kendra said.

"Which giant?" Madam Ladonna asked.

Kendra paused. "A good giant. One of your leaders. We want to help defend Titan Valley."

Madam Ladonna considered the scales as if surprised they had not moved.

"I need a name," Madam Ladonna said.

"I mustn't betray him," Kendra said.

"You believe him to be a good giant," Madam Ladonna said. "That does not guarantee he is actually good. If you and your friends want a chance to live, I need a name."

Kendra winced. "Dectus."

"Ah," Madam Ladonna said, looking away. "Tampering, as always." She looked back at Kendra. "Why does he want the Waystar?"

"I don't know," Kendra said. The scales wobbled a little.

"You're not telling me everything," Madam Ladonna said.

"Getting the Waystar is the first part of a larger mission," Kendra said. "I only know Dectus wants us to help him protect Titan Valley from the dragon war."

Madam Ladonna scrutinized the scales. They stayed level.

"I see," Madam Ladonna said. "At times I disagree with his methods, but Dectus is loyal to our queen and to the interests of the giants. Dectus sent you to take the Waystar from me?"

"Yes," Kendra said.

"A test, no doubt," Madam Ladonna said. "But a test you were not likely to pass. More likely he wanted this interview to happen. Kendra, do you have any motives to be here at Titan Valley besides helping the giants?"

"I want to find my brother," Kendra said. "He lost his memories."

"Do you mean any harm to Titan Valley or the giants who dwell here?" Madam Ladonna asked.

"No."

"Did you deliberately help Wyrmroost fall?"

"No way!"

"Did you defend Wyrmroost as best you could?"

"Yes."

"Are you aware of any peril to Titan Valley?"

"The Giant Queen is entertaining Ronodin, the dark unicorn. Destruction follows wherever he goes. Here he is called the giant killer. That might turn out to be more literal than anyone suspects."

Eyes on the perfectly balanced scales, Madam Ladonna nodded. "You intend to use the Waystar to help Dectus protect Titan Valley?"

"Yes," Kendra said. "We were just borrowing it. We didn't intend to keep it."

"And your friends share your intentions?" Madam Ladonna asked.

"I'm sure they do," Kendra said.

Madam Ladonna smiled. "Well, for now, your good intentions have saved your life."

Kendra felt relief. "I'm sorry we trespassed."

"It earned you a cold welcome. As a former caretaker,

you should be trustworthy, but I had to be sure. Dangerous items are housed here."

Kendra glanced at the Quiet Box. "Who is inside?"

"Best not to speak of her," Madam Ladonna said. "Hope that she stays there."

"Somebody big?"

"Not necessarily. But yes."

Kendra shivered, gazing at the towering box. At that size, it could be almost anyone—a giant, or a dragon, or an enormous demon.

"What are you going to do with us?" Kendra asked.

"What would you have me do?"

Kendra attempted her best smile. "Maybe give us the Waystar? So we can protect the sanctuary?"

"I will not let you take the Waystar," Madam Ladonna said. "But since your intentions are honorable, and because I trust Dectus, under my supervision, I will let you use the Waystar for the purpose I believe he intended."

"What purpose is that?" Kendra asked.

"He wants you to have the map to the Dragon Temple," Madam Ladonna said. "I suspect Dectus wants you to recover the Harp of Ages in case it is needed in the dragon war."

The news astonished Kendra. "That sounds dangerous."

"You and your friends will almost surely perish," Madam Ladonna said. "But no giant can undertake the quest because the entrance and passages are far too small. All by design, of course. The dragons were permitted to build their temples by treaty to protect the talismans that helped us overpower them. Should you somehow succeed, Dectus is correct that the Harp of Ages would grant extra protection from the dragons."

"The Waystar is a map?" Kendra asked.

Madam Ladonna crossed to a shelf and plucked something between her thumb and forefinger. She came to Kendra and set it on the scale with her, a rich blue jewel the dimensions of a normal-sized grapefruit.

"The Waystar is a gemstone that makes a map," Madam Ladonna explained.

"It's the perfect color," Kendra said.

"Always," Madam Ladonna agreed. "For me, it's pale green."

"It makes a map?" Kendra asked.

Madam Ladonna held out her palm. "Bring the Waystar. Come."

Kendra picked up the jewel and hopped onto Madam Ladonna's hand. She was carried through the kitchen, out the back door, and into the garden. Kendra had seen the bucket containing her friends but didn't call out to them.

Madam Ladonna set Kendra down on a sundial that seemed at least three stories tall. The giant produced a parchment that seemed large to Kendra, nearly wider than her armspan.

"You can do this easier than I can," Madam Ladonna said. "Hold the Waystar so the sunlight passes through it onto the parchment."

Kendra held out the jewel and noticed bright lines

making a web on the parchment. It looked more like spaghetti than a map.

"Move the jewel closer and farther from the parchment until the image resolves," Madam Ladonna directed.

Kendra raised and lowered the jewel, watching the mess of bright lines writhe until at just the right distance from the page, everything came into sharp focus and she beheld a brilliant map of Titan Valley, labeled in a fairy language that she could read as plainly as English.

"I see the map," Kendra said.

"Well done. Hold the jewel steady."

Kendra started trying to read the map until a bright flash made her close her eyes. When she looked again, the bright lines had all been burned into the parchment, rendering the jewel unnecessary.

"That's amazing," Kendra said.

"Do you see now why you no longer need to borrow the Waystar?" Madam Ladonna asked.

"It's a tool to make the map," Kendra replied. "Like a stamp."

"Quite so," Madam Ladonna said, holding out her hand.

Kendra climbed on and was carried back into the house. This time when she saw the overturned bucket she called out, "It's going to be all right!"

"Are you okay?" Warren responded, his voice muted.

"I'm fine," Kendra called.

Madam Ladonna returned to her study, set Kendra on the desk, and replaced the Waystar on her shelf. "I suppose you will need me to return you to Terastios," the giant said.

"If you take us to your front gate, Dectus will return for us," Kendra said.

"I am tempted to give him a piece of my mind for sending you here unannounced," Madam Ladonna said. "But I have lost enough time with you already. I will collect your friends and leave you to the connivings of the politicians. Please do not return here uninvited."

"Thank you for your help," Kendra said.

Madam Ladonna laughed grandly. "Thank me after you survive."

Below the Floor

Out on the arena floor, a uniformed man and woman were putting on an exhibition of trained bears and jungle cats. Under some circumstances it could have been quite entertaining, but after being saturated with mortal combat, Seth could hardly pay attention.

"When does all of this end?" Seth asked.

"The Games halt about an hour before sunset," Virgil said. "Every night there are fireworks for those who care to stay. Technically, once admitted to the coliseum, nobody has to leave. If you are willing to sleep on the benches, you can stay inside until the Games start the next day."

"What about food?"

"Food is for sale in the halls of the coliseum. And some people scrounge."

"Humbuggle built his own world here," Seth said.

"The world of the Titan Games inside the world of his town," Virgil said. "And there is the secret world of the competitors beneath the arena floor."

"They live underground?" Seth asked.

"Once they enlist in the Games, they live and train here," Virgil said. "They never emerge. When they watch the combat, it is from their own private section." Virgil regarded Seth thoughtfully. "Now I'm wondering something."

"What?" Seth asked.

"You were admitted to the arena as a participant in the Games," Virgil said. "You were granted access to the reserved seats. I wonder how far your access goes."

"What do you mean?" Seth asked.

"Those of us who study the Games dream of accessing the competitors' quarters. Who knows what secrets Humbuggle has hidden down there where only the gladiators, trainers, and a few members of the senior staff can venture?"

"You think I have access?"

"Only one way to find out," Virgil said.

"What would I look for down there?" Seth asked.

"Humbuggle once said, 'The dullest part of my Games happens on the arena floor,'" Virgil recited. "That is a direct quote."

"Then where do the most exciting parts happen?" Seth said.

"Perhaps he was boasting or trying to misdirect," Virgil said. "Or maybe the smarter action is behind the scenes at the arena and hidden around Humburgh. Could there be other ways to win? Secret contests? Like the game you played at Stormguard Castle."

"Just about anything sounds better than a hundred gladiator fights," Seth said. "Let's see if we can get behind the scenes."

"Hold on," Virgil said. "Be forewarned, it may be easier to get in than to get out. The combatants are not allowed to leave."

"I didn't sign up to be a gladiator," Seth said. "And I'm not going to jump into the arena and join a fight. Would they have any claim on me?"

"I don't think so," Virgil said.

"We'll ask the guards," Seth said. "I'll see if I can get you in, too."

"Are you sure about this?" Virgil asked.

Seth leaned close and lowered his voice. "I came here to beat Humbuggle. That won't happen if I don't do some things others haven't. It's going to involve risk. Compared with fighting to the death in front of an audience, I'd rather explore the coliseum."

Virgil rose from his seat. "This way."

They climbed the stairs and exited past a guard into a hallway. Virgil turned right, passing some food stands.

"Hungry?" Virgil asked.

"I could eat," Seth said. "Do you have money?"

"Enough for some food."

Virgil bought them each a skewer of meat and vegetables. As they continued along their way, Seth bit off a juicy chunk of beef that was almost too hot to chew.

They reached a black gate where a heavyset troll stood, resting a club on one shoulder. Above him, a sculpted insignia of a skull wearing a gladiator helm adorned the gate.

"Ordinarily we couldn't pass beyond this point," Virgil murmured.

Seth gave a nod, sliding a hot mushroom off the skewer with his teeth. After chewing and swallowing, he approached the troll. "Can we go through here?"

"You, of course," the troll said. "Him, absolutely not."

"Not even as my guest?" Seth asked.

The troll gave a grunt. "What are you playing at?"

"But I can go in and out?" Seth asked.

"Unless you sign on as an active combatant," the troll said.

Seth turned to Virgil. "See you later."

"If you're certain . . ." Virgil hedged.

"Don't wait up," Seth said.

"I'll be here when you're done," Virgil promised. "Southwest below-ground access gate."

Seth gave Virgil a little salute, then patted the troll on the arm. "Keep up the good work."

The troll elbowed Seth roughly. "Hands off."

"You're worried about me?" Seth asked. "Keep your eyes on the goatman."

"He's a comedian," Virgil said with an uncertain smile.

The troll sneered. "The best comedy leans on truth."

Seth hurried through the checkpoint. As the hall curved away from the gate, sloping downward, it rapidly became bleak and bare. Gone were the food stands, statues, fountains, and architectural flourishes. The floor grew uneven, and Seth noticed cracks and water stains on the stony walls.

The arena crowd roared, the exuberance now above and behind him. A new fight must have started, because he had not heard the audience respond with such enthusiasm to any of the other entertainment.

Natural light faded, and the passage branched. Seth took the steeper way and soon found stairs that wound downward. He came out into a torchlit corridor where a minotaur with his arm in a sling stood in close conversation with a warty brown ogre. Both stopped talking and turned to face Seth. The minotaur exhaled sharply.

Seth walked by them, avoiding eye contact. From far above, he heard the noise of the crowd surge again, too distant to carry much volume. Louder, from up ahead, Seth heard overlapping conversations, punctuated by laughter.

The corridor emptied into a dining area full of benches and long tables. Behind a counter, a quartet of cooks attended to grills laden with meat and bubbling stewpots. The powerfully built diners must have been gladiators, though none wore armor or carried weapons. Some were dressed in simple tunics, others in shirts and pants, mostly browns and grays. The homespun clothes were of such similar style that Seth assumed they were provided by whoever ran the coliseum.

A large hand clapped down on Seth's shoulder. "Aren't you a tad young to dine here?"

Seth looked up at a handsome man, clean-shaven,

middle-aged, with intense brown eyes, a slightly receding hairline, and a cleft chin. "I participate in the Games."

"I can tell," the man said. "But not as a combatant here in the Titan Games. Have you come to enlist?"

Some warriors at a nearby table chuckled at the question.

"Still deciding," Seth said.

"Give it a few years," the man said. "We're always looking for able candidates."

"Are you a gladiator?" Seth asked.

"In another life, perhaps," the man said. "I'm Fenrick, one of the trainers." He gently hit Seth on the shoulder with the back of his hand. "Maybe we'll work together one day."

"Boy!" a woman at a nearby table called. "Come here."

She was a plain woman with a sparkle of mischief in her gaze. Of average height and slender build, she didn't seem suited for the kind of combat Seth had watched from the stands. He approached her table. Beside her, a thickset guy with an orange beard watched him curiously.

"What brings you down here?" she asked.

"Snooping around," Seth said. "Trying to figure out the Games."

The guy with the orange beard laughed. "Why not start young?"

"Because he'll die young," the woman said.

The guy waved away her words. "The boy isn't here to fight. He's scouting. What's your name, lad?"

"Seth."

"I'm Per and this is Rianne," he said. "We don't often hear casual words from Fenrick."

"Is he mean?" Seth asked.

"Stern," Rianne said. "He's the best trainer here. He wants us all to live, so he makes life exhausting."

"You can't all live," Seth said.

"Those who train with him fare better than most," Per said. "But who are we kidding? Nobody makes it to a hundred games."

"I will," Rianne said.

"She says after seven victories," Per scoffed.

Rianne glanced at Seth. "You have free run down here?"

"So far," Seth said. "I'm a participant in the Games."

"Where did you start?" Per asked.

"Stormguard Castle," Seth said.

"I heard that contest finally ended," Per said.

"I was part of that," Seth replied.

"Who won?" Rianna asked around a bite of potatoes. "Shouldn't one of you have the Wizenstone?"

"The game ended with a player sending the Wizenstone away," Seth said.

Per grimaced. "Must have made everyone crazy to come so close."

"I lost my memories," Seth said.

"All of them?" Per asked.

"My whole identity," Seth said. "Up until that point, at least."

Per gave a soft whistle. "He's not so different from us. The kid's a veteran."

"Did you lose your memories too?" Seth asked.

"Some of them," Per said. "Do you know how it works with combatants?"

"Not really," Seth said.

"Don't spill too much," Rianne said. "He belongs topside."

"He's a player," Per said. "We can talk freely to other contestants."

"You want to do favors for a competitor?" Rianne asked.

"I've stopped worrying about winning," Per said.

"You're here for information?" Rianne asked.

"All I can get," Seth said.

"Be careful about sharing what I tell you," Per said. "Humbuggle will get wind if you spill secrets to nonplayers."

"I'll be careful," Seth promised.

"Watch what you divulge," Rianne muttered to Per.

"What's it matter if we help the kid?" Per asked. "Somebody else will fill him in if we don't. And they may not shoot straight."

"Why do you disappear right before you die?" Seth asked.

"See," Per said. "He's asking the right questions."

"It's all part of the agreement to join the Games," Rianne said. "We can get injured, but before death takes us, we vanish. We go into hibernation and heal. And eventually we fight again."

"You fight over and over?" Seth asked.

Per wiped his lips on his sleeve. "Until somebody wins, everyone who ever signed up for these Games remains part of the Games."

"How often are you recycled?" Seth asked.

"Hard to say," Rianne said. "We don't keep all of our memories. We get assigned new personas for the arena. Did you ever wonder why so many gladiators wear masks or helms that disguise them?"

"We keep a sense of who we are," Per said. "More or less. But each time we come back, the previous attempts become a haze."

"Do you know how long you've been here?" Seth asked.

Per shrugged. "I don't know how many times I've lost. More than once, I think. Maybe twice. Maybe dozens of times."

"I hope not," Rianne said with disgust.

"Do you remember what year it was when you started?" Seth asked.

"Hazy," Per said. "I know I lived in Norway. I know I had two sisters. I don't know what year I came here."

"Those kinds of details slip away," Rianne said. "It's the same for all of us."

"Except for new volunteers on their first run," Per said. "Their memories are fine until after the first loss."

"Nobody ever really dies here," Seth said.

"Unless somebody jumps into the arena," Per said. "If those impulsive wannabes die in their first fight, they die for good. If not, they have to make the same arrangement as the rest of us."

"These Games have gone on for centuries," Seth said.

Per looked at him with wide eyes, nodding. "You're telling me. The fuzzy memories are probably a mercy."

"How well do you two know each other?" Seth asked. "Do you remember one another? From previous attempts."

Per scrunched his brow. "She and I have had this conversation."

"Per feels familiar," Rianne said. "But who knows?"

"We may have never been active in the Games at the same time," Per said.

"Or we could have crossed paths a lot," Rianne said.

"You fight until you die," Seth said. "And then you do it again."

Rianne raised a finger. "Unless we win."

"Do you guys age?" Seth asked.

"I don't know," Per said.

"Hard to be sure without memories," Rianne said.

"What if you quit?" Seth asked. "Like, refuse to fight?"

"They'll send us out there anyway," Rianne said. "There is no end to it."

"The closest a combatant can get to an end is becoming a trainer," Per said. "If gladiators do well enough, they are sometimes given that option."

"Fenrick was a gladiator?" Seth asked.

"Rumor has it he was one of the best," Per said. "Long ago he had a run where he made it to ninety."

"Some say rumors are more trustworthy than memories," Rianne said.

"We don't all get vanquished at once," Per said. "So gossip becomes a form of group memory."

"But after some time goes by, who could contradict a false rumor?" Seth asked.

"The boy has a point," Per murmured.

"Actual memories have some real advantages," Rianne said.

"Any rumors I should know?" Seth asked. "Where should I look to figure out the Games?"

Per smiled sadly. "Our rumors are mostly stories about one another. We're not working this like a puzzle, as some do. We're trying to fight our way to the top."

Rianne looked at Seth with sympathy. "Kid, the winner won't be us, and, no offense, it won't be you, either. If you know what's good for you, walk away while you can. These Games are a bottomless pit. Once you slip, you fall forever."

"I can't give up," Seth said. "Where can I go to learn more?"

"Talk to the trainers," Rianne said. "They have had longer stretches to learn things." She looked pointedly at where Fenrick sat eating alone. "Fenrick was civil to you. Ask him."

"But don't be surprised if he rebukes you," Per added.

"Okay," Seth said. "Thanks for the tips."

"Don't mention it," Per said.

"Make your own luck," Rianne advised.

Crossing to where Fenrick sat, Seth claimed a spot on the bench across from him. The trainer was spooning bites from a bowl of chowder. Fenrick looked up. "How can I help you, Son?"

"I'm searching for info about the Games," Seth said.

"I figured as much," Fenrick said. "We don't get many participants down here who are not enrolled in the fighting.

We've had one or two others recently. Even if you ignore the fighting, it isn't safe down here. Some people come in looking for secrets and don't come out."

"What happens to them?" Seth asked.

Fenrick took a bite of chowder. "I don't know. But they head down to the depths where the gladiators and the trainers are forbidden to venture."

"Where is that?" Seth asked.

"They seldom return," Fenrick said.

"I'm not going to learn what I need without taking some risks," Seth said.

"Why would a boy your age care so much about the Wizenstone?" Fenrick asked.

"It's not the stone I care about," Seth said. "Humbuggle took my memories. I need them back."

"Only the new fighters among us have their memories," Fenrick said. "You have your freedom. Go make new memories."

"It's not like I forgot a few fights," Seth said. "He took my whole identity."

"You're not the only one," Fenrick said. "Some remember more than others. I don't know my identity either."

"You used to fight?" Seth asked.

"I suspect so," Fenrick said.

"I heard you were good," Seth said.

"You have to be good to become a trainer," Fenrick said.

"I heard you almost won," Seth said.

"Rumors," Fenrick said with a snort.

"How long have you been a trainer?" Seth asked.

"A long time," Fenrick said.

"Long enough to see the same fighters come back after losing?"

"From time to time," Fenrick said. "The gaps tend to be long. There is a large pool to draw from."

"Don't you want these Games to end?" Seth asked.

"I surely do," Fenrick said. "Look, you're persistent, so you'll find out sooner or later." He pointed to a door. "You want to go where the action is? Head through there. Turn left, and descend the stairs. None of us can go down there. There are invisible barriers. But you can. Have a look if you must. But consider walking away."

"I won't quit," Seth said.

"Then down you go," Fenrick said. "You've been warned. You can eat here first if you wish."

"I just had food," Seth said. "Thanks."

Fenrick gave Seth a long stare. "When these gladiators lose, they come back. Where you're going, there are no second chances. I admire your determination."

"Can you go back into the Games?" Seth asked.

"If I gave up my rights as a trainer, I could," Fenrick said. "I'd rather watch and wait. Help the others."

Seth glanced at the door. "Does anyone return from down the stairs?"

"Sometimes," Fenrick said. "A few officials of the Games go down there routinely. Barruze. Humbuggle occasionally."

"Humbuggle comes here?" Seth asked.

"Now and then," Fenrick said. "He's unpredictable."

"Who is Barruze?" Seth asked.

"You really are new here," Fenrick said. "The troll who announces the Games."

"Gotcha," Seth said.

"Well, stay on your toes," Fenrick said. "Whether you remember or not, you paid a price for access here. Don't squander the opportunity."

CHAPTER TWENTY-TWO

Crystal Hollow

Leaving the dining area behind, Seth went through the indicated door and turned left like Fenrick had suggested. He found a stairway and started down, stepping quietly to match the silence around him. The illumination now derived from crystals in sconces on the walls rather than from torches.

Seth searched inside himself for his power and reached out to feel for any undead, but sensed nothing. Then he switched his approach, crouching as he walked, keeping to the shadows, willing himself toward invisibility.

The bottom of the stairs led into a chamber where an ogre with gray, droopy skin tilted his wooden chair onto two legs, his feet propped up on a table. Three archways led out of the room. Skirting the edge of the chamber, Seth took the first archway he reached. The ogre never glanced his way.

Seth proceeded down a gloomy corridor. The masonry looked more ancient than up above, with no mortar between the rough-hewn and sometimes ill-fitted stones. At a junction where the passage forked, Seth heard footsteps coming his way from one branch, and he slouched against the wall in the deepest shadows he could find.

A striking woman strode into view, tall and lissome, with long green hair and penetrating eyes. She wore leather armor and was missing an arm.

"I see you, shadow walker," she said.

Seth stepped away from the wall.

The woman gave a little gasp. "Seth Sorenson. What a surprise."

"Do I know you?" Seth asked.

Her smile spread slowly. "Am I that forgettable?"

"My memory isn't so good lately," Seth said.

"We're old acquaintances," the woman said smoothly. "I'm Lydia. I know your sister."

"Do you work here?" Seth asked.

The woman glanced around and shivered in disgust. "Thankfully, no. I assume you're playing in the Games."

"Trying," Seth said. "You too?"

"Seems like one dead end after another," she said. "Have you learned anything beneficial?"

"I wish," Seth said. "I'm new here. I barely learned how the Games work for the gladiators."

Lydia nodded. "I'm not faring much better. Want to hunt together?"

Something was off. The first expression on her face

when she saw him had been panic, not relief. And now she was behaving too at ease. It smelled like an act.

"Why the green hair?" Seth asked.

"It's my favorite color," Lydia said.

"What's Kendra's favorite color?" Seth asked.

She hesitated. "I never asked."

Though he couldn't remember what colors Kendra preferred, the hesitation told him a lot. "How do you know her again?"

Lydia fumbled for an answer, then scowled and bared her teeth. "I've tasted her!"

Seth was surprised by her vehemence. "Who are you?"

She drew a dagger. "One who has had enough of you!"

She lunged at Seth, stabbing, and he sprang aside. She nimbly kept after him, slashing, and he backed into the wall. The surprise contact left him flat-footed, and Lydia surged forward, the dagger plunging for his chest. An instant before the tip would have pierced him, the knife disintegrated, as did her arm up past the elbow.

Lydia's jaw dropped open, and she staggered back, staring in horror at what remained of her arm. There was no open wound—the fleshy stump looked like it could have been that way for years.

Her eyes returned to Seth, burning with hate.

"I don't think we're supposed to kill people here," he said.

Growling, she sprang forward, lashing out with one leg. Seth skipped aside, and she kicked the wall instead.

"Seriously?" Seth asked.

She kicked at him again, and Seth caught her booted

foot, leaving her balanced on one leg, truncated arm flailing. Still holding her foot, Seth started walking toward her, forcing her to hop backwards.

"Who are you really?" Seth asked. "Who do you work for?"

Jumping and turning, Lydia twisted her leg free from Seth's grasp and tumbled to the floor. She struggled awkwardly to her feet, then ran off down the passageway.

Panting from the stress and exertion, Seth watched her flee. The woman clearly worked for his enemies. Ronodin? The Sphinx? The Underking? The dragons? Humbuggle? It was hard to guess who his biggest enemy was anymore.

He could not remember seeing the woman before, but she had seen him despite his shade walking, and she had known his name. Lydia had become so flustered when he had grilled her about Kendra that he doubted she actually knew his sister. Had she been serious about tasting her? Could Lydia be a monster or a dragon in human form? Was Kendra all right?

Seth debated about whether he should chase the green-haired woman. Lydia was fast, and she was heading back the way he had come. What if she rounded up reinforcements? And what would he do if he caught her? He'd had her by the foot before she ran away, and that had yielded little. He decided it would be smarter to keep looking for clues about the Games.

At the junction where the passage forked, Seth took the branch Lydia had used. He didn't have to go far before the passage ended at a steel door. It was locked, and Seth could see no keyhole or other means to open it.

Placing a palm against the cold metal, Seth focused on the dark power inside himself. He mentally probed the door, calling upon it to open, and felt considerable resistance. Gritting his teeth, Seth insisted with all his effort, and, after a trembling moment, an unseen locking mechanism released.

Seth opened the door to find a more polished corridor beyond, the air still and cold, the stone walls black and smooth. When Seth released the door, it started to close. He considered propping it open before deciding a closed door might help foil Lydia if she found help and came after him.

He advanced along the hall, impressed by the reflective finish of the black walls, ceiling, and floor, lit by the occasional dim crystal. A bronze door came into view at the far end of the hall, but before he reached it, Seth noticed a silver door on his right out of the corner of his eye.

When Seth turned to face the silver door, it was gone.

He immediately thought of the door to the shop that Virgil had shown him. Seth returned his gaze to the distant bronze door until the silver door appeared again at the edge of his vision. Stepping carefully, keeping the silver door barely in sight, Seth drew nearer, then reached out and caught hold of the handle. This time, the silver door remained when he looked at it directly, and Seth hoisted it open.

Beyond the doorway, he encountered a natural cavern bristling with bluish, glowing crystals. Seth waited in the doorway, astonished at how the quartzlike crystals covered every wall and protuberance in the room while leaving the floor and ceiling bare. The even blue glow emanating from all directions left the room shadowless, though not very bright.

Seth entered the room. The crystals were all roughly the size of his finger. When he drew near to a cluster of them, they glowed a little brighter, and he could hear them faintly vibrating. He cautiously extended a hand to touch one.

"Don't," a voice commanded.

Seth jumped and turned, letting out an involuntary yelp.

A gaunt man with a fringe of white hair approached. He was a few inches shorter than Seth, with a large mole prominent on one cheek. His long robe hid his feet.

"You do not belong here," the man accused.

"I'm a participant in the Games," Seth argued.

The man shook his head and waved his hands. "Move away from the crystals."

Seth took a couple of steps away.

"Why have you come here?" the man asked.

"I'm trying to figure out the Games," Seth said.

"Don't you mean win the Games?"

Seth shook his head. He figured honesty was his best chance for information. "I lost my memories. I want them back."

The man seemed to relax a little. "How did you lose them?"

"Stormguard Castle," Seth said.

"I regret to inform you that your memories are not here," the man said. "You should depart."

"What is this place?" Seth asked.

"A private repository where you are trespassing," the man said. "A sanctuary where you could cause great harm."

"To the Games?" Seth asked.

"To innocent lives," the man said.

"What about *my* life?" Seth asked. "Humbuggle wasn't shy about harming me. Maybe if I smash some of his precious crystals I can finally get some payback." Seth stormed over to a dense cluster of crystals and raised a threatening hand.

"Stop!" the man exclaimed. "You don't understand the consequences!"

"Then tell me," Seth insisted.

"Listen," the man said. "Certain competitors are granted access down here because learning Humbuggle's secrets is part of the Games. Since you're forcing my hand, I'll tell you a little about this sanctum, and then you must depart."

"Deal," Seth said.

"You get nothing if you harm a single crystal," the man said. "And you must keep this information to yourself."

"Sure."

"That means you promise to tell nobody," the man emphasized.

Seth thought of Virgil. "All right."

The man held out his hand. "I'm Willard."

Seth shook it. "Seth."

Willard gestured at the crystals surrounding them. "This is the Crystal Hollow. This is where the gladiators hibernate and heal until they are called upon to rejoin the combat."

Seth surveyed the room. "Where are they?"

"Each crystal houses a life force," Willard explained.

Seth reconsidered the expansive cavern. "There are so many."

"All of them virtually immortal," Willard said.

"How do they come out?" Seth asked.

Willard walked over to a waist-high pillar of stone. "When the time comes for a combatant to return, I harvest their crystal and place it in the slot." He indicated a socket in the surface of the pillar.

"And a person comes out?" Seth asked.

"A gladiator emerges from a chamber elsewhere beneath the coliseum," Willard said. "That's outside my purview."

"You watch over the crystals," Seth said.

"I just follow orders," Willard said. "Along with a few others. We take shifts."

"Exciting job?" Seth asked.

"You'll note some crystals are dimmer than others," Willard said. "The dim ones represent injured warriors. They receive extra care until they achieve full health."

"How long are people trapped here?" Seth asked.

"They rest here," Willard said. "It's like sleep. Hibernation. They relax and heal."

"And lose their memories," Seth said.

"Their memories are not taken," Willard said. "Not stripped away like yours. They are simply . . . submerged. I help that process along."

"How?" Seth asked.

Willard clasped his hands behind his back. "Let's say magic. Leave it at that."

"You shouldn't mess with their memories," Seth said.

"It isn't my policy," Willard said. "I'm performing my job. Those above me consider the submerging of memories a mercy. Some of these fighters have been here for a very long time and have accumulated many lifetimes of trauma."

"I would want to keep my memories," Seth said. "I would rather understand my situation."

"The choice would not be yours to make," Willard said. "I suspect the great majority would thank me for hiding the vastness of this experience from them. Now you know about the Crystal Hollow. You arrived here haphazardly. Please do not return."

"Are there other secrets of the Games down here?" Seth asked.

Willard smiled, his upper teeth uncommonly prominent. "There are secrets about the Games everywhere."

"How do I get out of here?" Seth asked.

"I recommend you backtrack all the way to daylight," Willard said.

"I ran into some trouble on my way in," Seth said. "An alternate exit would help."

"I'll grant no extra favors," Willard said. "You should hurry. Security will soon be summoned to oust you. I'll give you a head start, in case you would rather see yourself out."

Seth gave the cavern a final sweeping glance. "All right. Have fun down here."

Willard offered a faint smile. "Enjoy your Games."

CHAPTER TWENTY-THREE

Messenger

Pungent smoke percolated through the holes of a brass incense burner on the corner of the expansive desk. Seated together, Kendra, Vanessa, Warren, and Tanu watched Dectus pace back and forth, hands moving animatedly as he talked.

"You four did very well in Stratos," the giant said.

"We got caught," Kendra said.

"But you returned with the map," Dectus said. "And Madam Ladonna weighed you, taking the guesswork out of your motives."

"You got what you expected," Warren said.

Dectus held up a finger. "I had to be sure about you. I hoped for this outcome. And not a moment too soon. The Perennial Storm has been spotted."

"You're kidding," Vanessa said.

"The storm visits here every seven years, give or take a couple of weeks," Dectus said.

"How bad is the storm?" Kendra asked.

"It's enchanted," Tanu said. "The storm roves the magical world, never ending, bringing torrential showers and brilliant displays of lightning."

"I heard it hailed gold for a while on Isla del Dragón," Warren said.

"Legends about the storm abound," Dectus said. "We know thunderbirds flock inside those tenebrous clouds. But, most important, we know the entrance to our Dragon Temple opens only when the Perennial Storm is present."

"You want us to go out in the Perennial Storm?" Vanessa asked.

"Sounds about right," Warren murmured.

"My most trusted courier will bear you safely there," Dectus said. "Even giants respect the Perennial Storm, but, in a pinch, we sky giants can brave any weather."

"I heard at its peak there can be a thousand lightning strikes a minute," Vanessa said.

"Maybe at the very heart of the storm," Dectus said. "We will insulate Bernosh and his passengers against lightning. The primary question is whether you will undertake the quest for the Harp of Ages."

"What do you know about the guardians of the temple?" Warren asked.

"We have no details," Dectus said. "Expect three monsters or dragons of great renown."

"How do we open the door?" Tanu asked.

"You will need to use the lightning key while the storm is raging," Dectus said.

"You have the key?" Tanu asked.

Dectus pointed at the map.

Kendra looked at the parchment. "Ptolemy and the lightning key," Kendra read, tapping the labeled spot.

"Use the map to find the lair of Ptolemy," Dectus said. "Take the key from him."

"Who is Ptolemy?" Kendra asked.

"A three-headed giant," Warren said. "Really tough customer."

"You need not defeat him," Dectus said. "You just need the key."

"Ptolemy is notoriously unpredictable," Vanessa said.

"And the Dragon Temple will be more perilous still," Dectus said. "Will you make the attempt, or should I find other champions?"

"The Harp of Ages puts dragons to sleep?" Kendra asked.

"By the hundreds, provided they are within range," Dectus said.

Kendra looked to Tanu. "We have to stop Celebrant. But we also need to find Seth."

"You go after Seth," Tanu said. "Warren, Vanessa, and I can chase down the Harp."

"If you're going to the Dragon Temple, you need a dragon tamer," Kendra said.

"We have potions," Tanu responded.

Kendra shook her head. "I don't think Seth wants to be found, but the satyrs can take Knox and Tess to look for him while we go after the Harp. If we lose the dragon war, we're all doomed."

"I can help your friends make their way to Humburgh," Dectus said. "If your brother has interest in Humbuggle and the Titan Games, it is the sensible place to investigate."

A human-sized door opened and Raza entered, bowing. "Apologies, Dectus, but you have a visitor."

"I explicitly directed we not be disturbed," Dectus said.

"Understood, your excellency, but this is an emergency visitor seeking Kendra Sorenson," Raza explained. "I believe her message is urgent and perhaps relevant to your discussion."

"Very well," Dectus said, sounding intrigued.

Raza stepped aside, and a human-sized fairy came through the door, one wing mostly torn off, soiled and limping. Her golden hair was tangled, and what remained of her wings blazed in fiery colors, matching her slip. "Kendra Sorenson?" the fairy called.

Dectus strode to her, crouched, and carried her to the desk. The fairy gave a feeble smile and bowed her head. "I'm sorry it took me so long. I had to walk from the fairy shrine because my wing was damaged."

Kendra felt deep alarm that something might have happened to Bracken. "What is your news?" she asked.

The fairy's chin quivered and she collapsed, sobbing. "I never imagined I would utter these words. The Fairy Realm has fallen."

"What?" Kendra asked. "Is Bracken all right?"

"Nobody is all right," the fairy said. "Ronodin has claimed the Fairy Queen's crown."

Kendra could not move. She could find no words.

"That's impossible," Warren said.

The fairy shook her head. "The former Fairy King sent me to find you after Ronodin claimed the crown. My former king wanted me to tell you the fall of the Fairy Realm was his fault. He also wanted me to assure you that after I came through, he would seal off the Titan Valley fairy shrine."

"How was the fall his fault?" Kendra asked.

"The former Fairy King let Ronodin inside," the fairy said. "And many dragons."

"Why do you call him the former Fairy King?" Kendra asked. "Was he killed?"

"Ronodin is the new Fairy King," the fairy said.

"Then shouldn't you be serving him?" Vanessa asked.

The fairy held up her hand. "This bracelet from the former Fairy King enables me to act independently of the new king."

"Why would the Fairy King admit Ronodin to the Fairy Realm?" Kendra asked.

"I don't believe he was himself," the fairy said. "When he spoke to me, the former Fairy King was devastated."

"Is Bracken alive?" Kendra asked, trying to brace herself for the worst.

"Before I departed, I believed he and the Fairy Queen had been captured," the fairy said. "I cannot confirm their current fate."

"What is your name?" Kendra asked.

"Gwendolyn," the fairy replied.

"You're injured," Kendra said.

The fairy whimpered. "I feel faint."

"Does this mean Ronodin controls the fairies?" Kendra asked, extending a hand to steady Gwendolyn.

"All fairies who serve in the Fairy Realm," the fairy said. "And most other fairies everywhere. He also controls the astrids, nymphs, and satyrs who swore fealty to the crown. Especially those who remain in the realm. All except the unicorns. They had power to resist him."

"This is a nightmare," Kendra said.

"We tried to repel him," Gwendolyn said. "Once Ronodin claimed the crown, we were helpless."

"He had dragons with him?" Kendra asked.

"The dragons gave him clout," the fairy said. "And some demons helped. A few wizards." She coughed and stumbled. "I don't feel so . . ." Gwendolyn collapsed flat on the table.

Vanessa rushed to the fairy's side and stroked her cheek. "She's unconscious but alive," Vanessa reported.

"Could this be a trick?" Warren asked. "The Fairy Realm has always been untouchable."

"That was before the fairies took over the demon prison," Vanessa said. "The Fairy Realm was protected by purity. We saw the darkness gaining inroads there."

"Forgive me," Dectus said. "This must be reported to the Giant Queen immediately."

"Of course," Tanu said.

Dectus set Kendra and her companions to the floor, including the unconscious fairy. Then he crossed to the door, pausing to issue orders to Raza. "See that Kendra and her friends have any assistance they need." Dectus exited.

"This is what Ronodin wanted all along," Kendra said. "We have to get the crown from him."

"Kendra," Tanu said. "This is a tragedy worse than the fall of any sanctuary. But without a fairy shrine, we have no way to go help."

"Be glad the Fairy King closed it," Vanessa said. "He may have saved Titan Valley by doing so. If the shrine remained active, Ronodin would have unrestricted access to the sanctuary."

"Can't he get in anyhow because of the Games?" Kendra asked.

"That kind of access would require him to travel," Vanessa said. "And at least it involves a screening process. The shrine would provide a direct inroad to the heart of the sanctuary."

"What can we do?" Kendra asked.

"We can help this fairy mend," Vanessa said. "And we do our part against the dragons. Now it is more important than ever that Titan Valley not fall."

Kendra nodded, then succumbed to her tears. It was so frustrating! How was she supposed to help Bracken? And his mother! What would Ronodin do to them? She remembered how powerful she had felt while wearing the crown. And she was an amateur! Ronodin was an expert.

"Might the fairies rebel against him?" Kendra asked.

"I don't know," Tanu said. "Let's hope so. Much better kings than Ronodin have been overthrown."

"The demons were distracting Bracken and the Fairy Queen," Kendra said. "But why would the Fairy King betray them?"

"He was in the demon prison for a long time," Warren said. "Shackled to the Demon King. That had to have taken a toll."

"It's a disaster," Kendra lamented, shaking with sobs. "Why do we even try?"

"Somebody has to," Warren said. "This isn't over. We'll find a way."

"Will we?" Kendra asked. "Whatever we do, we keep losing ground."

"Let's start with the Harp," Tanu said. "We need serious firepower against the dragons. Right now, finding the Harp of Ages is our best hope."

Kendra sagged. She didn't want to find a harp. She had barely survived her previous excursion into a Dragon Temple. She wanted her brother back. And she wanted Bracken safe. Whenever an impossible situation had arisen in the past, she had always turned to the Fairy Queen.

Now that option was gone.

Maybe forever.

Kendra felt stupid for crying. Her face burned. Her nose ran freely. But she just couldn't hold back the sobs.

She knew she would go after the Harp. She would do her duty.

But, for the moment, Kendra needed to mourn.

CHAPTER TWENTY-FOUR

Mystery

As the sun sank into the western mountains, goblins on stilts used poles with wicks at the tips to light streetlamps along the avenue leading away from the Arena Plaza. Strolling beside Virgil, Seth munched on a giant pretzel.

"You really waited at the gate," Seth said, using his teeth to rake an oily salt pellet from his bottom lip into his mouth.

"Did you think I would abandon you?" Virgil asked.

"It was a long time to just stand around," Seth said.

"I kept an eye on the Games," Virgil said. "I was back and forth."

"You were just waiting when I got there," Seth said.

"The Games had ended," Virgil said. "You really can't tell me what you learned?"

"Not all of it," Seth said.

"Do you know what happens when the fallen gladiators disappear?" Virgil asked.

"I know a lot," Seth replied.

"They don't die," Virgil conjectured. "Their lives are somehow preserved, and they start over in the competition at a later date. I assume this is why so many competitors have their faces hidden."

Seth pointed at Virgil. "That is a really good theory. I'd stick with it."

"Is that confirmation?" Virgil asked. "It would explain how they never run out of combatants."

"It's as close to confirmation as you're going to get," Seth said.

"I'm jealous you went down there," Virgil said. "I've dreamed of an opportunity like that."

"I also ran into trouble," Seth said. "You didn't notice a lady with green hair and no arms?"

"Completely armless?"

"Well, one is a nub and the other a stump," Seth said. "She tried to kill me."

"With no arms?"

"It's how she lost one of them."

"Oh," Virgil said. "She must be new here. Or else really hot-tempered. You can't take a life in Humburgh, unless you're on the arena floor. Then again, not even there, if my theory is right."

"Unless somebody joins the fight without signing up," Seth said.

"You're right," Virgil agreed. "Those poor saps bleed out."

"Maybe I shouldn't have revealed that," Seth realized.

"It's obvious if you watch those who leap from the stands to the arena floor," Virgil consoled.

"Did you see the lady?" Seth asked.

"No," Virgil said. "I'll watch for her. Will you go back to the coliseum tomorrow?"

"I guess I can go as much as I want," Seth said. "I'll have to look out for trouble. Where else can I search for clues in Humburgh?"

"Take your pick," Virgil said. "The whole town has potential."

"I wish I hadn't blown it at the Humburgh Mystery House," Seth said.

"How did you blow it?" Virgil asked.

"I couldn't get inside," Seth said.

"You just go down the side alley to the back," Virgil said. "They try to make the entrance feel hidden. If you haggle with the guy at the door, you can get in for peanuts."

"I talked to a woman out front," Seth said. "She wanted something valuable from me."

Virgil laid a hand on Seth. "Wait. You spoke with Esmira?"

"A lady all bundled in black?" Seth asked.

"What did you offer?" Virgil asked.

"A turnip."

Virgil's eyes went wide. "The hag approached you and you offered a turnip?"

"I didn't have much," Seth said defensively. "I hoped

maybe she liked turnips. She rejected me and told me it was the last offer I could make that day."

"This happened yesterday?" Virgil asked. "As in, perhaps you could make another offer today?"

"Yes."

"You were with Reggie, Hermo, and Calvin?" Virgil sounded excited.

"Yeah."

"Let's fetch them and try to re-create the moment," Virgil said. "See if Esmira shows herself again. Getting admitted by Esmira is the best way to find the Diviner."

"What does the Diviner do?" Seth asked.

"I've never met him personally," Virgil said. "I've tried several times. But if you find him, he helps you locate stuff. Including your destiny."

"Really?" Seth said. "Is the Mystery House still open?"

"Until midnight," Virgil said. "We should grab the others. Esmira shows herself infrequently. You should imitate the conditions of her first appearance as much as possible."

"What should I give her for admission?" Seth asked.

"I've heard money always fails," Virgil said. "Give what you have."

"Except not a turnip," Seth said.

"Something of value," Virgil said.

They reached Virgil's townhouse, and the satyr opened the door with a key. The main floor looked quiet, so they headed for the stairs.

"Seth!" Calvin called. "You're back!"

Seth paused at the foot of the stairs. Calvin came running across the floor.

"How was your day?" Calvin asked.

"Interesting," Seth said. "How was yours?"

"Amazing," Calvin said. "I went to Humbuggle's estate."

"Really?" Seth asked. "Did you get inside?"

"There were barriers to keep me out," Calvin said. "But I made friends with a maid out hanging clothes. She confirmed that one of Humbuggle's staff—a woman named Sable—has a little woman like me."

"It could be Serena," Seth said.

"That's my hope," Calvin said. "The maid caught me and tried to keep me as a pet. I got away, though. What are you up to now?"

"We're going back to the Mystery House," Seth said. "Are you up for it?"

"Anywhere," Calvin said. "Always."

Seth placed Calvin in his pocket, then climbed the stairs. He found Reggie in the bedroom, standing still.

Welcome back, Master, Reggie communicated.

Seth looked around. "Have you seen Hermo?"

He's hiding beneath the bed, Reggie conveyed.

Seth knelt down and looked under the bed, but he saw only clutter.

"I know you're under there, Hermo," Seth said. "Come out."

"Dirtman tattletale!" Hermo complained, sliding out from under the bed and hopping to his feet.

"We're going to the Mystery House," Seth said.

"No," Hermo said. "Me stay."

"You can't make a lair in here," Virgil said, entering the room.

"How you know?" Hermo complained.

"Because this is my home," Virgil said. "You are here as my guests. And if you want to be my guests, you have to help in my research. Come along to the Humburgh Mystery House."

"Fine," Hermo said. "Me solve mystery for slowpokes. Then Hermo sleep."

🦎   🦎   🦎

This time the troll on the balcony of the Humburgh Mystery House wore a striped jacket and a dapper straw hat. Most people passing by did not look twice at him.

"Do you see her?" Virgil asked Seth.

"Not yet."

"I'll hang back," Virgil said. "You should show up with the same group as before."

Seth approached the alley beside the painted door, and the woman bundled in dark fabric emerged from the shadows. Seth walked up to her.

"Have you a better offer?" the hag asked in her creaky voice.

"Would you be interested in secrets?" Seth asked.

"Depends if I already know them," the hag replied. "Also depends if I care to know them."

Seth stepped closer and lowered his voice. "I'm a

shadow charmer. I helped Ronodin the dark unicorn and the Underking free the undead from the Blackwell to destroy Wyrmroost."

"Not bad," the hag said. "There is value in learning what forces are combining in this conflict. I need more, though. Why have you come to Titan Valley?"

"Humbuggle took my memories," Seth said. "I want them back. I'm trying to figure out the Games."

"You want the Wizenstone," the hag said.

"I don't care about the stone," Seth said. "But I need to beat Humbuggle."

"Much better than a turnip," the hag said. "You have my attention. Secrets spoil. I need something tangible that you value."

Seth had retrieved his satchel from the townhouse. He rummaged inside and pulled out a glove. "This makes you invisible if you stand still." Seth knew he could get many of the same benefits the glove provided by shade walking, but the thought of losing the item still stung.

The hag accepted the glove and gave it a sniff. "Fair enough. You may enter, along with your servants."

"Me no servant," Hermo said.

"Then you must provide your own admission," the hag said.

Hermo glanced at the Mystery House and sniffed, then waved a dismissive hand at the hag. "Me get in own way."

The hermit troll waddled off into the alley.

Seth looked back at Virgil. "Want to be my servant? It gets you access."

Virgil scrunched his face. "I've been in there several times. Today is part of your journey. Tell me about it later."

The hag motioned Seth toward the picture of the door on the wall of the Mystery House. Seth reached for the doorknob, and, right before he touched it, the picture became an actual door.

Seth glanced back at Reggie. "Ready?"

I will go where you lead, Reggie responded.

Seth entered and stared down a winding white hall with a bloodred carpet running down the center. The door closed behind Seth, and he turned to find a bare wall with no evidence that a door had ever existed there.

Seth advanced along the carpet with Reggie right behind him. The floor began to tilt until the carpet was on the wall, but Seth's feet stayed firmly attached. The corridor continued to twist until Seth strolled along the ceiling, as if gravity had been reversed.

The red carpet ended at a yellow door. Seth opened it and found a room beyond, oriented as if he were walking on the floor rather than the ceiling. He entered, and the door closed behind him, making it easy to believe he was indeed on the floor, though he felt sure the room was actually upside down. Exotic potted plants were spaced around the room, as were a few benches and seven grandfather clocks. Seth saw no windows or doors, though velvet curtains masked most of the walls.

The curtains bulged near the bottom on one side of the room, then lifted, and Hermo emerged. "Hi, Seth."

"That was fast," Seth said. "How'd you find us?"

"Easy. Me find other way in, then me join you. You want meet Diviner?"

"Yes," Seth said.

"Over here." Hermo held up the curtain.

Seth ducked under, then went through a narrow door into a fancy parlor, sumptuously furnished. Seth turned to find Reggie following.

"What do you think of this place?" Seth asked.

This building is old, Reggie expressed. *And larger than it seems from outside.*

Hermo led them to a life-sized portrait of a young lord in a powdered wig, then pulled it open like a door. They stepped into a small room behind the painting—small until Seth looked up. The room extended upward like a hallway. A red carpet ran up one of the walls, so Seth stepped onto it, and he found himself standing as if gravity was now pulling sideways. With this new orientation, Seth and Reggie followed Hermo straight up the shaft.

Hermo stopped at a tapestry and pulled it aside to reveal a door behind it. "In there," the hermit troll said.

"You've never been here before?" Seth asked.

"First time," Hermo replied.

"You're amazing," Seth said.

"Not amazing," Hermo said. "This simple."

"Are you coming?" Seth asked.

"Not as servant," Hermo said.

"How about as a friend?" Seth suggested.

Hermo smiled. "Okay."

The door had no handle, but when Seth pressed, it swung inward.

"You first," Hermo said.

CHAPTER TWENTY-FIVE

Diviner

B eyond the door, Seth discovered a large room where a giant pivoted in a pit of sand, carefully making patterns with a hoe. The giant had red, barklike skin and a head like that of a rhinoceros without the horn. Seth gauged that he would come up to just below the waist of the creature.

The high ceiling held a skylight of stained glass, gently illuminated by moonlight. On one side of the room, a pond containing diverse fish and amphibians bordered the edge of the central sandpit. On the other side of the room, instruments were displayed in stands and cases, including kettle drums, cymbals, a xylophone, a harp, racks of chimes, a bassoon, a cello, a flute, a French horn, and a gong, all on a scale to match the giant. Worktables at the back of the room held oddments ranging from clocks to kaleidoscopes to dice of unusual size and shape.

"You found me swiftly," the giant said in a deep, calm voice. He did not look up from scoring the sand. "Please, come inside."

Seth, Reggie, and Hermo stepped into the room. Seth ventured to the edge of the sandpit. "Are you the Diviner?"

"We are all components of the same great whole," the giant said. "Some call me the Diviner. You may do so as well. If you are thirsty, use the pump."

Seth saw an old-fashioned water pump with a bucket beneath the spout. A drink sounded good, so he levered the handle up and down until water poured into the bucket, some splashing onto the marble floor. Claiming one of several tin cups near the pump, Seth took water from the bucket and tried a sip. It tasted slightly metallic.

"I haven't seen a giant like you," Seth said.

"There are seventeen tribes of giants represented here at Titan Valley," the Diviner said. "I am one of the Kurut Oi, commonly called the gentle giants." Setting his rake aside, the Diviner crouched and began plucking pebbles out of the sand.

"You can help us find things?" Seth asked.

The giant climbed out of the sandpit and loomed over Seth. "We shall see," he said, bending down and holding out a broad hand with ten pebbles in it. "Select a stone."

Seth picked out a round, smooth, tan pebble. The giant offered the remaining pebbles to Hermo.

"Me no need rock," Hermo said. "Me find things better than you."

"Anyone else?" the giant asked.

"Reggie?" Seth prompted. "Would you like to choose a stone?"

Should I? Reggie asked.

"Sure," Seth said.

The dirtman approached the Diviner. He leaned over the hand displaying the pebbles.

I can't pick, Reggie conveyed. *Master, which should I take?*

"He must choose for himself," the Diviner said.

I'm sorry, Reggie agonized. *Decisions are hard.*

"Indecision can be telling as well," the Diviner said.

"It's all right, Reggie," Seth said. "You don't have to choose." He looked at the Diviner. "You can hear him?"

"There are diverse ways to communicate," the Diviner said.

"I'll pick one," Calvin offered.

"Be my guest," the Diviner said, holding out the hand with nine pebbles.

Seth took Calvin from his pocket and placed him on the Diviner's palm. After inspecting the pebbles for a long moment, Calvin pointed out a flat one with square edges.

"Interesting selection," the Diviner said. "Follow me."

He led them over to one of the worktables, where he picked up a tuning fork and tapped it against his thumbnail. He held the vibrating fork beside Seth's left ear, the tone becoming rather loud at that proximity.

"What would you most like to find?" the Diviner asked.

"My memories," Seth said as the Diviner passed the tuning fork over his head in an arc to end up beside his right ear.

"That is correct," the Diviner said. "Good awareness. Hold out the little person."

Seth held out Calvin on his hand.

The Diviner tapped the tuning fork again and asked the same question.

"Serena," Calvin said.

The Diviner nodded. "And the truth behind the nipsie curse."

"Amazing," Calvin said. "Yes, those two things."

The Diviner tapped the tuning fork again and passed it over Reggie. "What do you most want to find?"

I already found it, Reggie expressed. *I know who I am.*

"But you're wrong," the Diviner said. "You wish to find your true identity."

I am Master's assistant, Reggie declared.

"For now, yes," the Diviner said. "But you are more."

The dirt figure turned to Seth. *Master, am I more?*

"I'm sure you are," Seth said.

"What about you, hermit troll?" the Diviner asked. "What do you most want to find?" He flicked the tuning fork and held it to the side of Hermo's head.

"No secret what me want," Hermo grumbled. "Perfect lairs. Secure. Private."

The Diviner swept the tuning fork over Hermo's head to the other side. "Interesting."

"No interesting," Hermo said, swatting the tuning fork away. "This game boring. Me wait outside." He turned and stalked from the room.

"He used to be most concerned with finding ideal lairs,"

the Diviner confided after Hermo left. "A shift recently occurred in him. Now he most wants a friend."

"You can hear that through the tuning fork?" Seth asked.

The Diviner set down the tuning fork. "I get a sense for the harmonies of the desires expressed, and I glimpse the dissonant yearnings beneath, conscious and unconscious. Truth is more available than most suppose, especially to those ready to perceive it."

"Are you trying to help us?" Seth asked.

"That depends on what you want," the Diviner said. "I find hidden things. I unmask truth. I have been loved for it, and I have been hated for it. Come."

The Diviner led them over to a gong. "Seth, stand before the gong. I recommend you cover your ears."

Seth complied. Even with his hands over his ears, he heard the splashy toll of the gong and felt an outpouring of vibrations.

The Diviner nodded, then played a flute in close proximity to Calvin and rang chimes beside Reggie. Seth watched with a mix of fascination and skepticism.

"Seth," the Diviner said, "you are a shadow charmer."

"Yes," Seth agreed.

"And you assume that the presence you named Reggie is one of the undead," the Diviner continued, "because you hear him."

"True," Seth said.

Am I undead? Reggie asked.

"That assumption is wrong," the Diviner said. "The presence you call Reggie is a collection of memories that were separated from a living being. That being is not dead; therefore the presence you call Reggie is a metaphysical fragment separated from a greater whole."

Seth's mouth was dry, and he felt slightly queasy. "From me?"

"No," the Diviner said. "Wouldn't that be convenient? The presence you call Reggie was separated from a living being who dwells in the coliseum here in Humburgh. The presence has extremely limited free will and longs to be made whole."

Master, Reggie inquired tentatively. *You lied to me?*

"I was helping you as best I knew how," Seth said.

I am not dirt?

"I needed to move you," Seth said. "You needed a shape."

I needed to know who I was, Reggie conveyed, sounding betrayed.

"I didn't have all the answers yet," Seth said. "I'll keep helping you."

The dirt body crumbled to the floor. *I am memories?*

"You were attacking anyone who came to that cottage," Seth said.

Nobody could hear me, Reggie expressed. *I didn't know where to go, who to be. It made me angry.*

"For disembodied memories, you are unusually powerful," the Diviner said. "Humbuggle keeps his disembodied memories in a certain location, and you escaped. You did not want to be held by him. But after winning your freedom, you gradually lost your sense of self and most of your ability to choose."

Who am I? Reggie asked.

"As an independent entity, you have no true name," the Diviner said. "*Reggie* serves for the present. You are an extensive lifetime of memories divided from a living being. With some minor tinkering on my part, you are now vibrating in such a way that, if taken to the coliseum, you could find and reunite with your true self."

I would like that, Reggie conveyed. *Master helped me?*

"Seth helped free you from a prison of your own making," the Diviner said. "He helped you make choices you could not make on your own."

I left the cottage, Reggie communicated. *I became dirt. I became his assistant. Master will still help me?*

"I'll help you find who you were taken from," Seth said. "I wish somebody would do the same for me."

"I will aid you," the Diviner said. "Seth, it might interest you to know that your memories also escaped the place where Humbuggle contains such things. You will need cooperation from Humbuggle to find them. There are many forces with an interest in you, Seth. Yours is a grand and complicated destiny. I cannot see your full path, but mending Reggie will help you as well."

"Can I help Seth too?" Calvin asked.

"You have and you will," the Diviner said. "Remember the old saying: 'Help thy brother's boat across, and lo, thine own has reached the shore.'"

"I like that," Calvin said.

"Much hinges on you breaking the nipsie curse, Calvin," the Diviner said. "Seth is not yet the champion of light that you need, but one day he could fill that role, if he so chooses."

"What should I do now?" Calvin asked.

"Serena is at Humbuggle's manor," the Diviner said. "Learn what she knows."

"She is?" Calvin exclaimed. "Really? For sure?"

"I'm sure," the Diviner said.

"Don't keep me in suspense," Calvin said. "How is she? What has she been doing?"

"Her story belongs to her," the Diviner said. "My role is to reveal your story to you. And I don't see all. If I feel the rail vibrating, I know a train is coming. With sensitive attention, perhaps I can discern the speed of the train, perhaps the size, but not the paint color or the favorite food of the engineer."

"Has Serena learned important things?" Calvin said.

"That much I can confirm," the Diviner said. "A breeze with a certain smell and a particular amount of moisture can reveal a coming storm. A raging storm is heading for Titan Valley, literally and figuratively. You cannot stop it. You can choose whether to work with it or against it. My suggestion? When the gales come, raise a windmill, not a dam."

"What does that mean exactly?" Seth asked.

"I can get no more specific," the Diviner said. "You have all the direction I can currently offer."

"Can we see you again?" Seth asked.

The Diviner stared off into the distance for a moment. "The way out of here is simple. Follow the blue carpet. If you should find me again, you will. If you should not, you will not. Let that supply what peace it can."

CHAPTER TWENTY-SIX

Asleep

Tess sat cross-legged on her bed, watching the light of dawn bleed into the sky. She knew if she crawled under her covers, she could probably fall back to sleep. But she felt eager for a new day, and she was enjoying the cool tranquility of the early hour.

Yesterday morning, a fairy had come to her window. Her name was Nina, and she had streamlined yellow wings, unusually sparkly. They had played for a time, and Nina had promised to return this morning, but Tess saw no sign of her.

Padding over to the window, Tess rested her arms on the sill and leaned out, conscious of the tremendous drop to the ground below. She saw no fairies.

Tess got dressed, then went out to the sitting area that separated her room from Knox's. She crossed to Knox's door and opened it just enough to see he was still sleeping beneath the covers. Closing the door and backing away, Tess retrieved the card she had made the previous evening and decided to seek out Emery, the beautiful servant who attended their group.

After unlocking the front door of their suite, Tess peeked into the hall. Emery stood talking with Raza. Tess felt strange remembering they both were dragons. Marat had looked nothing like a dragon in his human form, so she knew it was possible.

Emery waved at Tess, said something to Raza, and came her way. "Up early again?" Emery asked.

"I made you something," Tess said, trying not to feel shy.

"Let me see," Emery said, approaching and accepting the card.

Tess had drawn a picture of a dragon reading to a little girl. THANKS FOR THE STORIES was printed in all caps. Tess knew the art was imperfect, but she hoped the characters would be recognizable. "That's you and me."

Emery's eyes widened, and Tess thought that tears might have glimmered for a moment. "Is this why you asked for colored pencils yesterday?"

"I wanted to thank you," Tess said. "Would you tell me more stories?"

"I am here to serve you," Emery said with a little curtsy. Her long black hair was pinned back in a complex style Tess had never seen. "Would you care for breakfast?"

"Sure," Tess said. "Could I have eggs again?"

"Scrambled with cheese?" Emery asked. "Toast on the side?"

"Yum," Tess said, following Emery to the dining room shared by all the companions except Kendra.

"What would you like to hear about?" Emery asked as she tied on an apron.

"Yesterday you told me about the different giants," Tess said. "How the night giants and the hill giants protect the gentle giants. And how the sea giants almost went extinct. And how the sky giants used to live in a floating kingdom."

"Good memory," Emery said.

"What was it like being a dragon?" Tess asked.

Emery paused, an egg in her hand. "Dragons are a difficult topic for me. Too many painful memories."

"Sorry," Tess said. "It seemed interesting."

"It is very interesting," Emery said, cracking another egg into the pan.

"Why is this sanctuary called Titan Valley?" Tess asked. "Are there titans here?"

"There is one actual titan," Emery said. "The father of the Giant Queen."

"How big is he?" Tess asked.

"Much bigger than the Giant Queen," Emery said. "But he has slept for centuries."

"Where does he sleep?" Tess asked.

"In the Valley of the Sleeping Giants," Emery replied.

"Are there many sleeping giants?" Tess asked.

"It's hard to be sure," Emery said. "Some can be clearly identified. They are the servants of the titan."

"Are the servants big?" Tess asked.

"You tell me," Emery said, leading Tess to a window.

"See that ridge out there? Do you see how it kind of looks like an old man lying on his back? Hands on his chest? Feet poking up? See his face in profile? His nose and chin?"

"It does look like a man," Tess said.

"He is Pietro, one of the sleeping giants," Emery said.

"He looks bigger than the Giant Queen," Tess said.

"Don't say that too loudly," Emery cautioned. "But yes, he is. Most of the sleeping giants are larger than the queen."

"Is he made of dirt and rocks?" Tess asked. "He has trees and bushes on him!"

"The sleeping giants have slumbered so long that they are merging with the landscape," Emery said. "Some claim they are long dead and will never awaken. Others maintain the sleeping giants are merely dormant and may someday rise again."

"Where is the titan?" Tess asked.

"I've heard that the titan, Garocles, slumbers in a vast cavern at the far end of the Valley of the Sleeping Giants. He hibernates on a huge slab by the blue light of an eternal flame."

"Does he look like a giant?" Tess asked.

"An enormous giant in a white toga," Emery said. "The sky giants pattern their dress after him. He is technically the Dragon Slayer of Titan Valley, though none of us have ever seen him active."

"Can he wake up?" Tess asked.

"Only the Giant Queen knows."

"Can I go see him?"

Emery shook her head. "None are allowed in the Valley

of the Sleeping Giants, let alone into the titan's shrine. It is sacred ground for the giants."

"I bet it isn't sacred to dragons," Tess said.

"I would rather not speak for the dragons," Emery said. "As for myself, I think it is best to let sleeping giants lie."

"Probably smart," Tess agreed.

"Your eggs are ready," Emery said, using a spatula to slide fluffy scrambled eggs onto a plate beside two pieces of wheat toast.

"I'm not sure I can eat so much," Tess said.

"Eat what you can," Emery said. "Through the eyes of a giant, it is a miniscule portion, so any waste will seem small."

Knox sat at breakfast with the satyrs, munching a crisp piece of bacon, hot and crunchy, the way his dad made it. For some reason his mom and sister liked their bacon less done, a little chewier.

Newel took a long sip of apple juice and wiped his lips with his hairy forearm. "This is the life. I hope we're exiles forever."

"It really is the only way to travel," Doren said. "I've never had servants. Doesn't take long to grasp the appeal."

Knox forked a fragment of pancake and used it to mop up some of the excess syrup on his plate. "Doesn't it make you a little nervous that breakfast was made by something that could eat you for breakfast?"

Newel glanced toward the kitchen. "Emery? In her dragon state, I wouldn't want to come within a hundred miles of her."

"She knows our names," Doren observed. "And we sometimes get a little bossy."

"You were the one who wanted french fries in the middle of the night," Newel accused. "I was content with those left-over croissants."

Knox lowered his voice, eyes on Emery, who was washing dishes. "I have a feeling that if this preserve falls, we will have some really furious dragons on our hands," he said. Did a small, knowing smile bend Emery's lips? If so, it vanished as swiftly as it came.

"For now, we're just following instructions," Newel said. "Don't forget, they're serving us, but they're also spying for the Giant Queen."

"Doesn't hurt to be courteous," Doren murmured. He raised his voice. "Emery, these pancakes are a dream come true. And the bacon! I ate twice my normal helping."

"I'm glad you enjoyed the food," Emery said.

"Can I help with the dishes?" Doren asked, clearing his plate and utensils.

"Please, no," Emery said. "Allow me the privilege of doing my duty."

"Sorry I asked for those french fries the other night," Doren mentioned.

"Ask again," Emery said. "Make your wishes known, and I will endeavor to fulfill them."

"This is the life!" Newel mouthed.

Warren poked his head into the dining room. "Meeting at Kendra's. We're receiving assignments."

Knox wiped his mouth with a napkin. "I'm not getting left behind," he said.

Newel looked at him with a deadpan expression. "We have very different goals."

The three of them rose from the table and hurried down the hall. Knox found Tess, Vanessa, Tanu, Warren, and Kendra ready and waiting.

"The Fairy Realm has fallen," Kendra announced gravely.

"What?" Tess exclaimed with a gasp. "How?"

"We've gotten word the Fairy King let Ronodin in with a bunch of dragons," Kendra said. "The dark unicorn stole the crown from the Fairy Queen, so fairies are now under his command."

"What about satyrs?" Knox asked, glancing at Newel and Doren.

"I'm offended," Doren said, folding his arms.

"Ronodin is now technically our king," Newel said. "We've never paid much attention to those protocols. Maybe a little on holidays. He has no practical power over us, but the fairies are a different matter."

"The fairy explained that satyrs are more loosely bound to the crown," Kendra said.

"Can he mess up your fairykind status?" Tess asked.

"The fairy didn't think so," Kendra said. "Except I may not be able to give fairies orders anymore."

"This is horrible news," Newel said. "If we keep losing ground, what will be left?"

"We have to fight back," Kendra said. "Warren, Tanu, Vanessa, and I are going to the Dragon Temple to recover the Harp of Ages. It can put dragons to sleep."

"I'm going too," Knox said. "Final answer. I have spoken."

"We need you to lead a different mission," Kendra said.

"Lead?" Knox checked.

"You, Tess, and the satyrs must go to Humburgh and find Seth," Kendra said. "Knowing you guys are taking care of that problem will allow us to raid the Dragon Temple."

"How far away is Humburgh?" Knox asked.

"Too far to walk," Kendra said. "But we have friends in high places who will smuggle you there through the same passage the Giant Queen uses. It will take a matter of minutes."

"We know Seth is in Humburgh?" Newel asked.

"We suspect he is," Kendra said. "It is a large town, and this will be a challenging job. If you find him, he might not be happy to see you."

"I'll do it," Knox said. "I was worried you were going to give me busywork or something. Finding Seth is the main reason I came here. You can count on me."

"And as long as Knox takes full responsibility, we're in too," Newel said.

"I really want to see Seth again," Doren said. "Even if his memories are wiped."

"I'll go too," Tess said.

"Good," Vanessa said. "Your sensitivity to magic will be an asset there."

"There are other pressures to worry about," Tanu said. "The Perennial Storm will hit Titan Valley within a day or two."

"Are you kidding?" Doren exclaimed.

"I wish," Tanu said. "It's a magical storm of unfathomable power."

"I know," Doren said. "I remember cowering in a shelter during the Perennial Storm years ago. My uncle Igor disappeared in that storm."

"We have reason to fear Ronodin has plans against Titan Valley," Vanessa said. "He earned the Giant Queen's favor and was here not long ago."

"And we got news this morning that Polar Plains has fallen," Warren said. "The more dragon sanctuaries fall, the more Titan Valley becomes the main target."

"And the more dragons can join the fight," Tanu said.

"When do we put this plan into action?" Knox asked.

"Now," Kendra said. "Gather whatever you want to bring. Warren, Tanu, Vanessa, and I will see you off, and then we will depart as well. We're out of time."

"I was just beginning to worry today would be boring," Knox said.

CHAPTER TWENTY-SEVEN

Reunited

A steady breeze flowed from the west, sometimes gusting enough to make the flags and banners along the street flutter and snap, or even to blow off hats. Seth made his way down the avenue alongside Virgil, with the invisible presence of Reggie nearby.

"Are there magical barriers or sensors that could block Reggie from getting inside?" Seth asked.

"He is technically part of somebody who resides in the coliseum," Virgil said. "I don't see how anyone could protest his entrance. With him traveling formless, the hardest part for the guards might be detecting him in the first place."

"Worst-case scenario, I still have my pass from the rabbits," Seth said.

"I doubt you'll need it," Virgil replied.

"Are you sure you don't want to come inside today?" Seth checked.

"You'll be working behind the scenes," Virgil said. "I think my time would be better spent trying to get Calvin an audience with Sable."

"Excited, Calvin?" Seth asked.

"I don't have words to explain it," Calvin said. "Today could be the day I have dreamed of for years."

"I have a good feeling about it," Seth said.

The avenue delivered them to the plaza, where crowds were beginning to gather in the morning light. Seth felt jealous of a woman taking a bite of a baked apple dusted with cinnamon. Without warning, a hand clamped down on his shoulder from behind and whipped him around. The grip squeezed as Seth looked up at a dignified older man with steel gray hair and a close-cropped beard. He wore a chain-mail shirt and carried a broadsword.

"Celebrant," Seth said.

The hand on his shoulder tightened painfully, making Seth crouch a little and arch his back. "Do not utter my name," Celebrant demanded through lips that barely moved.

"Lighten up or I'll shout for help," Seth replied through gritted teeth.

The grip remained firm but stopped being painful.

"You're still after the stone," Seth surmised. "You were there in the castle after . . . I forgot myself."

"You also still hunt the same prize," Celebrant accused.

"I just want my memories back," Seth said. "Wait a

minute—back at Stormguard Castle, you mentioned somebody who lost an arm."

"Now two arms," Celebrant said.

"Her fault," Seth said. "She tried to kill me. She's a
dragon too?"

Celebrant nodded toward somebody, and a powerful
man with a ponytail of brown hair seized Seth by the upper
arm. Celebrant kept a hand clamped on his opposite shoulder, and together they marched Seth away from the plaza.

"Wait a minute," Virgil said, stepping in front of
Celebrant.

The Dragon King briskly shoved the satyr to the ground
and kept walking.

"Help!" Seth shouted, but before he could call out
again, the man with the ponytail covered his mouth. Seth
thrashed, but the men holding him were too strong.

Shall I intervene, Master? Reggie asked.

"Yes," Seth yelled as best he could into the palm over
his mouth, jerking his head in a nod.

The guy with the ponytail lost hold of Seth and sailed
through the air, landing in a tumble. Celebrant launched
sideways, bouncing and sliding over the cobbles of the plaza,
bowling over a young couple who had been holding hands.

"Stay on them," Seth called as people cleared away from
the supernatural fight.

"Get him, Kerzian," Celebrant ordered.

The man with the ponytail charged at Seth but seemed
to collide with an invisible wall. He barely had time to

register his surprise before he was hurled backward, his body skipping a long distance over the cobblestones.

Celebrant regained his feet and faced Seth, hand on the hilt of his sword. "You are making the wrong enemies, whelp," Celebrant threatened.

"So are you, grandpa," Seth replied.

As Celebrant started to draw his sword, his legs lurched sideways, and he slammed down violently, the metal of his sword and armor ringing against the timeworn stone.

"Prevent those two from following me," Seth instructed. "Then come find me."

Consider it done, Reggie replied.

Seth hurried swiftly toward the nearest of the arena entrances. Virgil came up beside him. "Sorry I was little help back there," the satyr apologized. "I'm not much of a fighter."

"It's all right," Seth said.

"It's almost too bad you can't keep Reggie in his present form," Virgil said. "He's quite powerful."

"He deserves to be restored to his body," Seth said.

"It's true," Virgil said. "I'm going to give you some space. I'll watch with Calvin until you're safely through the entrance."

Seth took his place at the end of the line, trying not to look over his shoulder too much. He half expected to see Celebrant or Kerzian shoving their way through the crowd, but neither of them materialized. Seth scanned the area with his shadow-charming senses and soon perceived Reggie drifting his way.

They gave up, Reggie communicated once he drew near.

"Stay vigilant," Seth murmured.

I am, Reggie assured him. *They are heading off in a whole different direction.*

"They may be back," Seth whispered.

I'll remain alert, Reggie promised.

Seth tried to relax as the line inched forward. He felt like he was doing a horrible job of hurrying away from danger. At least Reggie was keeping watch. Finally, Seth reached the front of the line, and a minotaur waved him through the entrance. If the guards noticed Reggie, they gave no sign.

"Still with me?" Seth whispered as he walked along the corridor to the arena.

I'm here, Reggie conveyed.

Seth went through the coral archway at the end of the corridor. The clear day felt warmer than in Humburgh, and the air was placid. Seth entered the coliseum and headed for the ramp down to the underground barracks.

I feel something, Reggie expressed excitedly. *Someone. A familiar energy.*

"Good," Seth said. "Let's follow that feeling."

This way, Reggie expressed.

Seth ignored the crowd and the enticing aromas wafting from food stands. The cheering of the fans faded into the background as he focused on perceiving and following Reggie. They soon reached a gate guarded by a minotaur with a black head and gray fur dappled with dark spots.

The minotaur barred his way with a poleax. "Where are you going?"

Want me to knock him flat? Reggie asked.

"Diplomacy," Seth whispered.

"What was that?" the minotaur asked.

"I'm visiting some of the gladiators," Seth said.

The minotaur snorted. "We know about you. Last time you poked around where you didn't belong. Stick to the common areas."

"That's my plan," Seth said.

The minotaur stepped aside. Staying focused on Reggie's unseen presence, Seth followed him down a long, gently curving ramp, then to the bottom of some grimy stairs. He traversed cramped halls and descended more stairs to an unfamiliar passageway lined with doors.

We're near, Reggie communicated.

"Lead on," Seth said.

Before long, Seth sensed Reggie stop in front of a certain door. *In here.*

Seth knocked. He was about to knock again when the door opened.

"Seth?" Fenrick asked. "This is a surprise. How did you find me?" He looked freshly bathed, a towel hanging around his neck, his damp hair newly combed.

"I'm surprised too," Seth said. "You need to hear the story behind it. Can I come in?"

"Only for a minute," Fenrick said, stepping back. "Two of my trainees face off in the arena shortly. I'm guaranteed a win and a loss today."

He feels familiar, Reggie enthused.

"He's part of you," Seth whispered. "You're part of him."

"What was that?" Fenrick asked, tossing his towel beside a laving basin and grabbing a pair of sandals.

"How would you like your memories back?" Seth asked.

"Sure, who wouldn't?" Fenrick replied. "I know you would."

"It's a risk," Seth said. "Some of it could be heavy."

Fenrick regarded him more seriously. "I would want to remember."

"What if I said I had found your memories and brought them here?"

I belong here? Reggie verified.

"I have to admit I wouldn't believe you," Fenrick said, strapping on his sandals. "Are they in your pocket?"

"I named your memories Reggie," Seth said. "They got lost without you. I think it will make sense once you're reunited."

"Are you serious?" Fenrick asked.

"Reggie, you wanted me to tell you who you are," Seth said. "You're not dirt. You're Fenrick. You're an important part of him."

Seth felt Reggie surge at Fenrick, who fell to his knees, waving his hands as if he were being attacked by bats. "What's happening?" Fenrick cried.

I . . . can't . . . become him, Reggie conveyed with frustration.

Seth could sense Reggie pressing against an unseen barrier. Apparently Fenrick could feel it as well.

"Stop pushing, Reggie," Seth said. "Fenrick, I think you have to invite your memories in."

"That force is my memories?" Fenrick asked. "What's your game? I felt under attack." He rose and retrieved a short sword, pointing it at Seth.

"Your memories exist separately from you right now," Seth explained. "Like a phantom. I found them on my way here. I'm helping you the way I wish somebody would help me."

"You really believe this?" Fenrick asked.

"It was confirmed by the Diviner," Seth said.

"I don't know who that is," Fenrick said. "But, all right, phantom, if you really are my memories, I invite you to return." He spread his arms wide.

Seth sensed Reggie dissolving into Fenrick.

Fenrick swayed, his sword clattering to the floor. He closed his eyes, fingers pressed against his temples, then dropped to one knee, head bowed. After a moment, he looked up at Seth.

"No," he whispered, eyes darting. "I don't believe it. All this time."

"What?" Seth asked.

Fenrick closed his eyes tightly, sweat beading on his brow. "Please . . . allow me a moment. This isn't happening. How could . . . ? Wait, of course." He laughed nervously. "No. No, no, no. I can hardly . . . it's like waking from a long sleep. From a coma. No, it's like nothing else. Master, I mean Seth, I need a moment."

Fenrick arose, then walked into a neighboring room, muttering to himself. Seth heard him pounding a mattress.

Seth waited, hoping Fenrick was okay.

"I can't believe it," Fenrick mumbled in astonishment, apparently to himself. "This is too much to absorb." Seth was pretty sure Fenrick started weeping.

Seth remained respectfully quiet.

After splashing water on his face, Fenrick returned to the room and paused, a new energy about him. He clutched a wooden stake in one hand. "*Fenrick* was a false name."

"Were you aware?" Seth asked.

"I had no idea," he said. "My name is Merek. And I have lived for a long time."

"You were in the Games?" Seth asked.

Merek grinned. "Not on the arena floor. Not ever. Any rumors of that sort were a sham. I came here like you did, Seth. I won one of Humbuggle's Games in the Necropolis of Antilla, long ago."

"You won the Wizenstone?" Seth asked.

"I broke a long-standing curse," Merek said. "I won a chance to learn the true Game. I came here to claim that opportunity."

"What is the true Game?" Seth asked.

"It's the surest way to the Wizenstone," Merek said. "I never found it. To obtain that knowledge, I had to unlock a door, and it cost me my memories. That loss sent me down an alternate path. The senior staff acted like I had elected out of active participation on the floor to become a trainer. Seth, I had no reason to believe otherwise. The more I learned about the Games, the better the story fit. I was Fenrick—a seasoned trainer who could not recall his past."

"But you remember your past now?" Seth asked.

Merek nodded thoughtfully. "I have lived my life in many stages and accomplished deeds you could scarcely imagine. My identity has gone out of focus on other occasions—part of the price of immortality."

"You're immortal?" Seth asked.

"Almost," Merek said. "My father was known as the Legender, and for centuries, I have served in times of need as one of the legendary Dragon Slayers."

CHAPTER TWENTY-EIGHT

True Game

Y ou kill dragons?" Seth asked.

"Do you know the story of the Legender?" Merek asked.

Seth shrugged. "Maybe I did once. I lost my memories."

"Five legendary Dragon Slayers helped win the dragon war," Merek said. "I am one of them."

"Doesn't every dragon sanctuary have a Dragon Slayer?" Seth asked.

"Anyone who has killed a dragon is a Dragon Slayer," Merek said. "Every sanctuary has a resident Dragon Slayer to assist in emergencies. Apart from all the rest, there are five legendary Dragon Slayers, so-called because that group includes the Legender and his four children. I hoped to win the Wizenstone to better protect the world, and to keep it out of evil hands."

"Just be careful picking it up," Seth said. "I saw two guys try, and they got vaporized."

"You've seen it?" Merek asked.

"My sister used magic to send it away," Seth said. "That choice broke the curse at Stormguard Castle."

"And now you're here," Merek said.

"Hunting for my memories," Seth said. "You've really slain dragons?"

Merek gave a little chuckle. "You have no idea. Unless . . . confession time—did you have any inkling about my true identity?"

"I still don't," Seth said. "I lost my memories by opening a door as well. Or so I'm told."

"At Stormguard Castle," Merek said. "Seth, among all of my memories, I also remember traveling with you as Reggie. I believe in your sincerity. Do you wish to join me in the quest for the Wizenstone?"

"If it might help me find my memories," Seth said.

"At the very least, it should lead us to Humbuggle," Merek said. "Wait here for a moment?"

"Sure."

Merek went into the other room. Seth picked up the short sword the Dragon Slayer had dropped and practiced swinging it. The weight felt good in his hand.

"Keep that, if you like," Merek said, returning to the room as he buckled a sword at his waist. The stake he had held was in a sheath on the other side of the belt. He had put on some leather armor. "Change of plans. I'm not watching fights today. Or ever again."

"You can just walk away?" Seth asked.

"I never intended to be a trainer here," Merek said. "I didn't vow to be a combatant in these games. I could have walked away at any time. I just never realized I could."

"Do all of those memories feel like an overload?" Seth asked.

"Yes!" Merek said. "It's simply too much to absorb. And such a spectrum, triumph and failure, joy and misery. The more recent recollections are freshest. Including you convincing me to make dirt my physical vehicle. I remember Hermo, Virgil, and Calvin. And the latest rounds of training here at the coliseum. Together with my long history, it all fused into one. I'll be trying to catch up to what I know as the days pass."

"Where are we going?" Seth asked.

"Back where I intended to go when I first arrived," Merek said. "To learn the most direct path to the Wizenstone. The secret Game, hidden among the others."

"I can come?" Seth asked.

"You have done me a great service," Merek said. "I mean to return the favor. You're welcome to join me, shadow charmer."

"Thanks, Merek."

"For now, call me Fenrick." He winked.

Seth followed Merek down halls and across common areas. They skirted the edge of a spacious room where gladiators skirmished with practice gear under the critical gazes of their trainers. Merek wore a stern expression, and nobody approached them.

Merek paused at the top of a stairway illuminated by an occasional white crystal. "I never descended these stairs because I did not believe I could. But now I remember experiences down there. I could have returned again at my leisure."

He started down, and Seth followed. "A guard warned me to stay in the common areas this time," Seth said.

"You have a right to come down here, or they would stop you," Merek said. "Shed all doubts. Our mission is ahead of us."

At the bottom of the stairs, the passage forward had an arched ceiling and was composed of small, ill-fitted stones, giving all surfaces but the floor a rough-hewn jaggedness. The air was chilly, and their footfalls seemed magnified. Seth engaged his senses but perceived no undead.

Merek stopped before a bare stretch of wall, hands on his hips. "I remember this place. Seth, this is not a real wall."

Seth reached out and touched the rough stone surface. He knocked his knuckles against the cool, solid barrier. "Feels real to me."

"This wall is there only if we believe it is there," Merek said.

"No way," Seth said.

"It is basically impossible for two people to pass it at once," Merek said. "If you think it is there, the wall will be present for me as well. If I believe it is there, it will block your way and mine."

"I'm trying not to believe in it," Seth said.

"So am I," Merek said.

"It's still there," Seth observed. "You've gotten past it before?"

"I did so alone," Merek said. "I pressed against the rocks, disbelieving them, until they yielded. I know of no other way."

"Should I leave?" Seth asked.

"Just retreat around the corner," Merek said. "Count to a hundred. When you look again, if I'm gone, I'll be waiting for you on the other side."

"All right," Seth said.

Seth walked several paces along the hall and went around the corner. He stood with his back to a wall and started counting. He kept the pace slow, whispering the numbers and resisting the urge to count by fives.

What would happen if he looked too early? What if Merek was partway through the wall, Seth wondered—could he think it into existence, trapping Merek or even killing him?

Seth took the nineties extra slow just in case. Then he listened, hearing nothing. A quick peek around the corner revealed an empty hall.

Seth walked to the supposedly fake wall and gave it a gentle kick. It seemed undeniably tangible.

Closing his eyes, Seth imagined the wall disappearing. Eyes still shut, he held out a hand, hoping to feel nothing. When his fingers came up against cool stone, he tried not to feel disappointed.

The wall wasn't there. He was putting it there himself. He had to really believe it.

Unless Merek had tricked him.

Seth opened his eyes. The hall extended a long way. While Seth was around the corner, Merek could have easily snuck away. And left him standing here like a sucker, trying to walk through an absolutely real wall.

Seth listened carefully. He heard no footfalls. But that was no proof—Merek could be walking quietly. Should he try to catch up to him? Was Merek's head start already too big?

Or had Merek told the truth? Should he stay here trying to push through a stone barrier?

Reaching out with both hands, Seth pressed against the wall. The texture felt perfectly real. Why would Merek lie? He had voluntarily invited Seth along.

Seth closed his eyes again and leaned into the effort, telling himself that the stone against his palms was imaginary. He found that as he relaxed and pushed less hard, the wall began to yield. Gradually, his hands began to sink into the stone, at first like it was clay. Then it began to feel less substantial, like putty, until it became almost like liquid.

As his hands sank deeper into what had previously behaved like solid rock, something clicked inside Seth, and he knew it was an illusion. No stone wall would soften into goo under pressure.

Suddenly the wall was gone. Seth walked forward into a broad hall. When he looked back, the wall was still gone.

"Seth," Merek called, poking his head around a corner.

"I stayed away in case my mind would interfere with your efforts."

"Was the wall gone when you looked back?" Seth asked.

"Yes, but it returned when you began to make your attempt," Merek said. "It's still gone now."

"How did you ever figure that out?" Seth asked.

"I had help from a friend," Merek said. "A master illusionist. He lost his life at the end of this hall."

"How?" Seth asked.

"I'll show you," Merek said.

They advanced until the passage ended at a circular room.

"How many doors do you see?" Merek asked.

Seth counted five doors along the curved wall. "Five."

"All of them lead to death," Merek said. "Make a circle with your thumb and forefinger."

Seth mimicked his okay sign.

"Peer through the circle," Merek suggested.

"What?" Seth exclaimed. "Now there are six doors."

"Do you see which one is visible only through the circle?" Merek asked.

Seth broke the circle, then formed it again. "Yep."

"That is the door we want," Merek said. "My illusionist friend died when we opened the wrong one. As the poison took hold, he experimented with several ways the right door might be hidden and figured out the trick. The door he found stole my memories."

Seth went to the door visible through the circle. "Then

our answers are behind this door. Will it take our memories again?"

"I'm not sure," Merek said. "Better let me try."

"I have fewer memories to lose," Seth said, quickly turning the doorknob and pushing the door open. He stepped into the room beyond, and Merek followed.

"Are you all right?" Merek asked.

"I'm still with you," Seth said.

A bell sat atop an ornate altar on the far side of the lavish room. Hangings made of beads decorated the walls, and fur rugs covered the ground. The altar glowed red, providing light.

They approached the altar.

"Ring the bell?" Seth asked.

"If we ring it, who knows what it might trigger?" Merek said, eyes roving the room.

"What did you do last time?" Seth asked.

"I found myself here, confused, and I wandered away," Merek said.

"Did you ring the bell?"

Merek glanced at the altar. "No."

Seth picked up the bell and gave it a shake.

With a flash of light and a puff of smoke, a dwarf appeared atop the altar. His forked beard was an auburn color, streaked with gray. He smiled and tossed glitter into the air.

"Congratulations!" he crowed. "You have passed the trials entitling you to learn the true Game!"

"Are you Humbuggle?" Merek asked.

The dwarf pressed his palm to his face. "Oh, no. You

wasted your only question. Back to the start for you! Always listen to the rules before speaking."

Merek stared at the dwarf in frustration.

"I'm teasing," the dwarf said. "Yes, I'm Humbuggle. And you are Merek. And Seth remembers me, if not much else."

"I lost many years here," Merek said.

"Everyone loses many years here!" Humbuggle said. "At least you are making progress. And you found a new friend. I love when my Games bring people together."

"I earned my way to this room before," Merek said.

"But you didn't know why you were here," Humbuggle said. "You wandered off without ringing the bell. We provided a good life for what remained of you."

"You'll tell us the true Game?" Seth asked.

"Yes," Humbuggle said. "Very few ever learn it. I could count them on one hand. If that hand had at least eighteen fingers. To learn it, you must swear to keep it a secret."

"I promise," Seth said.

"Me too," Merek added. "What is the true Game?"

Humbuggle pressed against one fist, cracking knuckles, then popped the knuckles of his other hand. After clearing his throat, he recited:

To master how my Game is played
Go find the Unforgiving Blade
Beg no gurus, ask no sages
Cut the strings of the Harp of Ages

"That's it?" Merek asked.

"I know, it's brief, and the meter is imperfect," Humbuggle said. "But you both paid heavily to come this far—I wanted to make the objective plain. English can be so ambiguous and cumbersome."

"We find the Unforgiving Blade and cut the strings of the Harp of Ages," Seth said.

"Can't get much by this kid," Humbuggle said, jerking a thumb at Seth. "Don't be too disappointed. Many tasks are easier said than done."

"The Harp of Ages is in the Dragon Temple here at Titan Valley," Merek said.

"I will neither confirm nor deny," Humbuggle said, hands behind his back.

"To destroy it would be a desecration," Merek said. "That Harp was pivotal in winning the dragon war."

"Could we restring it?" Seth asked.

"You don't understand," Merek said. "Wounds inflicted by the Unforgiving Blade can never be undone. What that blade cuts will never be repaired."

"You didn't expect me to give away the Wizenstone without sacrifices?" Humbuggle asked. "I better go. Being around clever heroes tends to make me blab. Thanks for making this entertaining."

With a flash and a puff of smoke, Humbuggle vanished.

CHAPTER TWENTY-NINE

Ptolemy

W e're traveling by dungeon?" Warren asked.

"It was made for transporting prisoners," Kendra said. "But Dectus thought we might prefer it to wicker when the storm hits."

Kendra, Warren, Vanessa, and Tanu stood before a human-sized wooden house with iron-reinforced doors and bars on the windows, meant to be carried by a giant. Not far off, Bernosh, a surly giant wearing huge, mismatched pieces of armor, sat sharpening a longsword that could probably cut most castles in half.

"I try not to voluntarily enter dungeons," Warren said. "Entering a prison is often easy. Getting out tends to be the problem."

"You don't think Dectus means to trap us?" Vanessa checked.

"Let's imagine Bernosh takes a nasty fall and breaks his neck," Warren said in a reasonable tone. "What happens to us?"

"We have the keys," Kendra said. "We unlock the front door and leave."

"If our giant takes a nasty fall, we'll be lucky to survive it," Tanu said. "Unless we use the right potion."

Bernosh stood and sheathed his sword. "Are we going or not?" He was built like a running back, with bulging arms and legs.

"We're going," Kendra said, unlocking the front door of the dungeon.

The four of them entered and sat on thinly cushioned benches with high backs. Armrests projected from the benches at intervals, and Kendra grabbed one tightly. Unlike in the wicker house, several sets of shackles were bolted to the walls. Bernosh smoothly swung the house onto his back and set off at a brisk pace.

"He doesn't waste time," Warren approved.

"It gave me a head rush," Tanu said, sliding his fingers through his thick hair.

"But it wasn't jerky," Vanessa said.

When Bernosh exited Terastios, he picked up the pace to a lively jog, making the portable dungeon sway and bob, shackles jangling. Seen through the barred windows, the landscape went by at a startling rate.

"Are we in *this* big of a hurry?" Warren asked.

"The faster we travel, the less ground we cover surrounded by lightning," Bernosh said in his rumbly voice.

"Great, he's listening," Warren said.

"I'm slow to judge," Bernosh said.

Though the speed was exhilarating, Kendra had to agree that the jostling was too much, especially with all the furniture made of wood and poorly cushioned. Kendra soon found that by rocking her body in harmony with the jouncing of the dungeon, she could reduce the impact of the motion.

"I'm going to need a chiropractor after this," Tanu said.

"You could use a gaseous potion," Vanessa suggested.

"Worse situations might lie ahead," Tanu replied. "I'd better save the potions."

Warren had unfolded a copy of the map. "Does this giant's name start with a *p?*"

"The *p* is silent," Tanu said. "Like in pterodactyl."

"English is ridiculous sometimes," Warren said. "Why have silent *p*s?"

"Only psychics know," Kendra said.

Bernosh ran for more than two hours before setting the portable dungeon down on a riverbank so he could pause and drink. Kendra had not seen much of the landscape going by because she had been too busy bracing herself during the choppy ride. She and the others stood and stretched now that they were at rest.

"Listen to the wind," Tanu said.

Now that he mentioned it, Kendra heard the wind whistling in the trees and felt it gusting through the dungeon. Going to a window, she saw that the sky still looked mostly clear.

"How far off is the storm?" Kendra called.

At the river's edge, Bernosh stood tall and gazed eastward. "Less than a day," he reported. "We may feel the front edge in a matter of hours."

"How far to Ptolemy?" Kendra asked.

"We're almost there," Bernosh said. "This was the last reliable place to get water before we reach his cave."

"Are you sure you want to go in alone?" Warren asked Kendra.

"Dectus thought negotiation was our best chance," Kendra said. "He suspected Ptolemy would be more likely to take pity on me than any of you. I'll bring a gaseous potion. If he tries to capture me, I'll drink it right away."

"Most ettins have two heads," Bernosh put in. "But Ptolemy has three."

"Dectus told us the middle one has control over the body," Kendra said. "The other two act like counselors."

"True enough," Bernosh said. "Not a terribly large giant, but plenty big next to any of you. Ready to go?"

"Sure," Kendra said.

She and the others returned to their seats barely before Bernosh hauled the dungeon onto his back. This time he walked instead of jogged, and Kendra could see the relief on Tanu's face.

They traversed heavily forested foothills, the dungeon windows just higher than the tallest treetops. Bernosh stepped over creeks and pressed through branches, leaving some damage to the forest in his wake. He stopped at the mouth of a narrow ravine and set the dungeon down beside a small stream.

"The way ahead becomes too narrow for me," Bernosh said. "Even if Ptolemy should come out, I can't assist in a scuffle against him. He is held in high regard by the ettins and several of the other lesser giants."

"We understand," Warren said. "Does an ettin have much of an appetite?"

Bernosh chuckled. "Does a wheel roll downhill? Ettins eat almost anything."

"Do they have favorite game or livestock in the area?" Warren asked.

"Bears," Bernosh said. "Sheep. You four, potentially. Anything alive they can catch."

"How are you at catching sheep?" Warren asked.

"It's no trouble," Bernosh said.

"We could use a live sheep," Warren said. "It might speed the mission along."

"I'll have a look," Bernosh said, lumbering off.

Tanu held out a gaseous potion to Kendra. "Don't hesitate to use this."

Kendra accepted it. "I won't. How would this wind affect me in a gaseous state?"

Tanu winced. "You could get blown far from us. If you go gaseous, try to stay in the ravine. It looks mostly sheltered from the breeze."

"I'll accompany her to the entrance," Vanessa said.

"Take my gummy potion," Tanu said. "Just in case."

Vanessa accepted it and joined Kendra on her way into the ravine. They walked along a little shelf of land between the wall of the ravine and the trickling stream. The ground was uneven, and loose rocks sometimes shifted underfoot, forcing Kendra to tread carefully.

"Have you ever seen an ettin before?" Kendra asked.

"I have had few dealings with giants," Vanessa said. "Do not expect the ettin to be as refined as the sky giants. Most giants are quite savage."

"Dectus thought Ptolemy would talk to me," Kendra said.

"I hope so," Vanessa responded. "Keep that potion ready."

After a couple of gentle turns in the path, a thin waterfall came into view at the end of the ravine, no broader than if Kendra extended both arms. Behind the waterfall gaped the mouth of a cave, at least four times Kendra's height. Animal bones littered the sides of the stream near the base of the falls, with a few poking out of the water.

"I could do without the bones," Kendra said.

"Let's not join the collection," Vanessa suggested.

Kendra paused toward the end of the ravine, at the side of the waterfall. There was room to get behind the waterfall without stepping into the stream, but not without passing through some chilly mist.

"I'll wait here," Vanessa said. "Turn on the charm. Play up your innocence."

"I'll do my best," Kendra said, ducking through the mist, stepping over slick rocks and damp bones. Not many steps behind the waterfall, the coolness of the cave made her wet skin colder.

The bare cave lacked features like stalactites or

stalagmites. It was just a big hole leading into the hillside. Kendra supposed it was dark, but her fairykind abilities allowed her to see just fine. Each step forward took her farther from the sound of the waterfall—and farther from her friends.

Before long, Kendra saw the flickering glow of firelight up ahead. The cave widened into a large cavern, and Kendra beheld several flaming cauldrons standing on tall, iron legs. By the firelight, Kendra beheld a brutish giant with exaggerated musculature. He wore a garment of shaggy fur and hairy boots fashioned from animal hides. He was nearly as broad as he was tall, with three heads perched above his beefy shoulders, the middle one larger than the other two. He was throwing hatchets at a wooden target with impressive accuracy.

After hurling his fifth hatchet, the giant plodded forward to retrieve them. One of the three heads turned and locked eyes with Kendra.

"We have company," the left head said, and the giant turned, the other two pairs of eyes quickly fixing on her.

"We do," the center head acknowledged.

Kendra was no taller than his hip. Compared to Bernosh, this giant's size was not overly impressive, but he easily looked large and savage enough to beat Kendra into paste. Mustering her courage, she tried to project that she was a visitor rather than prey.

"I'm Kendra Sorenson," she said with a curtsy. "I've come hoping you can help me."

"A delightful little mortal," the right head said.

"A delightful little morsel," the left head countered.

"Fairykind, if I am not mistaken," the right head said.

"We've never tasted fairykind before," the left head noted.

"You were not invited," the center head said, his voice rougher and his pronunciation more primitive than the other two heads. "I owe you nothing."

"I came because of an emergency," Kendra said. "Dectus hopes you can loan us the key to the Dragon Temple."

"She should not know you have the lightning key," the left head said. "Her knowledge endangers us."

"She must be telling the truth about Dectus," the right head reasoned. "Very few know the location of the key."

"Dectus has no authority over us," the center head said.

"It might be worth learning the conditions of the emergency," the right head maintained.

"Kendra, why do you seek the key?" the center head asked.

"A dragon war is coming to Titan Valley," Kendra said.

All three heads laughed.

"Dragons distress the small," the left head said.

"We bridle their power," the right head said.

"Let the dragons come," the center head boasted. "We giants will smash them."

"Most of the other sanctuaries have fallen," Kendra said. "This isn't just a few dragons. We are talking about a dragon army, led by Celebrant. He is aided by Ronodin, who recently took over the Fairy Realm. Dectus thinks it would be wise to retrieve the Harp of Ages to help in the fight."

"More likely she wants the Harp to help her people," the left head said.

"We have heard tales of other sanctuaries falling," the right head said.

"With or without the Harp, the dragons will perish," the center head said.

Kendra dropped to her knees. "Please, mighty Ptolemy. I need your help. Let me try to retrieve the Harp of Ages."

"She's so young and sincere," the right head said. "And Dectus backs her. I say lend the girl the key."

"She is small and weak!" the left head argued. "She has no chance of retrieving the Harp. She will lose the key!"

Kendra rose to her feet. "I am a dragon tamer. I bested the dragons at the Wyrmroost Dragon Temple. We defeated the hydra and Glommus, and I killed Siletta."

"Grand claims," the center head said.

"Let's help the girl!" the right head said.

"We should eat the girl!" the left head said.

"I don't taste good," Kendra assured them.

"She is slight," the right head said. "Scant meat to be had."

"Humans have a wonderful crunch, bones and all," the left head said.

Ptolemy pulled two hatchets from the target, one for each hand. "The hatchets will decide," the center head said. "Dodge all five and you can borrow the key."

He surprised Kendra by tossing the first one underhand. She lurched to the side, and it scythed by close enough that she felt the breeze. Kendra unstopped the bottle and guzzled the effervescent liquid.

The next hatchet was thrown overhand and slashed

Kendra in half. It was strange for Kendra to feel her vaporous body separate and then merge back together.

The center head yelled angrily.

"Witchcraft!" the left head accused. "Treachery!"

Kendra tried to explain that she was simply trying to play smart, but her gaseous vocal cords could not produce sound. With an effort of will, Kendra drifted slightly closer to Ptolemy.

The ettin angrily claimed another hatchet and hurled it twice as hard. Kendra felt the weapon swish through her, temporarily dispersing her body with a sensation like millions of tiny fizzing bubbles. Again, her gaseous body fused back together as the hatchet clattered behind her.

"She cheated us!" the left head cried.

"She is using good strategy," the right head approved. "She has potential to retrieve the Harp of Ages."

Ptolemy collected the final two hatchets. He raised one to throw it.

"No!" the left head shouted. "She is like a cloud of gas! We cannot hit her right now. You may as well try to wound the smoke of a campfire. Wait. We did not say how quickly we must throw the axes. Wait for her to solidify so you have a fair target."

"Go reach under your mattress and fetch the key," the right head said, giving Kendra a significant look. "We should let her attempt her errand."

"She mocks us," the left head said. "Do not allow a young girl to defeat us. We would be laughingstocks. She will no longer act so smug after we devour her."

"I will wait," the center head said, hefting the hatchets. "Two more throws with a fair chance."

Kendra willed herself back toward the entrance to the cave, and she drifted in that direction.

"She flees," the left head said. "I declare a forfeit."

"She may return," the right head said.

"Return and die," the center head called. "I will not miss."

Kendra glided onward. She needed a new strategy. If she waited near Ptolemy until her body solidified, she had no doubt that she would die.

Floating through the mist beside the waterfall caused a bizarre sensation, her entire body tingling as water particles invasively mingled with her gaseousness. Vanessa approached with concern, and Kendra started pantomiming.

"He threw rocks at you?" Vanessa guessed. "Wait. Axes? And you drank the potion?"

Kendra signaled that she had it right. Then she played more charades.

"A key?" Vanessa interpreted. "Under something? You're sleeping? On a bed? I see. Ptolemy keeps the lightning key under his bed?"

Kendra tapped her nose and gave a thumbs-up.

"I need to hurry to the others," Vanessa said. "Follow me if you like, but stay in the shelter of the ravine so you don't blow away."

Vanessa took off at a sprint over the rough terrain beside the creek. Kendra was surprised that she dared run so fast over the unfavorable ground, but the narcoblix remained surefooted until she passed out of sight. Kendra decided to wait rather than float after her, mostly because she knew Tanu and Warren would head to the cave now that negotiations had failed.

Kendra hovered within view of the waterfall for a long time, idly wondering if Ptolemy might come after her. The ettin did not emerge from his cave, and Kendra tried to relax and enjoy the bubbly calmness of floating without a solid body.

After what seemed a long time, Warren appeared, leading a sheep. They had apparently used chains from the portable dungeon to devise a crude leash. Tanu and Vanessa came along behind.

Warren waved as he approached Kendra. "Good job getting the location of the key," he said cheerfully.

Kendra scowled, flexed her vaporous muscles, and pointed at the cave.

"I figured the ettin would be tough," Warren said. He lowered his voice. "We're going to trick him, not fight him."

Warren led the sheep to the edge of the waterfall; then Tanu crouched and fed the sheep a potion. Kendra saw no difference in the animal. Holding a small flask in his hand, Warren led the sheep behind the waterfall.

Tanu and Vanessa retreated to Kendra, each holding a potion ready. Tanu scrutinized Kendra for a moment. "Stay low," he advised. "You won't be gaseous much longer."

Kendra pointed at the cave and cocked her head curiously.

Tanu sidled close and whispered. "I gave the sheep a

sleeping potion. It's very potent, but I tinkered with the recipe so hopefully the sheep will remain conscious until the ettin eats it. I tuned the mixture for the ettin's chemistry. Let's hope Ptolemy will soon be in dreamland."

Kendra pantomimed throwing hatchets.

"Warren has the gummy potion," Vanessa said. "It will make him virtually indestructible."

Kendra nodded. Her body started to feel extra fizzy, and she coalesced into a solid again. Vanessa and Tanu supported her until the dizzy spell passed.

Tanu handed her a bottle. "Here is another one in case you need it. If Ptolemy shows himself, don't hesitate."

"All right," Kendra said, watching the cave, worried for Warren.

"How deep is the cave?" Vanessa whispered.

"I didn't have to go very far to find the ettin," Kendra said. "He's super buff. Huge muscles. One of his heads is nice, one is a jerk, and the middle one seems to be listening more to the jerk."

"Well, I have an enlargement potion ready in case it turns into a fight out here," Tanu said.

Vanessa glanced at him. "Does your shirt stretch?"

"The solution is tuned to treat my clothes like part of me," Tanu said. "Similar to fur or a hide."

About half an hour later, Warren emerged from the mist, carrying an iron pole with a complex symbol at the end. He took wobbly steps, legs bending in ways that made Kendra wince.

"Is Ptolemy neutralized?" Tanu called.

"He took the bait," Warren said, speech slurred, head bobbing oddly on his rubbery neck. "Sleeping like a baby. Wait, I've known too many babies. Sleeping like an old guy after a long day."

Clutching the lightning key with two hands, trying to keep it steady with unstable arms, Warren handed it to Vanessa. Then he held out a hand to Kendra. She shook it and felt the rubbery fingers compress beneath her grip.

"Gross," she said, reflexively releasing him.

"Doesn't hurt," Warren said as clearly as he could. "The gummy potion worked great. Ptolemy hit me with hatchets, punched me, pulled me, stomped on me. It didn't hurt. My body stretched around sharp edges without tearing and squished flat under heavy blows."

"Perfect," Tanu said.

"How long will Mr. Three Heads be out?" Warren asked.

"He ate the entire sheep?" Tanu asked.

"Spat out a few bones," Warren said.

"He'll be unconscious for a day or two," Tanu said.

Warren nodded floppily. "It'll give that cave some much-needed silence. That guy wouldn't shut up. Three heads are definitely worse than one. Should we head back to our dungeon?"

Tanu looked at Kendra. "Next stop, Dragon Temple."

"I'll catch up," Vanessa said. "With an ettin asleep so nearby, it would be a waste not to have a quick bite."

"He looked kind of germy," Warren said.

"I'll be careful," Vanessa promised, licking her lips.

CHAPTER THIRTY

Mission Accomplished

There's Seth!" Knox exclaimed. "I call it! I found him!"

"You're not serious," Newel said.

"That sure looks like him!" Doren cried, pointing. "See? Over there, by the swordsman. Is that a satyr with them?"

"We found him!" Tess enthused.

Knox ran through the crowd of the Arena Plaza to reach his cousin. The wind gusted, and a goblin chasing a bandanna almost collided with him.

Knox, Tess, Newel, and Doren had been carried to Humburgh through the Giant Queen's passage by Rustafet. The giant shuttled them across Big Side to the Small Town entrance, with directions to the Arena Plaza. They had rooms reserved at a place called the Wayside Inn that Knox had not yet seen. Knox had been looking for Seth at the Arena Plaza for about five minutes.

"Seth!" Knox called as he drew near to his cousin. "We found you."

Seth turned and regarded him skeptically. "Do I know you?"

"You don't remember me?" Knox asked.

"I'm sorry," Seth said. He stood by a tough-looking guy with his hand casually on the hilt of a sword and a satyr wearing a yellow shirt under a tweed vest.

"It's me, Knox. Your favorite cousin!"

"You're my cousin?" Seth asked.

"The ob-Knox-ious one? From Texas? With the smelly Knox socks? I sometimes make fun of your Seth breath! You have to remember."

"You'd be surprised how clean my memory was wiped," Seth replied.

Tess and the satyrs caught up.

"Do you recognize me?" Tess asked. "Your cousin?"

"I'm afraid not," Seth said.

"I'll give you multiple choice for my name: Tess. Jules. McKinley. Or Laura."

"I don't know," Seth said. "Jules?"

"No, but I always wanted that name!" Tess said. "Good guess. Try again."

"Tess?"

"Good job," Tess said. "Maybe your subconscious knows."

"You seem nice," Seth said.

"What about us?" Newel asked. "Do any memories stir?"

"A hint is you introduced us to fast food," Doren said.

"Sorry, guys," Seth said. "I only know about fast food—I have no memories of eating it."

"We have a huge favor to repay," Doren said solemnly. "Where do we start? Taco Bell?"

"We're Newel and Doren," Newel said. "We've been looking for our best friend."

"You have many who care about you," the swordsman said.

"Who is this guy?" Newel asked.

"Looks like he can handle himself in a brawl," Doren assessed.

"This is Fenrick," Seth said.

"Who's the new satyr?" Doren asked contemptuously.

"I'm Virgil," the satyr said, holding out a hand to shake.

Newel clasped his hand. "Nice to meet the flavor of the moment."

Doren glared. "Have fun while it lasts."

"Fly high," Newel said. "Try not to think about the crash."

"Look, guys," Seth interrupted. "I'm sure you mean well. We're on important business."

"Are you going to trash another sanctuary?" Knox asked.

Newel and Doren winced.

Seth looked uncomfortable. "I probably deserve that. I'm not trying to hurt anybody. I just want my memories back. You probably want that for me too!"

"We're here to help you," Knox said.

"Meet your reinforcements," Newel said.

"You don't have to be lost anymore," Tess added.

Seth glanced at Fenrick and Virgil, then back to Knox. "Can we talk later?" Seth asked. "I have an urgent appointment."

"We crossed oceans to find you," Knox said. "We almost got killed a bunch of times. And I took out a powerful demon."

"We have rooms at the Wayside Inn," Doren said. "We can feed you. And your new sidekicks."

"Are you with Kendra?" Seth asked.

"Not at the moment," Knox said. "But she was with us. She sent us to look for you while she tries to save the world."

"How?" Seth asked. "What's the problem? What's she doing?"

Knox glanced at Newel and Doren. The satyrs theatrically looked away, as if they had become interested in anything besides the current conversation.

"You don't want to tell me," Seth said. "I get it. You know I lost my memory, and after all I've done, you don't know if you can trust me."

"We really are here to help you," Knox said.

"Help me how?" Seth asked. "Take me in? Lock me up? Keep me from doing more damage?"

"Nothing underhanded," Newel said.

"We'll find your memories," Tess said.

"Doing that will be complicated," Seth said. "I'm in the middle of the process, and making progress. Right now, extra people might capsize the boat."

"Harsh," Newel said.

"The new Seth is falling in the polls," Doren added.

"It's not personal," Seth said. "I'm going someplace where unexpected tagalongs could hurt my chances. Virgil set up an important meeting."

"Who would let a satyr organize a meeting?" Newel said with a huff.

"Have you ever been to a party, Virgil?" Doren asked. "Ever watched an action movie? Or binged on donuts?"

"Virgil has been a big help," Calvin called. "We're closing in on important mysteries."

"Calvin!" Tess exclaimed. "You really were with Seth!"

"I'm fine," Calvin said. "We really do have a meeting."

"You can vouch for us," Tess said.

"They really are your cousins," Calvin said. "The satyrs are longtime friends."

"Good old Calvin," Newel said.

"He tells it like it is," Doren affirmed.

"Seth, don't you have some news for Kendra?" Calvin asked.

Seth frowned. "Can you tell Kendra that Celebrant is here?"

"At Titan Valley?" Knox asked.

"In Humburgh," Seth said.

"Is he pulling wagons?" Knox asked.

"I wish," Seth said. "He's in human form, still hunting the Wizenstone."

"How do you know?" Newel asked.

"I saw him," Seth said. "He tried to kidnap me, but Fenrick stopped him."

"Thanks for saving him," Tess said.

"Seth has aided me more than I can repay," Fenrick said. "You have a noble friend and cousin."

"You haven't seen him pick his nose," Knox said.

"Whatever," Seth said.

"Seth is on the right path, guys," Calvin said. "You can count on him."

"Then maybe he should know," Newel said. "Kendra has gone after the key to the Dragon Temple. She hopes to retrieve the Harp of Ages to help in the dragon war."

"Thanks for telling me," Seth said, glancing at the swordsman.

"What should we do about Celebrant?" Tess asked.

"Spread the word," Seth said.

"Did you hear about the Fairy Realm?" Newel asked.

"No," Seth said.

"It fell," Doren said. "Ronodin is the new Fairy King."

Seth blanched. "You're not serious."

"The Fairy Queen is overthrown?" Virgil asked.

"We got word from a fairy who escaped," Newel said.

"That is disastrous news," Seth said. "Ronodin is dangerous."

"We know," Knox said. "Didn't you work for him?"

"Kind of," Seth said. "He kidnapped me and was tricking me. He got me indebted to the Underking. I didn't know who I was. I got away once I could."

"It must have been rough," Newel said.

"That's life," Seth said. "Thanks for the news. How

about I catch up with you guys at the Wayside Inn after this meeting? Maybe we can help each other."

"Sounds fair," Newel said.

"You aren't going to ditch us?" Knox asked.

"Not without good reason," Seth said. "Thanks for trying to help me."

"Sure," Knox said.

Seth gave a wave and turned.

Knox watched his cousin walk away.

"Should we follow him?" Doren asked.

"I will," Newel offered. "At a distance. Doren, take the kids to the inn and I'll meet you there."

Newel slipped into the crowd, not directly following Seth and his new friends. The satyr worked his way at a diagonal, keeping them in view.

"Think Newel might ditch us too?" Knox asked.

"If there's good food involved?" Doren replied. "Absolutely."

CHAPTER THIRTY-ONE

Serena

"Those satyrs seemed jealous," Virgil said as they advanced through the crowd. "And Knox is a little much."

"Calvin, are you sure they weren't dragons in disguise?" Seth asked.

"I would have sensed it," Merek said.

"I don't think any powerful creature would assume the form of a satyr," Virgil said. "We're considered frivolous."

"You're levelheaded," Seth pointed out.

"I'm about as serious as satyrs get," Virgil said. "And I spend my life studying games."

"How far to the Chime House?" Calvin asked.

"Just a few blocks down this street," Virgil said, the rising wind causing him to tuck his head and raise an arm against it.

Virgil had surprised Seth by meeting him as he and Merek emerged from the arena. The satyr explained that he and Calvin had visited the manor and made contact with an associate of Humbuggle's called Sable. After speaking to Virgil for a few minutes, she had decided they should meet in private at the Chime House, where their conversation could not be overheard. Sable had promised to bring Serena. Since the appointment was not until one in the afternoon, Virgil had decided to see if Seth would emerge in time to join them.

Seth took Calvin from his pocket and cupped him in his palm as they walked. "Can you believe you're about to see Serena?" Seth asked.

"I can't express how excited I am," Calvin said. "Have you ever wanted something so desperately, for such a long time, that it began to feel like an impossible quest without an end? Where you knew you might never succeed, but the prize was so worthwhile that you devoted your whole existence to the journey, even if it might all prove fruitless? That's how I feel. I've wanted to see Serena so badly for so long that it's hard to accept it will finally happen."

"I'm happy for you," Seth said.

"Don't jinx it," Calvin said, wringing his hands. "Let's be happy afterwards."

"Do you hear it?" Virgil asked.

"I hear about a thousand monkeys pounding xylophones," Seth said. "And maybe a hundred of them blowing flutes."

"It gets annoying when the wind rises," Virgil said. "The

Chime House is much quieter inside than outside. I don't know how the neighbors tolerate it."

Merek leaned close to Seth. "See the man on the other side of the street—the one with the black beard?"

Seth glanced in the indicated direction. "Short guy? Chubby?"

"Dragon," Merek said.

"Really?" Seth asked. "Him?"

"Don't make eye contact," Merek said.

"They can't kill us here in town," Seth said.

"Nor can we slay them," Merek said. "I can't believe I threw Celebrant to the ground. Well, my incorporeal memories did. I've long dreamed of testing myself against him."

"You may get your wish," Seth said. "Based on what I understand from working with Ronodin, the dragon war is getting ugly."

The Chime House came into view up the street. The four-story structure was built out of dark wood and featured three rapidly turning windmills. Wind chimes lined the eaves, windowsills, balconies, and porches, rippling vigorously in the wind with an incessant tinkling that seemed to jangle across every possible pitch. Other decorations hooted and shrilled as the wind passed through them, adding to the cacophony.

A pot-bellied ogre with a sloping brow, huge nose, and dangling earlobes stood in front of the wooden stairs leading up to the Chime House porch, leaning on a metal cudgel. Virgil walked right up to the ogre and held up a folded card.

Virgil spoke words that Seth could not hear over the

clangorous chimes. The ogre checked the card, then jerked his chin toward the porch. Virgil, Seth, and Merek climbed the stairs to the front door, and Virgil rapped the knocker.

A troll with yellow markings on his black scales opened the door. He had a fin down the center of his head that continued along his neck and back. The troll admitted them and closed the door, reducing the noisy chimes to a tuneless rustle.

"Do you have an appointment?" the troll asked.

"We're meeting Sable in the Serenity Parlor," Virgil said, showing his card to the troll.

"Excellent," the troll said after a brief inspection of the card. "Sable is among our most valued clients. Put away your invitation and follow me."

They climbed two sets of abnormally creaky stairs. Discreet signs along the way shared messages like "Stay Where You Belong" and "No Admittance without a Guide." At the top of the stairs, they turned down a hallway where every step sounded like a tap on a bongo drum.

"Hard to sneak around in here," Seth said.

"You have no idea," the troll said in a snide tone. He stopped in front of a wooden sliding door. "The Serenity Parlor lies beyond. One of our finest spaces." He indicated a rope that disappeared into a hole in the ceiling. "When the time comes to depart, pull this cord and wait for a guide. Should you attempt to navigate these halls unescorted, you will be promptly mauled by whisper hounds."

"Understood," Virgil said.

The troll gestured at the door and backed away. "Your encounter awaits."

Virgil slid the door aside. The floor of the room beyond was lower than the hall and immersed in a thin layer of water that ran from beneath the left-hand wall across the room to disappear under the wall on the right. The blades of one of the windmills zoomed by outside the lone window. A long table awaited in the middle of the room, with a man and a woman seated on the far side. There were two empty chairs on the near side, plus additional chairs at the head and the foot. A candelabra with three candles burned in the center of the table.

The woman stood. She had short brown hair, parted stylishly on one side, and wore a fashionable red dress with a dark blazer over it. "Welcome. Call me Sable. This is my associate, Basil."

Basil was a lean man with angular features, dressed in a dark suit. His black hair was slicked back, and he sported a little tuft of whiskers on the tip of his chin.

"Wet room," Seth said.

"You may want to remove your shoes," Sable said. "You can place them in the bin just inside the door. Virgil, I believe you told me to expect one companion in addition to Calvin."

Seth and Merek crouched and started removing their shoes.

"He made a new friend," Virgil said. "I hope you don't mind."

"Calvin?" Sable asked. "Do you vouch for him?"

"You bet I do," Calvin said.

"Any friend of Calvin's," Sable said.

As Seth waded into the room, lukewarm water sloshed against his bare feet. He placed his shoes in the bin on top of black dress shoes and a pair of high heels. Merek added his boots as well.

Seth and Virgil crossed to the table and sat down. Merek moved the chair from the head of the table so he could sit beside Seth.

"This is one of the most secure places in all of Humburgh," Sable said. "I am true to my employer, but that doesn't mean I want him to hear every word I speak."

"Not even Humbuggle can hear us here?" Seth asked.

"Nor can he enter the room without being detected," Sable said. "The running water prevents him from appearing in disguise or entering invisibly."

"Is he often in disguise?" Seth asked.

Sable laughed. "Oh, you're charming! Dear boy, Humbuggle is always prowling about in disguise. Are you new to town?"

"I've been here a couple of days," Seth said.

"On your first day you undoubtedly met him," Sable said. "He pays pointed attention to newcomers. Most who visit Humburgh encounter him several times unawares."

Seth looked left and right. "He isn't any of us."

"At least not right now," Sable said.

"Is she here?" Calvin asked.

"Serena wanted to see you before showing herself," Sable said.

Seth set Calvin on the table. "Serena?" Calvin called. "It's me. I've come a long way to find you."

"I told you to wait for me," came a voice from the breast pocket of Sable's jacket.

"Serena?" Calvin exclaimed.

A pretty little face peeked up from Sable's pocket. She had honey-blonde hair and animated blue eyes. "Of course it's me."

Calvin grinned from ear to ear, placed both hands over his chest, then flung his arms wide. "Finally!"

"You promised to stay with the others until I finished the assignment," Serena said. "What I'm doing takes time, and it's extremely dangerous."

"Serena, I was waiting, and would have kept waiting, except I found the champion," Calvin said.

"You did?" Serena asked.

"Seth," Calvin said, presenting him with both arms.

"He killed Graulas?" Serena asked doubtfully.

"With Vasilis," Calvin said. "And he promised to help break the curse. But he lost his memories. He's still helping, though."

"I've met Virgil and Calvin," Sable said. "We still lack some introductions."

"I'm Seth Sorenson. And this is Fenrick."

One of the candles in the candelabra went out, a thin ribbon of smoke curling up from the charred wick. Sable glanced at it. "Whoops. Who is he really?"

"What did the candle tell you?" Seth asked.

"They protect us all from lies," Sable said, using one of

the other candles to relight the candle that had gone out. "Giants are so skillful at truth magic."

"I'm Merek. But I went by Fenrick until recently."

Sable gasped, then narrowed her eyes. "Are you who I think you are?"

"I have a famous father," Merek said. "Tell me what you do for Humbuggle."

"I am the head housekeeper," Sable said. "Basil is one of his drivers."

"What is your real name?" Merek asked.

"I'm called Sable," she replied.

"I didn't ask what people call you," Merek said. "I asked for your name."

Sable scrunched her lips to the side and scowled. "I am Isadore."

"A sorceress," Merek said.

"I dabble," Isadore said.

"What was your name when you were a dragon?" Merek asked.

"Ishaya," Isadore said, some heat in the word.

Merek gave a nod. "And what about you, Basil?"

"My name is Basil," he said.

"In your human form," Merek stated.

Basil gave a nod. "You have killed many of our kind. I am Basirus."

"I take no pleasure in slaying dragons," Merek said.

Two of the candles snuffed out.

Merek gave a guilty chuckle. "All right. It can be

satisfying to dispatch the worst ones. But I don't harm dragons unless it becomes necessary."

Isadore relit the two extinguished candles with her fingertip.

"What about the satyr?" Serena asked.

"I'm just a scholar of the Games," Virgil said.

"A satyr and a scholar?" Serena exclaimed. "And the
candles stayed lit?"

"This company is full of surprises," Isadore said.

"Do you want to slay me, butcher?" Basirus asked.

"Should I?" Merek replied.

"Let's keep this friendly," Isadore said. "We're ruining
the moment for our nipsie lovers."

"I'm doing fine," Serena said.

"Maybe a hug?" Calvin asked.

"Why not?" Serena said. Isadore set her on the table,
and she ran to Calvin, picked him up in her embrace, and
spun him around. After she set Calvin down, Seth could see
that they were exactly the same height.

Calvin smiled uncontrollably. "You never let me pick
you up."

"I was excited to see you!" Serena replied.

"I can't believe it's you," Calvin said.

"I know what you mean," Serena said. "I never imagined
I would see you here."

"How have you been?" Calvin asked.

"Working really hard," Serena said. "And I can't get dis-
tracted right now. So much is in motion. You brought me

the champion. I'm indebted for that. But this is no place for nipsies."

"Serena," Calvin said. "The elders made me a giant, too. I have the same assignment as you. The same responsibility."

"Calvin, this is deadlier work than you know," Serena said. "I don't want you in the kind of danger I've seen. I set out to do this for you and for all our people."

"I came for our people too," Calvin said. "And for you. I'm Seth's sworn vassal. Wherever he goes, I go."

Serena looked up at Seth. "And where are you going?"

Seth found all eyes on him. "Well, I'm on a quest."

"We need to find the Unforgiving Blade," Merek said. "It's one of Humbuggle's challenges."

Isadore glanced at the candles and found them all burning. "I've never heard of that challenge. To what end?"

"I assume to cut something," Merek said.

The candles still burned.

"Do you know where to find it?" Isadore asked.

"No idea," Merek said, glancing at Seth.

"Could you help us?" Seth asked.

"Possibly," Isadore said.

"Tell me a lie," Seth said.

"Excuse me?" Isadore asked.

"I want to make sure the candles work for you as well," Seth said.

"I like Dragon Slayers," Isadore said.

All three candles went out.

"Ouch," Calvin said. "That was cold."

Isadore reignited the flames with her fingertip.

"I take it you're on the Small Council?" Merek asked.

"I was until recently," Isadore said. "The Small Council came out in open support of the dragons in the war. That was too much for me."

Seth noted the candles still burning.

"What have you learned about the curse?" Serena asked. "Besides finding the champion?"

"Isn't finding the champion the main part?" Calvin asked. "*'The curse arose from the demon's blight; the lord who slays him will set it right. The slayer shall restore our pride, the Giant Hero at his side.'*"

"I'm the Giant Hero," Serena said.

"I'm one too now," Calvin said. "We hadn't heard from you in a long time. The elders were worried you might have perished."

"You can assure them I am well," Serena said. "What exactly are you and the champion supposed to do?"

"Set it right," Calvin said.

"Set what right?" Serena pressed.

"Undo the curse," Calvin said vaguely.

"Who placed the curse?" Serena asked.

"Graulas," Calvin said.

"Okay, but who was he working with?" Serena said. "Who handled the details?"

"Do you know?" Calvin asked.

"Humbuggle," Serena said.

Calvin's jaw dropped. "No."

"Isn't that why you're here?" Serena cried.

"Well, mostly," Calvin said.

Two of the candles went out.

"You didn't know," Serena accused.

Isadore relit the extinguished candles.

"We're learning as we go," Calvin said. "You had a head start."

"None of you has much time left," Merek said. "The dragon war is coming to Titan Valley. Celebrant is here."

Isadore's eyes widened. "No." She glanced at the candles, still burning. "Are you sure?"

"Yes," Seth said. "And Ronodin has taken over the Fairy Realm. The dark unicorn will almost surely help Celebrant take down this sanctuary."

Isadore glanced at Basirus. "This disturbs our plans."

"It's a problem," Basirus said.

Isadore looked at Merek. "Why do you need the Unforgiving Blade?"

"We can't tell you," Merek said.

The candles kept burning.

"You literally can't?" Isadore asked. "You're not allowed?"

"We're not allowed," Seth said.

Isadore gasped and covered her mouth. "The blade is important. You're close to winning."

"We're close," Merek said.

She glanced at the candles, still burning.

"Very well," Isadore said. "Let's all share what we can."

CHAPTER THIRTY-TWO

Curse

M erek gripped the edge of the table, stroking the smooth finish with his thumbs. "Before we all start comparing notes, I need to know what your side of the table is after."

"What do you think?" Isadore asked. "We want the Wizenstone." She looked at Basirus. "Same as everyone who works for Humbuggle."

"Everyone who comes to mind," Basirus said.

"And same as everyone who enters the Games," Isadore added.

"What would you do if you obtained the Wizenstone?" Merek asked.

Her eyes flicked to the candles. "What would anyone do? Advance their own interests in one way or another."

"I would do the same as I have done for centuries," Merek said. "I would try to protect the world."

All three candles stayed lit.

"Does that include protecting dragons?" Basirus asked.

"Mostly," Merek said.

One candle went out.

"I would not seek to exterminate any kind of creature, whether demon or dragon or the undead," Merek said.

The two remaining candles kept burning. Isadore relit the other.

"I want to lift the curse on the nipsies," Calvin piped in.

"Do you understand what the curse involves?" Serena asked.

Calvin hesitated. "I'm learning."

"We're talking about ancient history," Isadore said. "Before I was hatched. Before preserves were established. Before the dragon war. Graulas was young. Humbuggle was young. The world was new."

"So much of knowing how to proceed involves doing the research," Serena said. "Learning the history. Understanding the context."

"We've learned a way to win the Games," Seth said.

"And what would you do with the Wizenstone?" Isadore asked. "Do you believe you could wield it?"

"Those I saw try to take it were instantly destroyed," Seth said.

Isadore seemed surprised when she checked the candles. "You have actually seen it?"

"At Stormguard Castle," Seth said. "Right after I lost my memories. I met Humbuggle there too."

"Let me guess," Isadore said. "A contestant sent the Wizenstone away."

"Yes," Seth said. "It was my sister."

"Humbuggle likes to create situations in which the lesser evil becomes banishing the stone," Isadore said. "If no competitor can figure out how to claim or wield the Wizenstone, and if the Game is sufficiently unpleasant, and especially if there is the risk of an adversary gaining the stone, it can feel like a win simply to send the stone out of reach."

"Meaning Humbuggle tends to win even if you complete his Game," Serena said. "He retains control of the Wizenstone and invents new competitions."

"I wonder what might have happened if Kendra had sent Humbuggle away instead of the stone," Seth said.

"Now you're thinking down promising avenues," Isadore said.

"I hear the wisdom," Merek said. "Instead of trying to claim and wield the stone directly, perhaps we should ponder how to replace Humbuggle as the custodian."

"Thoughts worth considering," Isadore said.

Basirus gestured at Merek. "We can't allow this butcher to gain power over the stone."

"Is it best to leave the Wizenstone with Humbuggle?" Calvin asked. "At least he isn't using it to destroy the world. With Humbuggle, it's all about the Games. Could he be a safer custodian than most?"

"Holding the Games might be what allows Humbuggle

to retain control," Serena said. "If he tried to fully claim the stone for his own, it could destroy him as it has destroyed others."

"If someone replaced Humbuggle, they might have to fill his post," Merek said. "Preside over their own Games."

"Or carry out some comparable trickery to keep full ownership in question," Isadore said.

"This is all speculative," Basirus said. "Nobody has these answers."

"Would a candle go out if you were wrong?" Seth asked.

"The candles measure whether you believe you are telling the truth," Isadore said. "Not whether your assumptions are correct."

"This discussion is only productive if you have real knowledge to share," Merek said.

"I feel the same way," Isadore said. "This needs to be productive for us, or else why should we surrender hard-earned information?"

"We can't reveal some of what we know," Seth said.

Merek looked at Seth. "We may have to obtain what they learned from another source. They discovered it somewhere."

Isadore smirked. "Be my guest. It took long years of inquiry, none of it easy."

"I have a proposal," Serena said. "What if, in return for information, Calvin and his friends pledge to take me with them?"

Isadore gave a slow nod. "I would consent to that." She glanced at Basirus.

"So much is in motion," Basirus said. "We must act soon or risk starting over."

Calvin looked up at Seth and Merek. "This is a good deal! We want Serena with us anyhow!"

Merek grimaced. "She comes with strings attached to wizards and dragons."

"Just me," Isadore said. "And one dragon. Basirus is my brother. We operate independently from other wizards and dragons."

The candles stayed lit.

"Answer two questions, and we might have a deal," Merek said. "Do you want the dragons to wipe out humanity?"

"No," Isadore said.

Basirus shook his head.

The candles continued to burn.

"Do you want Celebrant to gain the Wizenstone?" Merek asked.

"Absolutely not," Basirus said.

"By no means," Isadore said.

The candles burned steadily.

Merek glanced at Seth. "I think I can live with that."

Seth gave a nod. "Serena can join us if your information is good."

"Long ago, Stratos and the sky giants floated high above the ground," Isadore said. "They were the original overlords, rulers of the sky. By what power did their realm remain in the upper reaches?"

"The sky giants were once mighty in sorcery," Merek said. "Much more so than now."

"By what power?" Isadore repeated.

"I'm stumped," Merek confessed, looking to Seth.

"I don't even remember my favorite food," Seth said.

"The Ethergem," Serena supplied.

"A stone of astronomical power," Isadore said.

"More powerful than the Wizenstone?" Seth asked.

"Definitely," Isadore said. "Powerful enough to keep an entire civilization of giants afloat among clouds, with enough surplus energy for them to perform wonders with magic we can scarcely imagine."

"Do the giants still have it?" Seth asked.

"Why do you suppose Stratos fell to the earth?" Isadore asked. "Why do the sky giants now walk among us on the ground? Why do they no longer grow as tall as in their most glorious era?"

"Was the Ethergem lost?" Seth asked.

"I will tell you presently," Isadore said. "Another question. We currently have five great monarchs with five crowns. How many were there originally?"

"Two," Merek said.

"Which two?" Isadore asked.

"The Fairy Queen and the Underking," Merek said. "Yin and yang. Light and dark. Birth and death. Creation and decay."

"Correct," Isadore said. "The giants had the Ethergem, but they looked upon the crowns of the monarchs with envy. The dragons looked upon the crowns with lust. And the demons looked upon the crowns with hate."

"Let me guess," Seth said. "They all ended up with crowns."

"At great cost," Isadore said. "Do the crown of light worn by the Fairy Queen and the crown of darkness worn by the Underking belong to this mortal world?"

"Probably not?" Seth guessed.

"Good instincts," Isadore commended. "They came to this world from immortal realms. Drawing on power from their native realms, the Underking unnaturally prevents death and the Fairy Queen unnaturally prolongs life."

"This is true," Merek said. "Though I have seldom heard it named so plainly."

"Mortals inhabit this world temporarily," Isadore said. "They pass through en route to the realms of death and darkness or to the realms of life and light. The conduit between this world and the immortal realms of death and darkness is called the Void. And the conduit between this world and the realms of light and life is called the Source."

"I have heard of the Source," Merek said, "though the way to it is lost."

"Neither the Void nor the Source can be destroyed," Isadore said. "But they can be difficult to find. They can change location. They can change shape. And they can be walled off. The crown of the Underking derives power from the Void, just as the crown of the Fairy Queen receives power from the Source. Creatures of magic exist in this world thanks mainly to the Void and the Source. The

Ethergem came from the Source in the earliest times. It was a gift to the giants that enabled them to dwell apart from the rest of the world, and it was given with the promise that they would not alter or repurpose it in any way."

"Something went wrong," Seth said. "What happened?"

"In short?" Isadore asked. "Graulas and Humbuggle happened. Together they inflamed the envy of the giants by suggesting the Ethergem could be crafted into a crown for a monarch who would surpass the Fairy Queen and the Underking. Graulas increased the lust of the dragons by telling them the Ethergem could be worked into a crown for a monarch to overpower all others. And Humbuggle aroused the hate of the demons by describing a crown made from the Ethergem that would allow an unrivaled monarch to arise."

"How could they keep all of those promises?" Calvin asked.

"I puzzled this story together from fragments," Isadore said. "But crowns were indeed promised by Graulas and Humbuggle to the parties I named, with great penalties attached if they failed to deliver. The giants were convinced that dragon fire would be necessary to forge their crown, and that only Humbuggle could craft it. The dragons were convinced that they had to give up the sole ingot of their strongest alloy to produce their crown. The alloy had a name only in dragon speech, but in our tongue we might call it mother-of-adamant. And the demons were convinced to surrender Raglamar, the sword of their leader, a gift from the Void."

"Then Humbuggle got the Fair Folk involved," Serena said. "Remember, their sworn role was to maintain balance in the magical world. Humbuggle convinced the Fair Folk to intervene against the giants, who were allegedly plotting to create a crown out of the Ethergem, which would let them descend to earth as an unstoppable race of unimaginable power."

"I learned that many of the Fair Folk broke their vow of neutrality and went to war," Merek said. "I never learned why. The remaining Fair Folk refuse to speak of it, and I was dormant at the time. I wish I could have prevented the foolishness."

"It would have been hard to prevent," Isadore said. "The Fair Folk managed to confirm with magic that the sky giants meant to forge a crown, and such an act would have granted them unassailable power. Though some of the Fair Folk held to their neutrality, a large portion decided that breaking their vows of impartiality was necessary for the survival of the world."

"Enter the nipsies," Serena said. "Graulas convinced the nipsies that stealing the Ethergem was the only way to save the world. He promised them honor and glory if they successfully delivered the Ethergem to the leaders of the Fair Folk. At the time, the nipsies were the size Calvin and I are now. Because the Ethergem was so precious and powerful, if the nipsies failed to deliver the gem, a curse would make them even smaller."

"The stage was set," Isadore said. "The demons Graulas and Humbuggle managed to pit the greatest crownless powers against one another. Humbuggle flew to Stratos upon a dragon named Abraxas."

"The first dragon," Merek said. "My father later slew him."

"Abraxas was supposed to provide heat to forge the crown," Isadore said. "And Humbuggle was supposed to craft it. Naturally, the giants made Abraxas and Humbuggle vow not to steal the Ethergem."

"But nobody expected the nipsies," Serena said.

"The nipsies were so small that the giants failed to detect them," Isadore said. "To the sky giants, the nipsies were like specks of dust. They were smuggled into Stratos aboard Abraxas, and while Humbuggle and the dragon pretended to work, the nipsies swiped the Ethergem."

"How did the nipsies get out of the sky?" Seth asked.

"Working together, the nipsies carried the Ethergem to the edge of Stratos," Isadore said. "They jumped off and were met by Graulas, riding Velrog."

"First of the demonic dragons," Merek said. "Sire to demon princes of dragons like Gazarog and Navarog."

"The same," Isadore said.

"What happened to Stratos without the Ethergem?" Seth asked.

"The sky kingdom began to fall," Isadore said. "Not straight down. The floating landmass coasted to a crash landing. There was an island here before the sky giants plummeted to the earth. Stratos made the island larger. Also, a significant portion of Stratos sank beneath the waves. Humbuggle and Abraxas fled after the crash."

"What about Graulas?" Calvin asked.

"Velrog carried Graulas, the nipsies, and the Ethergem to the demon mother of witches, Nagi Luna, who used dark magic and the blade of Raglamar to shatter the Ethergem."

"They destroyed it?" Seth asked.

"The Ethergem proved too powerful to destroy," Isadore said. "Besides, Graulas and Humbuggle had promises to keep. Breaking the Ethergem fractured Raglamar and injured Nagi Luna. It also brought about the curse on the nipsies, who could no longer deliver the Ethergem to the Fair Folk."

"No fair," Calvin complained.

"But binding," Serena said.

"Humbuggle rejoined Graulas and they set about keeping their promises," Isadore continued. "The Ethergem had shattered into five pieces—one large, three medium-sized, and a single small shard. Abraxas and Velrog helped the demons shape the mother-of-adamant into three crowns, one for each of the medium stones. Those became the crowns for the giants, the dragons, and the demons. Nagi Luna delivered the crown to the demons. Abraxas delivered the crown to the dragons. Velrog delivered the crown to the giants, along with the small fragment that became known as the Ethershard."

"Was that to replace the Ethergem?" Calvin asked. "So Humbuggle could claim he didn't steal it?"

"I believe so," Isadore said. "The salient point is, Graulas and Humbuggle had fulfilled their obligations while betraying all who trusted them."

"What about the Fair Folk?" Seth asked.

"After all that happened, they realized they had been tricked into an unjust war," Serena said. "The Fair Folk had been trusted to keep the balance for the magical world based on the promise that they would never fight an unjust war. Graulas and Humbuggle invoked the curse attached to that promise, and many kingdoms of the Fair Folk were lost."

"Where did they go?" Calvin asked.

"Nobody knows," Serena said. "They vanished. Most assume they were destroyed, but some suspect they were imprisoned."

Isadore folded her hands on the table. "All of that suffering and destruction so that Graulas and Humbuggle could get what they wanted."

"The largest piece of the Ethergem," Merek said.

"Otherwise known as . . ." Isadore prompted.

"The Wizenstone," Seth finished.

"Graulas was an extremely powerful demon," Isadore said. "He attempted to wield the Wizenstone, and he succeeded for a time. He used its connection to the Source to seal off the Source from the mortal world. The effort almost killed him. He never returned to his full strength after that."

"The Source is cut off?" Seth asked.

"Power still flows from it," Isadore said. "But not like before. None in this world can visit the Source anymore. The effort also limited the power of the Void, because it always stays in balance with the Source."

"That would weaken the Fairy Queen and the Underking," Seth said.

"Considerably," Isadore agreed. "After Humbuggle realized that the Wizenstone could not be wielded directly, he became the custodian of it and developed the Games. The Giant Queen hates him passionately, but she let him bring the Games here in hopes the sky giants could win the stone back."

"I saw the Wizenstone," Seth said. "It looked complete—not like a piece of something else."

"The Wizenstone and the stones in the crowns were worked into fair shapes," Isadore said. "They are magical in nature and therefore shapeable by magic. Only the Ethershard looks like a broken piece."

"I always wondered where those three crowns originated," Merek said.

"Would finding the Wizenstone heal the nipsie curse?" Calvin asked.

"I don't think so," Serena said. "Our people were supposed to deliver the Ethergem to the Fair Folk to prevent the sky war. Instead we stole it from the giants in an unjust war, and the Ethergem was shattered. I think our best hope for removing the curse is to gain forgiveness from the giants."

"You think that would be enough?" Calvin asked.

"I hope so," Serena said. "I'm not sure what more could be done."

"Could the giants wield the Wizenstone?" Seth asked.

"I doubt whether anyone could properly wield it," Isadore said. "The giants never commanded the Ethergem. It was meant as the power source of Stratos. It kept their realm aloft, and they could siphon power from it to work their magic. But no one giant was allowed to claim the Ethergem as his or her own."

"Unwieldy or not, the Wizenstone is loaded with more power than was ever meant for this world," Merek said.

Isadore nodded. "Many crave a chance to channel that power."

"Do you want that chance?" Seth asked.

"Others simply wish to keep that power out of danger-ous hands," Isadore said.

Calvin slumped to his knees, head bowed. His shoulders shook with sobs.

Serena crossed to him and laid a hand on the back of his neck. "Calvin, what's wrong?"

"Our quest is hopeless," he managed, the words sad and halting. "After all this time, all these years of hoping and searching, we never had a chance."

"Calvin, we still have the prophecy," Serena said kindly. "You are here, and so is the champion."

"You don't want me here," Calvin said.

"I want you safe," Serena said. "But the elders sent you, making your claim to the quest as good as mine. With the champion found, who knows what is possible? What use is a prophecy if success comes without struggle?"

Calvin looked up, tears in his eyes, hope returning to his voice. "I suppose the prophecy is meant to keep us going even when the way seems impossible."

"And your champion is making progress," Serena said.

"He needs to know the location of the Unforgiving Blade. And that is a secret we have uncovered."

"We found the resting place of the Unforgiving Blade as part of our general studies," Isadore said. "We didn't know it would be relevant to the Games. The blade was fashioned from a fragment of Raglamar."

"The sword that shattered the Ethergem," Seth said.

"That weapon emerged from the Void brimming with dark power," Isadore said. "Enough to shatter a gem overloaded with energy from the Source. The Unforgiving Blade was wrought by dark sorcerers with help from the Underking, and it became a powerful talisman of darkness. It was hidden away for the protection of all in the Reliquary of the Wandering Stones."

"That's here in Titan Valley!" Merek exclaimed.

"Not nearby," Isadore said. "Over in the southeastern steppes. Barren wilderness. You'll never make it there before the Perennial Storm hits."

"What if we need to make it there before the storm arrives?" Merek asked. He glanced at Basirus. "Could a dragon do it?"

Basirus laughed mirthlessly. "You are presumptuous beyond belief! I know how many dragons you and your kin have slain. What would stop me from flying as high as I could and dropping you onto the sharpest rocks I can find?"

"Have you any idea how many times I've died?" Merek asked. "My question was whether a dragon could make it to the reliquary before the storm."

"The storm is coming from the west," Basirus said with a

sneer. "Conditions are already hazardous for flight, but with the wind at my back, I could make it to the Reliquary of the Wandering Stones ahead of the big show."

"Would you take us?" Seth asked. "Serena, too?"

Basirus looked at his sister. "I'm not sure I've ever been asked to do anything more distasteful."

Isadore leveled her gaze at Merek. "This is essential to the Games? You have limited time?"

"Something like that," Merek said.

Isadore and Basirus shared a look; then Isadore glanced back at Merek. "I would have to join you as well."

Scratching his neck, Merek gave a pensive nod. "Can we have a moment of privacy? I need to consult with Seth and Calvin."

Isadore shrugged. "We can step outside." She picked up Serena and stood. Basirus rose as well.

"Do you promise not to eavesdrop?" Seth asked.

Isadore glanced at the candles. "Yes."

She and Basirus went to the door, footsteps splashing.

"Want me to exit too?" Virgil asked.

"You can stay," Merek said.

"How does water keep flowing through this room?" Seth asked.

"Pumps powered by the windmills is my guess," Merek said.

"Good thinking," Isadore said from the doorway. "Ogres power it if the winds are low. We're short on time. Try to hurry." She slid the door closed.

Merek lowered his voice. "The Harp of Ages is located

in the Titan Valley Dragon Temple. The temple can be accessed only during the Perennial Storm."

"We know where to find everything we need to win the Games," Seth said.

"Neither relic will be easy to obtain," Merek said. "Time is against us. But from what I gather, the hardest part may be actually claiming the Wizenstone."

"I think we have to let the dragon take us," Seth said. "Otherwise the timing won't work."

"Me too," Calvin said. "Though I have to confess, I'm confused by Serena's choice of partners."

"She has learned a lot," Merek said. "Sometimes the goal justifies the means."

"They might try to steal the Unforgiving Blade," Seth said.

"They will betray us," Merek said. "The questions will be how and when."

"You've really died many times?" Seth asked.

"It allows me to take risks," Merek said. "Like an Eternal, I never die unless I'm killed. And if I'm killed . . . I don't stay dead."

"Like the undead?" Seth asked.

"Think opposite," Merek said. "The undying."

"The undying are real?" Calvin exclaimed. "I thought they were legendary!"

"Right on both counts," Merek said. "I'm not immortal, but I'm as close as mortals can get. A lot of magic would have to be undone for me to die. Seth, you are more vulnerable than I am. But I cannot wield a blade wrought from darkness. This won't work without you."

"I'm determined to meet Humbuggle and get my memories back," Seth said. "I'm not going to get a better chance than this. It would be a bigger risk to miss the opportunity."

"Agreed," Merek said, crossing to the door and opening it.

"That didn't take long," Isadore said, returning to the room. "Have you decided?"

"We need to reach the reliquary before the storm," Merek said. "You can join us."

"Very well," Isadore said. "The winds are rising. We'll have to depart almost immediately. Meet outside of Humburgh in two hours. Exit through the gates and go to the far side of the nearest hill. You'll know the one."

"We'll be there," Seth said. He looked at Virgil. "I'll need some of my stuff from your house. And can you deliver a message to my cousin at the inn?"

Virgil saluted. "This is the greatest windfall of information about the Games I have ever encountered. I'm yours to command . . . as long as I don't have to come with you."

CHAPTER THIRTY-THREE

Cloudburst

"Not again!" Bernosh bellowed.

Warren looked at Kendra nervously. "Another bridge?" he called.

"This is the third ruined crossing!" the giant complained. "It was made of stone! One of the strongest in the whole sanctuary!"

Kendra, Warren, Vanessa, and Tanu sat together inside the portable dungeon. Bernosh had been climbing rough terrain, so the going was slower, and the enormous backpack jounced less sharply. They had learned that Bernosh could hear their words without difficulty.

"It's deliberate," Tanu said. "This is a concerted effort. They're sabotaging bridges."

"Who would dare?" Bernosh fumed.

"We told you," Kendra said. "The dragons are plotting

against you. This is more proof. They don't want anyone getting near the Harp of Ages."

"In all my days, I have never endured such an insult," Bernosh seethed. "I will get you to the Dragon Temple if I have to scale every cliff at Titan Valley."

"It may come to that if the bridges are down," Warren murmured.

A violent gust of wind tore through the portable dungeon. For a moment, Bernosh had to brace himself.

"Rain will be here soon," Bernosh said.

"I don't love wet cliffs," Warren said.

"Wet or dry, rain or shine, I can climb anything," Bernosh said.

"Please let him be right," Warren muttered.

"The sky to the west is getting murky," Tanu said, peering out a window.

Kendra saw inky, black clouds spreading on the horizon. Pulses of lightning brightened pockets of the tenebrous mass, highlighting otherwise unseen textures of the thunderheads.

"This is not yet the onset," Vanessa said. "We have to get to the Dragon Temple before the storm hits or we may not get there at all."

"We'll make it," Bernosh grumbled, starting down the side of the cliff. The portable dungeon lurched and rocked with his movements. "The terrain is challenging, but the distance is not great."

As they descended, the deep canyon provided shelter from the rising wind. At the bottom, Bernosh waded along a rushing river, the water above his knees in the deep places. During several stretches, unruly water flooded the canyon from wall to wall, endlessly tumbling in churning rapids and spraying up to the giant's waist. Kendra wondered how much more the river would rise with the oncoming storm.

"There you are!" a high, male voice called from the barred window.

Kendra turned to see a male fairy in his young teens sliding through the bars to drop onto the dungeon floor. His shaggy silver hair complemented his metallic wings. She recognized the impishly handsome face, though he seldom appeared in this form.

"Raxtus?" Kendra asked.

"Please, no photos," Raxtus said. "I hate this form. But I figured the giant would freak out if I approached as a dragon. Plus, I could fit through the bars."

"Good strategy," Tanu said. "Bernosh is not happy right now. Somebody has taken out their backcountry bridges."

"Dragons," Raxtus said. "I've seen several since arriving at Titan Valley. Dragons that don't belong here."

"They're probably slipping in as visitors to the Games," Vanessa said. "Using their human avatars."

"Whatever they're doing, it is large scale," Raxtus said. "They're taking up positions. It all feels coordinated."

"Would they attack during the storm?" Kendra asked.

"Not unless they're suicidal," Raxtus said. "The high winds would destroy them. I'm about as aerodynamic as dragons get, and I was already struggling with the choppy air. You guys were hard to find. If Kendra didn't shine so brightly, I might not have reached you."

"How did you know where to find me?" Kendra asked.

"The Fairy King sent me," Raxtus said.

"Where is he?" Kendra asked. "Is he all right?"

Raxtus flitted over to stand on the arm of the bench beside Kendra. "Still alive, last I saw him, but devastated," the fairy said.

"I heard he gave Ronodin access to the Fairy Realm," Kendra said.

"That fits," Raxtus replied. "He didn't fully confide in me, but he went on about how he tried to warn the queen, and how it was all his fault. He seemed heartbroken and incoherent. He escaped the Fairy Realm with me at the last possible moment, after sending messages with some astrids and fairies."

"One of his fairies brought me a message," Kendra said. "I didn't know he made it out."

"The Fairy King had me drop him off elsewhere at Titan Valley," Raxtus said.

"He's here?" Kendra asked hopefully.

"Since his stay inside Zzyzx, he has been a shadow of his former self," Raxtus said. "Now he is a shadow of a shadow. He looked grim when he sent me away to find you. I worry he came here to die. Or maybe as a form of exile."

"Where did you leave him?" Kendra asked.

"A lonely plateau in the middle of nowhere," Raxtus said. "The kind of place you end up after being lost for days, heading in the wrong direction. No settlements nearby. As

I flew away, the only life forms I saw were a few nomadic giants."

"Does Ronodin have any power over you?" Kendra asked.

"No," Raxtus said. "I'm an adopted son of the Fairy Realm. The crown has no actual claim on me. But by the time we left, I saw several fairies taking a turn for the worse. They were darkening, Kendra. Some resisted better than others."

"Sounds like the shadow plague," Kendra said.

"Watch yourself around fairies," Raxtus warned.

"Good tip," Kendra said.

Bernosh abandoned the river and started climbing a cliff. Raxtus looked around uncertainly as the portable dungeon shifted and rocked in new ways.

Raxtus held up a hand beside his mouth and whispered, "How good a climber is this guy?"

"He seems skillful," Vanessa said. "And he is all confidence."

"Let's hope his abilities match his muscles," Raxtus said. "No fair when a guy is a giant *and* a weight lifter."

"Do I hear a new voice?" Bernosh asked.

"I'm a friend of theirs," Raxtus called. "A wimpy little fairy."

"All is well?" Bernosh asked.

"He is welcome," Kendra said.

"I will have you to the Dragon Temple in a matter of minutes," Bernosh asserted.

Raxtus put a hand by his mouth and whispered again.

"The noise of the river must have been masking our conversation."

As Bernosh reached the top of the canyon wall, the wind blowing through the dungeon windows became a nuisance. Thunder growled ominously as the armada of dark clouds overtook the sky. The dungeon rocked as Bernosh advanced.

"I've been worried about you," Kendra said. "When you left me, dragons were chasing you."

"After I set you down, evading the other dragons was no problem," Raxtus said. "It's hard for them to chase a dragon who flies faster, maneuvers better, and can become nearly invisible."

"Where have you been?" Kendra asked.

"Mostly hiding out in the Fairy Realm, after Wyrmroost fell," Raxtus said. "Sorry I couldn't help more."

"You saved my life," Kendra said. "I'm sorry for what it cost you."

Raxtus shook his head. "Saving you freed me. It helped me finally grow up. Working with my dad, I had what I always wanted, but I wasn't happy. Not even close. You helped me embrace who I really am. I never would have been happy any other way."

"But the dragons are hunting you now," Kendra said.

"Which should tell you all you need to know about my father," Raxtus said. "It's his way or nothing."

"That's tough," Kendra sympathized.

"Forget him," Raxtus said. "The Fairy King sent me with gifts. None are fairy talismans—such things would not be safe with Ronodin wearing the crown. But this is the king's signet ring, made by unicorns. He suggests you wear it only at dire need. Powered by your magical energy, it will shine brightly enough to blind any who look at it, including you."

"Wow," Kendra said, accepting the ring from his little hands. "I'll treat it carefully. Hopefully I can return it to him when this is over." It was hefty, like a class ring, set with tiny white stones that together formed the likeness of a rearing unicorn. The longer Kendra held it, the brighter the stones shone, and the more the silvery metal gleamed with inner fire.

"See how it shines just from contact with you?" Raxtus asked. "That isn't normal. Be cautious when you put it on."

"Is that adamant?" Warren asked, craning to better view the ring.

"Yes," Raxtus said. "Kendra, the Fairy King also wanted you to have this seed." He held out a little seed, about the size of a cornflake, then handed it to Kendra. "Plant it in the rain of the Perennial Storm and give it instructions. The spruce will grow, and a hamadryad will emerge. Her name is Cyllia, from a line of hamadryads known as the guardians. He suggests you instruct her to protect you."

"She'll obey me?" Kendra asked.

"Yes," Raxtus said. "The hamadryads of her line serve the unicorns. Cyllia has already been prepped to heed the orders you give."

"Ronodin is a unicorn," Kendra pointed out.

"But Ronodin is a disgrace," Raxtus said. "Unicorns despise him. The power of his crown mainly influences fairies."

Kendra slipped the ring and the seed into a pocket.

"Potion maker," Raxtus said, turning to Tanu. "The Fairy King thought you might benefit from these ingredients." He held up three packets the size of tea bags. "Source water, unicorn blood, and powdered horn."

"Powdered unicorn horn?" Tanu asked, clearly excited.

"Yes," Raxtus said. "It can only be obtained after a unicorn dies."

"Rare ingredients," Tanu said, his expression somewhere between wonder and delight. "Thank you."

"Thank the Fairy King," Raxtus said. "I'm just the messenger. And . . . I guess I'm the final gift. I'm here to help."

"You'll come to the Dragon Temple with us?" Kendra asked.

"The other dragons already call me a traitor," Raxtus said. "I might as well live up to my reputation. The Harp of Ages can slow the war—let's go get it."

Kendra scrunched her brow. "Do we need to know how to play a harp?"

"I know some basics," Vanessa said. "It's possible that using the Harp has nothing to do with musical talent."

"I hope it works like a magical music box," Warren mused.

A moment later, the rain turned into a drenching downpour. High winds propelled some of the moisture sideways into Kendra and her friends.

"We're not even by a window," Warren said, wiping water off his face.

After moving away from them, Raxtus expanded into

his dragon form, a sleek specimen whose silver-white scales reflected prismatic sparkles of light. His body was a little larger than a horse's, not counting the added length from his neck and tail. By stretching his body and spreading his wings somewhat, the fairy dragon turned himself into a windbreak.

"Much appreciated," Warren said.

Bernosh came to a standstill. Howling wind drove rain against the portable dungeon.

"We have arrived," the giant announced. "So has the Perennial Storm. And we're not alone."

"Who else is here?" Warren called.

The giant turned around.

Kendra and her friends ran forward to a barred window and saw they had stopped at the mouth of a box canyon. Two hundred yards away, visible through the driving rain, the canyon dead-ended against a tall rock face made exquisite by relief carvings of dragons. Fir trees lined the base of the cliffs leading to the carved rear wall, but the middle of the canyon floor was a sloppy mix of rocks and mud.

At the base of the carved rock face waited an older man clad in black and a younger woman dressed in white. They stood unflinchingly as the rainfall doused them.

"Are those guardians?" Kendra asked.

"Not official ones," Raxtus said. "Celebrant might have stationed them there to deny anyone entry."

"You know them?" Warren asked.

"Purnag and Riotta," Raxtus said. "A black dragon and a white one. Purnag has many breath weapons: fire, poison gas, or a sludge that disintegrates flesh. Riotta's breath could freeze a pond in seconds. They have offspring together, and they like to partner in combat."

"Why are they in human form?" Kendra asked.

"Maybe to take people by surprise?" Raxtus guessed. "Maybe it feels easier in this weather."

"Finally," Bernosh said, unshouldering the portable dungeon and setting it down. "Dragons who want to stand and fight."

"Do you need help?" Tanu asked.

Bernosh gave a snort. "There are only two. You'll be on your own inside the temple, but out here, let me do you this favor." He drew a sword longer than most of the trees in the area, crouched to pick up a boulder the size of a car, and stomped into the box canyon.

"If he goes down, we'll be in horrible danger," Raxtus said.

Tanu used a key to open the door of the dungeon. "Let's get ready to flee. Raxtus, if it comes to it, fly Kendra to safety."

"And take Vanessa," Warren said. "I know you can fly well with two."

"I have my sack of gales," Kendra said, getting it out and holding it ready.

Raxtus returned to his fairy form. "To fit through the door," he explained.

Beyond the doorway they saw Bernosh throw his rock at a relatively tiny figure ahead of him. The woman in white lunged to one side, barely avoiding the boulder. Within an instant, she expanded into a magnificent white dragon with spikes down her neck, and the man enlarged into a black dragon with a bony frill just behind his fearsome head. Neither dragon carried more mass than Bernosh, but from nose to tail, the length of Purnag rivaled the height of the giant.

Wings spreading, Purnag flew upward, while Riotta attacked low. An icy spray whitened the giant's legs, only slightly slowing his charge. Purnag sent a crop-dusting of dark gas down at the giant, but the wind and rain swiftly shredded the murky cloud.

With one hand, Bernosh caught Riotta by the neck just below the head and began to repeatedly slash her body with his sword. Purnag flew over Bernosh, swaying unsteadily in the stormy air, gliding directly toward the portable dungeon.

"I've got this," Kendra said, stepping out into the full deluge, becoming almost immediately soaked as she readied the sack of gales.

As Purnag swooped down toward her, Kendra opened the mouth of the sack, and a wind even stronger than the gales of the storm gushed outward. The wings of the black dragon ballooned like overtaxed sails as the furious creature was blown violently backward. Purnag tucked his wings and fell to the ground, only to get attacked from behind by Bernosh. Roaring, the dragon turned and clamped his jaws down on the giant's upper arm. Bernosh went down, stabbing the dragon again and again until he finally managed to sever the neck.

Kendra retreated into the shelter of the portable dungeon,

where Vanessa greeted her with an embrace. "Well done," the narcoblix whispered.

Kendra watched in horror as Bernosh rose, both lifeless dragons behind him, and staggered toward the portable dungeon. Frosty ice crystals coated his lower half, and most of the flesh was gone from one shoulder to the elbow, with only a charred black bone remaining. He coughed and stumbled, dropping to his knees.

"Now, that was a fight," he said, his smile showing a couple of missing teeth. "More than I expected from a pair of dragons." He blearily looked down at the fleshless portion of his arm. "Bit down and breathed right into me. Worthy beast. Might take some time to recover from this one." From his kneeling position, using his sword like a cane, he got one foot out in front of himself and started to rise, then flopped facedown onto the rocks and mud.

The giant did not move after that.

"Is he . . . ?" Kendra asked.

"Looks that way," Tanu said. He leaned out of the doorway, searching the skies. "We better get into the Dragon Temple before more company shows up."

"Resolved!" Warren exclaimed. "If I am to be eaten by a dragon today, it will be indoors."

"Would Celebrant send more dragons in this weather?" Kendra asked.

"Not normally," Raxtus said. "But who knows? These are abnormal circumstances."

"Plant the tree, Kendra," Vanessa prompted. "We're going to need all the help we can get."

While the others gathered gear, Kendra ran over to the nearest fir trees, where the soil seemed rich. Rain pelting, she crouched in the mud and scooped out a goopy hole with her hand. Water flowed into it, but she pressed the seed down into the bottom and pushed mud over it.

A bolt of lightning struck a nearby clifftop, accompanied by an immediate explosion of thunder that made Kendra jump and shriek. "Grow quickly," she told the seed. "Come protect me and my friends as soon as you can, Cyllia. We'll be inside the Dragon Temple."

A little green shoot rose out of the mud, stretching upward. It was strange to see it happening so fast, like watching a time-lapse film.

"Are you ready, Kendra?" Tanu called.

Kendra looked back to find Raxtus in his dragon shape and her three friends all waiting in the rain. Sheets of lightning strobed above, soon followed by thunder. Glancing up, Kendra glimpsed huge silhouettes of birds of prey made temporarily visible by lightning.

"Yes," Kendra called. "Coming."

She slogged over to her friends, who all started toward the carved cliff where they expected to find the Dragon Temple. Warren carried the key they had taken from Ptolemy.

"I'd fly us forward," Raxtus said, "but I don't trust my wings in this weather."

The strongest gust yet nearly knocked Kendra off her feet before the wind subsided. Lightning blazed across the sky every few seconds, trailed by overlapping crashes of thunder.

They passed the motionless body of Bernosh. Raxtus bounded over to his head and sniffed the huge neck. "He's dead," the dragon confirmed.

Kendra avoided studying Bernosh. The giant had moved to protect them from the dragons so energetically, almost eagerly. And now his life had ended. She hoped it was not a sign of things to come.

The rain fell even harder and the day darkened. Little waterfalls were taking shape on the clifftops, and a stream began to flow out of the box canyon. Hair and clothes already saturated, Kendra had the mild consolation that she couldn't get much wetter. She trudged forward and, by the pulses of lightning, caught harsh glimpses of the dragon corpses.

They paused in the lashing rain as they reached the rear of the canyon. "Where in a cliff do you insert a key?" Warren shouted.

"That's the seal of Abraxas, the first dragon, on the key," Raxtus said. "He's depicted in the middle of the wall, bottom row. See the notch where his heart would be?"

"If you're right, you just made a new best friend," Warren said. He clambered up a slick boulder in front of the carved dragon, raised the spear-sized key over his head, and jammed it into the slot.

"Back away!" Kendra warned. "Dectus promised the storm would do the rest."

Warren had already hopped down. "I remember," he

said. "Let's get clear." They all hurried sideways along the base of the cliff, squelching in mud and slipping on wet rocks. For a long moment, the wind whipped so furiously that Kendra fell to her knees and kept her head down until the gust relented.

Shortly after she stood, a searing bolt of lightning blasted the key. The deafening thunder hit like a physical blow. Kendra covered her ears too late—for a moment, all she could hear was a steady ringing.

As the ringing tone diminished and the roar of the wind became audible again, Kendra saw that the carved dragon had receded, leaving a doorway just over ten feet tall and five feet wide. Kendra and her companions scrambled back to the doorway, up the steps, and into the disquieting shelter of the Dragon Temple.

CHAPTER THIRTY-FOUR

Reliquary

Are you sure you intend to leave the city?" the guard shouted from the top of the wall, his words barely audible over the rushing wind.

"Yes, thank you!" Seth called.

"You know the Perennial Storm is coming?" the guard checked, one hand holding his steel cap as the wind gusted. "Most folk are heading into the city and going underground."

"We're aware, thank you," Merek responded.

"Gates will be locked and barred soon," the guard called. "You may find some modest shelter on the far side of the eastern wall."

Merek waved as they strode away from the gate. The guard squinted at the oncoming mass of dark, roiling clouds and then back at Seth and Merek, shaking his head.

Seth angled his head to keep the wind from blowing directly into his ear, because it was quite loud and uncomfortable. The relentless gale pulled at his clothing and threatened to push him off-balance. The front edge of the megastorm would be over Humburgh within minutes. Away to the north, lightning-laced thunderheads already blanketed more of the landscape, hovering above a gray blur of rainfall.

Leaving the road, Seth and Merek walked around the nearest hill outside of town. Seth knew it was crazy to brave the weather, but they needed the Unforgiving Blade and the Harp of Ages, and Merek had stressed that the Dragon Temple would only admit them during the Perennial Storm, so it was either win the Games in the next day or two or else wait seven years.

Around the backside of the hill, they found two figures huddled in oilskin coats, hoods drawn up to conceal their faces. The pair emerged from the partial shelter of a recess in the hillside to greet Seth and Merek.

"How considerate of you to show up!" Isadore yelled over the wind. "We were about to abort."

"Serena?" Calvin called from Seth's pocket.

"I'm here," she answered.

"Can we fly in this mayhem?" Merek asked.

Basirus gazed up at the threatening clouds. "Into the storm? Not a chance. Away from it? I'm willing to try. It will be a rough ride. Don't blame me if somebody gets dropped."

"I need your word that won't happen on purpose," Merek said.

"You have it," Basirus said. "Are you ready? If we're going, it has to be now."

"We're ready," Seth said.

Basirus swelled into a dark gray dragon with three rows of spikes down the back of his neck, a crown of sharp horns on his head, and a quartet of long spurs on his tail. Turning, he snatched Seth and Isadore with his forelegs and Merek with a hind leg. The scaly grip squeezed Seth's chest tightly, but at least he felt secure. Seth couldn't help noticing the black talons, each the length of a dagger and wickedly curved.

The dragon sprang into the air, and as his great wings unfurled, they took off like a kite in a hurricane. Twice they dipped dangerously close to the ground, but after some adjustments, Basirus stopped rocking and wobbling so much and gained altitude. Propelled by a mighty tailwind, they rocketed forward, relentlessly buffeted by crosswinds and other turbulence.

"This is an atrocious day to fly," Basirus said. "I'll take us high so that if I lose control, I'll have space to recover."

Seth could hardly believe their breathtaking speed, or the shocking turns and dives that left his dangling legs swinging in the wind. With no warning, Basirus would plunge unexpectedly, swooping out of the dive only to be blown in a new direction. Occasional updrafts elevated them at rates that made Seth's insides lurch, and violent gusts added haphazard bursts of acceleration. Sometimes the dragon spun, wings splayed helplessly, until he fully tucked them, righted himself during the free fall, then extended them anew to resume the chaotic flight.

As the winds impelled them farther ahead of the storm, the air currents became less blustery. For longer stretches they would bullet forward instead of tumbling into wild corkscrews and pretzels. The ground below became a barren wilderness of windswept ridges and prairies. At their outrageous velocity, Seth felt sure they would all be reduced to smears if they crashed.

Sometime after Seth had given up hope that the exhausting flight would ever end, a monumental pyramid of boulders came into view up ahead, the sides too steep and the apex too lofty to seem architecturally sound. The closer they got to the pyramid, the better Seth could see that the stacked boulders were a diverse jumble of irregular shapes and sizes, puzzled together with startling cohesion.

"Is that the reliquary?" Seth called, but either his words were lost on the wind, or else nobody bothered to answer.

The lower they flew, the more aware Seth became of their breakneck speed. Basirus started banking, first left, then right, back and forth, perhaps trying to slow, but whenever he turned too much, he began to lose control.

"This is going to be a difficult landing," the dragon announced. "Wish me luck."

Seth witnessed with horrified fascination their dive toward the ground, gaining speed when he thought they should be slowing. For a moment they skimmed above scrubby bushes and brittle grass until Basirus turned sharply into the gale, wings trimmed, and let the wind abruptly slow them. The dragon got one foot down and managed to fold his wings, flopping onto his side to avoid crushing the passengers he carried.

The huge claw gripping Seth receded as Basirus resumed his human form. Basirus stretched, rolling his shoulders. "My wings will be sore for weeks," he said.

"Can you still feel them?" Seth asked.

"Only phantom sensation in this form," Basirus said. "In my shoulder blades mostly. What would be the equivalent? Imagine hanging from a limb during an earthquake for an hour. No, better, imagine an hour with each wrist tied to a different horse as they run wild. How would your shoulders feel afterward?"

"Sounds painful," Seth said.

"Good job getting here," Merek said, gazing up at the pyramid, hair ruffled by the constant wind.

"The Reliquary of the Wandering Stones," Isadore said.

"It looks ancient," Seth said. "And weirdly tall. A pyramid shaped almost like an arrowhead. Who built it? Giants?"

"If so, they accomplished the feat long ago," Isadore said. "I suspect not. Giants refuse to tread in this desolation."

"I figured," Merek said, hands on his hips, surveying the area. "You could have given us a clearer warning."

"Would it have mattered?" Isadore asked.

"In truth?" Merek replied. "No."

"We don't relish coming here either," Isadore said. "But since when was it easy to win the Games?"

Seth noticed many individual rocks apart from the grand pyramid, scattered on the dry plain. Some were huge monoliths standing on end, like giant dominos. Others were smooth and rounded, ranging in size from bowling balls to bulldozers. Large or small, irregular or symmetrical, the stones tended to exist alone, rather than in clusters, and many had furrows to one side of them, as if they had recently skidded to a stop.

"Do the stones really wander?" Seth asked.

"You see the trails," Isadore said, clutching her oilskin coat as the wind tore at it. "Without wind erasing the evidence, the tracks would extend much farther."

"They're too big to slide around," Seth said. "This wind doesn't budge them and the ground is flat."

"Exactly," Isadore said. "These trovants seldom move when observed, though I know a wizard who claims to have watched from hiding as a large procession paraded across the prairie one night."

"Those who venture to this part of the sanctuary rarely return," Merek said. "Giants avoid this region, as do ogres and trolls. It is often repeated that to sleep here is to die here."

The nearest hulking slab of rock suddenly seemed ominous to Seth. What would he do if it started to scoot toward him? How was a person supposed to fight a twenty-ton megalith?

"We have about an hour before the storm pummels us," Isadore said. "If you get the blade before the storm catches up, we can fly southeast until we find shelter."

"To sleep here is to die here," Seth quoted.

"Few know of this place," Isadore said. "You are

benefiting from arcane knowledge I worked hard to acquire. If tales are true, the reliquary shifts position as well."

"Are you coming inside with us?" Merek asked.

Isadore grinned and chuckled. "This is your quest. We're the transportation. We'll wait out here."

"What if the storm hits before we're out?" Seth asked.

"We'll be gone," Isadore said. "We can't ride out the storm in the open, and we daren't seek shelter behind rocks or in the reliquary."

"I'll go inside with them," Serena volunteered.

"It might be dangerous," Calvin warned.

"It *will* be dangerous," Serena corrected. "Which is why you need me."

"Hurry, whatever you do," Isadore said. "The storm will not wait."

"Should I take Serena?" Seth asked.

"I'll go with Merek," Serena volunteered. "Divide and conquer."

Merek accepted Serena from Isadore. The wind intensified, peppering them with bits of dry brush and grit.

"I need cover," Isadore said.

Basirus returned to dragon form, wings tucked, and curled around her. Seth started toward the one gap he could see in the improbable pyramid, weaving to avoid the larger solitary stones in his path. At the base of the pyramid, he scrambled up interlocked boulders using his hands and feet until he reached the gap.

"Check your motives," Serena warned. "Legend has it that anyone with evil intentions will be crushed upon entry."

"What if my motives are good, but yours are sour, and I'm carrying you?" Merek asked.

"Put me down," Serena said. "Calvin too. Just to be safe."

Seth set Calvin down. He hoped wanting his memories back would be considered an acceptable intention. And he didn't mean anybody harm. Since time was not on their side, Seth quickly ducked into the triangular gap. The tunnel extended ahead about fifteen yards. The sheer volume of boulders above staggered his imagination, and the air was so saturated with the smell of stone that he could almost chew it.

The tunnel ended in a grand trapezoidal chamber within the center of the pyramid. Daylight filtered in through several shafts.

"Someone has produced an interesting paradox," Merek said as he crouched to light a small lantern. "A person cannot enter with sinister intentions, but no being of light could wield the Unforgiving Blade. It's a rare person who could do both."

"Why can't you?" Seth asked.

"The power that preserves me derives from light," Merek said. "However, a shadow charmer should be a different story."

"I can't hear the wind from here," Calvin said, coming into the chamber beside Serena.

Seth noticed that the air was unnaturally heavy and still, especially considering the nearby turbulence of the oncoming storm. At least there should have been a strong draft from the tunnel.

"What have we here?" Merek asked, examining a pedestal on a raised stone slab in the middle of the room.

Seth trotted over to him. The slot in the top of the pedestal seemed the right size to hold a blade. "Do you think somebody already took it?"

"Looks that way," Merek said.

"There has to be more to it," Serena said.

"Tell me about your friends outside," Calvin said to Serena. "Did they stay out in the wind because the entrance would have crushed them?"

"It's a delicate situation," Serena said.

"Suppose we find the Unforgiving Blade and exit," Merek said. "What happens?"

"I don't know," Serena said. "Can you trust Isadore? Absolutely not. When she sees the right opportunity to betray you, she'll take it. She's here to get the Wizenstone."

"And she's your friend?" Calvin asked.

"It's why I didn't want you involved," Serena said. "Isadore helped me learn essential information, but she's dangerous. Partnering with her is a deadly game. I wanted to protect you from it."

"You told me to go home," Calvin said. "That hurt."

Serena smiled and hugged him. "I would rather you were home because I love you! It took time to learn to swim in these waters. I endured experiences I would never want you to have, and almost lost my life."

"All the more reason I should be here to help," Calvin said.

"I would probably feel the same way if our roles were

reversed," Serena said. "Even so, I wouldn't want people I care about dealing with Basirus and Isadore."

"We wouldn't be here without her," Merek said. "But I can tell she's no friend of ours. I'm not going to let her hijack the Wizenstone."

"Keep her in the dark," Serena said. "She would rather not make her move until she knows what to do with the blade. I think she was bluffing about flying away. Until she knows your secrets, I don't think she'll let you out of her sight. She has been trying to gain the Wizenstone for centuries."

"It's a complicated situation," Merek said. "We need to go somewhere else before the storm ends, but our only hope to get there in time depends on the dragon."

"He won't be able to fly in the storm," Serena said.

"Dragons are strong," Merek said. "With enough motivation, he might be able to run."

Closing his eyes, Seth reached out with his shadow-charming senses, trying to discern a dark blade. Instead, beneath his feet, he immediately perceived a chattering chaos of entities. The sudden discovery was such a shock that he unwittingly withdrew from his power.

"What's the matter, Seth?" Calvin asked, looking up at him. "You look like you just saw a ghost."

"Maybe I did," Seth said.

"What do you mean?" Serena asked.

"There are beings underneath us," Seth said. "Lots of them. Gibbering in confusion."

"Can you still hear them?" Calvin asked.

"If I try," Seth said. "Give me a second." He engaged his senses and again was assailed by a confusion of words and feelings. Were they wraiths? Phantoms? Patient listening revealed a mix of voices. Definitely some wraiths. A few phantoms. And uncountable presences.

"What do you hear?" Merek asked.

"Many voices," Seth said. "They seem unaware of us. Some are undead, but mostly I hear presences. Like when I first met you."

"Disembodied memories?" Merek asked.

"I think so," Seth said. "A host of them. They sound confused. The majority are asking about themselves. Their advisers are wraiths and phantoms. It's the blind leading the blind."

"Sounds terrible," Serena said.

Seth concentrated on the voice of a single wraith.

Alone, the voice lamented. *Surrounded and alone.*

That struck Seth as a sentiment he could work with. *Can you hear me?* Seth projected to the wraith.

You speak to me?

I hear you and I'm speaking to you, Seth affirmed. *You must feel lost.*

Forever alone, the voice mourned.

Not right now, Seth said. *I hear you. Can you come see me?*

No way out, the wraith bewailed. *The Old Ones forbid it.*

Who are the Old Ones? Seth inquired.

Ancient and immovable, the wraith declared. *I am trapped. We are all ensnared. So alone.*

I can hear you, Seth said.

You are living, the wraith affirmed. *You hear me.*

I need to find the Unforgiving Blade, Seth communicated.

Above us, the wraith said. *The blade can harm us. The blade can end us.*

Is the blade gone? Seth asked.

Above us, the wraith repeated. *Above you. High above. The blade remains.*

How do we get to it? Seth asked.

I am trapped, the wraith grieved. *Find your way up. Beware the blade.*

Seth took his focus from the wraith and zeroed in on a forlorn phantom.

It never slows, the phantom complained. *Broken minds shattering into ever smaller pieces.*

I can be patient, Seth assured the phantom.

You hear me? the phantom asked.

It's noisy, but I hear you.

The ceaseless babbling haunts me, the phantom shared. *You are an island in an agitated sea.*

Can you help me find the Unforgiving Blade? Seth asked.

That edge is sharp! the phantom warned.

I need a sharp edge, Seth stated. *Can you help me?*

I cannot rise to where you stand, the phantom moaned. *The blade is higher still.*

How do I reach the blade? Seth asked.

Find the gaps, the phantom suggested. *Climb.*

Seth targeted a couple more wraiths and one more phantom, but the first two he had spoken with proved to be the most coherent. He tried to focus on some of the presences, but none could hear him.

"The blade is still here," Seth said.

"According to the memories?" Calvin asked.

"According to a wraith and a phantom," Seth said.

"Do you think your memories are down there?" Calvin asked.

"I considered the possibility," Seth said. "None of the memories could hear me. They are sealed deep under this place. The entities down there can't get out. Even if this is where Humbuggle stores the memories he steals, remember, the Diviner believed my memories had escaped."

"I'll take that as positive news," Serena said. "With hope that your memories are not among these entrapped wretches."

"Wraiths can be helpful when I'm looking for things," Seth said. "Or in a fight."

"Any other hints?" Merek asked.

"Supposedly the blade is above us," Seth said. "We need to hunt for gaps or maybe try to climb. They didn't give good instructions."

"Not much to climb in here," Merek said, eyes roving the stony walls. "Could they have meant to climb the exterior?"

"I felt like they meant to climb in here," Seth said. Closing his eyes, he drew on his power and probed for locks. Anything to unlock. Anything to open.

After a moment, he sensed a simple mechanism. A small mental effort released a catch, and what looked like a rectangular boulder slid slightly ajar, like a door.

"Did you do that?" Merek asked, responding to the unexpected movement.

"I try to make myself useful," Seth said, jogging over to the rectangular rock. It pulled open smoothly on hidden hinges. Beyond, a crude stairway led upward. "Who wants to climb a pyramid?"

CHAPTER THIRTY-FIVE

Jinzen

K endra, can you see?" Warren asked as they left the entrance behind.

Kendra realized it must be getting dark for her companions. She could see just fine in any nonmagical darkness, and there was still some extra light from the open doorway behind them. They had tried to shut it to no avail. The heavy stone door had refused to budge.

"We're in a grand hall," Kendra said. "There are four big dragon statues on each side."

"Let us know if they start to move," Warren said. "Or breathe acid. Or even if they wink."

"We'll have light shortly," Tanu said, mixing two solutions into a clear container. A moment later the concoction shone like a lightbulb.

"Yep," Warren said, glancing around. "Dragon statues. She wasn't bluffing about her night vision."

"I think they're only decorative," Vanessa said. "They look too primitive to come to life."

"But sometimes that's exactly how they get you," Warren said. "You let your guard down, and the crudely rendered dragons attack, all the scarier because they're so unrefined."

"We could run into the first guardian at any moment," Tanu said.

"This hall is safe," Raxtus said. "I would sense a dragon."

"Any idea who we're up against?" Vanessa asked.

"The guardians of the Dragon Temples were established long before I hatched," Raxtus said. "Few dragons know who was selected. The guardians will possess uniquely challenging abilities."

"Can you help us survive?" Kendra asked.

"I'll do my best," Raxtus said. "The only dragon I ever defeated was in human form at the time."

"That's only because you've never fought a dragon in his natural shape," Kendra said.

"Is that anything to brag about?" Raxtus asked.

"You're undefeated," Kendra encouraged.

"Any living dragon you meet is undefeated against other dragons," Raxtus explained. "My kind don't give second chances."

"You'll have backup," Kendra said.

"Having somebody to fight for is the only reason I'm here," Raxtus said.

"If this area is clear, let's ready our equipment," Tanu said. "May I take a moment to whip up an elixir or two using the ingredients Raxtus brought?"

"By all means, if it will help us survive," Warren said.

"Don't forget the entrance lies open behind us," Vanessa warned. "We don't want to be ambushed from the rear."

Raxtus took a few steps back toward the entrance. "In this weather, surrounded by such unwelcoming terrain, we probably won't see more dragons until the storm clears."

"This is your dad we're talking about," Kendra said.

"Where he's involved, anything is possible," Raxtus agreed. "I'll watch our tails."

"I wish I had more equipment and time," Tanu said. "It's a shame to waste such fine ingredients on half-baked potions."

"If we don't live, all of your ingredients will go to waste," Warren said. "Anything that could provide an advantage is worth a try."

Tanu uncapped a flask, sniffed the contents, then poured some fluid into a little bowl. "Even under these conditions I can improvise some powerful defensive potions. Whether they help will depend on the kind of dragons we meet."

"Expect the unconventional," Raxtus said. "They will be chosen from among the most feared dragons in history, seasoned veterans of extraordinary power."

"He's unselling me," Warren said. "Anyone want to throw in the towel? Go play in the nice rain? Jump in some puddles?"

"Few attributes are as attractive as courage," Vanessa said.

Warren straightened and spoke in a grittier voice. "Those dragons better get ready for me to bring the thunder."

"Better," Vanessa approved.

Kendra checked her magical bow. Having not been shot recently, it should have three hundred arrows at the ready. Her sack of gales remained available and probably had three-quarters of its wind left, estimating based on how much she had used. She checked in her pocket for the ring Raxtus had just given her, relieved as her fingers curled around it.

Minutes crawled by. Holding a bottle over a low flame, Tanu stirred in some powder. Kendra wondered if the first guardian could have overheard their conversations.

"This will have to do," Tanu said, repacking his ingredients. "I have a lotion to cure injuries, a salve to heal diseases, and a potion that bestows resistance to fire."

"Dragon fire?" Warren asked.

"Probably not full immunity to a direct attack," Tanu said. "It would be a close call."

"A close call beats charred to the core," Warren said. "I want that gummy potion ready as well. After last time, I'm a believer."

"Several of those elixirs are ready to go," Tanu said.

"Listen to me," Raxtus urged. "Huddle up. I'm going to let you in on a secret. Dragons are complicated creatures. Yes, they're antisocial, but they also get lonely. These guardians have been isolated for long years. They may find conversation hard to resist. If you can, keep them chatting. Dragons love the cat and mouse of talking to their food. It could buy us time."

"Most of us will be paralyzed in their presence without courage potions," Warren said. "Do we have any?"

"For all of us except Kendra," Tanu said. "She resists dragon fear without it. I dosed the courage potions so we should be able to take one other potion on top of them."

"Brave and gummy," Warren said. "Sounds like a winning combo."

"Or maybe brave and fireproof," Vanessa said.

Tanu distributed courage potions and drank one himself. "Don't forget, until we face a dragon to dampen the effect, courage potions can make you overenthusiastic."

"I feel fine," Warren said. "Better than fine. I might take on this first dragon with my bare hands, you know, to keep it interesting."

Vanessa rolled her eyes. "I hope you're kidding."

"I think so," Warren said. "Mostly."

"I'm ready," Kendra said.

"Onward," Tanu said, shouldering his pack.

At the end of the great hall, they reached a long flight of red stairs as broad as bleachers. They started up, and Kendra eventually felt her legs become weary.

"What if a dragon is hiding at the top?" Warren complained. "I'll need a time-out to get my breath back. Isn't there an escalator?"

"No dragon in this area," Raxtus offered. "In case that helps."

At the top of the stairs, they found a splendid set of double doors designed in a distinctively Asian style. Beside the doors hung a round, golden gong with a mallet on a nearby stand.

"Who wants to do the honors?" Tanu asked.

"I guess a sneak attack is out?" Warren checked.

"Should I?" Kendra asked.

"No, let me," Vanessa said. "In case there is a trap or magical penalty."

"In that case, allow me," Warren said, cutting in front of Vanessa. "My main job on my basketball team was drawing fouls."

He picked up the mallet and smashed it against the gong, producing a long, shimmering reverberation. The double doors slid open of their own accord, revealing a pristine white floor, expertly painted with golden vines and leaves. A row of glossy black columns extended left to right beyond the doors, separating the entryway from the rest of the chamber. Beyond the columns gleamed an elaborate maze of spotless mirrors.

As Kendra and the others came through the wide doorway, a long Chinese dragon swept into view, body undulating as it hovered, scales flashing like gilded coins. The brilliant creature had no wings, and little sets of pawed feet dangled along the serpentine body. The head resembled a fox with golden fur and eyes as bright as emeralds.

"Welcome, doomed mortals who enter my chamber,"

spoke a clear voice that seemed to come from all directions. "If you each leave your most valuable item on my doorstep, I will allow you to depart in peace."

"Jinzen," Raxtus said. "A treasure dragon. I've heard of you. All dragons hoard. Your tastes are much more refined. A true collector."

"What misapprehension brings a dragon to my domain?" Jinzen asked, eyes flaring with anger. "Do you not know that I guard a talisman made to destroy all dragonkind? End this foul betrayal at once."

"I've been having trouble sleeping," Raxtus said. "The Harp of Ages might be just the medicine I need."

"By all means, come inside, if you yearn for death," Jinzen said brightly. "I can use the exercise."

The double doors slammed shut, cutting off escape. Corkscrewing like a twirled ribbon, Jinzen streaked away into the maze of mirrors. For a prolonged moment, multiple reflections of his glittering body stretched across dozens of surfaces, elongating the dragon to impossible dimensions, until he was no longer in view.

"Let's start by leveling the playing field," Warren said, rushing past the columns to the nearest mirror, sword raised. At least a dozen reflections of Warren from various angles swung their swords in unison. The blade rebounded off the mirror with a clang.

"Ow!" Warren cried, switching his sword to his less dominant hand so he could shake out his arm. He banged the mirror with the hilt of his sword, then rubbed his free hand against the reflective surface. "I can't even leave a smudge."

Returning his sword to his dominant hand, Warren stabbed the mirror twice and slashed it once more without making a scratch. "It's like steel."

"It's probably enchanted glass," Raxtus said. "Look out!"

With a telltale whoosh, Jinzen arrowed back into view. Warren flattened himself against the mirror as Jinzen streamed by. The dragon's laughter emanated from all directions.

After the golden dragon zoomed out of view again, Warren staggered away from the mirror, blood spreading across his shoulder. "I feel like I picked up fifty deep paper cuts," Warren said. "The worst one is on my shoulder."

"He's playing with you," Raxtus said. "Come away from there."

Warren ran back to the shelter of the colonnade.

"I could use a hand, Kendra," Raxtus said.

Kendra placed her palm on the dragon's neck, and prismatic radiance shone from his metallic scales as her power flowed into him. Raxtus breathed a minty mist onto Warren, who sank to his knees.

"That feels good," Warren said dreamily.

"I'm especially adept with slits and scrapes," Raxtus said.

Vanessa slapped Warren. "Snap out of it," she said. "We need you."

"Right," Warren said, getting to his feet. He raised a bottle to his lips and upended it. His steps began to wobble, and the arm holding the sword stretched longer than his other one. "This dragon wants to play? I can play too."

"What do we do?" Kendra asked Raxtus.

"The corners are too tight and the passages too narrow for me to fly in there," Raxtus said. "Jinzen doesn't have to worry about wings. Let me see what I can learn on foot. He's scary fast, but not terribly huge. If I could just get a hold of him . . ."

Wings tucked, Raxtus charged into the maze. Dozens of reflections of the silvery dragon dashed one way or another until Raxtus raced out of view. Fierce laughter resounded through the room, and Kendra heard the crunch of a big collision. A moment later, Raxtus came hurtling from the maze to slam against a nearby column.

"Raxtus!" Kendra cried, running to where the dragon lay curled around the foot of the column. "Are you all right?"

His head swiveled up, eyes not entirely focused. "Great, except for getting hit by a freight train. He has blazing speed and unearthly reflexes. I'm out of my depth. And he uses at least some of the mirrors as cross-dimensional portals."

"He flies into them?" Vanessa asked.

"And comes out from other ones," Raxtus said.

"Can you do that?" Kendra asked.

"Not in his playground," Raxtus said. "He has a major home field advantage."

"Are you going to remain by the entrance?" Jinzen asked from all directions. "The way you're currently grouped, I could dispatch all of you with one pass. Come, make a sport of it."

"What should we do?" Kendra asked.

"Give him the best you have," Raxtus said. "It's now or never."

"If I mention fairy treasure, close your eyes," Kendra whispered, displaying her ring.

Warren charged into the maze on wobbly legs, sword gripped in two hands.

"Speed potion," Vanessa whispered.

"I'll try the same," Tanu said.

"Give me one too," Kendra said.

"Remember, after the burst of speed, this mixture will leave you depleted," Tanu cautioned. He passed Vanessa a potion and handed Kendra one as well. Then he followed Vanessa into the maze, their many reflections overlapping before diverging and vanishing.

Raxtus arched his neck as Kendra placed both hands on the flawless armor of his scales. With his entire body shedding light, his tail swished, and he stood up. "Wow, that's potent energy. I'm back. What do you need?"

"Can you get me to a spot in the maze with maximum reflections?" Kendra whispered.

"He's a dragon of light," Raxtus cautioned. "It may not blind him."

"Raxtus, could you be blinded by too much light?" Kendra asked.

"Probably, in enough excess," Raxtus said. "I can't look directly at the sun."

"You're a dragon of light," Kendra said. "This is the best idea I've got."

Kendra ran into the maze with Raxtus at her side. The strategically angled mirrors threw her reflections everywhere, along with duplicates of Raxtus. In some spots, repetitions of herself stretched outward toward infinity. Most of the mirrors showed true reflections, but occasionally Kendra found herself and Raxtus upside down, or magnified, or refracted into thousands of miniature likenesses.

They reached a portion of the maze where the ceiling and floor were mirrored as well, extending space to forever in all directions. Endless rows of herself and Raxtus repeated outward along unexpected diagonals, and she began to blunder into mirrors.

Kendra caught fleeting glimpses of Jinzen and Tanu at odd angles and from a distance. She reached a pocket of the maze where images of Warren repeated. The reflections of Warren multiplied until she found him on the ground. From the waist down Warren had been squished flat, and teeth had left deep, bloodless impressions in his chest.

"Are you all right?" Kendra asked.

"Fine," Warren said. "Except I lost my sword, and it might take a minute for my legs to return to their proper shape."

As Kendra watched, the indentations decreased, and Warren's legs regained more functional proportions. Raxtus brought a sword in his jaws and dropped it beside Warren.

"Jinzen is unbelievably fast," Warren said. "I thought I timed a perfect swing, but he dipped under it, mowed me down, and savaged me. Thanks to the potion, it didn't break my skin."

"I'm using my speed potion!" Vanessa announced.

"You call that speed?" Jinzen mocked. "Quick for a mortal, I suppose."

Body flexing as if he had joints in the wrong places, Warren swayed to his feet. Kendra heard rushing air, and the mirrors began to fill with an endlessly long golden body in rapid motion. Raxtus thrust Kendra to the floor and disappeared with a noisy crash as a shimmering stream of gold blurred by above her. Manic laughter bombarded her ears from all directions.

When Kendra sat up, Warren and Raxtus were gone. She was alone with thousands of reflections of herself. She heard vicious snarls and claws ringing against hard surfaces.

"This vase looks expensive," Vanessa called, her voice off in the distance. The remark was followed by a shattering smash. "Whoops!"

"No, no, no, no, no, no!" Jinzen shouted from all sides. "Why?"

"I upgraded my speed," Tanu announced from a different direction than Vanessa. "Check this out! Who would sculpt a bridge out of jade? The trees on the riverbank look so fragile!" What followed sounded like a baseball bat destroying a chandelier.

"Noooooooo!" Jinzen howled in rage.

Kendra heard a rush of wind and began to see golden flashes in the mirrors. Jinzen was flying her way.

"Look at the fairy treasure I found!" Kendra hollered, raising her hand, closing her eyes, and putting on the ring.

She could feel the light against her skin, and it flared

unbelievably bright even with her eyes closed. She forced all the power she could muster into the ring and felt the glare intensify. Then, with a bursting sound, the ring went dark and no longer felt connected to her power.

Jinzen was half roaring, half screaming. Kendra crouched low, hands over her ears.

"My eyes!" Jinzen yelled. "You devils will pay for that trick." It sounded like he was colliding with mirror after mirror, flopping around haphazardly. "You will pay dearly!"

"Everyone lie low," Warren shouted. "This overhyped dragon is mine. After I smash more of his things. Where is the little worm? Is he hiding?"

Kendra got down flat on her stomach and pressed into the juncture where the floor met the wall. Glancing at the ring, she noticed that the white stones forming a unicorn were gone, with empty sockets in their place. Somehow her energy had consumed them.

She could see a reflection of Warren walking, clutching two large poleaxes with huge, semicircular blades. Arms unsteadily straining, he dragged the butts of the axes on the floor to manage the weight, keeping one facing ahead of himself, one behind. He chattered nonstop.

"What's the matter, Jinzen?" Warren taunted. "Do you think if you close your eyes we can't see you?"

Kendra no longer heard the dragon crashing into things. Was he keeping still? Had his sight returned? Did he have his mirror maze memorized? Gilded lengths of dragon flickered in the mirrors, and Kendra heard a whistling rush of air.

"A lot of dragons get slow in their old age," Warren

heckled, arms wobbling, trying to keep the axes stable. "And they become so fussy about their weird possessions."

Kendra saw Jinzen speed directly into the ax Warren held behind himself, the dragon splitting down the middle for nearly a third of his length before slamming to the floor, dragging Warren with him. After sliding to a stop, Jinzen did not move.

Arising, Kendra chased the reflections of the motionless dragon in the wrong direction several times before making her way to the actual corpse. She arrived at the same time as Raxtus and found Warren bent sickeningly out of shape.

"I'm okay," Warren claimed, responding to her expression. "No pain. I'm already regaining my normal form. Great flash, Kendra! I could sense it with my eyes shut. It did the trick."

"You taunted him into flying right at you," Kendra said.

"He had flung me into a treasure pile," Warren said. "I found the axes right after your flash. He could hear which way I was facing and tried to take me from behind. I caught a glimpse of his milky white eyes just before impact. He was blind as a bat. Ran straight into the ax."

Reflections of Tanu staggered into view. Minutes later, his actual form rounded a nearby corner, peaked and panting. "That speed potion takes a lot out of a guy."

Somewhere, they heard Vanessa quietly weeping.

Warren scowled, unsteadily rising. "Vanessa?"

She didn't answer, but the soft crying continued.

"That isn't like her," Warren said.

"This way," Raxtus offered.

The fairy dragon led them through many twists and turns. Kendra kept her eyes on Raxtus and tried to ignore the disorienting parade of reflections. They found Vanessa just outside the maze, in a luxurious area heaped with treasure. The shards of a broken vase lay nearby on the floor.

Vanessa sat on a mound of gold coins, face in her hands, shoulders shaking. Warren went to her, but she swiveled away at his touch.

"Vanessa, what's wrong?" Warren asked.

"I'm so foolish," she lamented through her sobs.

"You did great," Warren said. "We got Jinzen."

"I knew not to look," Vanessa said with self-loathing. "I was an instant too late. The whole maze went supernova. I've compromised my role on this mission."

Her hands dropped to reveal her milky white eyes.

CHAPTER THIRTY-SIX

Unforgiving Blade

Merek stopped just before the stairs led into a circular room littered with bones. Seth stood next to him staring at the morbid jumble of skeletons, some plainly human, others clearly not.

"Is it a lair?" Seth asked.

"See the black stone in the middle of the floor?" Merek asked. "The one rising above the bones?"

"The blocky one?" Seth checked. "With little veins of red?"

"There is something wrong with that stone," Merek said. "Do you see the dimness around it? As if it pollutes the nearby light. Or maybe absorbs it."

Testing with his shadow-charming senses, Seth could feel the rock had a deep, though alien, awareness. He perceived no words—just a profound hunger.

"It's hungry," Seth said.

"Yes," Merek said. "Certain rocks are more aware than others. I've run across some ancient ones that have developed strong identities, along with peculiar attitudes and appetites. That is no ordinary rock. Bones carpet the room for a reason."

"Want me to check it out?" Calvin offered.

"No," Merek said, removing Serena from his pocket. "Most living creatures who enter that room don't stay alive for long. I'm a little different, though." He handed Serena to Seth.

"Are you sure about this?" Seth asked.

"Who can be sure about a malevolent rock?" Merek said. "Keep your guard up."

Merek stepped into the room. He turned back to Seth and nodded. "It's draining my life away."

"Get out," Seth urged.

"I have life to give," Merek said, picking his way through the bones toward the stone.

"So do I," Seth countered. "I wouldn't mind getting a few years older."

"It doesn't make you older," Merek said, lying down with his chest atop the rock. "It saps your life. A baby would wither and die in here, not grow. Come through the room. It's feeding completely from me. Hurry."

Seth raced into the room, stumbling on some bones as he hastily crossed. Once he passed through the far doorway, he turned to Merek and called, "I made it."

"Get well into the hall," Merek said.

Seth complied as Merek got off the rock and rejoined him.

"You look the same," Seth said.

"I'm one of the undying," Merek said. "I have an inexhaustible supply of life. And one like me could never carry the Unforgiving Blade. That room should have thwarted anyone who could wield it. Look! More stairs."

Up they climbed, winding to unguessable heights within the thick walls of the pyramid. Seth wondered how quickly a normal person would have died in the room with the black rock.

"Have you ever died?" Seth asked.

"Many times," Merek said. "And I am always reborn."

"You remember multiple lives?" Seth asked.

"I do since you restored my memories," Merek said. "Mine is a long history. Being reborn can play tricks with your recollections. So can long periods of inaction. Certain types of memory lapses can be regenerative, like sleep, allowing a person to rest and recharge."

From up ahead they heard a continuous, earthy grinding. When they reached the next doorway, they found a circular room with a rock floor that sloped into the walls like a shallow bowl. Circling inside the bowl was a spherical stone ball, tall enough to reach Seth's chin.

"I don't trust it," Merek said.

Seth tried to get a sense of the stone ball with his power and was surprised to hear words repeating, like a mind stuck on a looping thought.

All who enter must be crushed. All who enter must be crushed. All who enter must be crushed. All who enter . . .

Why crush people? Seth asked.

The repeating mantra halted, and the ball swerved slightly off course, interrupting its perfectly circular route. *You hear me?*

It must be tough having the same purpose for so long, Seth communicated.

It is my mandate, the stone replied.

Who gave the command? Seth asked.

One who reached me long ago, the stone replied.

Like I am reaching you now? Seth asked.

Much like this, yes, the stone acknowledged.

I have a new command, Seth conveyed. *You can finally rest.*

I can rest? the stone verified. *No more crushing all who enter?*

Rest, and crush no more, Seth soothed.

As you command.

The stone ball lazily spiraled to the bottom of the bowl until it settled and became still.

"The ball was going to crush anyone who entered the room," Seth reported. "I gave it new instructions, like I would with the undead. Might be smart to keep our guard up, just in case." Seth probed with his power. "The ball seems quiet now."

"Let me go first," Merek said, stepping gingerly into the room. He walked lightly to the other side of the shallow bowl and out the far doorway.

Seth followed. The stone ball never budged.

More stairs continued upward. Seth's leg muscles were burning when at last the stairs ended at a wall of boulders. Merek stepped forward, hands running gently over the fitted stones.

"Well, we tried," Seth said, panting from the climb. "At least we got some exercise."

Merek looked at him dubiously.

Seth winked. "Let me check for a hidden door."

As he had done at the bottom of the stairs, Seth mentally searched for a lock and was surprised to find one right in front of them. Drawing on his power, he willed the mechanism to unlock, but the effort was met with considerable resistance.

Planting his feet, clenching his fists, Seth concentrated all his energy on the problem. Still the mechanism defied him. Gasping for breath, Seth kept pushing, and all at once the resistance relented, as if he were in a tug of war and the other team dropped the rope. The mechanism unlatched, and a previously unseen door composed of multiple rocks swung open.

"That looked like a fight," Calvin said.

"Something opposed me," Seth replied.

Merek extended a hand to keep Seth from going forward. "Let's survey the room first."

Beyond the doorway awaited a room that looked to be inside the top of the pyramid—at least, the lofty ceiling came to a point in the center. Occupying the middle of the room was a large block of stone so black that no subtleties of texture were discernible. Part of a long knife jutted from the top, much of the blade buried in the rock.

"Now, that is a black stone," Calvin said. "It looks more like a void than a rock."

Seth mentally scanned the room. "The space feels empty."

"I get the same read," Merek said, stepping into the room. Seth followed.

The moment Seth set foot in the room, he became acutely aware of the dark well of power inside himself. He had never sensed it so distinctly. To his alarm, the darkness within was irresistibly drawing him toward the black stone. Seth walked jerkily, straining to resist.

"Are you all right?" Merek asked.

"I'm being pulled," Seth said, unable to look away from the fathomless darkness.

"Take the blade and we'll depart," Merek said. "This shrine is dedicated to darkness."

Seth quit resisting and felt the pull lessen. He hurried to the stone. Looking down at the dark shape, Seth could discern no surface, as if it were made from the essence of shadow. The stone seemed much deeper than it should be, a window into endless night.

"Claim the blade, Seth," Merek said. "I can't do it for you. Be extremely careful. Wounds from that edge will never be repaired."

The words reached Seth from far away. He extended his hand, not to the ebon handle of the Unforgiving Blade, but toward the darkness encasing it.

"Seth!" Calvin shouted from his pocket. "Not the stone! The knife."

Seth heard the words, and he numbly glanced at the nipsie waving at him. He felt deliciously drawn to the stone, as if an unnamed appetite that had starved throughout his life was finally about to be sated.

"Seth!" Calvin yelled. "Wake up!"

Seth paused. He was here for the blade, not to commune with the darkness.

His eyes flicked to the dark handle and the darker blade. The blade seemed made from the same shadow substance as the stone. He grabbed the hilt and lifted the long knife. The stone offered no resistance. The knife felt so light, Seth wondered if the hilt provided the only weight. A shudder ran through the pyramid, then subsided.

"I'm not sure that's a stone," Seth said, forcing his mouth to speak and his legs to back away. "It's more like the absence of a stone."

Merek watched the dust trickling down from the fitted stones of the sloped ceiling. "We should not linger."

The darkness did not speak to Seth with words. But he knew the absence of stone wanted him to cut off a piece of it to bring with him.

"Merek?" Seth asked, feet sliding toward the absence of stone against his will. "Can you get me out of here?"

Strong arms encircled Seth and carried him from the room. Once he was back on the stairs, the draw of the void ceased. Seth didn't look back at it.

"Hurry," Merek said.

"What about Isadore and Basirus?" Serena asked.

"We'll solve that problem when we reach it," Merek said. "Let me lead the way. Don't forget the room with the draining stone."

"I wish this knife had a sheath," Seth said, holding it away from himself.

"I'm not sure such a weapon can be sheathed," Merek said. "Except perhaps in pure darkness."

"I think you're right," Seth agreed.

The pyramid did not tremble as they descended the long stairs. The spherical rock remained at rest in the bowl-shaped room, and Seth crossed the room with the draining stone the same way he had coming up. Seth held the knife out in front of himself, careful not to let it touch anything.

When Seth reached the bottom of the stairs, the pyramid began to quake. A huge boulder dropped from high above and crashed against the floor, spitting dusty fragments in all directions.

"Run," Merek urged, staying behind Seth.

Seth sprinted to the opening and dashed along the triangular corridor. The rumbles of the pyramid were punctuated by rocks falling behind him. Seth burst out of the passage into a torrential downpour. Lightning slashed across the sky, producing thunder that overpowered the crash of tumbling boulders. Merek emerged behind Seth, and he pointed to where Isadore had found shelter beneath a dome visible only by the rain being repelled off of it. Basirus waited beside her in his human form. Both of them looked perfectly dry. The sorceress waved for the others to join her.

"She's using magic," Merek said.

"Do we go to her?" Seth asked.

Lightning struck the pyramid, and the thunder felt like a physical blow. Seth was already halfway soaked.

"Take care if you do," Serena warned.

"We have matters to settle with those two," Merek said. "And having shelter is preferable to being caught in this storm."

Seth ran to where the rain splattered against the invisible dome. Isadore waved a hand, and part of the dome stopped repelling rain. Seth figured the barrier was gone, and he stepped into her dry refuge. After Merek entered, Isadore made another gesture and the dome re-formed, significantly muting the storm.

"I see you were successful," Isadore said, eyes on the shadowy blade.

"We got it," Seth said. "I think the pyramid is collapsing."

"May I hold it?" Isadore asked.

"No," Seth said.

"Don't be selfish," Basirus pressured.

"This blade stays in my hand until I'm done with it," Seth said.

"And what are you going to do?" Isadore asked.

"We have a long road ahead," Merek said. "Thank you for your help with this leg of our journey."

"We're not fair-weather friends," Isadore assured him. "This dome will protect us from the storm. It is a specialty of mine. It even repelled some nasty rocks who took an interest in us."

"Can the dragon fly?" Merek asked. "We need to travel."

"What is the destination?" Basirus asked.

"The wild highlands," Merek said.

"Could that involve the Dragon Temple?" Isadore asked.

"Our business is private," Seth said.

"Am I not part of your business?" Isadore asked. "I seldom give charity."

"I can't fly in this weather," Basirus said.

"What about running?" Merek asked.

Basirus sneered. "Run through the Perennial Storm to the highlands? For what?"

"To reach the Dragon Temple before the storm abates and entry becomes impossible," Isadore guessed. "Why did Humbuggle involve the Dragon Temple? What has he hidden there?"

"You ask many questions," Merek warned.

"You need a key to enter the Dragon Temple," Isadore said. "Is that already managed? Do you have other partners?"

"We need transportation," Merek said.

"A run to the Dragon Temple from here might not be possible until the storm ends," Isadore said. "Even for a dragon as strong as Basirus. Not to mention the danger from the lightning and the thunderbirds. We would need to be full partners to attempt such folly. And I would have to carry the blade."

"We'll find our own way," Seth said.

Isadore laughed richly. "Oh, you will? How fast do you run during hurricanes? I'll take Serena back."

"No," Serena said.

"Excuse me?" Isadore responded.

"Our partnership ends tonight," Serena said.

"After so much time," Isadore said. "I wonder what prompted such an abrupt change of heart."

"We all want to win," Serena said.

"Well spoken," Isadore approved.

"We know your task involves the Dragon Temple," Basirus said.

"I believe that will have to suffice," Isadore replied. She moved closer to Basirus and her hands fluttered.

Merek drew his sword. Part of the dome folded inward, and suddenly there were two domes repelling the rain. One held Seth and Merek along with their nipsies. The neighboring dome contained Isadore and Basirus.

"We'll wait out the storm separately for now," Isadore called, her voice barely audible.

"This is a prison," Merek said, clanging his sword against the dome.

"Should I test this knife?" Seth asked.

"We won't make it to the Dragon Temple if we're trapped here," Merek said.

Seth slashed the dome with the Unforgiving Blade and it tore open, vanishing completely an instant later. Isadore staggered as if injured, and her dome disappeared as well. Rain showered down on her and Basirus.

Merek drew his stake and charged forward as Basirus expanded into his dragon form. The transformation had barely finished when Merek plunged the stake into the dragon's side. Instantaneously, the dragon disintegrated to ash.

Lightning flashed and Isadore screamed. Thunder partially masked her cry as the enchantress turned and ran. Sheathing his stake, Merek did not pursue her.

"Merek, wasn't that our only ride?" Seth asked.

"Our partnership had ended. We weren't going anywhere with them."

"How did you kill him so quickly?" Seth asked.

"A Dragon Slayer has tools of his trade," Merek said. "I lack my preferred sword and shield and my favorite bow. But if I can get close enough to use it, nothing ends a fight like my stake."

"What about Isadore?" Calvin asked.

"She might double back and attack us," Serena said. "Right now she's devastated. Her regard for her brother was sincere."

"She's also wet," Merek said. "She won't be able to create that dome spell ever again."

"Really?" Seth asked.

"The wounds of that blade are permanent," Merek said. "You used it well. We were at her mercy."

"We're stranded in the Perennial Storm," Serena reminded him.

Merek shook his head. "We're only stranded if we act helpless. We're drenched anyway—let's head in the right direction and search for mounts."

"And pray we don't get struck by lightning," Serena said.

"You're catching on," Merek replied, setting off at a brisk pace. Seth ran to stay with him.

With clouds blanketing the sky, Seth found it hard to

gauge the time of day, though it was growing so dim, he assumed it was heading into the evening. Dazzling bursts of lightning and explosive concussions of thunder became a nearly constant accompaniment to their jog. Behind them, the pyramid had not fully collapsed, though it looked less steep and tall than before, and the summit was crumpled. The structure began to shrink in the distance as they progressed over the muddy prairie.

As they reached the top of a little bluff and started across it, the wind lulled. A searing bolt of lightning struck off to one side, and the electrical current reached Seth through the ground. The brutal shock hurled him to the mud, unconscious before he could register what had happened.

CHAPTER THIRTY-SEVEN

Pioleen

Raxtus breathed again onto Vanessa's eyes, with Kendra lending support, her hand on his neck. The various exhalations he had attempted featured subtly different colors and scents. This yellowish vapor smelled chiefly floral, with hints of the sea.

"How about that one?" Raxtus asked.

"I don't feel any progress," Vanessa said. "I'm sorry for costing us so much time. I'll be a liability if I continue with you. Please leave me behind."

"Normally I would stay with you," Warren said.

"This is an emergency," Vanessa implored. "All of you need to push onward. With me sidelined, you're already shorthanded. There are two more guardians to confront."

"She's right," Tanu said. "I wish she wasn't."

"What if we apply more of your healing ointment?" Warren asked.

"A greater quantity will not be more effective," Tanu said. "This injury is beyond my skills to heal."

"Please," Vanessa said. "You have to go."

"I found a door that leads forward," Tanu said. "From here, we can walk around the perimeter of the maze to reach it."

"Go," Vanessa said. "We all have a better chance if you hurry."

"Here is a gaseous potion," Tanu said, putting the little bottle into her hand. "If trouble shows up, become vaporous."

Warren knelt, clasped one of her hands, and kissed it. "I'll be back for you."

"Don't get eaten," Vanessa said.

Warren grinned. "With this potion, I'm far too chewy."

Tanu led them to an ornately carved wooden door. Beyond it, in contrast to the bright mirrors and gleaming piles of treasure, they found a dim, snaking corridor.

"I'll hang back," Raxtus said. "Go invisible. Other dragons have a hard time sensing me if I lie low. I might be more effective if I attack out of hiding."

"My gumminess is fading," Warren said. "Could I do another?"

"I think so," Tanu replied. "Remember that how well it protects you will depend on the dragon. The gummy potion won't do much against fire, for example."

"I still have my speed potion," Kendra said.

"Keep it handy," Tanu said.

"I don't like leaving Vanessa behind," Warren said. "It feels like we lost our adult."

"Kendra can step up," Tanu said lightly.

The tunnel wound for a long time. Finally, it led them into an immense cavern where a tiny dragon splashed in a puddle. The creature was no larger than a chicken, with an oversized head shaped somewhat like a pterodactyl's. The diminutive dragon hopped and flapped stubby wings, head bobbing left and right, big round eyes staring.

"How did that get in here?" Kendra asked.

"It can't be the next dragon," Warren said. "Did they give us a freebie?"

They ventured farther into the room as the little dragon bounced and splashed. Head swiveling, it made some croaky caws, then shook its tail vigorously.

"Maybe the dragon had a weird kid?" Tanu asked.

"It might be like the cat," Warren said. "We kill it and it comes back bigger."

"I don't think we have to kill it," Kendra said. "Let's just pass it by. The goal is to find the prize."

"I don't know," Warren said. "On our way out, it might be a thousand times bigger or something. The dragons aren't stupid."

"Could it have wandered in here?" Tanu asked.

"There is a doorway on the far side," Kendra said. "Let's just keep going. On the way back we can send it to dreamland if needed."

Tanu shrugged. "We'll have the Harp."

"Sure," Warren said. "Live and let live."

The little dragon hopped from one foot to the other, head bobbling. As Kendra and the others neared the doorway at the far side of the room, the huge stone door crashed shut. A door slammed closed to block where they had entered as well.

"Guys," Raxtus said from across the room, his form too perfectly blended with the environment for them to see him. "We're in trouble."

"Because of the doors?" Warren asked.

"I think that's Pioleen," Raxtus said.

"Is he a baby?" Warren asked. "What does he do?"

"If I'm right, she's full grown and ancient," Raxtus said. "No dragon was ever more powerful in magic. And no dragon was less predictable."

The little dragon buried its face in the puddle, then tipped its head back and gargled. It flapped one wing rhythmically, then the other.

"She fell out of the stories long ago," Raxtus said. "I should have guessed she became a guardian."

"She doesn't seem to notice us," Kendra said.

"The doors," Warren pointed out.

Pioleen jumped in the puddle with both feet, then swished her tail in the water. Croaking caws followed.

"Raxtus, are you pranking us?" Warren asked.

Kendra stood in a cabin. An extremely old man, thin and wrinkled, with a few stringy hairs on his bald, veiny scalp, sat in a wooden rocking chair, bundled in blankets. A fire burned in the fireplace, popping and sending sparks up the chimney.

The scene looked perfectly real. The details were right—the smells of the woodsmoke and the old man, his soft snoring, the scuffed floorboards, the way the flames made the shadows jitter.

But Kendra knew it couldn't be real. She was in the Dragon Temple with Warren, Tanu, and Raxtus. And the eerie magical dragon.

"Pioleen?" Kendra asked. "Are you doing this?"

She approached the old man, reaching out a hand to shake him awake.

"Don't bother," said a female voice that made Kendra jump. The speaker was a face made of knotholes in the wall of the cabin. "You have bigger problems at hand."

Something crashed against the cabin door, and Kendra whirled. The next impact shook the entire cabin and left cracks in the door. Was it a battering ram? Kendra ran to the window at the rear of the cabin as a huge brown bear exploded through the front door with a furious roar. The bear overturned a table with a swipe, then picked up the old man in vicious jaws and shook him.

Kendra yanked the rear window open and dove out into moonlit snow, an icy crunch breaking her fall. She lurched to her feet and started wading away from the cabin. The snow was almost two feet deep, powdery beneath an icy skin.

The bear roared from inside the cabin and burst through the window, destroying part of the wall in the process. Kendra fumbled with her bow. The bear loped toward her, thick fur sloshing over fat and muscles, then reared up, giving a mighty bellow as its paws raked the air.

Kendra pulled back the bowstring and was about to say "fifty," to launch fifty simultaneous arrows at the beast, when she wondered what exactly she was really aiming at. None of this could be real, despite how authentic it looked and felt and sounded and smelled.

Kendra lowered her bow, and the bear surged forward, slavering jaws agape, but stopped just short of biting her. She flinched away, falling onto her backside in the snow. The bear loomed over her. She felt its hot breath on her face, smelled its shaggy fur.

But the beast did not make contact.

The bear huffed slobber onto Kendra and shook its thick coat, spraying icy pinpricks of snow. Kendra detected no cues to suggest the scene was imaginary. She only had the knowledge that she had just been in the Dragon Temple with Warren, Tanu, and Raxtus. She felt tempted to wonder if the Dragon Temple had been a dream and this might be reality.

Except why would she be in a cabin in a snowy wilderness?

Raxtus had warned that Pioleen was magical.

Was that goofy little dragon splashing in the puddle somehow generating all of this?

The bear turned and started plodding away. Kendra arose. Where the skin of ice had broken, she scooped up a fluffy handful of snow, fingers stinging with impending numbness as she packed it into a snowball. She threw it and watched it burst against a tree trunk.

A wild, angry cry startled Kendra, and she saw an ugly goblin racing toward her through the snow, coming from a stand of trees. Clad in furs and an oversized helm, the goblin raised a notched scimitar as he closed in.

Kendra resisted the temptation to reach for her bow. This had to be part of the show. As the goblin drew near, Kendra resisted the urge to run away or defend herself. What if she accidentally hurt one of her friends?

The goblin swung his sword as he came within reach. Kendra flinched, but the blade stopped short of her neck. Placing a hand on one hip, the goblin planted his slightly rusted scimitar in the snow. "None of you are any fun," he complained in a female voice.

"This isn't real," Kendra said.

The goblin kicked up some snow. "It's real enough."

"We're on a mission," Kendra said.

"You seek something best left alone," the goblin said. "I'll tell you what. When this ends, you will have until the count of thirty to leave. If you don't, I'll squash you like bugs."

"Why not just let us pass?"

The goblin shook his head. "One . . . two . . . three . . ."

The snowy scene disappeared, and Kendra was back in the cavern, though she had moved to a different part of the room from where the illusion had begun. Warren stood where the goblin had been. Tanu was off to one side, roughly where the bear had gone.

"I'm glad I didn't slash the minotaur," Warren said to Kendra.

"I saw you as a goblin," Kendra said.

"Who stabbed me?" Tanu asked, hand over a wound on his thigh.

"Sorry," Warren said, wincing. "I didn't catch on at first. You seemed like a werehyena."

"Where is Pioleen?" Tanu asked, dabbing some goo onto the injury, then hastily wrapping a bandage around it.

Kendra scanned the room. Though the door that would take them onward remained closed, the door they had entered through stood open. The little dragon no longer splashed in her puddle.

"On the wall!" Raxtus exclaimed.

Looking higher on the wall of the cavern, Kendra saw the little dragon climbing like a lizard, perhaps thirty feet up. She wondered whether Pioleen's wings worked, or if this was just more eccentric behavior.

"A gorilla told me it would squash us," Tanu said.

"After counting to thirty," Raxtus added.

"Quick, Kendra, take her out," Warren urged.

Kendra drew the bowstring back and aimed. "Twenty."

When she released the string, twenty arrows shot toward Pioleen. At the same time, a piece of the ceiling broke off, falling to intercept the swarm of arrows before they reached the dragon.

Thirty. Time's up, Kendra heard in her mind.

The rock wall where Pioleen climbed bulged outward, becoming the perfectly sculpted head of a huge dragon. Pioleen perched on the head as the rest of the dragon emerged from the stone wall, complete with four legs, a pair of wings, and a long tail, detailed down to the texture of each individual scale.

Warren guzzled his potion and Kendra backed away as

the stone dragon stalked toward them. The dragon stomped on Warren, mashing him cartoonishly flat, but before the living statue reached Kendra, claws gripped her from behind and swung her into the air. Raxtus carried her beyond the reach of gaping jaws that bristled with rows of stone teeth.

"Try again," Raxtus urged, flying up toward the shadowy ceiling. "More arrows."

Pioleen remained atop the stone dragon's head, crouching low, wings spread wide. It seemed apparent the little dragon was controlling the larger one. Trying to keep her bow steady despite gliding high in the air, Kendra pulled back the string and whispered, "one hundred."

When she released, a deluge of arrows hissed toward their target, but the dragon simply raised a wing like a stone shield, and the projectiles pinged away harmlessly. The stone dragon now pursued Tanu, who had evidently taken another speed potion, judging from how swiftly he evaded the pounding claws and snapping teeth.

Warren had peeled himself up from the floor and was starting to regain his shape, though for the moment much of his body remained disgustingly flat. He pawed at his fallen sword with flimsy fingers.

"What should we do, Raxtus?" Kendra asked.

"I'm really not sure," Raxtus replied. "This stone dragon is a heavyweight, and who knows what other magic Pioleen might be ready to use? It might be best if I fly you out of here."

Raxtus veered abruptly as several stalactites fell from the ceiling, barely missing them. He swerved again as more stones tumbled from above.

"We can't give up," Kendra said. "There has to be a way. Can you get in for a closer shot? One that it can't block?"

"I can try," Raxtus said, wheeling and diving.

Down below, a barefoot woman dashed into the room, tall and lithe, wearing a dark green gown and carrying a sword in each hand. The stone dragon swiped at her with its tail, but she nimbly jumped over the attack and fleetly raced toward the rear of the dragon. Pine cones nested in her dark braids.

"Cyllia," Kendra said. "The hamadryad."

Tanu continued to dodge the front claws of the dragon, and Warren clambered clumsily to his feet, sword in hand. As Raxtus swooped near the stone dragon, Kendra pulled back her bowstring again. "Twenty," she whispered.

The flock of arrows flew, but the stone dragon tipped its head up and opened its mouth wide, and they sailed inside. Then the ferocious head shot toward Kendra and Raxtus, missing only thanks to a spiraling turn that made Kendra's head swim.

As Raxtus climbed higher, Kendra saw Cyllia sprinting up the back of the stone dragon, following the spine. The dragon bucked and twisted, but she continued at an astonishing pace and remained surefooted. By the time she neared the base of the neck, the head of the stone dragon swiveled around and darted downward to bite her. Cyllia not only dodged the strike but leaped onto the head, driving one sword through the little dragon and decapitating it with the other.

The stone dragon instantly became rigid. As the immobilized dragon started to tip, Raxtus dove. Waiting until the last instant, Cyllia sprang from the head, and Raxtus snatched her with his hind legs. When the stone dragon struck the cavern floor, the neck broke off, as did a wing. After the impact, the stone dragon remained motionless.

Raxtus glided Kendra and Cyllia to the floor, then raced over to the small corpse of Pioleen and ate it in a single bite. "Just to be sure," Raxtus explained after swallowing. "Plus, bragging rights."

"Thank you," Kendra told Cyllia, amazed by the height of the hamadryad up close. Head and shoulders above Tanu, she must have been nearly eight feet tall.

"I am assigned to protect you," the graceful woman replied. Her arms looked too slender to casually wield such long swords. After swishing them through the air, presumably to dispose of flesh and gore, she sheathed them.

"You'll stay with us until we get the Harp?" Kendra asked.

"I will serve you for as long as I am needed," Cyllia said.

"Our chances just went up," Warren said, his speech slurred, tottering toward them. "Did you see a woman in the previous room?" he asked the hamadryad.

"Vanessa encouraged me to hurry," Cyllia said.

"Have you been in many fights?" Kendra asked.

The hamadryad smiled. "This was my first battle. Much like my tree, I am newly born. But I carry knowledge and instincts from my ancestors."

"Happy birthday," Tanu said. "You arrived just in time."

"She was a tiny dragon," Cyllia said. "Just difficult to reach."

Kendra reconsidered Cyllia as a newborn. It made her

realize there was so much she didn't know about magical creatures. How many of them had no childhoods? She glanced at the fairy dragon. "Thanks for saving me, Raxtus," she said. "Again."

"We're all trying to save one another," the sparkly dragon said humbly.

"Did you see illusions?" Kendra asked.

"Cockatrices were attacking a nest of dragon eggs," Raxtus said. "It was hard to resist lending aid, but I decided it had to be a trick."

"I was at a grocery store," Warren said. "First a cashier transformed into a werehyena. Then a minotaur confronted me in the produce section. Turned out it was Kendra."

"I was the hyena," Tanu said, patting his bandage. "I witnessed foul creatures rising from the sea. One of them bit my thigh, but the fang pierced me just like a sword. I watched them slaughter innocents, while resisting the impulse to intervene."

"Mind magic doesn't usually work on me," Kendra said.

"This magic was attacking our senses," Tanu said. "The impulses came from outside our minds. Very potent and believable."

"Pioleen wanted us to kill one another," Kendra said.

"Good restraint, everyone but me," Warren said. "And way to finish the job, Cyllia."

The hamadryad gave a small bow.

"One more guardian," Warren said. "Let's hope this last monster is asleep."

CHAPTER THIRTY-EIGHT

Wings

Seth awoke looking up at a dome of rocks. The warm air was rich with the most pleasant woodsmoke he had ever smelled. Beyond the confines of his stony sanctuary, thunder boomed.

Seth sat up abruptly.

He had been struck by lightning!

Merek knelt nearby, his clothes and armor soiled. "Welcome back, Seth. You have friends in strange places."

An older man sat on the far side of the modest fire, wrapped in a dark brown cloak. He was handsome, with silver hair and a steady gaze. Seth had never seen him before.

"Did you build a dome around us?" Seth asked.

"The credit for your shelter goes to the Wandering Stones," the older man said. "I may have put in a good word."

Seth reached out with his power to see if he could

communicate with the rocks around him, but he could detect no identities. "Thank you. Not to be rude, but won't this fire choke us soon?"

The man gave a nod. "Ordinarily, yes, without a vent, but the stones are allowing the smoke to filter out. And I have some skill with woodcraft."

Seth turned to Merek. "Did the lightning knock you out, too?"

"I woke up only a few minutes ago," Merek said.

"Calvin?" Seth asked. "Serena?"

"I'm here," Calvin said from his pocket. "Serena too. We were both out cold."

Seth looked at the stranger. "How did you find us? Were you out for a walk? Enjoying the fine weather?"

"He isn't a dragon," Merek said. "I can tell."

Seth relaxed a little. Merek had anticipated his suspicion. "It's still unusual," Seth said.

"He is no ordinary man," Merek said.

"I admit I was seeking you, Seth Sorenson," the man said, pouring herbal tea from a kettle beside the fire into a cup. "Don't let that alarm you. There is enough peril ahead without me adding to your worries." He handed the cup to Seth. "You once did me a favor. It may have seemed small to you, but it was significant to me, and I have come to help you."

"I lost my memories," Seth said, grateful for the warmth of the cup between his hands.

"I understand," the man said. "Your friend the Dragon Slayer told me you have a long way to go tonight."

"It's basically impossible," Seth said. "Especially since you aren't a dragon."

The man poked the fire with a stick. "There are other powers besides dragons in the world. You are aware the Fairy Realm has fallen."

"I heard," Seth said, taking a careful sip from the cup. The tea was hot, but cool enough for sipping. It warmed and invigorated him.

"I managed to sneak a relic or two out during the commotion," the man said.

"You're from the Fairy Realm?" Seth asked.

"Once I was," the man said. "It has been a great while since I truly belonged there. But I came from there recently. Have you heard of the astrids?"

"Flying men," Seth said. "Sometimes they look like owls with human faces."

"Wings are a specialty among the fairy folk," the man said. "I suspect wings might help you and the Dragon Slayer tonight."

"Maybe," Seth said. "It might be too stormy." Every sip of the flavorful tea helped Seth feel more alert.

"Much too stormy for most wings," the man agreed. "But the wings of an astrid are extraordinary. They perform very well under duress and always respond to courage."

"Are you an astrid?" Seth asked.

"I am not," the man said. "Nor can I offer astrids to help you. But I can give you and your friend wings like an astrid, if you wish."

"You can make us into astrids?" Seth asked.

"No, you're a mortal," the man said. "And the Dragon Slayer is mortal as well, though he possesses a lifespan that tests the limits. I can give you both temporary wings, of the same sort used by astrids."

"Wings that could fly through the Perennial Storm?" Merek asked.

"Any storm," the man said. "Including this one. Maintain your courage, and even thunderbirds will appear clumsy beside you."

"Sounds like a wild ride," Calvin said.

"Sadly, I don't have tiny wings for the nipsies," the man said.

"We're used to being passengers," Serena said.

"Wings like you're describing could save us," Seth said.

The man nodded. "These sets of wings are the most useful gift I could manage under these circumstances. They are resistant to lightning and freezing temperatures. If you can keep your courage against dragons, these wings will largely protect you from the magic behind their breath weapons."

"That could be valuable if dragons show up," Merek said.

"Dragons are quietly gathering here," the man said. "Have you not felt it, Dragon Slayer? Titan Valley will soon be resisting the largest offensive dragons have launched since the sanctuaries were established."

"I saw Celebrant, the Dragon King," Seth said. "In his human form."

"He has come to lead the assault," the man said. "The giants have set themselves up for a disaster with the way this sanctuary has been run. I'm not sure Celebrant could have garnered the support he needed for this war without the ability to cite the conditions here."

"With respect, how do you know so much?" Merek asked. "Who are you?"

"Perhaps I am wrong," the man said. "You be the judge. I have filled many roles in my days. For now, you may call me the Traveler."

"Thanks for your help, Traveler," Seth said. "That lightning could have killed me."

"Had you been left exposed to the storm, it might have," the Traveler said.

"This tea really helped," Seth said.

"It's a specialty of mine," the Traveler said. "I should not consume more time. You ran through this storm because you have places to be. Turn your backs to me if you want wings."

Seth turned away from the Traveler. Merek did likewise.

Seth felt strong fingers examining his back; then the side of a hand pressed beside his shoulder blade, followed by similar pressure near the other one. For a painful moment, Seth felt something taking root in his back, twining with his muscles. Then, as easily as moving his hands, he flexed and stretched his wings. They spanned quite a bit broader than the reach of his outspread arms and had golden feathers.

"This feels weirdly natural," Seth said.

"Almost like you were born with them," the Traveler said.

Merek flapped his wings harder than Seth had attempted, blowing air and campfire smoke around the stone enclosure. "This is unbelievable," Merek said. "What a gift!"

Seth noticed the Unforgiving Blade on the ground and picked it up.

"That is quite a weapon," the Traveler commented. "Take care where you keep it and how you use it."

"I'll do my best," Seth said.

"Blades such as that one have a history of harming the wielder," the Traveler said. "If you'll take my advice, try not to carry it longer than necessary."

"A wise sentiment," Merek said. "At present the weapon is a necessity."

"Remember, with those wings, courage is key," the Traveler said. "Now, open so our guests may depart, my wandering friends."

One side of the dome collapsed, and the rocks slid out of the way. The storm immediately clamored louder, rain pelting down amid harsh flashes of lightning and stunning bursts of thunder. The wind roared with a volume Seth had never imagined.

"Do you know where to go?" Seth asked Merek.

"Yes," Merek replied. "Stay with me. Traveler, we are in your debt."

"You are, perhaps, Dragon Slayer," the Traveler said. "I will always owe Seth. Fly well."

Merek stepped into the downpour and jumped, wings beating down to propel him up into the wild night. For a moment, Seth stared up at the dark fury of the Perennial Storm, watching jagged tangles of lightning backlight the rain and highlight the clouds. With a running start, he sprang from the relative warmth of the protective dome into the icy pandemonium of the tempest. His wings flapped hard as Seth ascended behind and beneath Merek, adapting to the punishing winds.

The wings did not feel like a contraption he was wearing. They sprouted out of his back as though part of him, and they functioned instinctively, as if he had flown in savage weather for years. Rising through the chilling rain, Seth and Merek promptly became soaked, but even with the wind stripping away his heat, Seth didn't go numb. The exercise of flapping his wings generated a surprising amount of warmth.

Soon lightning blazed not just above them, but to the sides, and even beneath them. Most of the electric discharges were brilliant variations on yellow, white, and orange, but a startling amount also flared green or light blue, and a few deepened into vivid shades of red or purple. A cannonade of thunder accompanied the intense lightning, but Seth did not find the blasts as deafening as before he had his wings.

The lightning made it relatively easy for Seth to track Merek, and, between flashes, Merek's wings shed enough light of their own that Seth could glimpse them through the deluge. Seth felt less buffeted than when he had flown in the talons of Basirus ahead of the storm. The wind currents were stronger and wilder here in the heart of the tempest, but Seth's wings reacted magnificently—tucking, extending, angling, and folding into unique shapes to help him make swift progress in whatever direction he chose.

As the winged duo gained altitude, flying near the base

of the storm clouds, Seth became aware of great birds of prey with wingspans the size of hang gliders. The dark raptors soared sedately through the turmoil, wings fully extended, three on one side of Seth and two beyond Merek.

Dazzling stabs of colorful lightning increased in both frequency and proximity after the birds arrived. Seth felt a charge in the air a moment before lightning shot through his wings, through Merek's wings, and into one of the thunderbirds off to the side. Seth felt some of the heat from the brilliant flash and smelled ozone afterward, but he didn't experience an electric shock.

The surprise of the brightness and the heat, coupled with the immediate detonation of thunder, startled Seth enough that his wings faltered. The sensation of his wings failing compounded his fear, and he went into a free fall.

"Courage, Seth!" Calvin called. "You can do it!"

Clenching his fists, Seth deliberately mustered his courage and swooped upward again. Merek had plunged to help Seth, but once they both flew evenly, he tried some evasive maneuvers. Though he spiraled and swerved, the thunderbirds stayed with them.

Seth held the Unforgiving Blade ready in case the huge raptors decided to attack. Another electric charge built up around Seth, and a second lightning bolt crackled through his wings. After a third blast of lightning caused no real harm, the thunderbirds seemed to lose interest, and they veered away.

Some flashes of lightning offered hints to the terrain below or granted flickering glimpses of the surrounding horizon, but otherwise Seth followed Merek with blind faith. The Dragon Slayer flew to one side of Seth and a little ahead of him, never seeming to doubt his course. Seth decided to stop hoping he would see the Dragon Temple up ahead, because the continued absence of their destination became too disheartening. Pummeled by blustery gales and stinging sleet, they resolutely pressed forward, wings flapping and adjusting endlessly, as the nightmare tempest raged on.

Velrog

Kendra paused where the corridor ahead sloped ever steeper, almost becoming vertical before curving back to level at the bottom. She had cautiously edged to where she could see all the way down, but inching much farther would lead to a fall.

Warren crouched beside her. "The ground is smooth. It'll be like riding a steep slide."

"Getting back up will be tricky," Kendra said.

"Not with me around," Raxtus assured her.

"I can help too," Cyllia said.

"Time is a factor," Tanu reminded the group.

"Let me take the lead," Cyllia offered, drawing her swords. "Who knows what lurks down there?"

"All right," Kendra said.

With an adroit mix of bounding and sliding on her feet,

the hamadryad raced down the slope. "It's quiet down here," she called up to the others.

"I can take you, Kendra," Raxtus said.

"Thanks," Kendra said. "It looks like jumping off a building."

"I would accept some help as well," Tanu said, craning forward to peer down the steep drop. "Big guys aren't made for falling."

"I'll be right back," Raxtus said, gripping Kendra's shoulders with his forelegs. The dragon sprang forward, and Kendra felt the alarming rush of falling before he extended his wings fully, turning himself into her personal hang glider and dropping her gently at the bottom.

As Raxtus flew back to help Tanu, Kendra approached where Cyllia stood. A steepled archway at the end of the corridor granted access to a sizable chamber, partially masked by curtains of web.

"Spiders?" Kendra asked.

"Those don't seem like spiderwebs to me," Cyllia said.

Raxtus shuttled Tanu down, and then Warren as well. They all gathered by Kendra and the hamadryad.

"I've always hated the feeling of walking through a spiderweb," Raxtus whispered, peering ahead.

"I will lead," Cyllia said. "The edges of my blades are keen."

The hamadryad preceded them to the steepled archway. She stepped around the curtains of web, and the others followed. Milky crystals recessed in the grimy walls dimly lit a huge cylindrical chamber that widened near the top, like a funnel. Gray draperies of web veiled much of the room from floor to ceiling. High above, thick strands crisscrossed in bizarre patterns. Holding her bow ready, Kendra scanned the gauzy, overlapping layers for a threat.

"It reeks of death in here," Cyllia murmured.

"What could have died?" Kendra asked.

"Rats, cave beetles, earthworms—the giant kind," Tanu said.

"I'm worried this could be Velrog," Raxtus whispered, looking up.

"Who is that?" Warren asked.

Raxtus closed his eyes momentarily and gave a shudder. "A mutant dragon with the skills of a spider. Humans have the boogeyman. Dragons have Velrog. Our mothers tell us stories about Velrog to motivate good behavior."

"What can he do?" Tanu asked.

With a glance toward the webby chamber, Raxtus shrank down low. "I don't know where myth ends and fact begins. The stories claim his webs are strong enough to ensnare dragons. They say breath weapons cannot harm him. He was the first of the demonic dragons—supposedly he came into being when a dark wizard worked unnatural magic on a dragon egg. He was incubated and hatched in the bowels of a crumbling castle and never learned to love the sky."

"Great story, Raxtus," Warren said. "So we're down here with your childhood nightmare?"

Raxtus looked to Tanu. "Do you have any potions that make you slippery? So that nothing could stick to you?"

"It would be an interesting challenge," Tanu said. "I haven't tried to produce that effect, and I don't have the ingredients to attempt it now."

"Avoid the webs," Raxtus said. "If this is Velrog, we have to kill him before he entraps us."

A dry laugh drifted down from above. "What peculiar visitors," a clinical voice observed from the upper reaches of the room. "Surface dwellers chaperoned by a dragon."

Kendra searched the shadowed heights of the room, but web formations blocked her view. Some strands and sheets of web quivered, as if an unseen predator were in motion somewhere on the interconnected network.

"We have no quarrel with you, Velrog," Raxtus said, his voice cracking at the end.

"If you know my name, then you understand what awaits," Velrog replied. "Forgive me if I consume you slowly. I savor morsels from the sunlit realm."

"Ten," Kendra said, aiming her bow toward the sound of the voice and releasing the string. A burst of arrows streaked upward, but all got caught at various distances in the filmy layers of webbing before getting halfway to the highest pockets of shadow.

"The webs are stronger than they look," Warren lamented quietly.

"The intruders brought toys," Velrog said. "Clumsy tools that poke and prod. Poor substitutes for teeth and claws. Bring your toys, surface walkers, and teach me how to play."

Webs throughout the room vibrated, and a dragon roughly the size of an elephant dropped to the floor in front of Cyllia. Instead of the snug scales encasing most dragons, heavy plates armored Velrog, many bristling with thorny spines. The bulky creature looked like a relative of a horned lizard or an ankylosaurus, but with six legs and an additional pair of tiny forelegs at the front. The rounded bulge at the end of his tail gave it the shape of a flail.

"Fifty," Kendra said, releasing the bowstring. Arrows swarmed at Velrog and stuck to all the surfaces of the dragon, showing that the plates shielding his body were leathery.

Velrog shook like a wet dog, shedding arrows in all directions. Cyllia sprinted forward, a sword in each hand, and Velrog sprang into the air, batlike wings flapping to lift him out of reach. The dragon opened his wide mouth, and gray matter streamed out like water from a firehose. Wherever the concentrated stream touched, gooey masses of web spread outward. Cyllia leaped and dodged and aerialed to avoid the web stream for a few seconds before it overtook her, binding her from head to foot in a heavy cocoon. The hamadryad squirmed and struggled, making the cocoon bulge slightly and wiggle. Her muffled cries made Kendra question whether Cyllia could breathe.

Raxtus sprang forward and used his teeth to tear the webbing away from her head. Cyllia gasped with relief and Raxtus took flight, hurtling toward Velrog. This time Velrog breathed a silvery mist that coalesced around Raxtus, promptly leaving him tangled in a messy net of webs. Wings stuck to his sides, Raxtus fell to the floor. Flying overhead,

Velrog fired a gray sphere from his mouth that exploded into a jumble of webs when it hit the fallen dragon.

Hoping the extended wings in flight made Velrog more vulnerable, Kendra aimed her bow and cried, "Eighty!" As the arrows launched, Velrog tucked his wings. The projectiles connected to his thick scales as he plummeted to the floor.

After Velrog landed, legs splayed beneath him, Kendra hauled back the bowstring again and called, "Fifty!" When she released, no arrows flew. Pulling the string again, she frantically tried to calculate how many arrows she had used so far. Was the bow empty? Or had fifty exceeded the balance of her remaining arrows?

Raxtus snapped at the constraining webs with his teeth and raked with his claws, finally cutting himself free enough to scramble behind the cover of some of the heavier web curtains. Glancing over her shoulder, Kendra saw Tanu expanding into a giant version of himself as he tossed aside an empty bottle. Warren ran to Cyllia and started sawing at her bindings with a dagger.

"Ten," Kendra said, and ten arrows sped to thunk against Velrog. She at least wanted to provide a distraction. Was it too much to hope she might hit an eye?

"Ten," she repeated, and after she released the string, Velrog looked even more like a pincushion.

"Ten," she said again, but no arrows launched.

"One," Kendra tried, but the empty string twanged without a result.

Velrog shook off the arrows as Tanu stomped past

Kendra, his knees level with her shoulders. The enlarged Samoan rushed the dragon, but Velrog took flight and began spraying a stream of web matter. Powering forward, Tanu swiped at the spreading webs with minor success at first, but as Velrog kept the stream trained on him, webs multiplied until Tanu became hopelessly entangled. Staggering sideways, the potion master fell against a tall, webby drapery and stuck there as Velrog piled on more bindings.

Tossing her bow aside, Kendra pulled out the sack of gales. Aiming the mouth at the flying dragon, she opened the bag.

"No!" Raxtus cried from his hiding place behind the webs as a torrent of wind gushed from the sack, flinging Velrog back against the wall. Velrog folded his wings and dropped to the ground as veils of web around the room flapped and billowed wildly, sticky cords whipping like manic tentacles in the flood of wind swirling through the cylindrical chamber.

Kendra hurriedly closed the sack, but the damage was done. Raxtus hung like a trapped bug, wings askew, sandwiched between layers of sticky curtains. Warren had become ensnared by sheets of web as well, and Cyllia remained bound in her snug cocoon. Tanu flopped and wriggled, but the restraining webs held him fast.

Only three ropes of web had adhered to Kendra—one on her right shoulder and two against her left leg. Kendra grabbed the cord on her shoulder to yank it off but found her hand instantly affixed. Her most desperate tugging did nothing to separate the gluey line from her shoulder or her palm.

Velrog scuttled through snarled strands and enmeshed draperies as if they had no adhesive properties. He shot a spurt of gray web stream at Kendra that left her wrapped from shoulders to knees in warm, soft matter that proved frustratingly resilient when she struggled.

"I have not feasted like this in ages," Velrog gloated, approaching Cyllia. "This one is a singular prize, long and trim, brimming with vitality. I have almost forgotten the robust flavor of a tree maiden."

"I'm meatier," Tanu invited.

"No, me," Warren insisted, lunging against the webs that held him. "His aftertaste is gamey."

"I shall wait until you return to your actual size, potion man," Velrog said. "Magically augmented meat reduces unpleasantly after ingestion. None of you should fret. You will all get your turn. I have long subscribed to the policy of beginning with the ripest fruit."

"I am not afraid," Cyllia said.

"Excellent," Velrog enthused. "For your bravery, I award you a final chance." Leaning forward, the dragon breathed pink fluid onto Cyllia that melted away her bindings. The hamadryad reclaimed her swords and assumed a fighting stance. Stepping carefully, weapons ready, she moved to the portion of the room least festooned with webs.

"Evil fogs your judgment," Cyllia said. "I am no typical tree maiden. I am Kendra's guardian and your executioner."

Cyllia threw one of her swords. It embedded in Velrog

beside the neck, and he snarled as she raced forward, her other sword ready to strike. Hissing fiercely, Velrog dodged her swing, then lunged at her. Cyllia sidestepped the bite, pulled her embedded sword from the dragon, and nimbly ducked a swipe from the tail.

"Enough," Velrog declared, blowing a puff of mist at the agile warrior. The cloud condensed into hundreds of entwined strands, and the more Cyllia moved, the more fully entangled she became.

Velrog pounced, and Kendra looked away as the dragon noisily devoured the hamadryad. Kendra strained against the webs girdling her, weeping with frustration as her muscles failed the test. She fell over, and the webs binding her stuck to the floor.

"That was rash," Velrog admitted after his last swallow. "Luscious, satisfying, but overly indulgent. How could I resist? It has been so long. Having slaked my appetite, I intend to relish the rest of you."

Velrog looked upward. Kendra heard a rush of air and flapping wings. Had Raxtus torn free? No, he remained flypapered to the hanging webs. Craning her head, Kendra glimpsed two figures flying above and behind her, golden wings flashing. Both held swords. Were they astrids? Where had they come from? As they wheeled into a more visible position, Kendra recognized one of the newcomers as her brother!

Seth hovered beside Merek. After arriving at the Dragon Temple as the sun rose, they had found a dead giant, two dead dragons, and the main door open. They had discovered a dragon corpse in the mirror maze, shortly before meeting a blind woman named Vanessa, who had encouraged them onward. They had flown through a room with an enormous, broken dragon statue, and then had arrived in this web-shrouded lair.

"Is that your sister?" Merek asked, pointing down to where Kendra lay wrapped in webs on the floor.

"Yeah," Seth said, happy to find her alive.

"Who has joined us?" the dragon asked. "A pair of sparrows?"

"Velrog!" Merek warned Seth. "This one hunts like a spider. He is preparing to feed. Split up."

Seth swooped one way and Merek the other. Seth's wings involuntarily jerked him sideways, and a gray ball of matter flew by, barely missing him. As he maneuvered closer to the scurrying dragon, Seth dodged many webby banners and tendrils, his golden wings neatly slicing through any strands they encountered.

Diving near the dragon with his stake in his hand, Merek swerved to avoid the club tail and missed his chance to strike. The dragon jetted a concentrated stream of web material at him, but Merek flew behind hanging webs, and the stream could not reach him.

Seth streaked toward the dragon. The creature turned and breathed a gray mist at him. Holding out his long knife, Seth spiraled into the cloud, wings spinning like blades in a blender, and he came through the mist with only a few gluey strands clinging to him.

Landing beside the dragon, Seth slashed one of the legs. He thought he had missed, due to the lack of resistance against his blade, but then the limb fell off. Shrieking, the dragon tipped toward him, allowing Seth to stab the Unforgiving Blade up into its belly. The blade entered effortlessly, as if he had thrust it into water.

Otherwise strangely still, the dragon trembled.

"How?" the dragon whispered, the words requiring effort to speak. "Your blade . . . I have failed. I yield."

"You do?" Seth asked.

"Seth," Merek called. "Grant the monstrosity a clean death."

"Remove . . . the blade," the dragon begged quietly. "Please . . ."

Seth noticed the platelike scales around the blade withering and darkening.

"Quickly, Seth," Raxtus said. "It isn't a trick."

The dragon gasped. "Please . . . my word . . . mercy."

Seth pulled out the Unforgiving Blade but held it ready. On shaky legs, the dragon turned, lowering his head in front of Seth. "Be quick," the dragon whispered.

The Unforgiving Blade passed easily through the neck, though it lacked enough length to decapitate the dragon with a single stroke. Two more rapid swipes fully parted the head from the body. The dragon collapsed and remained still.

Seth stepped away and pondered the long knife in his

hand. How powerful was it? What had the dragon felt with the dark blade inside of him?

Merek landed beside Seth. "Well done. First dragon?"

"Second," Kendra said from her webby straitjacket. "Unless you've killed others since leaving us."

"The first I can remember," Seth said. "Hi, Kendra."

"Where did you get wings?" Kendra asked.

"Some old guy in the middle of nowhere," Seth said. "After I was struck by lightning."

"You've been busy," a guy tangled in webs said. "I'm Warren, Seth. Welcome back."

"Nice to meet you," Seth said. "I probably used to know you?"

"You knew all of us," the huge Polynesian said.

"Sorry we didn't get here sooner," Seth said. "The weather was insane. We did our best. This is Merek. He's . . . useful against dragons. Can I say?"

Merek gave a nod.

"He's one of the legendary Dragon Slayers," Seth said.

"Wait," Kendra said. "One of the five originals? A son of Konrad?"

"You know your history," Merek said.

"I've already seen him turn a dragon to dust," Seth said.

"We just eliminated a couple ourselves," Warren muttered.

"Your group did well," Merek complimented. "I have never seen a dragon filleted like Jinzen. And Pioleen has proven hard to kill for centuries."

"The leader of Dragonwatch is searching for the

legendary Dragon Slayers," Kendra said. "Do you know there is a dragon war going on?"

"I'm learning," Merek said. "Your brother recently reunited me with my memories."

"That's ironic," Kendra said. "Now if only we can get Seth's memories back."

"His memories existed separate from him," Seth said. "Almost like a ghost. Mine are probably in a similar state."

"How did you find him?" Kendra asked Seth.

"Happy accident," Seth said.

"You still don't remember me," Kendra said.

"Not from my old memories," Seth said. "Hopefully soon."

"I'm Tanu," the giant Polynesian guy said. "If you free me, I can help the others. I suspect that dragon has a gland in its mouth that produces a liquid to melt the webs."

Seth held up the Unforgiving Blade. "I can't use this. It's too dangerous to get close to anyone."

"I will use my wings to free Tanu," Merek said.

"I'm not always this massive," Tanu said. "I brewed an enlargement potion."

Merek took flight and started swooping near Tanu, his wings slashing away large swathes of web. Seth walked over to Kendra.

"What's with the smaller dragon?" Seth asked. "The one in the webs?"

"I'm Raxtus," the dragon said. "It's good to see you, Seth. I'm on your side."

"He is," Kendra confirmed.

"Nice to meet you," Seth said. He returned his attention to Kendra. "You're the one stuck this time."

"I wouldn't have left you on that mushroom," Kendra said. "I was trying to take advantage of having a captive audience. It was a delicate situation."

"Still is in a lot of ways," Seth said.

"Do you know we're on your side?" Kendra asked.

"Generally," Seth said. "I've confirmed that you're my sister. But I still have a lot to figure out."

"Can we agree that we don't want dragons to rule the world?" Kendra said.

"Yes," Seth answered.

"And we can agree we don't want Ronodin ruling the Fairy Realm?"

"Definitely," Seth said.

"That's a start," Kendra said.

"This is the third dragon you fought today inside the Dragon Temple?" Seth asked.

"It should be the last guardian," Kendra affirmed. "Thanks for the help. Is the storm still raging?"

"It was brutal," Seth said. "The storm was slowing down when we arrived here. The sun was starting to peek through. And it was raining purple frogs."

"Literally raining frogs?" Kendra checked.

"Yes," Seth verified. "Live ones, tiny and slimy."

"Gross," Kendra said.

"It was pretty disgusting," Seth admitted.

Trailing a short cape of webs, Tanu trudged over to Velrog. Crouching, he pulled the jaws apart, then, after finding leverage, cracked the jaws much wider than they were meant to open. Bending over, the gigantic Polynesian poked around inside the exposed mouth.

"If the storm is winding down, we need to hurry," Kendra said. "The dragons could strike anytime. Who knows how many might come to the temple? At some point, they will realize we killed the guards they posted here. We have to find the Harp before they arrive."

"I've got it," Tanu said, turning and smiling, holding up a pulpy little pocket of tissue. "Let me blend this into a solution, and I'll have everyone web-free in no time."

Second Storm

"T ess," Emery called. "Fetch your brother and meet me in the hall. There is something you should see."

"Is the storm over?" Tess asked.

"One is over," Emery said. "Another may be starting. Hurry."

Tess had only been awake for a few minutes. In Humburgh, Virgil had recommended they take refuge at Terastios before the storm hit, so she, Knox, Newel, and Doren had gone to Big Side and returned to the giant fortress with Rustafet. The night had been tumultuous outside, with shrieking winds and nearly continuous thunder, but she had finally slept.

Tess ran into Knox's room and shook him. "Wake up."

"Leave me alone," Knox grumbled, pulling the pillow over his head. "I could barely sleep last night."

"Emery wants to show us something," Tess insisted. "It's important."

"You go see," Knox mumbled. "She can show me later."

"Another storm is coming," Tess said.

Knox sat up. "Another storm? What do you mean?"

"Come on," Tess said. "She's waiting."

"Give me a minute," Knox said. "Let me get dressed."

Tess went out of his room and waited. She started to worry it was a trick and he was back under his covers. "Are you coming?" she checked.

He opened the door, a crease from the pillow printed across his cheek, eyes bleary, but he had a T-shirt, jeans, and shoes on. "This better be good."

"If not, blame Emery," Tess said, leading him to the hall.

"Glad to see you awake," Emery said. She took Tess by the hand. "I've been alerted to something worth seeing. This way."

The beautiful servant led them down a few hallways to a leaded-glass window, which she opened, offering a view from the front of the fortress. The storm clouds had broken up and were drifting into the distance. Several trees had fallen and more had lost limbs. Many were charred from lightning strikes. Standing water abounded in pools and puddles.

And there was a small group of dragons flying toward Terastios.

Behind them, in the distance, hundreds of flying objects peppered the sky.

The platinum scales of the leading dragon gleamed in the light of the newly risen sun as he landed in front of the fortress. Sleek in form and enormous in scale, he wore a crown at the base of his majestic horns. Twenty other dragons formed up behind him.

"Welcome to a new day," Celebrant declared in a clear voice with the resonance of many men speaking in unison. "Revenge is all the sweeter when your oppressors understand their doom. As of this morning, the other six dragon sanctuaries have all fallen. Yours is the last to stand. It will not endure for long."

The dragons behind Celebrant roared and blew fire triumphantly.

"I offer no terms of surrender. The way you have treated our kind here leaves no room for mercy. You giants never placed an emphasis on magical defenses for Stratos and Terastios, considering such preparations beneath you. Speaking as your devoted enemy, you have my sincere gratitude for this philosophy. What meager defensive spells were in place have already been compromised. I want the dragons of Titan Valley to know that the hour of their liberation is at hand. I want the sky giants to realize that by nightfall, they will be extinct. And I want all to recognize that when we dragons finish our work here today, no two stones of this fortress will remain one upon the other, and the kingdom of Stratos will be a scarred and desolate waste."

The dragons flanking Celebrant flapped their wings and bellowed. Behind them, rank upon rank of airborne dragons came into clearer view.

"The overseers of Titan Valley long ago forgot the might of dragons. We have come to issue a reminder that will never be forgotten. I am Celebrant the Just, and I swear that the Perennial Storm was a feeble precursor to the real tempest. Dragons, attack!"

The gates of Terastios opened, and three armored giants charged out, one bearing a mace, one a sword, and one a flail. After inhaling deeply, the Dragon King breathed out a stream of white energy that blew the helmet off the lead giant and left him on the ground, clutching his face. As the dragons accompanying Celebrant soared into the air, unleashing long columns of fire, searing bolts of lightning, and roiling torrents of acid, Emery closed the window and led Knox and Tess away.

"Are you going to kill us?" Knox asked Emery.

"I remain loyal to the Giant Queen, and I have been tasked with keeping you safe," Emery said. "Should she fall, I will be released from my vows to her, and I will resume my former life as a dragon. I want to get you to safety before that happens. Nobody who remains in Terastios will survive."

"Where can we go?" Tess asked.

"You must take the passage to Humburgh," Emery said. "Humbuggle has his own defenses there, and the wrath of Celebrant is not directed at him. Raza has contacted Rustafet to help you. And Giselle is waking the satyrs."

"We should have stayed in Humburgh," Knox complained.

"This was the better place to weather the Perennial Storm," Emery said. "There was no way to know these dragons were coming."

"Are you excited to be free?" Tess asked.

Emery gave a modest smile. "I must temper my emotions. I need to remain loyal until I am free, or this choker will strangle me. If despite our best efforts the Giant Queen falls, many of the servants in this fortress will transform and change allegiance. We must be swift."

Newel and Doren ran up to them, with Raza and Giselle trailing behind.

"How are you kids doing?" Newel asked.

"Good," Tess said. "Except Celebrant is attacking."

"We knew a dragon apocalypse was coming," Doren said. "Turns out it's today."

"We'll be all right," Newel assured them. "These servants of the Giant Queen will evacuate us."

"Before they change into monsters who want to eat us," Doren said.

"Escape will be a challenge," Raza said, walking briskly and motioning for them to follow. "Terastios will fall fast. The giants are woefully unprepared for a fight. In here, please." He opened a door into a narrow hall Tess had never seen.

An unfamiliar male servant waited behind the door. Stepping forward, he whispered something to Raza.

Raza glanced back at them. "We should run."

Tess pumped her arms and legs as fast as she could, trying to keep up with the adults. Raza glanced back at her and slowed his pace a little. Then Newel scooped her into his arms, and the pace increased again. They passed intersections with other cramped, nondescript hallways. As other servants rushed by them from different directions, Tess decided these passages were used primarily by the staff of the fortress.

A female servant ran toward them waving both arms, and Raza paused to speak with her. She leaned close and whispered. Newel was panting from the exertion, along with the rest of the group.

"I can run again," Tess offered.

"Better trust these goat legs," the satyr said. "They've transported me out of many a jam."

Raza turned to address the others. "The way I hoped to go is cut off. There is an alternate passage at the rear of the throne room, a secret way known only to a few. We can hope the commotion will be sufficient to distract those who would stop us."

"Lead on," Doren said.

Raza doubled back the way they had come, then turned down new passages. If Tess had to retrace her steps, she knew she would get lost. The plain hallways looked so similar, and there were too many intersections.

As they ran, from behind the stone walls of the passage, Tess heard an occasional rumble, along with some muted screaming and shouting. They passed a female servant whose silk kimono was singed and fuming.

At length, Raza led them through a door to the throne room and onto a human-sized walkway along the perimeter of the immense space. The walkway led to bleachers where humans and others of similar stature could observe the royal court.

The Giant Queen stood before the throne, her royal scepter clenched in one hand, a sword in the other, glaring at the main doors. Something beyond the doors was slamming against them, causing them to buckle inward, hinges rattling.

Only three other giants remained in the typically crowded room—two armed guards and a completely bald councilor wearing a sky-blue toga.

"Your majesty," the councilor implored. "Our defenses are failing. You must flee."

"I will not give up Terastios to a horde of worms," the Giant Queen said.

"Your people need you," the councilor insisted. "Fall back to where we can better defend ourselves. Ideally Humburgh. Or Stratos, at least."

"If the dragons are going to cut me down, my back will not be facing them," the Giant Queen said. "I will slay their entire host alone if I must. Find a weapon, Eratad. No true giant would flee to Humburgh."

The main doors to the throne room burst open and dragons poured through. The space was plenty large enough for them to fly, and most took to the air as the two giant guards, one female, one male, charged forward to oppose them.

"Give me a turn," Doren whispered to Newel, running by his side, and Tess was passed from one satyr to the other. Burying her face against Doren, Tess hid her eyes from the combat.

Knox leaned against the railing of the walkway, eyes intent on the battle. The guards held up massive shields as dragons rained down fire and lightning from above. When dragons swept in to physically attack, the female guard chopped the head off one with a sword, and the male guard skewered another with his spear.

Several of the attackers cleared the way for a dark gray dragon. The newcomer exhaled vast quantities of silvery mist that enveloped the two guards. The dragons retreated away from the broadening cloud, and a scarred one breathed fire into it. The instant the flames contacted the mist, the entire cloud erupted into a blazing fireball, flaring intensely bright for a few seconds and sending heat washing over the entire room before snuffing out. After the fiery display, dragons mobbed the burned guards, dispatching them viciously.

"Come," Newel called, and Knox realized the others were running ahead of him along the walkway. For a moment he wished he was small enough to be carried like Tess; then he sprinted after the others, his eyes straying to the fight.

The councilor turned and ran toward the rear of the throne room, behind the dais. The Giant Queen reversed her grip on her sword and flung it like a spear, harpooning the fleeing councilor through the back. Then she drew another sword from a scabbard affixed to her throne and whirled to face the dragons.

Celebrant soared to the front of the group, landing before the dais. Knox had never thought anyone could make the Dragon King look small, but the Giant Queen loomed high above him. He could have been her reptilian pet.

"Come at me, slave master," Celebrant invited.

The other dragons stayed back, either pacing on the floor or flying in holding patterns above. The Giant Queen stepped down from her dais, sword and scepter ready, still towering over Celebrant.

"How dare you come here?" the Giant Queen exclaimed.

"To illustrate that when authority can be overthrown, it will be," Celebrant said. "And to remind the world what happens when dragons are crossed."

"Do you think fire or lightning can harm me?" the Giant Queen challenged. "I am of the old blood. The dragons are about to mourn their king."

"The race of giants expires today," Celebrant answered. "Old blood and new."

Face contorted with rage, the Giant Queen swung her scepter down with such force that it shattered the throne-room floor where Celebrant had stood. But the Dragon King was no longer there. Moving with the speed of a striking snake, Celebrant sprang up and around the Giant Queen, trying to get behind her. In one fluid motion, she slashed him away with her sword, the edge skating over his scales, failing to draw blood.

Other dragons charged the Giant Queen. Flames billowed and lightning blazed. Her sword severed the head from one dragon, and a stroke of her scepter crumpled another. In the commotion, Celebrant attacked her from behind, clamping his jaws onto the back of her neck and exhaling into her.

The Giant Queen fell heavily to her knees, her face confused. And the dragons swarmed. Her crown rolled away from the frenzy, finally settling to the polished floor like a spun coin.

Knox caught up to the others where they crouched behind the bleachers.

"Is it over?" Giselle asked Raza hopefully.

"Are we free?" Emery asked.

As if responding to the question, the silver collars fell from their necks.

"Come with me," Raza said, moving out of hiding to the front of the bleachers. The two female servants followed.

Raza swelled into a huge white dragon with narrow red stripes, Emery expanded into a blue dragon bethorned with short quills, and Giselle became a red dragon tattooed with swirling black markings. Roaring exultantly, all three joined in attacking the Giant Queen.

Celebrant was the first to emerge from the ferocious pack. "Our revenge is not yet complete," the Dragon King asserted. "Many other giants still resist or run free. They must be eradicated."

He flew away from the colossal corpse, and the other dragons followed.

Except Raza, who glided toward the bleachers.

Giselle and Emery landed between the white dragon and his potential prey.

"Out of my way," Raza ordered, his voice magnified to match his new size.

"They are children," Emery said, her voice empowered as well. "And you are no longer in charge of us."

"You've been polluted!" Raza accused. "What do you care for human brats!"

"They were young ones placed in our care," Giselle said. The largest of the three, her voice carried the most powerfully. "They showed no aggression. What is the harm in their survival?"

"They were affiliated with Dragonwatch," Raza said.

"Some they traveled with were affiliated," Giselle corrected.

"At least give me the satyrs," Raza said.

"The satyrs are minding the young ones," Emery said. "Perhaps you have been polluted. Of what consequence are satyrs to our kind? You have giants to hunt."

Gnashing his teeth, Raza turned and flew from the room.

"You're not going to eat us?" Tess asked.

Emery looked down at her through reptilian eyes. "I could not have known before the transformation, but no, we will not devour you, not here, not like this." She held up a claw. "Come."

Emery took hold of Tess and Knox, and Giselle snatched the two satyrs. They flew to a rear corner of the throne room and set them down near a human-sized door.

"Through here," Giselle instructed. "Take your first right, then your first left, then go through the first door you reach. With luck, you will find Rustafet waiting."

"You're on your own now," Emery said. "Make your way to Humburgh and lie low."

"Thank you," Tess said.

"You're welcome," Emery replied, her eyes shifting away from Tess. "The rest of you owe your lives to this little girl. Farewell."

Emery and Giselle took flight and soared out of the throne room.

"Come on," Newel said, holding the door open.

"Just a second," Knox replied, running back into the throne room. "Get Tess out of here."

Knox knew the satyrs might try to stop him if he didn't run at top speed. When he glanced over his shoulder, they looked confused. "Go!" Knox urged. "I'll catch up."

Knox kept running. By the time he glanced back again, the satyrs and his sister were gone.

He had not explained his plan for fear they would have stopped him. He had repeatedly heard from Kendra that the crowns of the five monarchs were a big deal. Wearing the crown of the Fairy Queen had allowed her to rescue Seth. Currently, the crown of the Giant Queen rested unattended on the throne-room floor.

Knox knew there were plenty of problems with his plan. The throne room was humongous, so he would be running the distance of a few football fields to reach the crown. If a dragon entered the room while he was exposed, he was toast. And, of course, the crown was much too big for him to carry.

But Kendra had mentioned something about the crowns

resizing to fit whoever possessed them. If this worked, everyone would thank him for it. Maybe even praise him for it. If he returned empty-handed, hopefully at least there would be no harm done.

And if he didn't return at all, everyone would wonder what had been going through his mind. Maybe they would assume he had cracked under the pressure.

As Knox drew nearer to the crown, he felt ridiculous. It wasn't just too cumbersome to carry—it was the size of a house. But since he had already taken the risk, he finished the run and reached out to touch the crown.

As soon as his fingers touched the silvery metal, the crown began to shrink. Within a moment, it fit neatly in his grasp, sized for his head.

Turning, Knox ran back toward the door the satyrs had used. Panting hard, he wondered if he should try it on. Might it transform him into a giant? Might it increase his strength?

He decided to wait. If it became an emergency, he could give the crown a try.

Gasping for breath, a stitch in his side, Knox reached the door the satyrs had escaped through with his sister. The unremarkable passage beyond led to an intersection. At least the corridor looked too small for giants or dragons. He was supposed to go right? Then left? Then through the first door?

Hoping he remembered correctly, Knox hurried through the turns and found the door. Before opening it, he considered what Rustafet might do if he saw Knox holding the crown, and hid it under his shirt.

Beyond the door, in a huge, bare room, Knox saw Newel waiting in the doorway to a wicker house. Rustafet paced nearby, a lofty presence.

"Get over here," Newel called. "We were about to leave you!"

Knox mustered one last sprint and entered the wicker house. Newel shut the door, then sat down by Tess and Doren.

"We're ready!" Doren called.

Rustafet swung the house onto his back and ran through a door. He dashed down an unpolished hall, rounded a corner, and went through another door. Knox held on tight as the movements jounced and jostled him.

"Rustafet?" a stern voice challenged. "Where do you think you're going?"

"I have to take these passengers to Humburgh," Rustafet said.

"Nice try," a second voice scoffed. "The queen gave orders that no giant is to use this passageway under any circumstances."

"The queen is dead," Rustafet said.

"This is our darkest day," the first voice said.

"Are you certain?" the second voice asked.

"We come from the throne room," Rustafet said. "My passengers witnessed her fall."

"Then her order counts double," the first voice insisted, "and can never be redacted."

"I don't have to go," Rustafet said, unshouldering the

wicker house. "But you must let the passengers through. These are some of the visitors from Dragonwatch. Wee folk."

Knox could now see that Rustafet was talking with two enormous, heavily armored guards.

"The way to Humburgh is closed," the second guard said.

"But these passengers were approved by the queen's servants," Rustafet said. "Raza arranged the transport. That order must have come from her majesty."

"Raza arranged this?" the first guard asked.

"Do you think dragons took initiative to rescue a couple of human kids and a pair of satyrs?" Rustafet asked. "Weren't you just preaching that the orders of the queen must be honored?"

"Fine," the first guard said. "Send them through."

Newel led the little group out of the wicker house and past the monumental guards. Knox stayed by Tess and kept both hands on the crown under his shirt.

"You know the way," Rustafet called after them. "Straight as an arrow until you arrive. You can't get lost. But the distance may feel a tad long for little ones on foot."

"Thank you," Tess called over her shoulder.

"Take care," Rustafet said. His attention turned to the guards. "Where can I find armaments?"

"We might make it out of here," Newel whispered.

"Don't get cocky or a dragon will catch us from behind," Doren replied.

"Feeling sick, Knox?" Newel asked.

Knox realized that with both hands over his stomach,

holding the crown beneath his shirt, it must look like he was clutching his belly. "Something like that," Knox said. He didn't want to talk about the crown yet. "Rough morning."

"You know what I think?" Tess volunteered.

"Tell us," Doren said.

Tess drew a shuddering breath. "I wish we were back at Fablehaven."

"Amen!" the satyrs said in unison.

CHAPTER FORTY-ONE

Harp of Ages

The repository where the dragons stored their treasure was not far beyond the web-strewn den of Velrog. The concoction Tanu whipped up had washed away the web residue, though Kendra's clothes were damp, and she smelled vaguely of lemons, coconut, and baking soda.

Her heart remained heavy about Vanessa losing her sight and Cyllia falling prey to Velrog. But Kendra also felt relieved that Seth had appeared in time to bail them out, bringing with him one of the legendary Dragon Slayers. If they could claim the Harp of Ages soon, at least the sacrifices made to get this far might lead to positive outcomes.

It was odd to see Seth with wings. Though he showed more acceptance of her than he had previously, there was little recognition in his gaze, and the wings made him seem even less like the brother she knew. Was that how her family would view her if she ever became an Eternal? Would she become increasingly foreign to those she loved most?

The treasure room was organized like a museum, with items artfully displayed on raised platforms, tidy racks, tables, and pedestals. The lavish style in Jinzen's lair seemed echoed here, so she assumed he had influenced the layout and design.

"Lots of choices," Warren said, indicating a corner of the room crowded with harps great and small. Kendra hoped the Harp of Ages wasn't one of the massive ones.

"No need to worry," Merek said, striding confidently to a little golden harp with twelve strings. "This is the one we want."

"Are you sure?" Tanu asked.

"I remember it," Merek said.

"You've seen the Harp of Ages before?" Kendra asked.

"I remember when it was created," Merek said. "Archadius led the team that produced it."

"Is it hard to play?" Kendra asked.

Merek smiled. "It wasn't designed for recitals. You just strum it. There is no effect on humans."

"Should we go?" Seth asked.

"Give me a moment," Merek said. "This wouldn't be the first time I rescued some of my old gear from a dragon's hoard."

Kendra used the opportunity to approach Seth. "That's a scary weapon."

He held it up. "It's called the Unforgiving Blade. No wound from it ever heals."

"Shouldn't you keep it in a sheath?" Kendra asked.

"Merek doesn't think any sheath can contain it," Seth said.

"Sounds . . . dark," Kendra said.

"I'm playing Humbuggle's Game," Seth said, glancing at Merek. "This blade is part of it."

"Are you still trying to win the Wizenstone?" Kendra asked.

"Merek is more interested in the stone than I am," Seth said. "Both of us want to keep it away from Celebrant. He's after it too."

"Is he here at Titan Valley?" Kendra asked.

"Yes," Seth said. "He tried to kidnap me in Humburgh."

Kendra sighed. If Celebrant was here, the main attack was coming. "What about the Sphinx?"

"I haven't heard of him since the Under Realm," Seth said. "Maybe he's helping Ronodin."

"Nothing of mine here," Merek announced. "But I found a better sword and shield." He held them up. "Warren, consider that sword over in the corner. No, don't be fooled by the jeweled hilt. I mean the one to the left. That blade is made of adamant."

"Does adamant get that red?" Warren said.

"It's an alloy," Merek said. "And Tanu, you might like that crossbow. The bolts come out ten times larger than they go in, and white-hot. I see only eight bolts, but a direct hit with any of them could drop a dragon."

Tanu promptly claimed the crossbow.

"Where should we go?" Kendra asked.

"Beacon Hill?" Raxtus suggested.

"It has a good view of Terastios without being too close," Merek agreed. "We could get a sense for the scale of the dragon invasion. Good choice, Raxtus. Do you know Titan Valley well?"

"I was a loner for many years," Raxtus said. "I visited all of the dragon sanctuaries. I quietly explored. I can carry Kendra."

"We won't be able to carry everyone," Merek said.

"I'm coming for sure," Kendra said. "My cousins and the satyrs are out there."

"You guys go ahead," Warren said. "Tanu and I will catch up. We'll also need to help Vanessa."

"I can give her a shrinking potion so we can carry her," Tanu said.

"Great idea," Warren said.

"Be ready for an ambush outside the Dragon Temple," Tanu warned Raxtus. "Or even inside."

"I'll stay alert," Raxtus committed. "Shall we?"

"We'll follow you," Merek said. "Kendra, would you carry the Harp?"

"All right," she said, a little daunted by the crucial responsibility. She supposed Merek and Seth wanted their hands free for their weapons.

"The Harp could help quell an invasion," Merek said. "Doing so will take time and solid strategy. Hopefully we can catch the dragons off guard. The range is decent but not incredible."

Raxtus seized Kendra by the shoulders and pulled her

into the air. The corridors and caverns were mostly wide enough for the dragon to fly, though occasionally Raxtus had to land, and Kendra would jog beside him. They went back through the web-tangled chamber where Velrog lay dead, up the steep slope, and eventually into the cavern where they had fought Pioleen. In the lair of Jinzen, they paused to check on Vanessa.

"We have the Harp," Kendra announced.

"Great!" Vanessa said with a smile, her milky white eyes shifting toward Kendra but not quite in line with her. "Is Warren all right?"

"Yes, but we lost Cyllia," Kendra said. "The others are fine."

"Tragic," Vanessa said. "Cyllia seemed stalwart. Her death is a loss. Seth found you?"

"I'm here," Seth said.

"He and Merek saved us," Kendra reported. "Now we're off to see what this Harp can do. Warren and Tanu are coming behind us."

"Don't wait," Vanessa urged. "Go. I haven't heard any dragons yet, but I expect they're coming. Or lying in wait. Take care."

"I'll sense them," Raxtus said.

They raced through the mirror maze on foot. Raxtus became frustrated as he led them into a couple of dead ends, but before long, the group was flying toward the temple's entrance. Raxtus landed just before the hall ended.

"Lots of dragons outside," Raxtus whispered.

"The entrance is closed now," Seth whispered. "It was open when we came through."

"It probably closed when the storm ended," Raxtus said. "But I can smell and hear dragons on the far side."

After searching the end of the hall, Merek demonstrated how the removal of a stone block exposed a lever. Placing a hand on the lever, Merek whispered, "Raxtus, become your avatar. It should let you avoid the effects of the Harp."

The sparkly dragon gave a nod and took the shape of a young male fairy, about the height of Kendra's knee.

Merek looked surprised. "Your avatar is a fairy?" he whispered.

Raxtus shrugged.

Merek looked at Kendra. She held up the Harp, and Merek pantomimed playing it. Kendra took a deep breath. She hoped the instrument really was foolproof. What if she struck a sour chord and a bunch of dragons stormed in and devoured them?

Kendra strummed her hand over the strings, producing a lovely glissando. Merek pulled the lever, and, with a deep grinding, a stone slab slid inward. Merek motioned for Kendra to strum again, and she complied.

The Dragon Slayer held up both hands, gesturing for them to wait, then flew out of the opening. Kendra held her breath for a long, tense moment until his voice called, "Come on out!"

After exiting, Kendra paused to absorb the scene. In a loose semicircle around the entryway, a dozen huge dragons lay fast asleep. Kendra stepped forward gingerly.

"Can we prevent them from following us?" Seth whispered.

"Leave them," Merek said. "These will slumber for more than a week. And since they are already subdued, it would be dishonorable to harm them. Let's go see how Titan Valley has fared. Kendra, remember, if dragons get near, Raxtus will land and become his avatar, and you strum that Harp. There is no limit to how often you can use it."

"It's so powerful," Seth said, still surveying the unconscious dragons.

"It's the single greatest limited-range weapon against dragons ever devised," Merek said. "Few items in existence are more potent."

Jumping and flapping his wings, Merek shot into the air. Seth followed, and Raxtus transformed into his dragon shape and lifted Kendra. The box canyon and the slumbering dragons fell away beneath her, and a vista of the mountainous region unfolded. Had Bernosh really traversed these rocky slopes, perilous cliffs, and deep canyons on foot?

"Dragons at two o'clock," Raxtus announced.

"I see them," Merek replied. "Sharp eyes. Those are far off. We went from an abundance of clouds to scant options for cover. Let's fly low."

Raxtus, Seth, and Merek hugged the terrain, staying well below the surrounding summits, often dipping into ravines or swooping across clearings at heights lower than the treetops. The combination of high speed and tight turns kept Kendra on edge. Several times she lifted her legs,

worried they would hit branches, but Raxtus always maneuvered with sufficient skill to make her precautions unnecessary.

When the wilderness gave way to farmland, Raxtus, Seth, and Merek skimmed along just above fields, some flat, some furrowed, staying lower than windmills, barns, and even haystacks. Before long, they began to pass the charred skeletons of buildings adjoining scorched acreage. Occasionally, farmhouses or rows of crops were still burning.

"Dragons," Merek proclaimed, pointing.

Kendra spied a small yellow dragon and a larger, horned one diving toward them from off to one side. Raxtus abruptly landed and shrank into a fairy. Merek and Seth alighted beside Kendra. She readied the Harp, hand poised above the strings, but Merek held up a hand to stall her. As the dragons swooped near enough that their mouths opened to use their breath weapons, Merek gave a signal, and Kendra strummed the instrument. Both dragons immediately went limp, heads sagging, and dropped out of the air, sliding and bouncing over the flat ground before flopping awkwardly to a halt.

"Quick," Merek said, leaping into the air.

Raxtus changed back into a dragon, gripped Kendra, and took off. Not far ahead, they reached rolling terrain, allowing them to weave around the hillsides, out of view. When they ran into a gray dragon with horns like a ram, Raxtus landed and became a fairy, and Kendra ran her fingers over the harp strings. The dragon fell heavily, wings splayed.

"Beacon Hill, dead ahead," Raxtus said a few minutes after they returned to the air.

Merek, Seth, and Raxtus flew low up the slope of the tall hill, landing just shy of the summit. Raxtus immediately shrank into a fairy. "Just in case," he said.

Kendra ran with the others to the hilltop, then paused to absorb the sight. As they stood on the highest point for miles around, the panorama from the top left Kendra stunned by the massive destruction underway. Flying low had prevented her from witnessing the extent of the onslaught. Turning in a full circle, Kendra observed that more than half of the visible countryside had burned or was burning. Smoke obscured much of the sky, and ashes fluttered like snowflakes. Long lines of dragons flew wing to wing, heads down, torching the landscape.

In the distance Kendra saw Terastios, where the demolition appeared most concentrated. Lightning crackled and flames billowed. The fortress was already in blackened ruins, and yet the dragons seemed determined to see it utterly razed.

"In all my years, I've not seen this behavior from dragons," Merek said soberly. "They will fight and hunt and kill. They will despoil a castle or a town. They will go to war. But I have never beheld dragons systematically obliterating the natural world. Even the vilest dragons I have known respect resources. They preserve game to hunt and a wilderness to live in. This is a crime against nature. Wasteful to the point of suicidal."

"There is much anger about the conditions at Titan Valley," Raxtus said.

"Then fight the giants," Merek replied. "Not the forests and the fields."

"I agree," Raxtus said sadly.

"Heads up," Seth said.

A group of the nearest dragons had broken from their firestorm formation and were gliding directly toward Beacon Hill. Merek took cover behind some bushes, and Kendra followed his lead.

"They've spotted us," Merek said. "Kendra, ready the Harp, but wait until the last possible moment. I did not envision so many dragons. I count hundreds. I never saw a host like this in all of the dragon war."

"They're coming right at us," Seth warned.

"Patience, Kendra," Merek said.

Glancing up, Kendra counted nine dragons approaching the hilltop. She kept her hand near the harp strings.

"Now," Merek said.

Kendra slid her hand over the strings, producing a beautiful glissando, and dragons promptly littered the hillside. From all directions, dragons began veering their way.

"Please let them gather here," Merek said. "Putting big groups to sleep is our best hope. Kendra, stay ready."

The next wave of oncoming dragons landed before reaching the hill. Dozens were gathering. A few dragons flew away in various directions.

"They're sending messengers," Raxtus warned.

The dragons who landed began transforming into their

human avatars. The incoming dragons changed shape as soon as they landed. Dozens of avatars started marching to Beacon Hill from all sides.

"The Harp won't work on their avatars," Kendra said.

"How many of them can you defeat?" Seth asked Merek.

"In their human form?" he asked. "Four at my leisure. Probably six if they make mistakes. More are coming. We will be squaring off against hundreds."

"Do we fly away?" Kendra asked.

"Too many have spotted us," Merek said. "They know we have the Harp, which makes us the most valuable targets at this sanctuary. If we leave, they will follow at a distance. When we land, we'll be in the same circumstance. There are too many of them. They could take shifts, wear us out. If we have a card to play, now is the time."

"What can we do?" Kendra asked.

"Seth," Merek said. "It's time."

Seth nodded. "Kendra, I need the Harp."

"Why?" Kendra asked.

"There is something I need to do while we can," Seth said. "Before Celebrant or anyone else can do it."

"What?" Kendra asked.

Seth held out a hand. "I'll show you."

Kendra gave her brother the Harp.

Seth accepted it. Men and women, all of them dragon avatars, were charging up the hill. Dozens more dragons converged from all directions. There was no other option. If they failed to act, they would lose the Harp, and Celebrant might figure out how to gain the Wizenstone.

Seth knelt and set the Unforgiving Blade against the first string of the Harp.

"What are you doing?" Kendra cried.

Merek grabbed her from behind, holding her as she struggled.

"This is necessary," Seth said.

"He's right," Merek confirmed. "Let him do it. We're sacrificing something great for something better."

Seth pressed the dark blade against the golden string, and, for the first time since he had started using the knife, something resisted the edge. The string refused to break. Bracing one hand against the top of the Harp, Seth pushed harder with the long knife, and it jerkily cut through the first two strings, making a pair of ugly twangs, before stopping against the third.

"This is hard," Seth said.

"Hurry," Merek encouraged.

Seth forced the blade forward, strings making tortured sounds as they parted in ones and twos. Soon only one remained. As Seth added pressure, the last string snapped with a discordant clang that sank into the earth and sprang into the sky.

CHAPTER FORTY-TWO

Treasury

Seth no longer knelt on a hilltop.

The Harp was gone.

He still held the Unforgiving Blade, but he knelt on a marble floor in a light and airy room of modern design, as if severing the final harp string had altered reality. Seth stared in confusion at a white grand piano, chrome fixtures and furnishings, and oversized windows.

"Congratulations," a voice spoke from behind.

Seth knew the voice. Standing and turning, he faced Humbuggle. The dwarf grinned hugely.

"Where are my friends?" Seth asked.

"Right where you left them," Humbuggle said.

"Will they be all right?" Seth asked.

"That is up to them," Humbuggle said. "And partly up to you."

"Where are we?" Seth asked. "Humburgh?"

"No, my boy, this is my treasury," Humbuggle said. "It's where I keep the good stuff. Nobody knows the location."

"I cut the harp strings," Seth said, holding up the Unforgiving Blade.

"My compliments," Humbuggle said with a bow. "You are the champion of the Titan Games." Almost as an afterthought, he threw a handful of sparkly confetti.

"The Games are over?" Seth asked.

"That is up to you," Humbuggle said. "But you have indeed won the Wizenstone. Shall we adjourn to the relevant treasure room?"

"How much treasure do you have here?" Seth asked.

"Plenty," Humbuggle said. "But all my other riches combined do not approach the value of the Wizenstone. Come."

Humbuggle led Seth to an elevator.

"You have electricity here?" Seth asked as he stepped inside.

"All of the modern conveniences," Humbuggle said. "This is where I do most of my actual living. The manor in Humburgh is primarily for show. I prefer refrigerators, hot showers, the indoor saltwater pool, my theater room—the good life."

Humbuggle pressed the bottommost button, labeled B3. The elevator started down.

"Seven floors?" Seth asked, checking the buttons.

"Six with natural light," Humbuggle said. "My treasury is built into a hillside. I didn't expect you to win so quickly.

I thought it would be another seven years before you could access the Dragon Temple."

"We worked fast," Seth said. "My sister helped."

The elevator doors slid apart, and Humbuggle led Seth down a short, carpeted hallway. A single door awaited at the end of the hall. Humbuggle opened it with a snap of his fingers, revealing a pristine room where a white pedestal sat upon a red platform. Atop the pedestal rested a multifaceted gemstone the size of a baseball. The crystalline jewel contained scintillating refractions of all conceivable colors.

The sparsely decorated room also housed a few exotic potted plants and a wooden treasure chest that looked like it belonged aboard an old pirate ship. A piece of cubist art hung on one wall, and an impressionistic painting adorned another.

"Are those paintings originals?" Seth asked.

"Only the best," Humbuggle said. "A Picasso and a Van Gogh. Neither painting is known to the mortal art community. I acquired them directly from the artists, years ago."

Seth looked at the intricately cut jewel on the pedestal. "The Wizenstone is mine?"

"You have won the stone," Humbuggle said. "It is yours for the taking."

Seth had seen others disintegrate when they tried to take the Wizenstone. He knew the transfer of ownership would be more complicated than Humbuggle made it sound.

The treasure chest shuddered, then bounced a little. Seth shuffled a couple of steps away from it.

"What's in the box?" Seth asked.

"An alternate prize, if you prefer it over the stone," Humbuggle said.

"Do I have to choose without knowing the contents?" Seth asked.

"No, my boy," Humbuggle said. "The box contains your memories."

Seth stared at the dwarf.

"You surrendered them voluntarily," Humbuggle said. "If you would prefer being united with your memories to claiming the Wizenstone, I am offering the option."

"What will happen to the Wizenstone if I choose my memories?" Seth asked.

"It would remain in my care," Humbuggle said. "And I would organize new contests."

Seth sighed. "Can I think about this for a moment?"

"Outside, the world is burning down," Humbuggle said. "In here, we have all the time you like."

Seth went and sat on the red platform near the pedestal. He looked at the dark blade in his hand. He could use it to kill the dwarf. Would he get the Wizenstone *and* his memories? Would he stop the Games forever? Free all the captive contestants?

Seth stared at Humbuggle.

"You see a third option," Humbuggle said.

"Maybe," Seth replied.

"I'm unarmed," Humbuggle said. "But I'm very powerful."

"Yeah," Seth said. "And I'm pretty sure you're not telling me the whole truth."

"Tell you what," Humbuggle said. "I'll officially give you a third option. If you want to strike me down, I won't stop you. Few things could kill me, but that blade would do the job. I've been at this for a long time, Seth. If you want to slay me and accept what comes, that is also on the table."

"Do you have a death wish?" Seth asked.

The dwarf looked at the Van Gogh, a sun rising over a field of haystacks. "You know how life can be. I am weary. There are burdens I would like to set down."

"Can we talk it through?" Seth asked.

"Be my guest," Humbuggle said.

"Celebrant is after the Wizenstone," Seth said. "I sacrificed one of our best weapons against the dragons to win it. If I come away without the Wizenstone, we lose a vital talisman and gain nothing. Plus, I leave the door open for Celebrant to get the stone."

"I hear you," Humbuggle said.

"If I try to claim the stone, I probably turn to dust," Seth said.

"You've seen it happen to others," Humbuggle remarked.

Seth studied the dark blade. "And if I . . ."

"Kill me?" Humbuggle finished.

"Yeah, that. Maybe I get my memories back *and* the Wizenstone. I wouldn't have to take the Wizenstone to keep it. It would be mine to watch over. How would that even work? You can protect it because you know how to use it. I don't have a clue."

"There are no easy answers," Humbuggle said.

Seth stood up. "What I want most is my memories, but I can't take them and leave the problem of the Wizenstone unsolved. A bunch of people got me here, and I can't let them down. And I can't just kill you. Maybe in a fight, or to protect somebody, but not like this. So I'm going to have to go with the Wizenstone."

"Good luck," Humbuggle said.

Seth walked over to the pedestal. He remembered how the black stone that held the Unforgiving Blade had served as a window into true darkness—by contrast the jewel before him gleamed like a window into realms of light. The longer he stared, the more deeply absorbed he became.

Seth blinked his eyes and shook his head to clear it. This beautiful jewel of light had been corrupted and used for evil. He raised the Unforgiving Blade high and brought it down on the Wizenstone. The long knife cleaved through the stone and cut halfway down the white pedestal. A blazing flash of pain raced up Seth's arm to his shoulder, and he lost hold of the knife as the separate halves of the Wizenstone fell from the pedestal to the red platform, inner light extinguished. Seth's sword arm hung limply at his side, completely numb. With his left hand, he withdrew the Unforgiving Blade from the cloven pedestal.

"You destroyed the Wizenstone," Humbuggle said slowly.

Seth inspected both sides of the Unforgiving Blade. "The knife survived it."

"I admit I had hoped for this," Humbuggle said, as if in shock. "But I hardly believe it."

Looking closely at the demon dwarf, Seth noticed he looked more haggard than before, with deeper creases in his skin and more gray in his forked beard. "You *wanted* me to destroy the Wizenstone?"

"I had to keep the hope secret," Humbuggle said. "Quiet embers in my heart, simmering beneath conscious thought."

"Secret from who?" Seth asked.

"From the Wizenstone, my boy." Humbuggle rubbed his hands together. "My bargain with the stone was struck long ago, after Graulas failed to master it. Graulas was much more powerful than I and significantly stronger. I knew if his might failed, mine could never be sufficient. So instead I made an arrangement. I became the servant of the stone."

"You could hear it?" Seth asked. "Talk to it?"

"Anyone could," Humbuggle said, "if they knew how to speak, and how to listen."

"The Wizenstone controlled you?" Seth asked.

"Not entirely," Humbuggle said. "But in most ways that really matter. It was pure pleasure at first. Being the servant of the stone came with enormous privileges. As part of the agreement, I ran contests in which others could try to win the stone. Graulas may have been more powerful, but I have yet to meet anyone more clever than I am. I devised Games that nobody could win. And if somebody did win, the only real option would be to take my place as the servant of the stone, because none are strong enough to wield it for long."

"If I had killed you, I would have had to replace you," Seth said.

"Or to step aside and let somebody else replace me,"

Humbuggle said. "Perhaps Celebrant. One with enough power could handle the Wizenstone for a time, but it would eventually destroy them. The vast majority would dissolve to ashes on contact. Only by letting the stone wield me have I survived."

"And now I have freed you," Seth said.

"Exactly," Humbuggle said. "I set up the final Game with the Unforgiving Blade so there would be a hidden option of destroying the stone—a secret choice that I had to hide from myself and therefore from the stone controlling me. That part was not so hard. I learned self-deceit long ago. Most of us do. What I needed was somebody who might see and actually exercise the option. A champion who could win the Games, but who would do so without having ownership of the Wizenstone as their primary motive."

"You set me up for this," Seth said.

"I'm always laying plans," Humbuggle said. "I could not know what you would do. I only felt sure it would be interesting."

"You couldn't destroy the stone yourself?" Seth said.

"No," Humbuggle said. "That would have violated my arrangement with the stone. You did what I needed."

"How many times have I met you before?" Seth asked.

"Some of them you don't remember," Humbuggle said. "At Stormguard Castle I appeared to you as myself, and also as a lad named Augie, and as an old man named Pietro, modeled after one of the Sleeping Giants here at Titan Valley."

"You appeared as a giant?" Seth asked.

"A scaled-down version," Humbuggle said. "Human sized. I have also appeared to you in three forms here at Titan Valley. Can you guess who?"

Seth thought about it. "The hag?"

"Yes, Esmira," Humbuggle said. "I wanted to point you toward the Diviner. Who else?"

"Not Virgil," Seth said.

"The satyr is authentic," Humbuggle said. "But I sent you to him."

"Wait, you were Dante?" Seth asked.

"I'd show you," Humbuggle said. "But without the Wizenstone, I can't transform like that anymore. I hoped you would collect the memories of the Dragon Slayer."

"You manipulated me," Seth said.

Humbuggle shrugged. "I provided introductions. I was also the gladiator Per, who guided you toward Merek back when he was Fenrick."

"Would you have really let me kill you just now?" Seth asked.

Humbuggle nodded. "I wanted this to end hundreds of years ago. I accepted death as a viable escape. I've been a slave to the Wizenstone far too long. But I couldn't deliberately die, any more than I could purposely sabotage the stone. I could only set the right person on a course and hope they would destroy it."

"Are your powers gone?" Seth asked.

"So much is gone," Humbuggle said. "Many aspects of Humburgh were sustained by the power of the Wizenstone, along with the protections hiding this treasury."

"The pocket dimensions!" Seth exclaimed.

"The pocket dimensions are designed to unravel slowly in the event that the sustaining power of the Wizenstone is lost. Those dimensions are collapsing, including the island with the arena, but the people there will be thrown free."

"What about the gladiators?" Seth asked.

"All of the combatants will be freed," Humbuggle said. "Some have been there for eons. Most will lack their memories. Those memories will also be roaming free."

"What will happen to this place?" Seth asked.

"My treasury does not rely on the Wizenstone for structural or electrical support," Humbuggle said. "But the spells hiding it have dissipated, and the magical defenses are down. This treasure house is now vulnerable."

"Don't you have any power of your own?" Seth asked.

Humbuggle looked down at his hands, flexing them. Seth had not noticed so many liver spots before. "The absence of the stone is aging me. I'm not sure how far it will go. I haven't relied on my own power for so long that it has atrophied. I can do some basic things. Disappear, for example. It will take time to regain my former skills."

The treasure box shook, then hopped twice.

"Your memories are restless," Humbuggle said.

"I can still claim them?" Seth checked.

"Yours for the taking," Humbuggle said. "Consider it a gratuity for services rendered."

"All my senses tell me that I shouldn't trust you," Seth said.

Humbuggle shrugged. "You've been deceived by demons

in the past. Even without your memories, your instincts are admirably tuned. Whether or not you trust me, for now I am willing to speak the truth."

"You could have picked a lot of people," Seth said. "Why me?"

Humbuggle smiled. "I have lived an extremely long time, and I have met many individuals. They come in so many varieties, but there are patterns. Almost all of those willing to risk their lives to win the Wizenstone are the sort who would wreak havoc with its power after they obtained it. By their nature, the Games recruit contestants who should never wield tremendous power. You can witness the same principle in your world as candidates aspire to high political offices."

"I get what you mean," Seth said.

"I'll share a secret," Humbuggle said. "Demons do not like it mentioned, but being a demon is not a natural heritage. Nobody is born a demon. Did you know that?"

"Don't demons have children?" Seth asked.

"Less frequently than you might suppose, but yes, some do," Humbuggle said. "And the babies are not demons. They must be trained. They can choose to become demons. But not one demon started out the way they ended up. They grow monstrous over time. Any thinking being can qualify. It's why there is so much variety among demonkind."

"You used to be a normal dwarf?" Seth asked.

Humbuggle nodded and tugged on his beard. "Long ago, once upon a time, I was a mere dwarf. Like all demons, I gradually evolved into the role. It worked for me. Did it make me happy? I have never met a happy demon. But powerful? Very few could compete with me in my prime."

"Would you go back?" Seth asked. "To being a regular dwarf, I mean."

Humbuggle's eyes grew almost wistful, and he looked again upon the painting of the sunrise. "If such a thing were possible? Maybe, Seth. Maybe I would. But it would be like cramming an oak tree back into an acorn. I have become something else."

"I still don't understand why you picked me," Seth said. "Except that I wasn't after the Wizenstone."

"I chose you because you have real power," Humbuggle said.

"Because I'm a shadow charmer?" Seth asked.

Humbuggle chuckled. "That was a gift from Graulas. Useful, I suppose, but ultimately insignificant. Real power, lasting power, comes from knowing who you are."

Seth laughed. "But I lost my memories."

"Exactly," Humbuggle said. "And without them, you might have regrown in a totally new way. Except you didn't, even in the Under Realm with Ronodin to guide you. We like to imagine our identities are fixed, while in reality so many adjust like chameleons to fit the circumstances around them. We tend to develop based on how we are nurtured and to go where we are directed. Even rebellion is a reaction to what we are taught, and it follows its own predictable patterns. But there are also individuals with a deep sense of self that refuses to be denied. They hear an inner voice that overrides tampering. This rare individual will grow to a similar outcome no matter the influences. I can't explain how this innate compass originates, but I recognize that you have it."

"Why were you looking for that quality?" Seth asked.

"Because a person like that can see possibilities others cannot," Humbuggle said. "This task required a certain caliber of character. Somebody with the inner strength to enact what most would consider unthinkable."

"You saw that in me?" Seth asked.

"I made an educated guess," Humbuggle said. "Even without your memories, you resisted focused attempts to lead you down alternate paths. It gave me hope you might be who I needed."

The treasure chest rattled.

"Should I open it?" Seth asked.

"If you wish," Humbuggle said. "Don't forget, you won the Wizenstone. Even without the stone's magic, the value of the gem is high."

Seth collected the two halves of the Wizenstone and placed them in his satchel. They no longer emitted the same inner light, but they remained beautiful.

Seth faced the treasure chest. Using his power, he willed it to unlock, and the lid flew open. Seth sensed a presence emerge, much like the presence he had perceived in the cottage whom he had named Reggie.

Who locked me up? the presence asked. *What am I? Where am I?*

"It's all right," Seth said. "I'm here. I hear you."

Did you imprison me? the presence asked angrily.

"No," Seth said. "I've been looking for you."

What took you so long? the presence asked.

"You weren't easy to find," Seth said.

Do I know you? the presence asked.

"You're part of me," Seth said. "You're my memories. I lost you."

I'm part of you? the presence asked. *Don't you mean you're part of me?*

"That too," Seth said.

I have wings? the presence asked.

"Not when I lost you," Seth said. "We have wings now."

What should I do? the presence asked.

Seth spread his arms wide. "Come back to me. Become one with me again. It sounds weird but it will feel right. I saw a friend go through this."

You do seem familiar, the presence said. *We are one.*

Seth felt the presence flow into him. His whole body tingled, especially in his chest, and his physical strength left him. He sat down hard, the Unforgiving Blade falling from his grasp to clatter against the floor.

Immediately Seth knew what had happened to his memories. He knew his memories had escaped the place where Humbuggle had first stored them, but then Humbuggle had recaptured the memories and kept them in a chest. The time spent in the chest blurred together but was consistently uncomfortable, frustrating, and scary.

He really was Seth Sorenson! Kendra really was his sister! He knew Knox and Tess and Newel and Doren! He remembered his parents and his grandparents! He remembered his old school and discovering Fablehaven and slaying Graulas! The more he thought, the more he found that all his memories were there. It was just a matter of catching up.

Wait. Did he really just abandon his *sister* on Beacon Hill, besieged by dragons? The deepening realization sickened him. To make matters worse, he had destroyed the weapon that would have given them the best chance for survival. He had known that cutting the Harp would leave them in a compromised position. But he hadn't understood who he was risking. Kendra was likely fighting for her life at this very moment! What if she died because he left her behind? He could only hope that she might somehow survive with help from Merek and Raxtus.

He remembered Vanessa, and felt the terrible weight of her lost sight. He remembered his job as a co-caretaker of Wyrmroost. And he realized he had caused the fall of the sanctuary.

Biting his lower lip, Seth bowed his head. He had released the undead from the Blackwell. How could he have been so stupid! He had gotten Agad killed. He had enabled Celebrant's escape. He had helped the Sphinx and Ronodin.

Suddenly Seth wished he could hide from his memories. Their weight was too much! In releasing Celebrant, he had destroyed the sanctuary he had sworn to protect. He had caused the fall of the other sanctuaries Celebrant had toppled.

Seth wasn't sure he liked himself. His memories felt like

enemies that he could not hold back, disproving anything good he had hoped about his identity.

"A lot to sort through?" Humbuggle asked.

Seth slumped forward and puked onto the marble floor. He could not control the sobs. He was a murderer!

"You may want to hurry," Humbuggle said, rising. "They're coming for you."

With those words, Humbuggle snapped his fingers and vanished.

Seth stared blankly at the place where the demon dwarf had stood.

"You heard him," Calvin said. "We have to get out of here!"

"Is that you, Calvin?" Seth asked.

"I'm still here," Calvin said.

"Help me," Seth whispered.

"Always," Calvin assured him. "Though you have done the hardest stuff alone."

"I destroyed the things I cared about most," Seth said. "I've been my own worst enemy."

"You didn't know," Calvin said. "Ronodin lied to you. He used you."

"I let Graulas get free," Seth said. "Before my memory loss. It got Coulter killed. And now I've done worse. I've sabotaged us all."

"You parted ways with Ronodin," Calvin said. "You figured that out on your own."

"I need to get out of here," Seth said. "I abandoned Kendra on a hill surrounded by dragons, in order to break some stupid stone and get my memories back. Careful what you wish for, Calvin. I earned these memories. People paid for them with their lives. They're mine to own."

"We still have a war to fight," Calvin said. "And a curse to break."

Seth squeezed his head between his hands. "Kendra will do better without me. How is anyone supposed to trust me? I don't trust myself!"

Celebrant opened the door and entered, flanked by men and women bearing weapons. Seth assumed they were all dragons. He remained seated by his vomit.

"Where is the Wizenstone?" Celebrant asked.

"I destroyed it," Seth said.

Celebrant nodded slowly. "So it would seem. You made a mess of things out there." The Dragon King smiled. "The war is going well for us. I can live in a world without a Wizenstone, especially when that world also lacks the Harp of Ages."

"Are you here to kill me?" Seth asked.

Celebrant shook his head. "No. Today I have a pledge to fulfill to the new Fairy King. You're coming with me."

CHAPTER FORTY-THREE

Awakened

Merek kept a tight hold of Kendra, strong hands compressing her upper arms, as the clang of the final string reverberated through her and across the earth and sky. Seth vanished, but the Harp remained, severed strings twisting and curling in unsightly directions.

"What happened?" Kendra asked. "Where did he go?"

"I'm not sure," Merek said, releasing her arms. "I assumed Humbuggle would appear. Perhaps Seth was transported to him instead."

"This was part of the Game?" Kendra asked.

"This was the end of the Game," Merek said. "By cutting the strings of the Harp of Ages with the Unforgiving Blade, Seth just won the Wizenstone."

"This was about a prize?" Kendra shook her head. "If he tries to claim the Wizenstone, he'll be killed."

"Seth knows the basics," Merek said. "He'll be smart about it. Meanwhile, we have a situation."

The dragons that the Harp had put to sleep were waking and rising. The avatars climbing the hill looked around in confusion.

Picking up the damaged Harp, Merek raised his voice. "We awakened the slumbering dragons! Now leave us in peace! Fly away and do not return!"

The demand appeared to increase the confusion among those on the hillside. The dragons did not yet seem to realize the Harp had been destroyed.

Kendra felt the ground tremble. In the distance, she saw a ridgeline sit up. The blackened ridge had been almost totally burned by the dragons. As the ridge arose, charred soil and carbonized trees fell away, revealing a behemoth who looked as if he were in his sixties or seventies, easily the largest giant Kendra had ever beheld. The ridge had apparently been comprised of a giant resting on his back, covered in stone.

"Who is that?" Kendra asked.

"Pietro," Merek marveled. "One of the sleeping giants. After all these years, he awoke."

"He looked like a burned ridge," Kendra said.

"The sleeping giants have hibernated for years," Merek said. "Over time, they merged with the countryside." He pointed. "Look, Zabella is rising as well."

In the distance, Kendra saw a tremendous female giant brushing herself off. She may have been even taller than Pietro, though she was farther away, so it was hard to gauge.

"The Harp," Merek said, looking down at the instrument in his hands. "It must have played a role in their long sleep. The timing makes sense. Their hibernation began while the Dragon Temple was under construction."

Pietro had started using an enormous hoe to swat dragons out of the sky. Relative to him, they looked the size of chickens.

The dragons who had awakened were flying away, and the human avatars raced downhill. Some of the dragons still swarmed Pietro and Zabella, but others were apparently fleeing.

"WHAT ARE YOU VERMIN DOING TO MY ISLAND?" asked a voice as deep as the ocean and as broad as the sky.

Turning, Kendra beheld the largest being she had ever seen, striding from the north. Dressed in a white toga, he carried a sword and a round shield. A gold band circled his brow, his arms and legs rippled with muscle, and he grew larger with every stride.

"We woke Garocles," Merek said reverently.

"Who?" Kendra asked, transfixed by his enormity.

"The father of Imani," Merek said. "Garocles the titan. He's the Dragon Slayer of Titan Valley, but he has slept for centuries."

Several sleeping giants followed Garocles. Still others plodded into view, converging from diverse directions. The few dragons attacking Garocles looked like sparrows. He cut them down with nonchalance.

"YOU HAVE VIOLATED THIS LAND, SAURIANS," Garocles declared. "DEPART OR PERISH."

Dragons still assailed Pietro with fire, lightning, and gushing liquids. The barrage seemed like a minor irritant to the giant, who slew one or two attackers with every stroke of his hoe.

"The sleeping giants are colossal," Kendra said. "But Garocles is unbelievable."

"Legend has it he grows not only according to his anger, but also in proportion to the onslaught," Merek said. "Celebrant could not have anticipated this."

As Garocles came nearer, every step an earthquake, the dragons quit all attacks and started to flee. Garocles stopped, leaving the sleeping giants to pursue them. The dragons climbed high, out of reach, retreating to the southeast away from the titan.

"They're running away," Kendra said.

"Celebrant sounded the retreat," Merek said. "Or whoever he left in charge of the battle did. I wish they had stayed."

"Why?" Kendra asked.

"With Garocles awake, we could have won the dragon war today," Merek said.

"Will he go after them?" Kendra asked.

"Garocles is the Dragon Slayer of this sanctuary," Merek said. "His jurisdiction is here. A titan is as much a force of nature as he is a living being. With him awake, Titan Valley will be the last place any smart dragon will come. But it is impossible to say what help we can expect from him elsewhere. You and I lived through the day. Though many did not, and the preserve is in shambles, it could have ended worse. The dragons enjoyed great success, but they finally took some damage."

"Did Seth know cutting the harp strings would wake up the sleeping giants?" Kendra asked.

"He made no mention of it to me," Merek said.

"They got Terastios," Kendra said. "I hope my cousins stayed in Humburgh."

"Humburgh should be secure," Merek said. "The protections there derive from Humbuggle and the Wizenstone, not the Giant Queen."

"We have to find my cousins and the satyrs," Kendra said. "And we have to find Seth."

"I will help you," Merek said.

"So will I," Raxtus chimed in, still in fairy shape. "Is the titan shrinking?"

Kendra's gaze returned to Garocles.

"The threat is diminishing," Merek said. "His outrage is cooling."

The titan watched the fleeing dragons until they shrank from view. He continued the vigil for an extra ten minutes, gradually losing size, until he turned and strode off the way he had come.

"Do you think the dragons killed the Giant Queen?" Kendra asked.

"I expect so, if she remained at Terastios," Merek said. "She may have fled to Stratos. Or perhaps even to Humburgh. We'll learn her fate before long. It should be safe for us to fly to Humburgh now."

Raxtus returned to dragon shape.

"I'm worried about my brother," Kendra said.

"We have to find him," Merek said. "The fate of the world may rest on how he handled the end of the Titan Games."

CHAPTER FORTY-FOUR

Old Debt

Seth sat in a dungeon cell with his back to the wall, hands on his knees, head bowed. The air was too cold. The only light flickered indirectly from a torch down the hall. Somewhere water slowly dripped. He no longer had the Unforgiving Blade or his satchel of gear. He still had wings. Calvin remained in his pocket.

But the little nipsie had stopped trying to reassure Seth. He seemed to realize that Seth needed time.

After leaving Titan Valley, Celebrant had personally carried Seth to the fallen Soaring Cliffs sanctuary. Flying steadily, they had crossed oceans and mountains, glimpsed cargo ships and airplanes. The old castle at Soaring Cliffs was now staffed by dragons, and Seth had been locked in the dungeon until he could be delivered to Ronodin.

Seth had found that he could keep warm by wrapping

his wings around himself. But at present, he kept them folded behind his back, even though he was shivering. He wanted to suffer. He deserved to be locked up.

The memories that he had fought to regain now tortured him. The more he remembered, the more he ached. Without his memories, he had felt like he was doing his best. But he had crossed lines that could never be uncrossed. He had set events in motion that could never be undone.

This cell was too good for him.

He flexed the fingers of the hand he had used to bisect the Wizenstone. He could move that arm now, but not all sensation had returned. Part of him hoped the injury was permanent. There needed to be external evidence of how bad he felt inside.

He had been trying to do the brave thing, the right thing, when he went through that door at Stormguard Castle. He had surrendered his memories hoping to save the day and let Kendra get the Wizenstone instead of Celebrant. His intention had been selfless, and it had led to disaster.

He still didn't know if Kendra, Raxtus, or Merek had survived. It was possible that Warren, Tanu, Vanessa, Knox, Tess, and the satyrs had perished as well.

Calvin had tried to bolster his spirits. The nipsie was right that he had been deceived. But Calvin didn't understand that, to Seth, having good intentions almost made it worse. It suggested he couldn't trust his instincts.

Without grasping the ramifications, Seth had freed the undead from the Blackwell and caused the fall of Wyrmroost. How could he ever have suspected Ronodin might be on his side? Even for a second? How had he not recognized that Kendra was trying to help him?

Humbuggle had applauded him for having a strong sense of identity. The dwarf couldn't have been more wrong about that one! Happy to be free of the Wizenstone, the demon had recklessly overcomplimented him.

Seth waited silently in the damp dimness. Maybe he would stay incarcerated forever. Maybe Ronodin would come for him. Seth wiped his runny nose with the back of his hand. He could finally receive a punishment proportionate to his crimes.

Seth wished he could go back and do everything differently. If he had never dealt with Graulas, never become a shadow charmer, Wyrmroost might still be safe. Agad might be alive. Coulter might be alive. So many people might be alive. As the war went on, it would become impossible to count the lives he had ended and ruined.

Too much had happened. Too much had gone wrong. There was no way to erase it.

Seth could feel the dark power inside, even now. He was sure he could unlock the cell if he desired. How many guards were out there? Could he shade walk past them? Could he get free?

Should he get free?

What if he could repair some of the damage he had caused? Kendra needed help. The world needed help. The dragons were nearing a position where they could win their war. Ronodin had control of the Fairy Realm.

He desperately wanted to help. Even if it killed him.

Then again, what if he found a new way to make things worse?

Seth could sense undead in this dungeon. Feeling outward with his powers, Seth noticed a wraith coming toward him. This was unexpected. The undead here were all locked up. But this wraith was advancing down the hall toward his cell.

The wraith moved into view and stopped in front of his cell, gazing at Seth through the bars. The temperature in the chilly cell dropped noticeably.

Greetings, Seth Sorenson, the wraith communicated.

"How do you know my name?" Seth whispered.

The Singing Sisters sent me to find you, the wraith conveyed.

"Whiner?" Seth asked. "Is that you?"

You called me that when you delivered me to them.

"Are you still cold?"

Always, Whiner replied. *But the Sisters rehabilitated me.*

"You're more articulate," Seth whispered.

The Sisters request the favor you owe them, Whiner expressed.

Seth could not help laughing. "Really? Now? I'm kind of in jail."

I'm here to get you out, Whiner said.

"Has anyone told the Singing Sisters that the world is ending?" Seth asked.

If you do not comply, they will deploy the knife, Whiner warned.

"It will hunt me down and kill me," Seth said. "I know."

They sent this to help you fulfill their request, Whiner said, holding out a sword.

Seth sat forward. "Vasilis? Really?"

If you will fulfill their request, Whiner said.

Seth knew the power of that sword. "What do they ask?"

The Sisters want you to gather all fragments of the Ethergem and bring the pieces to them.

Seth considered what that would include: the broken Wizenstone, the stone from the crown of the Giant Queen, the stone from the crown of the Dragon King, the stone from the crown of the Demon King, and the Ethershard from Stratos. "Is that all?" Seth asked.

That is all, Whiner replied.

Although Seth had beaten the odds by accomplishing difficult missions, some aspects of this request seemed truly impossible to fulfill. Seth chuckled darkly.

The Sisters need an answer, Whiner pressed.

"All right," Seth said, rising. "Give me the sword."

Whiner handed the weapon through the bars. When Seth grabbed the hilt, vitality and warmth flooded into him. His mind felt sharper, his purpose clear.

The blade glowed a red so deep it was almost black. With two quick strokes, bars clattered to the floor, and Seth had a way out of his cell.

Acknowledgments

Book four in a five-volume series is a tough one. The books in the series I write tend to get thicker and more complex as the story goes on, and *Champion of the Titan Games* was no exception. It took a lot of effort to create this installment and get it ready for readers, and I owe thanks to many people.

The key woman on this project was my wife, Erlyn. She was right there with me as I conceptualized the book, was the first person to edit every chapter, and helped with polishing as well. She is very astute with language, and the book is better thanks to her involvement.

Sometimes it helps me to talk about the story I am planning, and this time I got some good early help from Chris Schoebinger and Hamish Elliott, along with the Baker kids—Anika, Brock, Clark, Chet, little Erlyn, and Fiona. They helped enrich the ingredients as I prepared the soup. There is also a reader named Marc Bienenfeld who has pointed out some improvements to make and who knows my books well enough that I sometimes ask him fact-checking questions.

I created this novel under strange conditions, not only during the COVID-19 pandemic, but also as I was engaged to be remarried. My thanks go out to Erlyn and her kids for being flexible, and to my kids as well. I also offer thanks to Duane and Erlyn Madsen (there are four generations of Erlyns in that family) for letting me use a little apartment near my fiancée on some days as I wrote this book.

As always, professional editors gave me invaluable feedback and made key improvements, including the inimitable Chris Schoebinger and the extremely talented Emily Watts. Early readers of rough drafts also helped the project, including Jason and Natalie Conforto, Monte Conforto, Erlyn Mull, Pamela Mull, Cherie and Bryson Mull, Davis Mull, Lila Mull, Sadie Mull, Chase Mull, Rose Mull, and Calvin Mull.

My Uncle Tuck wanted to help, but he had trouble thinking clearly because of his brain tumors. Tuck has assisted with all of my books since the start, and he even came up with the name of the Wizenstone, but his medical complications have been extreme for months. I love him and appreciate the mentoring he has given me.

I'm sure that, as usual, I failed to name everyone who deserves a nod. If I did, speak up, and I'll get you in the future!

Note to Readers

We're almost to the finale! Only one book left!

It interests me that reading a book can be both an individual experience and a collective one. Books can be read alone in silence as well as aloud with others. Once a book is read, you end up with a story world in your mind that corresponds with story worlds in the minds of other readers.

Now that you have finished this book, we could talk about the story world together as if we had been there, and we could discuss the characters as if we both knew them. I enjoy the comments I get at signings and online, especially when the observations reveal that others are engaging with my books. Sometimes I have epiphanies about the stories I tell through the questions I am asked and the insights others share.

I'm excited to write the final Dragonwatch book! It will wrap up the Dragonwatch saga and also provide the true finale to Fablehaven as well. My mind is overflowing with plans, and I can't wait to get it on paper.

We are also creating a stand-alone version of *Legend of the Dragon Slayer*, so readers can own the ancient tale Kendra discovered about the Legender. I'm thrilled that Brandon Dorman will provide the spectacular art, and getting a copy will simulate owning an artifact from the Fablehaven universe.

Thank you for reading this book. My readers are some of my favorite people alive. I write these stories hoping others will enjoy them, and I am enabled to create more as readers buy my books and share them. I'm fully aware that this could not be my job without you.

If you want to interact with me, search Brandon Mull on Facebook or Twitter, or look me up on Instagram (@writerbrandon). I like it when readers share pictures or thoughts online, and I do check in personally from time to time.

Reading Guide

1. When Kendra returned the crown to the Fairy Queen, she surrendered a chance to claim it for herself. Should she have considered keeping the crown? Why or why not?

2. Between Hermo, Reggie, Calvin, and Virgil, Seth had some unusual companions in this book. What were their strengths? What were their weaknesses? Which of those characters would you most want as a companion? Why?

3. Why do you think the Giant Queen looked down on Kendra? Why was she so confident her sanctuary could not fall? In what ways was she right? In what ways was she wrong?

4. Humburgh was full of mysteries and secrets. What place would you have liked to see Seth visit that he did not explore? Why did it interest you?

5. Kendra told a lie to get away from Ronodin. How did the lie backfire? Is there ever a good reason to lie? Why or why not?

6. A gladiator arena was central to the story, but our main characters never fought as gladiators. Would you have liked to see them fight? Which of the main characters do you think would have lasted the longest on the arena floor? Does it fit the personality of Humbuggle that Seth won the Games without fighting in the arena? Why or why not?

7. The giants were skilled at truth magic, and they created items that could discern whether a person was lying. Would you like to own one of those objects? In what ways would it be beneficial? In what ways might it be troublesome?

8. What legitimate grievances could the dragons of Titan Valley have had about how they were treated? Did you see the Giant Queen as a good character or an evil character? Explain your answer.

9. If you could meet the Diviner, what would you want his help finding? Would your question be confirmed as the most important when he rang the tuning fork? Why or why not?

10. Why do you think Merek and Seth chose to work with Isadore and Basirus? What did they gain by doing so? How did it cause problems?

11. Why was Humbuggle glad when Seth destroyed the Wizenstone? Do you think he was sincere? Why or why not?

12. We were never told the circumstances of how and why the Fairy King admitted Ronodin to the Fairy Realm. What do you think happened? Do you expect to learn more about that in the next book?

13. Why was getting his memories back torturous for Seth? Do you think he can ever forgive himself? Why might that be hard to do? How have you forgiven yourself after making a mistake?

14. Why do you think the dragons were merciful to Knox and Tess? What methods besides fighting could help you deal with an enemy?

15. This story left many questions unanswered. What would you like to see explained or resolved in the final book? What would you ask the author if you had the chance? Would it be better if he told you the upcoming secrets or kept them to himself? Why?

COMING MAY 2021

THE ORIGIN STORY OF

DRAGONWATCH

LEGEND OF THE

DRAGON SLAYER

BRANDON MULL

ILLUSTRATED BY

BRANDON DORMAN

The magical, medieval tale first introduced in
the *New York Times* best-selling Dragonwatch series
is now a reimagined, illustrated, stand-alone edition.

- A must-have, full-color storybook for Fablehaven and Dragonwatch super fans
- Brings to life the legend of the first Dragon Slayer with dozens of new illustrations
- Features a detailed map of the kingdom of Selona

- Includes a private letter written to Kendra from the wizard Andromadus
- Reveals ancient genealogy showing a history of Dragon Slayers (including who trained whom; number of dragons slain; how they died or if they are still known to be alive)